KEEP
HER

FAITH ANDREWS

Dear ~~████~~!
Beck's bringing sexy
back!! . xo
Faith Andrews

Keep Her by Faith Andrews
Copyright © 2014 by Faith Andrews

All rights reserved.

This book is a work of fiction. Names, characters, places, and incidents are either the product of the author's imagination or are used fictitiously. Any resemblance to actual persons, living or dead, events, or locales is entirely coincidental.

Except the original material written by the author, all songs, song titles and lyrics contained in the book are the property of the respective songwriters and copyright holders.

Interior Design by Angela McLaurin, Fictional Formats

DEDICATION

To my mother for being my rock, my voice of reason, my teacher, my role model, and my friend. You've always loved me unconditionally and without judgment, supporting all my dreams and even my mistakes. Thank you for accepting me for who I am and for helping me in ways I never imagined you could.

I'll love you forever,
I'll like you for always,
As long as I'm living
my Mommy you'll be.

~Robert Munsch, *Love You Forever*

PROLOGUE
5 years earlier

Dear God, let today be the day. Please take her with you. Bring her home to be with my Nanny. Let her be at peace.

The tears streamed down my face—I couldn't believe I had any left at this point, but praying for death... I guess that brings on tears no matter how depleted you are.

"Ry," Mom said, holding out her hand. "Where's Marcus?"

That was a good question. I looked around the room, as if he might be hidden in some corner, but from the sounds of the over-excited announcer and the loud roar coming from the television, it was obvious he was in the living room, watching the Yankees game with Dad and his best friend, Beck. Avoidance was his coping mechanism. He couldn't keep vigil by her side anymore. It was too painful for him. He didn't know how to handle his emotions—he was going to be lost without her. She was his best friend in the whole world, even if he was too macho of a teenage boy to admit it. Keeping busy kept him sane.

I stood, adjusting her favorite patchwork quilt so it covered my mother's bony arms. "He's watching the Yankees, why? Want me to get him?"

"No," she said on a whisper, her frail voice becoming less and less distinguishable as the lively one I'd grown up with. "I want to talk to you alone. There are things I need to say."

The tears that had finally subsided welled up again, this time lodging themselves in my throat and flooding my vision as well. I knew from experience that when people on their death beds started talking about things they needed to say or confessions they had to get off their chest, the end was near. As much as I needed to see her out of pain, I also wasn't quite ready to say goodbye. But I held back from begging her to hold on and nodded, gripping her fragile hand.

She squeezed mine back with the tiniest bit of strength. As weak as it was, it comforted me. I hoped her words would too. She spoke slowly, as if reciting a speech, something important she'd rehearsed. For all I knew, she probably had. "I know you think I'm going to miss so much—graduations, boyfriends, your wedding, your *babies*, but—" she paused, swallowing back her own tears and pushing forward with a loving smile. "I will be here, Riley Jo. I will be here to guide you and celebrate with you on every one of those journeys. Right now it might be hard to believe that's true but I'll fight with the man upstairs Himself just to make sure I'm by your and your brother's sides whenever I'm supposed to be."

"Mom—" I tried to interrupt, but she brought her hand up to my cheek and the touch of her cool, soft skin silenced me.

"Let me finish, sweetie."

I nodded, placing my hand over hers and encouraging her to continue.

"You've made me so proud, Ry. You're bound for greatness, I just know it. Everything you touch just seems to be improved because of you. You'll have that same impact on your father and brother and I don't want them to be a burden, even though I know it's your nature to step up to the plate and take over—that's just you, but... you need to remember to live this life for *you* too. Daddy will be okay in time and Marcus... he'll grow up—one of these days." She smiled the widest I'd seen in days, letting out the slightest chuckle.

As much as she adored her son, he was a handful lately. Rebelling because of his anger over our mother's health; taking advantage of his newfound stud status with the ladies. Now that they were finally taking interest in him, he was suddenly a cocky little son of a bitch. And they actually *liked* that about him.

I laughed alongside her, thinking about how much my mother and I could get a rise out of my little brother. I'd miss that—God, I'd miss so many things once she was gone.

Before I could tell her this, she swallowed back another gulp of tears to continue where she left off. "What I'm trying to say is—sweetie, be happy. You're smart, beautiful, and the most loving person I know, but you're also stubborn and sometimes *too* selfless. Do things just because they make you smile. Never settle, honey, but you need to kiss a lot of frogs and *then* marry your prince. Learn to let things go, even if you don't want to."

My mother and I had had a lot of heart to hearts over the

years, but she was always guarded with me because she thought I was sensitive. So, the vulnerability in her words of wisdom came as a surprise. "So," I said, wiping away a tear, "you wait 'til now to unleash it all, huh?"

I guided her up by her elbow, adjusting her pillows as she continued with a chuckle, "I know it seems that way, but I've told you these things—in other ways—your whole life. You're too serious, Riley. I know you feel you need to be, but it's okay not to be perfect all the time."

I wanted to believe that with all my heart. I wanted to be able to live this through, especially since these were the words my mother decided to leave me with. But even though I wanted to make that promise, it would be damn near impossible to simply "let my hair down" once she was gone. She was leaving us with big shoes to fill and if my father and brother—hell, all *three* of us—were going to survive her death, I would have to be more serious than I'd ever been.

Not wanting to disappoint her or give her any inkling that I wouldn't follow through on her wish, I leaned down to place a kiss on her forehead. "You are one wise woman, Mom. What the hell are we going to do without you?"

She raised her cold hand to my face, tucking a hair behind my ear and then resting her palm against my cheek. "Live. You're going to live."

That night, after giving my brother a similar speech of his own, whispering her secret recipe for meatballs in Beck's ear, and kissing my Dad with her last bit of strength, my mother passed.

The moment was absolutely surreal. In all the time I had prepared myself, I imagined crying and screaming and sobbing like there was no tomorrow. But after years of chemo and operations and months of painful suffering, the most amazing sense of relief washed over me as I watched my mother close her eyes and take her last peaceful breath.

The world was losing a remarkable woman, and heaven—God, I was so damn envious of heaven in that moment—was gaining an incredible angel. Our lives would never be the same without her. The healing process would take a lifetime, if I ever actually healed at all. But I had to do what my mother wanted most for me. After I mourned and grieved until I thought I'd break in two. After I got things in order and took care of my crumpled family so we felt whole again. After I screamed and cursed for hating the world and then learned to love it again for all its miracles, I had to keep her memory alive and just... live.

CHAPTER 1
Riley
5 years later

"Fallon, put down the damn tabloid and check my phone to see who just texted me. I'm waiting for a decision from Mrs. Ashworth about the wallpaper swatches we sent over earlier today."

My assistant/bestie ran his hand though his recently coiffed bro-hawk, gaping at John Travolta's alien baby. I snatched the rag mag out of his hands, threw it across the room, and reached for my phone.

"What?" Fallon rolled his pretty green eyes. "I know it's bullshit, but at least it's entertaining. You're as boring as watching paint dry, Miss Interior Designer Extraordinaire… all work, no play."

Oh, what did he know anyway? His idea of fun was prowling happy hour at Lucky Cheng's with the rest of his gorgeous-but-gay friends. Okay, even I had to admit that the last few times I tagged along I had a blast, *but* hanging out with Fallon and his "buds" on a regular basis wasn't going to help me end my dry spell.

I retrieved the incoming text and couldn't believe the irony. Fallon and Lucky Cheng's might keep things dry, but an invitation to that new bar on Fifth with Marcus, Beck, and Tessa—that sounded promising. Even if it did mean being kind of a third wheel. As much as they denied it, something was going on with Marcus and Tessa lately, and Beck... he was unavailable and dating that ice queen. I'd have to drag Tessa away from her infatuation with my little brother and make her my wing woman.

I texted the group back, letting them know I was in for tonight and a smile spread across my face—a hopeful one. I could use a night out, even if it didn't end up with a hook-up. In fact, I vowed to myself that tonight I would *not* entertain that random, sloppy, I'm-never-gonna-see-you-again kiss. I was in the mood to dance and have fun and forget this week of annoying clients and underqualified assistants. "Ha! I'm going out dancing tonight." I stuck my tongue out at Fallon and skipped across the office to pick the tabloid up off the floor. Returning the magazine to Fallon, who was staring at me unimpressed, I gloated, "You can resume your, uh, intellectual reading now while I decide on something to wear. God, do I need this night out."

"You're telling me," he whispered, snickering.

Planting my hand on my hip, I tilted my head. "Hey, what's that supposed to mean?"

"Riley, you're skipping around the office like a happy moron over going to a bar. I mean, *I* would be skipping just to be in the same room as that hot piece of man candy that is your little brother, but... most single people our age do this a few nights a week. Not once every four months."

Every four months? I had a date only a few weeks ago, albeit a lame one. But still, that counted as going out. Instead of sulking and whining about my lack of a social life, I chose to come back with my go-to excuse. Work. "Oh, I'm sorry, Mr. Party Animal, but I actually have a career... a flourishing one at that. I don't have time to go out and get trashed and canoodle with drag queens four nights a week."

"Hey, leave the queens out of this, missy. Listen," Fallon said, cocking an eyebrow as he stood and walked toward me. He placed a perfectly manicured hand at my shoulder and squeezed me against his small but muscular frame. "I've worked with you side-by-side, day in and day out, for the last two years. You are one bad-ass career woman who knows her color wheel and accent pillows, but... I also know you're lonely."

"I am not lonely," I insisted, pushing away from him. Okay, that was a lie, but I didn't need Fallon—the guy who had a random meaningless roll in the hay at least twice a week—as my life coach. "Tessa's back, and I have Dad and Marcus and..."

"And me. You have me too, love, but you don't have anyone to call your own and I *know* you want that. We're not enough and—newsflash, lady—that's okay! You deserve your knight in shining armor and everything that comes after it. I've heard you all goo goo, ga ga over Tessa's son. You want that—you want what all the good girls want, Ry. Marriage, kids, the picket fence. It's okay to admit it."

I did want all that. Everyone who knew me for more than five minutes knew that, but right now it just wasn't in my cards. I'd gone on blind dates set up by mutual friends, tried the internet thing, even gave a few exes a second shot—none of them measured up to my expectations. Well, I shouldn't say expectations. It was more of this need to feel like my mom would've liked the guy. None of them seemed mom-approved. Yet.

"I don't want to talk about my shitty love life, Fallon." It was easier to brush him off than to have this conversation *again.* "Why don't you come with tonight? You can drool over my brother. Maybe distract him from Tessa for a bit. I need to ravage the dance floor with my old partner in crime."

"As much as I'd like to ravish the dance floor *and* your brother, I have plans tonight," he said with wild, unruly, dancing brows.

"Cheng's *again*?"

"We don't only hang at Cheng's, you close-minded freak. Every once in a while I do have a subdued romantic evening with one of my gentleman callers."

"Well, your loss then. You would've fit in perfectly with me and Tess. You'll have to come along next time." I sat back down at my desk, pulling up my emails. It was only one o'clock in the afternoon and dancing the night away seemed like a lifetime in the future. "Now, seriously, Fal... go do some work before I have to fire yo' ass."

Beck

"Marissa, let me go. My texts are buzzing non-stop. There's nothing to talk about anyway. You already made your decision."

She'd made her decision two days ago and shocked the shit out of me. I understood how important passing the bar was to her, but I also thought after two years together, I was important too. This dead-end phone conversation had me replaying *that* one over again in my head.

"Baby, I've been thinking," I finally blurted out. I'd wanted this for a long time, but was too chicken shit to admit it. Marissa had me thinking things men my age shouldn't think about... like getting hitched, having babies, growing old together. I was in deep with this girl and wasn't too afraid to admit it.

"And what exactly is it you've been thinking about, Beck? Does it include you, me and a weekend away?—because Lord knows we could use that after all the studying I've been doing for this god-awful exam. Just a bit longer and we'll be back to normal."

Without hesitation, I manned-up and spit it out. "Move in with me." There, I said it. There was no turning back now. She was looking forward to a weekend away, but what I was offering was even better—waking up together every single morning. She was sure to say yes.

"Um..."

So not what I was expecting. That two-letter word nearly

had me dropping the phone. *Shit, maybe I shouldn't have done this over the phone. What an eager asshole. I should have done this on a romantic date. What the hell was I thinking?* "Baby, I'm sorry. I shouldn't have just blurted it out like that. I should've planned this better. Let me take you out tonight so we can talk about it over lobster—your favorite."

"No, Beck, it's not that, it's just…"

The hesitation in her voice had me on edge for the second time since I laid my heart on the line. *Why the fuck was I sensing a problem?* "Ris, did you not hear me? I'm asking you to move in with me. I think we should take this to the next step. Doesn't that make you happy?"

The silence on the other end didn't make me happy. When she finally said something, it wasn't exactly what I was anticipating. "Beck, baby. I've been a nervous wreck studying for this exam. Things are just so… I don't know… haphazard right now. Don't get me wrong, I love you, baby. I love you so much, but—"

"But the fuck what? You know what forget it, Ris. Forget I said anything. You're obviously too involved in your own shit to worry about what happens next with the two of us." My pride was burned. *Maybe it was my own insecurities biting me in the ass, but here I was giving her my whole heart, and she was consumed by her career, yet again. I know I sounded like a whiny brat, and I literally had to check inside my pants to make sure I still had a dick, but I felt wounded by her rejection. Still, it was no excuse to lash out at her for working hard at her dreams.*

Forcing myself to calm down and see things from her side, I took a different approach. "Babe, it's my bad. I know *you're stressed and I shouldn't have mentioned it right now. I just thought that since we've hardly seen each other, this would solve our problem. You could study, and even if you were locked away with your books all day, knowing we'd be sharing the same bed together every night—"*

"Beck, we need a break."

Two nights ago, those words shattered my dreams and now here she was trying, yet again, to make me see that it was bar over Beck.

"You're not being fair. You won't give me a chance to explain. You don't understand the pressure I'm under right now. You get mad when I can't come over because I'm studying. I feel strangled at all ends right now. I don't think you get how much is riding on this one test, Beck. I love you, I really do, but this is my career we're talking about. My life."

Strangled? Studying was putting her through the wringer, but what did being strangled at all ends have to do with it? And wow, her *career* was her life, but now that I wanted to move in together and make her a permanent part of *my* life, she was changing the game. For whatever reason, she thought I couldn't take her law school endeavors seriously. Maybe because to her I was just some lowly blue collar worker. Yeah, my aspirations weren't as high as hers, but I risked my life as FDNY every day and I wasn't about to defend myself to her for the millionth time.

I was tired of practically begging. I was done and what I was about to say would probably sound harsh and asshole-ish, but her rejection was harsh—it fucking stung and I didn't like it. "You know what, Ris, you're right. We do need this break. You got all weirded out when I mentioned moving in together the other night as if it were some fucking heinous crime that I wanted to make things more permanent with the woman I love. Then you throw this shit in my face and quite honestly, if you can't have me *and* your career as part of your life—then maybe we shouldn't be together. Study your heart out, honey. I hope you take the test and pass with flying colors and become the most successful lawyer there is, but remember that I wanted you to do all that with me by your side."

"Beck," she interrupted, without an ounce of sadness in her voice. She wasn't the best at showing her feelings, but this was an all-time low. Nothing she could say now would erase what had already been said, so I didn't let her continue.

"No. Don't. I've given you my all even when people thought that was impossible. I've been nothing but a good boyfriend to you—everyone thinks I'm fucking pussy-whipped and all changed and shit."

She wasted no time jumping in after that remark. "No, not everyone. Just Marcus, and you'd be smart *not* to take any relationship advice from that joker."

Marissa might have been dead on about Marcus, but hearing her talk about my best friend after making me feel like shit—it was my breaking point. "Ris, I gotta go."

"I'm sorry, Beck. I didn't mean to—"

"Enough! We'll talk later." I hung up the phone, feeling like a complete asshole. For the second time in two days.

I'd been Marissa's boyfriend for over two years. For those two years I made a point of proving myself and changing my former player ways. Marissa was the kind of girl you did that shit for. Not only was she gorgeous, but she was smart, accomplished, the kind of girl you took home to Mom. And let's not even talk about the hard-on my mom had for her. I had brought her home *once* and by the end of that night my mother was making it like my new girlfriend was her own flesh and blood and *I* was the outsider.

"Fuck!" I grunted, running my hands through my hair. This was so not how I'd envisioned any of this going. I felt crushed, I really did. How had it come to this? One minute I was asking her to move in and the next minute we were taking a break. A break—I felt like fucking Ross and Rachel from *Friends*, but I couldn't laugh about it because the idea of it being over with Marissa yanked at my heart.

And there was the damn phone again.

I contemplated ignoring it because I just wasn't in the mood to talk to anyone, but then realized it could be Marissa coming to her senses. It wasn't Marissa—stubborn, cold bitch. Instead it was a string of texts between Marcus, Riley, and Tessa, making plans for tonight.

I quickly read through all the messages and then typed back that I was game for a night out. Going to that new bar on Fifth tonight would be a good distraction. I needed a night with my friends. A night away from Marissa. A night to just let it all soak in and maybe understand why the hell I wasn't good enough for the girl I had called mine for the last two years.

CHAPTER 2
Riley

The loud thumping music washed over me like a renewing spring rain shower, pumping fresh, get-up-off-your-ass energy to my limbs. "Oh! I love this song!" Justin Timberlake was my man—I loved him, hated his snobby bitch of a wife, and always needed to move my feet whenever his words played through the speakers and filled the room. One bar of *Suit and Tie,* and the buzz from my second beer had me shooting up from my chair and pulling on Tessa's arm. "Come on, girl, let's dance!"

Staring into her Ketel and Cranberry and sitting a little too close to my brother, she all but mumbled, "No one's dancing, Ry."

An empty dance floor meant shit to me. "So, we'll start a trend. Come on, pleeeaaase?" I turned my lips into the obnoxious pout that usually got me nowhere, but when I saw Tessa's eye roll, I sensed she was about to cave.

"Fine," she huffed. "But only for this one song. I'm tired."

Marcus pulled her down to whisper something in her ear. Her cheeks blushed and a smile crept across her beautiful face. Damn these two... had the world gone mad? My brother was an asshat and no good for my naive friend. I pulled her back to me, as if it was a game of tug of war between Marcus and me. I was going to win this one. He had Beck—who looked extra sullen tonight—to talk to. I needed my girl to myself.

At the risk of sounding like a nag, I scolded her as we swayed onto the dance floor. "Stop flirting with him. You can do better. Like that guy over there." I pointed to the cutie bopping his head in our direction while he ordered his drink at the bar. I caught a look from Marcus, who was eyeing me and Tessa like an overprotective pitbull.

I hated to talk smack about my brother, but he was the last thing Tessa needed right now. Marcus went through my friends faster than a doctor went through latex gloves. Tessa was a fool if she thought she would be the one to change his man-whore ways.

Once she realized that and he got tired of her, she'd want nothing to do with any reminders of him—me included. I couldn't have my brother screwing things up between Tessa and me now that I finally had her back.

I'd missed her all the years Zack kept her from me as some hostage. Prisoner, rather. She'd put up with years of his domineering, alcoholic fits of jealousy and abuse before he finally checked into a treatment facility. And Tessa, thankfully, found enough strength to escape with her baby boy.

So it was a surprise to me that she'd even want to date so soon. Come to think of it... it wasn't just Tessa's wellbeing I was concerned with. She wasn't right for Marcus right now *either*. He needed to get his act together before he could even consider being semi-serious with anyone—Tessa was way too vulnerable after what she'd been through with her douche bag ex to be teaching Marcus the dating ropes.

So, that's why I dragged her in the direction of the guy in the suit who was making his way toward us with his beer.

"Ry, what are you doing?" Tessa was on to my game.

"We're using JT to help us flirt. Come on, this guy's been looking our way."

I caught her glancing back at the table where Marcus and Beck were sitting. If I didn't know any better, I'd say she and Marcus were having their own silent conversation with their eyes alone. *Screw that!* He didn't have any ownership over *my* friend.

"Hi, ladies," said the sexy suited man, distracting Tessa from my brother and Beck.

"Well, hello there," I answered back a little too eagerly.

"I'm Chris." He extended his beerless—and ringless (thank God)—hand to Tessa first, but when she hesitated a beat too long, I swooped in and grabbed it.

"Nice to meet you, Chris. Is that short for Christian, as in the dominating Christian Grey, or Christopher, as in the insanely ingenious Christopher Walken?"

Chris smiled a mega-watt grin, showing off a dentist's dream. "Cute. I like that," he laughed, making eye contact with me. "But it's actually neither. I'm just Chris. I guess my parents got lazy."

Feeling a little brazen, I flirted as I admired him from head to toe. "I wouldn't say they were lazy at all—they created quite a masterpiece."

Tessa chuckled, shaking her head. "Damn, you Grayson siblings are smooth."

I giggled to myself and then brought my attention back to Chris when he asked, "So, ladies, are you going to tell me your names or keep me guessing?"

"How silly of me." I took the initiative. "I'm Riley and this is my friend, Tessa." The music was getting louder so I wasn't sure if he heard me, but it obviously didn't matter because he decided to stick around and dance with us for the next song.

After a few sweaty minutes of fun, Chris's hands became a little freer. He cupped my waist and pulled me close to him, and then he grabbed Tessa's hands, encouraging her to move to the sultry hip-hop beat of the music. The boy obviously couldn't choose between the two of us. It didn't matter, though, because I was just having fun. I had to keep reminding myself that I'd vowed not to go through with the meaningless hook-up tonight. Riley Grayson was not going to meet her future husband in a bar. Even if the idea of Chris as said husband wasn't so unappealing.

As if I needed a blaring reminder as to the quality of men in clubs, at that exact moment Chris took it upon himself to start dry humping Tessa's behind. She was clearly uncomfortable, so I started to sandwich myself between them. I needed to salvage the little bit of fun we were having before Chris turned all bump-and-grind. I was buzzed and feeling the moment and just wanted to have a good damn time, even if this guy was all over my friend. I threw my arms around Chris's neck and wiggled my ass into Tessa's groin, but before I could actually get my threesome on, I saw Marcus making a beeline toward Tessa with Beck hot on his tail.

"Hey," he jabbed Chris on the shoulder. "Can I help you?"

Chris eyed him up and down. "Sure, are you taking drink orders? I'll take a Bud Light for myself and two Ketel and Cranberries for my new friends here."

If steam could've come out of his ears it would have. My brother's tattooed neck bulged so that it looked like his veins were about to pop. Through gritted teeth, he got right in Chris's face. "I'm not some bus boy, asshole. I'm her..." He paused, looking at Tessa but quickly darted his angry gaze back to me. "I'm her brother."

Chris seemed completely unbothered by Marcus's overprotectiveness. "Can't your sister speak for herself? And what about her friend, Jess, was it?"

Fuck! That set him off for some reason. This dude's top was about to blow! "Her name's Tessa and no, they're both spoken for, so... Get. The. Fuck. Away."

Whoa! Wait a minute. What the hell was that all about? "Marcus!" I finally scolded, giving him an ineffective punch in the arm. He didn't budge, but just kept staring at Chris with clenched fists and flaring nostrils. This was taking it too far. Why the hell would he want to ruin our good time? And my buzz!

"It's okay, Ry," Tessa finally spoke as the voice of reason, coming between Chris and Marcus as the music wound down. "Come on, Marcus. Song's over, we can go sit back down now."

My brother took a few deep breaths and appraised both me and Tessa before turning toward the table. Just as I thought the little scuffle was over, Marcus looked over his shoulder and spit out, "Good idea. Good night, prick."

Chris whooshed past me, nearly knocking me on my ass, and bumping chests with Marcus. "What did you just call me?" When Marcus didn't respond quickly enough, Chris wound up and threw a punch. "Fuck you, asshole," was the last thing he said before I saw tattoos and flesh and drinks flying in the air.

Tessa and I shrieked and Beck came running to his friend's defense, pulling him off the man I'd obviously misjudged for a gentleman.

In a calming tone, Beck held Marcus back and growled into his ear. "Dude, what the fuck? This isn't you... you're better than this. Come on, bro, before it gets ugly."

It was the first time I'd noticed how mature Beck had become. Back in the day, he would have thrown punches along with Marcus. They were partners in crime—sometimes *actual* crimes—but seeing him like this right now, calm and sensible, it was a pleasant surprise.

After a few more seconds of a standoff between Marcus and a panting Chris, the crowd that had gathered started to murmur. In our own little huddle of four, I watched as Tessa stared into Marcus's eyes, calming him. "Please, Marcus. Let's just go." I couldn't quite explain the exchange in words sufficient enough to capture the feeling, but it was like watching a vicious snake being charmed into submission.

When Marcus finally spoke, he never took his eyes off Tessa. "Let's go. Beck, you share a cab with Riley and make sure she gets home okay. Tessa, you're riding home with me."

"But..." What the hell just happened? We all came here

together. Why did I have to be babysat by Beck?

"But nothing. Good night, Riley." Marcus didn't give me time to retort. He grabbed Tessa's hand, and left me standing with Beck, completely baffled.

After a shot to calm my nerves and a trip to the ladies' room, I let Beck convince me that it was indeed time to call it a night. When we finally ambled outside to hail a cab, the fresh air just made my drunkenness more prominent. Feeling giddy and reckless for a change, suddenly I couldn't stop thinking of making up my own lyrics to *Cabaret* (one of Justin's not so well known tunes) and belting them out. "Cabaret... ohhhh! Even though I'm three sheets to the wind, I ain't hooking up with your hot ass." *Oops.* Did I just say that out loud?

"What the fuck are you singing?" He looked at me like I was growing a second head, but then laughed as he steadied me on my wobbly feet.

His strong hands clutched my waist, the pads of his fingers brushing along the exposed skin of my midriff. *Whoa. Shivers.* It had to be the alcohol making me warm and fuzzy. Couldn't be the thought of Beck's hands rubbing *all parts* of my body. Nope—not going there. I needed a quick save. *Sarcasm. Confidence. Justin!*

"Duh! It's JT... my man. It *always* leads back to JT, Beckster. Don't you know that?"

"Don't you know how much I hate it when you call me Beckster?"

"Do you really? I thought you liked my nicknames for you."

"Why? Are there more than one?"

"Of course there are, silly boy. You're the Italian Stallion, the boy with the dragon tattoo, and the one that makes Marcus squirm the most... Becks on a Stick. Get it? Like Sex on a Stick?" I snorted and then realized what I'd said. *Shit!* How many drinks did I have? I was being way too free with my words.

I stumbled backwards as I danced around while rattling off his secret pet names. He reached out to stop me from toppling off the curb. And then he was touching me again. *Sweet Jesus.* He had to stop doing that.

"Wow. Really? I never knew I did it for you, Riles," he said with the cocky, careless attitude that matched my brother's.

"Oh, don't go confusing a silly nickname with me having the hots for you. Yes, you're adorable in that best friend of my little brother's sort of way, but you most certainly do not do it for me, Beckster."

At that, he arched an eyebrow and gave me this smoldering look that caused a dampness between my thighs. *Shit... what the hell?* That was one dangerous weapon he'd been holding out on me.

He inched closer and my breath caught. Within seconds, he was backing me up against the wall and then caging me between his arms. Suddenly my heart was rapping so hard against my chest I could barely control my breathing. Beck was going to make me break out in hives from the way he was looking at me.

My words came out all choppy. "What are you—

why are you—"

"I know how to read women, Riles. I see how large those pretty pupils of yours are right now. Your chest," he zeroed in on my cleavage, licking his lips slightly, "is rising and falling rapidly as you try to catch your breath. That little ticking underneath that soft skin on your neck tells me your pulse is racing, and that delicious, sweet aroma... you're aroused as all hell. So, don't tell me I don't do it for you, baby. Because I know I most certainly do."

Um... *what?* "Uh... uh..." Suddenly I was a stammering mute. My fingers itched to bury themselves in his wavy brown hair, to touch the delicious stubble that covered his always tanned complexion. I stared into Beck's chocolate brown eyes, begging with my own for him to kiss me. *Kiss me?* Did I really want Beck to kiss me? God, his little speech had me so needy for him.

The alcohol in my system certainly played a part in my behavior, but honestly, I was so tired of doing the right thing and ending up alone. Maybe I needed to channel that inner wild side I'd always wanted to toy with. So what if I let my hair down this once? So what if I let the Beckster kiss me? It would only be this one time anyway. It would hold me over and satisfy this ridiculous craving just for one fleeting second. But as I was about to lift my arms and tangle my fingers in his sexy, unruly hair, the cab pulled up and Beck's warmth vanished.

Feeling his absence, I practically wilted against the wall, wanting to crawl under a rock when he started to snicker. "Cab's here, Riles. Wanna pick your chin up off the floor now?"

Mother fucker. He was teasing me. Beck had gotten me all hot and bothered and there was nothing I could do about it.

CHAPTER 3

Beck

Damn, she was a sloppy drunk. Sexy, hot, and making my dick hard, but sloppy all the same. The sleeve of her skimpy shirt hung off her shoulder, revealing a purple lace bra strap. Interesting... I never took the stick-up-her-ass Grayson sibling for wearing sexy tit huggers. Even in my wildest dreams of Riley (and there had been a few over the years, if I'm being honest here) she wore plain white cotton panties. There was no mistaking she was gorgeous, but she was also very safe when it came to her appearance. I found that odd, because her line of work relied so much on colors and boldness and taking risks. Riley had not been a risk taker in all the years I'd known her.

But tonight I was seeing a different side to her, with her sexy outfit, her bright nail and lipstick color—it was about time she let her hair down. And kicked off her shoes... literally. She'd abandoned her wedges and was resting her bare feet against the back of the cracked vinyl front seat. Her skirt rode up her lap, giving the illusion of mile-long silky legs. Shit, she looked gorgeous like that.

And she'd clearly made herself comfortable on the deep back seat, not only by half-undressing but by singing her heart out. After telling the cab driver her address, Riley continued rendition after annoying rendition of that *Cabaret* song. Pop wasn't my thing. In fact, music wasn't really my thing unless it was classic rock, but Riley had a way of making an irritating song (sung on repeat) sound pretty damn good.

"Riles, how about a new tune?" I all but begged. She was on key, and actually coming up with some clever lyrics that had me laughing, but I was on the verge of hunting down Justin Timberlake myself if I had to suffer through it one more time.

"Okay, then." She rolled her eyes, tapping her red-painted nails across her red-painted lips. "What do you have in mind?"

Silence was what I had in mind, but there were also a lot of other things swarming through my brain. Not so innocent things. Like dragging my tongue across her flawless skin from her ankle to her thigh. Like sucking that red lipstick right off her lips. *Shit!* Why was I thinking these things about my best friend's sister? Why was I thinking these things about someone other than Marissa? Why? Because we were on a break; because I was hurt; because my pride had been blown to smithereens. And quite honestly, at that moment I didn't want to think about Marissa at all. I was officially a pathetic chump forced into some sort of relationship limbo.

"Penny for your thoughts over there, Beckster?" She interrupted my silent tirade.

Oh, that was it! All thoughts of Marissa vanished at the sound of that fucking nickname again. "Stop calling me that," I growled playfully, lunging at her, and tickling the soft skin behind her knees.

"Oh my god, Beck. Stop that! Stop..." she trailed off, laughing uncontrollably.

For the first time in days, I allowed myself to laugh too. The musical sound of her contagious giggles and squeals only made my fingers move faster. In an attempt to back away from me, she fell against the seat so that she was lying beneath me as I continued my torture. I hovered over her for a split second, trying to get my brain to make a decision that I *wouldn't* regret later. But something else won over and drew me in. I inched my face closer to hers, the magnetic pull of our eyes never losing contact. I leaned down so we were nose to nose, and her breath hitched with the sweetest little gasp as my lips grazed hers, softly at first. But when she tangled her hands in my hair and wrapped her legs around my waist...

I was a goner.

This was Riley Grayson I was groping and devouring in the back of a cab. I should probably be delicate and sweet and kiss her like a gentleman. God damn it, even though I wanted to rip her clothes off and sink my cock between those delicious thighs, I tamed the urge as I gently cupped her face in my hands.

For a split second, our eyes locked and I saw past the fervent lust and the sudden craving. It might be nice to enjoy this the right way. Riley and I could...

Fuck being a gentleman! I wanted her legs spread open, her feet resting on my shoulders as I pounded into her and made her scream.

Unable to ignore my building urgency, I surged our bodies together, grinding my cock against her. Our tongues became wild, exploring unchartered, yet familiar, territory. I must've always wanted to kiss Riley and never knew how badly. Sucking her tongue and biting her lips while confined in this tight space was like feeding a hunger I never knew existed. The immediate friction of our writhing bodies had her arching her hips off the seat and grinding into the bulge trapped in my jeans.

"Mmmm," she moaned. These sounds were killing me and urging me to keep going.

As we continued our kiss, her breathing intensified while my hands roamed her body, finally making their way up her legs and under her skirt. Shit, she felt like heaven beneath my fingertips. I wanted to feel all of her. To taste all of her. To have my pulsing cock inside her. God, even though I'd never been with her before, it was like I couldn't get enough. I don't know—maybe it was the thrill of having a one-man audience, or the idea that she was forbidden fruit, but this was one insanely powerful first kiss. And I certainly didn't want it to end there.

Lucky for us, just as I was about to rip her skirt off—and she was gonna let me, too—the car came to a stop and the cabbie cleared his throat. "That'll be $18.55."

Still unable to disconnect myself from Riley, I reached into my pocket and threw the guy a few bills. "Keep the change." I was pretty sure it was two twenties—not only had we given the guy a free peep show, but he also got the best tip of the night out of us. I so did not give a fuck. I needed to be out of this cab and inside her pussy.

"Fuck! What am I doing?" Riley muttered as she smoothed down her skirt, readjusted herself, and sat up.

I was already standing outside the cab, with an outstretched hand and tented jeans. Was this where it ended? Was the magic over? Or was there a chance to convince her it was okay to try this on for size?

Shit! What the fuck was *I* doing? I was in love with another woman, even if things were a little messy right now.

But...

There it was. That dangling conjunction that could make or break any fucking sentence, any goddamn decision—right or wrong. In this case, my *but* was that I had to see this through—even if it was a dick move and a cop-out distraction from my problems with Marissa.

Trying to sound like a gentleman—let me rephrase that, a gentleman who wanted to try his luck at getting in her pants—I grabbed her hand and said, "Riles, we're just having fun. Come on, I'll walk you inside."

"Beck, if I let you walk me inside, I'm going to want you stay. I don't think that's a good idea."

It wasn't a good idea and I thought it was incredible that even after our heated kiss in the cab *and* in her tipsy state, Riley could still make a good judgment call.

I placed a hand at the small of her back, helping her up the cobblestone steps. "You sure? I can get you a glass of water and a few aspirin and tuck you in for the night." Bullshit. Once I was in her bedroom the only thing I'd be tucking was my dick inside her warmth.

Turning to face me, a smile spread across her stunning face. Even with glazed over eyes and lipstick smudged to oblivion, she was breathtaking. Why hadn't I noticed that until now?

"What are you smiling about?" I asked, grinning myself.

"That was fun back there," she admitted, biting on her lower lip, and running her hands through her trendy, short hair.

I walked up another step to meet her face to face again, reaching out to tuck a piece of her dark hair behind her ear. It was an intimate move, but my hands needed to touch a part of her again. I'd even settle for those few strands of errant hair. "Riles, let me inside so we can continue that fun."

She paused for a beat, staring at my lips, then licked her own. When our eyes met again, I swear I could see the desire raging behind those gorgeous blue orbs. "Fuck it," she finally said, reaching for her keys and unlocking the door. She looked over her shoulder and arched an eyebrow. "You only live once, right?"

We wasted no time getting our lips reacquainted. The door had barely shut behind us and I was mauling her again. Not that she was complaining—unless panting and moaning against my mouth was some form of complaint.

The house was dark, but I could see my way around, noticing a room with a large comfy couch and nothing that looked breakable. The cottony scent of just-washed-clothes mixed with a warm hint of vanilla was inviting—as if all my other senses weren't already making themselves at home.

Still kissing her, I clutched her waist to keep her steady, backing her into the room. When I started to guide her down on the couch, she broke away. "Beck, I—"

"Let me guess. Expensive upholstery?" I asked against her neck.

She laughed and backed up a drop, as she tried to fix the lipstick that was now fading from the frantic nature of our kiss. "No, but—wanna go upstairs?"

I was stunned for a moment, happy that she wasn't hesitating because she was having doubts. I was the one who should be having doubts, but I just couldn't bring myself to deny her invitation. I wanted this. More than I'd ever wanted a girl before, and I owed it to myself to find out why. But actually going up to her bedroom made it seem premeditated. I could live with myself and the guilt that was sure to creep up eventually if it seemed like a spontaneous act of lust. On the couch. It was all such bullshit—I knew it even as I thought it. There was no excuse, but I'd worry about the consequences later. When my brain wasn't high off images of fucking this girl to oblivion.

"I'm kind of digging right here, Riles. Is that okay?" Dim light seeped in through the windows. I watched her shadowed face for a reaction.

Without waiting a beat, she crossed her arms, curling her fingers inside the hem of her top and lifted it over her head. "Here's perfect. Just take me already."

Holy shit! I'd pegged her wrong all this time! She was an aggressive business woman, but she seemed shy and reserved in everything else she did. Guess I was wrong when it came to reading women. Mentally at least. Her hard pink nipples showed through the thin lace of her bra, begging to be tasted. Her pale, smooth skin was marked with thousands of tiny goose bumps, giving away her vulnerability. I knew how to read body language, and staring at her flawless figure—a perfect little bellybutton that I envisioned collecting the cum I wanted to squirt all over her smooth flat stomach—she was ready and willing. Did I really just think about coming all over Riley Grayson? There was no time to think about all the reasons we shouldn't be doing this, because none of those reasons could convince me it was wrong. As quickly and unexpectedly as it was happening, it felt right. It felt familiar.

"I like the sound of that, sweet thing."

Her hands crept into the waistline of her mini-skirt, but I inched closer, wanting the honor of undressing the rest of her. "Allow me," I said, kneeling down and pulling the skirt down her legs from the bottom. When I reached her feet, she stepped out of it one foot after the other, still wearing her heels. "These are pretty sweet too, but wouldn't you rather take them off?"

"Mmmhmm. Good idea. I can get kind of clumsy," she admitted with a giddy giggle.

As she kicked them off one-by-one with a thud against the carpet, she held my shoulders for support. I stroked her legs, up and down, finally stopping to cup her ass. She wore a barely-there lace thong, allowing my hands the much needed skin-on-skin contact. I lightly slapped one perky cheek and then gripped harder, pulling her closer to me.

When she felt my breath between her legs, her own breath hitched. I sucked in her scent through my nose, hypnotized by the sweet musky aroma of her arousal.

"Fucking amazing, Riles. I just know you're going to be delicious."

At my words, her legs opened ever so slightly, allowing me access to what I wanted most. Hooking my fingers in her panties, I slid them down her legs, stopping at her thighs. I couldn't even wait the half a second to taste her. My tongue darted out to caress her clean-shaven pussy, and when I skimmed it over her swollen clit I felt her legs go to jelly in my hands.

"Ohhhh, Beck. Please don't stop."

Pausing, I smiled up at her—hooded lids at half mast, her bottom lip between her teeth—she looked like she was in the best kind of pain possible. "I have no intention of it, baby. I'm just getting started." With that, I buried my face between her legs and grabbed her hips, moving her around so she could sit on the couch. "Sit down, baby. Get comfortable. I like to take my time."

"You keep doing that, it'll take no time at all."

"We'll see." I pushed her down against the plush cushion and spread her legs. She lifted one and draped it over my shoulder. I dug my fingers into her thigh, loving the idea of her anchoring herself to me. I'd imagined my face between Riley's legs, just never actually thought I'd get the chance. And never had I expected it to be so addicting after one sweet sample.

Her hips arched off the cushion in fucking harmony with each thrust of my tongue. I lapped at her arousal and circled her clit, while working my fingers in and out of her. I could tell she was close by the way she cried out my name and twisted her fingers in my hair, but I wanted this to last.

"Oh my god, I'm going to come. I swear to Christ,

Beck, you're going to make me come!"

Was it a surprise that I could do that to her? The way it came out of her mouth made it sound that way. Was it wild? I suppose. I'd known her since I was a little kid. But I didn't want her thinking of me as her brother's little pal right now. I was the guy who was about to give her the best orgasm of her life.

I stiffened my tongue to enter her and my hand crept around to cup her behind. I urged her to grind her pussy against my mouth as my fingers slowly trailed the crease of her ass. When she didn't move my hand away or give any indication that she didn't like where this was leading, I settled between her cheeks and found her other opening with one finger. She let out another melodious gasp and then her hand reached mine at her rear. But instead of stopping me, she urged me to continue thrusting in and out of the incredible tightness. "Mmmm, you like that, don't you?"

"Yes," she whispered, still guiding my finger with one hand, and keeping my head in place between her legs with the other.

"I can't hear you," I growled, pausing my licking. "Tell me that you like it."

I brought my tongue back to her flesh, and her head flew back as she screamed, "I fucking love it! Oh. My. God. I love it."

More sweetness erupted into my mouth and I lapped it up, like a starving man. Was I starved? No, not really, but there was something about getting that taste—that sexy, addicting, fucking glorious taste—of something I'd desired from afar, that was out of reach, the impossible victory. Shit, it felt like I'd just won the fucking lottery.

"Wow, babe. That was fucking hot as hell." It was and I wanted more, but I didn't want to push her. I rose from my knees and joined her on the couch. Leaning my head back, I closed my eyes and took it all in. How did this happen so quickly without so much as one thought about who we were to each other and how this would play out afterwards? You know what—how had this never happened *before*? There was always strong sexual tension between the two of us, but nothing I thought she'd want to act on. I guess there was a lot about Riley Grayson I didn't know.

Before I could open my eyes to make some kind of awkward-after-sex comment, Riley was straddling my lap and pulling my shirt up. "Is there more where that came from, Beckster?" she asked, tilting her head and giggling. It was her way of making light of the situation, but I had no intention of turning this night into a silly game.

"Riles, I hate that childish nickname," I said, gripping her wrists, causing her to look me in the eyes. "So how about we drop that, *but* I still make you come again."

"Sounds good, B." *B?* I liked that better. No one ever called me that—it felt like our own special thing. How the fuck did Riley and I have our own special thing already?

I didn't want to think about the emotional side of all this. There was no reason to. This would probably never happen again. It *couldn't* happen again. Marcus would kill me if he found out. Marissa would hate me for moving on after only a few days apart. So instead of worrying about those pesky things called morals, I thought about her screaming my name again. "Tell me how you want me to make you come?"

Removing my shirt and unbuttoning my jeans without haste, she said, "With you inside me."

"I think we can make that happen."

"Good, now stop talking and get those pants off."

Aggressive at work and play—Riley was full of surprises. "Yes, boss."

"Oh God," she laughed, as I shucked my pants. "I don't know what's come over me. I'm not usually like this. It's just—this is so—"

I brought my fingers to her lips. "Shhh. You have some coming to do." Her smile brightened and her cheeks reddened. I hooked my hand behind her neck and stared into her eyes. "I don't care how you usually are in bed. Tonight it's me and you and this crazy connection we've got going on. It feels good, doesn't it?" I ground my erection against her wet folds.

"So. Fucking. Good."

"Then let's keep going."

"Okay," she said, taking my cock in her hand and stroking it. She sat up tall and started to lower herself on top of me.

"Bareback, Riles? Are you sure?" I was clean and Marissa always made me wear a condom, but this was yet another surprise from the always straight-and-narrow Riley.

"I'm positive. I'm on the pill. Please, Beck, I need you inside me already."

I should've probably been more persistent—I wasn't the one in a cloudy alcohol haze—but I didn't even have any condoms on me, and I wasn't about to stop with the tip of my dick already making headway.

"Decisions, decisions," I pretended to contemplate the

pros and cons of living out the fantasy I'd had for a long time. When she tilted her head and rolled her eyes, I finally gave in like I intended all along. "Okay. I trust you. I know you're a good girl."

She arched an eyebrow and grabbed my hard-on with a tight squeeze. "Call me a good girl again and I'll have to go back to Beckster," she joked.

"Shit! Okay, you're a very bad girl, Riles. Now please, let me in."

Finally entering her slowly at first, I hissed with pure pleasure as she opened up for me and said, "Now, no more talking unless you're begging for more."

I stayed silent and rocked my hips so that we started to move faster. Her small but beautiful tits bounced as she sped up the pace, urging me deeper and deeper. I held on to her ass and encouraged her to grind against me each time she bounced up and down onto my lap. My dick felt like it was reaching unimaginable depths that way. I was buried in her addictive warmth and I never wanted to escape. "Shit, Riles. You feel so fucking good."

"You too, B. Don't stop."

There is was again. That cute little thing between only us. It made me tingle, and it had nothing to do with fucking her. Feeling connected, and nostalgic, and in complete ecstasy, I could go like this for hours—or at least I wanted to. But the way she was riding me, I would be exploding on that belly like I'd wanted in no time.

She leaned down and started kissing me again. Her urgency matched the way our bodies connected so forcefully. I wanted to feel more of her, so I reached my arms around her back to unsnap her bra. When her tits were free, I kneaded her nipples between my fingers, tugging with the tiniest of pressure.

"Oh," she moaned, arching her back while she continued slamming over me. "So good. So, so good."

I leaned down and sucked one breast into my mouth, pinching the pearl of her nipple with my teeth. She moved faster and more frantically—it made her fucking wild. Surprise, after surprise, after surprise. This was the most refreshing, unexpected, and rewarding lay I'd ever had.

"B, please tell me you're close, too," she panted in my ear. "I'm almost there and I want to make sure you come too."

For one of the first times I almost didn't give a fuck about finishing. Watching her have an orgasm was like witnessing a miraculous spectacle. It was fucking beautiful. But I wanted her to experience the same satisfaction I had, knowing that she made me come undone. One or two more powerful thrusts inside her tight pussy would do the trick.

"Turn around, Riles." I helped her swivel her body so that her back faced my front. I gripped her waist, guiding her up and down. I thrust my hips upward, meeting each movement with my own forceful penetration. It was heaven.

"Fuck, Beck! Oh my god," she screamed as I felt her walls pulse and then tighten around me. It was all I needed to push me over the edge, as well.

I lifted her from my lap so I didn't let loose inside of her. We would have enough to think about after this... we didn't need a pregnancy to further complicate things. I hated having to be on guard in this moment, but I guess that was the nature of cheating. Even though Marissa wasn't technically my girlfriend anymore. I just couldn't help feeling like a scumbag anyway.

Before I had the chance to bask in my guilt, Riley turned around, still straddling me, and rested her head in the crook of my neck.

She let out a sigh, and then I thought I felt tears. "I'm a horrible person. You have a girlfriend. What was I thinking?" Her shoulders started to shake—she was definitely crying. What a turn of events. This couldn't be happening—but it was, and I understood why.

"Please don't cry," I said, caressing her naked back and hugging her against me. "It's not like that. I promise you, it's not. Let me worry about... her." I couldn't even say her name. It would hurt Riley more if she heard it. And if I knew one thing, it was that I didn't want Riley to hurt because of me. "Riles, please, babe. Don't cry. Let's not ruin this."

She sat up, looking into my eyes. "Ruin what? Are you telling me this wasn't just some ridiculous one night stand, Beck? You have a girlfriend. You don't want me."

In the midst of all the guilt, lust, tears, and questions, the craziest thing was that I *did* want her. I wanted to be with her again. I maybe even wanted to be with her on more than just a sexual level. "I don't regret one second of tonight, babe, if that's what you're thinking. But it's late, you're still a little drunk, and we shouldn't talk about this now. Let's go to sleep and we'll talk in the morning."

She perked up again. "Wait. You're staying? Won't she be looking for you?"

If we lived together—like I'd asked her to—she'd be looking for me because she'd be home waiting for me. But that wasn't the case.

Pulling her closer to me with my hand at the nape of her neck, I whispered against her ear. "No, she won't. Can you show me to your room now, sweet thing?"

CHAPTER 4
Riley

Beck's phone ringing woke me up from a dead sleep. When I looked at the clock, I realized we'd slept for a pretty long time, considering all the times we wound up screwing around last night.

That first time on the couch just wasn't enough. We made our way up to my bedroom sometime past one a.m., after scarfing down half a pint of ice cream. After another glorious round of orgasms in my bedroom, we moved to the shower to clean up and indulge in some orally stimulating activities that had us wrinkled like prunes and the water running cold by the time we were moaning out each other's names.

There was no denying, after that first time, I felt like a home-wrecking whore. But Beck helped me believe it wasn't me who was at fault. Yes, I'd slept with him knowing his situation, but there was obviously something wrong in his relationship with Marissa if he was willing to go through with it.

I'd known Beck for a long time—as a cute child, through his gawky pre-teen years, his glorified high school quarterback days, and now his responsible adult days. He was a good person—not as reckless as my brother, taking random girls to bed all the time. Beck had morals and a conscience, so he had to be feeling like shit about now.

"B, your phone's ringing," I said, nudging his shirtless body.

He grumbled, pulling the covers over his head.

Oh, no, don't do that! I was admiring the view. I'd probably seen him shirtless millions of times, but this time— with him in *my* bed—it was so different. I'd always thought Beck was a good-looking guy, but suddenly I was more appreciative of his sexy dark features, his well-defined six pack, and those delicious, magical lips. God, I was swooning over Beck Matthews. What the hell was wrong with me?

Before I could wipe the drool from my lips, Beck was out from under the blanket, grabbing me.

"Come here," he said, tossing me around the bed so that I was wrapped in his arms.

Mmmm. I liked this, but I probably shouldn't get used to it. He was Beck. He wasn't available. He belonged to someone else. He was my brother's best friend.

"Stop thinking, Riles. That wheel is running marathons in your brain. I can actually hear it," he joked with his ear resting on my head.

"Yeah, well, for someone with such impeccable hearing, you didn't hear your phone buzzing for the last half hour."

He shot up from our cozy cuddling position to grab his phone from the nightstand and check the display. "Shit!" His fingers flew through his hair and then he banged his head purposely against the headboard.

"What?" I asked, like I didn't already know the answer to my question.

"She's been calling since last night. She's probably worried sick and—"

"Fucking pissed. I know I'd be." Reality was crashing in and I had to make like I didn't care. Even if I felt like the green-eyed monster and the other woman, both rolled into one.

He stood up from the bed, searching for his clothes.

"Over there." I pointed to the chair in the corner of the room. "And the rest is downstairs."

After he'd pulled on his boxers and T-shirt from last night, he came to sit next to me on the bed.

I couldn't help feeling so cheap at that moment. The room still smelled of hot sex and he was about to tell me all the things a cheater was supposed to say the morning after a night like ours. Like: please don't tell anyone; it was just a mistake; I never thought it would go that far; it was the alcohol talking.

What I didn't expect was what he actually *did* say: "Riles. Last night was—" He paused to scratch his head and take a deep breath. "Last night one of the best nights of my life, and I'm not just talking about the sex, babe," he winked and smiled, melting away the insecurities for a moment. "I don't want to talk about her with you, but you should know Marissa and I are on a break."

And then the insecurities were back. I pulled away from him, immediately thinking I was some rebound or a form of revenge. He must have sensed my fears, because he inched closer, cupping my face in his hands.

"I know what you're thinking and it's not like that. We have a lot to think about, but right now," he looked at his phone, shaking his head. "Right now, I have to deal with her. Can I call you later?"

I reached up to hold his warm hand in place at my cheek. It was a comforting show of affection from him and I didn't want it to end. "I'd love it if you'd call me later."

I could have said more, and maybe I should have. Maybe I should've let him off the hook and told him there was no way we could ever be anything other than two friends who had a little fun. I couldn't see this playing out any other way, but in that moment, I really wanted to hold on to the possibility of more.

"Fallon, answer your damn phone, you ass! Great news! My dry spell is officially O-V-E-R!"

I'd tried calling him at least ten times, and it just kept ringing with no answer. This was the first voicemail, and he wasn't the best at checking those. Fallon was notorious for having a bit too much fun on the weekends and going MIA for most of it.

I really needed to talk to him. Who else was I going to tell about what happened with Beck? I couldn't exactly keep everything I was feeling to myself. I might combust!

There was only one other person who would *hopefully* understand. Tessa. But I had no intention of calling her and asking permission to come over for some girl time. She'd given me a key for emergencies. *This* was certainly an emergency.

By the time I'd driven to her neighborhood and replayed my night with Beck over and over again in my head, I was starting to weigh all the repercussions. I was already in too deep, already feeling things I shouldn't be feeling.

I liked him. I liked the way we were together and the things he said to me. He didn't have to say those things. He could have left well enough alone, pretended it was what it really was... a one night stand between two old friends.

A mistake.

But was it a mistake? Something that felt so good couldn't be confused as a blunder in fate's workings. Yes, I was a deep thinker and circling the crowded Brooklyn blocks for a damn spot, was giving me *more* time to think.

When I finally made my way to Tessa's front door, I took out my key, reminding myself that she gave it to me with the intent to use it, and put it in the lock.

"Hello?" I bellowed as I walked in to the enticing aroma of freshly brewed coffee. "Tess? I really need to talk to you. You're not gonna believe what I—" I was laughing as I said it, but all humor vanished when I walked into the kitchen. There at the table sat a glowing Tessa, feeding Luca his breakfast—that part was normal. But the not so normal part was my shirtless brother, nonchalantly standing at the sink with a cup of joe.

"No. Fucking. Way." My mouth dropped to the floor when I realized what was going on. He'd obviously spent the night. These two were screwing behind my back, even though I'd told them what a disaster that would wind up being.

"Riley? How'd you get in? What the hell are you doing here?" Marcus remained frozen at the sink, looking like he'd been caught red-handed.

Fucking red-handed, alright.

My emotions were on such overload from my night with Beck and their blatant disregard for everything I'd tried to warn them about. I couldn't help but be angry. "Me? What're *you* doing here? And better yet, what the fuck is this all about?" I waved my arms all around, pointing fingers between the two of them. "Now you're playing house? Well, how fucking adorable." Marcus had no right pretending he could be what Tessa—and Luca—needed in a man. And I really never thought Tessa would fall victim to his seductive ways. "And you," I said pointing to her. "I thought you knew better. I warned you about this. Shit, Tessa! How stupid could you be?"

"Enough!" Marcus roared. "You have no right."

"Oh, the hell I don't!" I did so have a right. She was *my* friend and I'd just gotten her back. Once he was done messing with her, I'd lose her again. Marcus wasn't relationship material. This was just sex. And even though I felt guilty for ranting and raving at these two after pretty much doing the same thing with Beck, Beck was different than Marcus. I had hope. I'd seen it enough times to know that my brother was *hopeless.*

"You think you can just fuck whoever you want and leave me to pick up all the pieces, don't you? This won't work, Marcus, and when you decide you're done with her, like you did with all my other friends, she'll be devastated and she won't want to talk to me anymore. Again!"

Marcus glared at me with fury and rage in his eyes. His

fists clenched at his sides, and his breathing picked up so that his chest heaved. He was about to rip me a new one, but before he could open his mouth, Tessa was between us. "Okay, everyone calm down. Marcus, why don't you let me talk to Riley? We can catch up again later."

He eyed me with pure hatred, his nostrils still flaring, but when Tessa walked over to him and stroked the bulging muscles in his tensing arm and whispered something to him, he visibly calmed down. "You'll call me later," he barked like a Neanderthal, like he had something to prove to me.

I rolled my eyes, but didn't look away. I had to witness this whole ridiculous exchange for myself.

Tessa caressed his arm one more time and said, "Promise. Now, go cool off."

He bent down to kiss her—a long, lingering kiss right on the mouth—again, making a show of what he thought I needed to see. It meant nothing to me. It was all an act. He was trying to impress her. There was no depth—Marcus didn't do depth.

After he collected his belongings and walked out with a huff and the slam of a door, I sat down at the kitchen table next to a babbling Luca.

Tessa was the first to speak. I guess one of us had to break the ice. "Hey," she said with a small smile. I had to hand it to her—here I was barging in on her Saturday morning afterparty and she didn't seem the slightest bit annoyed with me. I guess, unlike my brother, she understood I only wanted the best for her. I didn't want to see her hurt again.

"He's bad news, Tessa."

With that, her expression changed from appreciative to

irritated. "Drop it. Please? I understand where you're coming from and I appreciate it with all my heart, but I like being with him."

Oh God, he'd gotten to her. "Ridiculous. I just can't see how—"

"Riley." She inched closer, locking her eyes with mine. "Leave. It. Alone." It was a stern warning and I knew better than to push my luck.

I looked away from her and down to Luca, who instantly made me smile. But then Tessa reminded me of why I'd been here in the first place and my smile grew even wider. "So, wanna tell me what you barged in here ranting about before you started your tirade on me and Marcus? I gave you that key for emergencies. Is there something you need to tell me?"

I found myself embarrassed by what I had to admit, yet I was giddy and couldn't stop smiling, thinking about the way Beck had made me feel. But Tessa only knew him as Marcus's friend—his *not single* friend. She would judge me for being with Beck, knowing he had a girlfriend.

And what about me being the world's *biggest* hypocrite? After the ass-chewing I'd just given her and Marcus—hadn't I'd done the exact same thing in reverse? I was probably about to get a well-deserved ass-chewing of my own. Pushing away the guilt, I feigned ignorance and played the drunk card. "I—shit, I was so dumb." My head dropped into my hands, trying to hide my embarrassment, *and* the big smile that just wouldn't go away. "I slept with Beck last night."

"You *what?*"

I'd never heard Tessa shriek that loud. In fact, I was

pretty sure her own son hadn't either, because at the sound of her shrills Luca was in tears.

"Oh, Luca. Don't cry, baby." I stood up to take him out of his high chair, but Tessa clamped a hand on my shoulder, pushing me back down.

"Oh, no. Not so fast. I've got him. You talk."

CHAPTER 5

Beck

So, now I was supposed to feel guilty, right? Was I supposed to call Marissa and tell her I made a mistake and that I was sorry for acting out my anger with a revenge fuck? Problem with that was—I didn't feel one ounce of remorse. Not one.

This was what *she* wanted. Marissa needed a break from me, and while we were on that break I should be able to do whatever and *whomever* I wanted. I didn't need to explain myself to her anymore. She had no right texting and calling me like a nagging mother—she'd given up on us. Didn't she have some studying to do or something?

So, after I made my way across town to my apartment and took a quick shower to wash off the night before, I dialed Marissa's number with pure ambivalence.

"Hi," she answered on the first ring.

"Hi. Everything okay?" I didn't want to care, but I did. You couldn't just turn off your love for someone.

"Yes. I tried calling you last night and when you didn't answer I stopped by, but you never came home. I'm not judging or even asking for an answer to where you were, but—can I come over? I want to talk." For the first time since she told me she needed a break, I could sense the urgency in her voice.

Maybe she wanted to come over to apologize and admit that she was overreacting when she broke up with me. That was all fine and dandy, except for the fact I'd just spent a really incredible night with my best friend's sister. It had me thinking things I wasn't sure I should be thinking.

I didn't owe Riley anything after one time together, but by the same token, I promised I'd call her. I wasn't going to hurt Riley Grayson. She was one of my oldest friends. She didn't deserve to be treated as a rebound fuck because she wasn't.

In fact, I wondered exactly what these thoughts were stirring up in my brain. I found myself replaying our night together with a huge smile on my face. And it wasn't just because of the smoking sex with a beautiful woman. Even in a drunken haze, we shared something that needed to be explored again. I wanted another shot with Riley.

So, where did that leave me with Marissa?

Regardless of my newfound interest in Riley, I gave in to Marissa's request. "Sure, come over. I'm here." I had no idea how this would play out, but I owed it to Marissa—and myself—after two years of being together.

When the doorbell rang, it was nothing like all the times before. In the past, when I was expecting a visit from Marissa I was actually giddy—yes, giddy—with anticipation. We rarely ever fought because there wasn't much time to do that. I worked crazy shifts at the firehouse and with her studying for the bar, lately we were lucky if we saw each other once a week. That worked for us. It made everything better when we did get to see each other. But I guess it was my stupid mistake for wanting to spend even *more* time with my girlfriend. Asking her to move in obviously wasn't on her radar. Her wanting a break wasn't on mine. But since that conversation a few days ago, a lot had changed and I wasn't exactly feeling all warm and tingly when I opened the door.

"Hi," she murmured. I could tell by the puffiness of her face and the redness in her eyes that she'd been crying.

"Hey," I said back, gesturing for her to come in. I was harboring so many emotions it was hard to react. I didn't like to see her upset, but I was hurt over the way we'd left things. Seeing her made it sting even more. But what was worse was the guilt that crept its way in. I didn't know what the reason for her being here was, but I wouldn't be able to lie to her if she asked questions.

And she wasted no time rambling them off. "Where were you last night? Why didn't you answer my calls? I think I made a mistake, Beck. Do you think we made a mistake?"

Whoa. Way to get right to the point. "Ris, calm down," I coaxed her, ushering her into the living room. "Why don't you sit on the couch and relax? I'll make you a cup of coffee and we'll talk." One of us had to be rational, otherwise this would be harder than it had to be. I just hoped I could do this the right way.

She simply nodded as she wiped away her tears. I turned my back to head into the kitchen.

I'd been making her coffee for two years. Cream and two sugars, with one ice cube so she didn't burn her mouth. It occurred to me that I really did know everything about

Marissa, except when it came to our future. I knew all her quirky, beautiful ins and outs—the way her feet rubbed together like a cricket's right before she fell asleep, the way her tongue crept out of the side of her mouth while she furiously wrote notes while studying, the way she sang terribly off-key in the shower when she was happy. I knew all those things and so many more, so how could I have missed that the two of us were not on the same page when it came to moving in?

Maybe part of me was an ignorant ass to not see this coming all along. She'd never really talked about marriage and always brushed off the idea of kids, but I still assumed she saw a future with me and that taking the next step would make her happy. I never imagined it would freak her out and have her second-guessing what I believed was a perfect relationship.

The refrigerator hummed in the quiet kitchen as I plopped the ice cube in the mug. It was my turn for second-guessing. I might not have been so keen on the break when she dropped that bomb on me the other night, but being with Riley made things different. Was it shitty that sleeping with another girl made me realize this? Maybe. But it wasn't just that. Being with Riley made me question things about my relationship with Marissa. I wasn't the cheating kind, and even though it wasn't *technically* cheating, I wouldn't have been so quick to jump in someone else's bed if I didn't have my own doubts about my future with Marissa.

Walking into the living room, balancing our Saturday morning coffee in my hands, I knew what I had to do. It wouldn't be easy since I figured she was here to convince me otherwise, but suddenly I needed this break as much as she did.

"You slept with someone?" she cried, jumping out of her seat on the couch. "We were broken up all of forty-eight hours and you fucked another girl? Beck, how could you?"

I glared at her from where I sat, realizing that my honesty might not have been the best segue into telling her our break was a good idea. I reached for her arm to pull her back down to her seat, but she yanked it away from me.

"Marissa, please. Can you sit down and let me talk to you?"

"This is unbelievable. I just can't believe—I'm not sure I want to hear what else you have to say. You're obviously not the man I thought you were if you need to go out and fuck away our issues."

What I took from that wasn't sadness, jealousy, or even anger. I heard the truth behind her words. "So, you *are* admitting we have issues. Not to mention that if I'm not the man you thought *I* was, then you're certainly not the woman I thought *you* were."

"What the hell's that supposed to mean?" she asked, narrowing her eyes.

I didn't want this to turn into a brawl, but I needed to be honest. There were things that needed to be said. "It means when I asked you to move in, you fucking clammed up. Not only did you reject my invitation to take the next step, but you reminded me of all the times you've pushed away my hopes for the future."

The look in her eyes went from hurt to defensive in a split second. "Beck, I'm sorry I hurt your feelings, but now is not the time for me to make this kind of decision. You have no idea the stress I've been under with this exam. I feel like I'm going crazy. And this is just the beginning. Once I pass, I'll be putting in hours that will seem ungodly to you. Your shifts at the firehouse have nothing on the torturous hours of a first year law associate."

"Yeah, okay." I rolled my eyes and scoffed at her. I was used to three days with no sleep, and as a probie... let's not go there. Rookie year on the fire department was worse than any fraternity hazing. "Just because I'm not some CEO hotshot doesn't mean I don't get what it's like to work hard."

"That's not what I'm saying, Beck. Why can't you understand where I'm coming from? How important this is to me? I'm sorry if I freaked out and made it like I didn't want to be with you. I love you. I *do* want to be with you. I want to make this work."

There was no denying our love for each other, and I did understand her need to focus on her career, but in the last few days I'd realized that we were on different paths at this stage in our lives. "Maybe you're not saying it now, but you've said a lot of things over the years that are just becoming clear to me now.

"Marissa, you don't want all the things I stand for. I don't expect you to drop your dreams for me, but I also don't want to drop mine for you. I took the job with the department partly because I saw the benefits of having a fireman for a dad, first hand. Mine was completely hands-on and retired when he was still young enough to toss around a ball with his kids. I want that. All of it. But, with the way things are going with you, when I'm retiring from the FDNY, you'll be a big-wig lawyer to the stars, still working twenty-hour days and making millions."

"And that's a bad thing?" she shrieked. "Please tell me that being a successful career woman is not a turn off for you, Beck. Here I thought I was making a decision for a solid future—for our future—and you're telling me I'm not?" I could tell by the way her hands were scrunched into fists at her side that she was furious. Rather than point out the obvious, it was time to ask her the question that could make or break everything.

"Do you want kids, Marissa?" It was a hefty question. One I never thought would matter to me at twenty-four, considering I wasn't sure I wanted a family before I met Marissa. But I had changed all my bachelor-for-life ways since then. It took spending time at my firehouse with some of the greatest husbands and fathers I'd known and falling in love with this girl to realize I wanted the all-American dream. But if she didn't want that, maybe I was with the *wrong* girl.

"Why are you bringing this up now? Why can't we worry about this later?"

"Why wait until later, Ris? Why prolong the inevitable?"

"Because I don't want to lose you. All I'm asking for is more time," she pleaded. Her tears welled up in her eyes and then flowed freely down her face. I wanted to reach out and swipe them away for her, but I didn't want to give the wrong impression.

But I also wasn't sure I was ready to say goodbye for good.

Wrapping my arms around her and cradling her face against my neck, I kissed the top of her head. *So much for wrong impressions.* I just couldn't pretend I didn't care, regardless of the disappointment I felt over things not going my way. She was a good person who had a lot going on. We both had shit to think about. "Can I make a suggestion?" I finally asked.

"What?" she replied, her voice muffled against my chest, her tears creating a wet spot on my T-shirt.

"Let's take this break—"

Her head popped up and I could already hear the words that were going to come out of her mouth. But before she could speak, I placed a finger to her lips and continued, "This test is warping your brain. You're stressed out—for good reason. You need to focus on that. You shouldn't have to worry about me and my demands or about making life-changing decisions right now. I'm sorry for adding more to your already overflowing plate.

"So, for now I say you study your ass off, ace the shit out of that exam, and then we revisit this. Things will be different then. Our heads will be clearer. You'll see." She stood silent, taking in my words. They were pretty rational for someone who was once so immature. *Damn, I'd grown up.*

She let out a huff of air as if she'd been holding her breath for some time and wiped the last of her tears from her face. Her features began to relax. "I can't believe I'm going to say this, but... I think it's a good idea."

Hearing her words was like having a ten ton weight lifted

from my chest. "See, I'm not as dumb as I look," I joked.

I inched closer to seal our deal with a hug, but she backed away, zeroing in on me. "Promise me this has nothing to do with the girl you slept with."

Her words cut into my heart like a razor sharp blade. I wasn't expecting her to say that and I didn't want to lie to her, but I'd be lying to myself if I said Riley wasn't part of the reason I was pushing this break. Marissa needed time to devote to her career and I needed time to see what else was out there before I settled down with someone who didn't necessarily want the same things I wanted. Maybe not even what else, but *who* else. Riley.

But I just couldn't bring myself to admit that I wanted more time with another girl to see if she was capable of giving me things Marissa wasn't willing to. So instead of starting a war, I did something I'd never done before. I looked Marissa right in the eyes... and lied.

CHAPTER 6
Riley

That prick wasn't gonna call me, was he? It was almost eight o'clock on the night after my little sexcapade with Beck, and I was sitting around waiting for his call like a hopeless, desperate, groupie. This was so not me. *Pathetic.*

When my phone did finally ring, I startled and swooped to grab it, only to feel my heart sink when Fallons' number flashed across the screen. I contemplated letting it go to voicemail, but then decided after my dead end discussion with Tessa, I needed some Fallon-inspired wisdom. "Yo," I picked up, answering after the third ring.

"Spill. Now. No beating around your non-existent bush."

"Ewww, and how the hell do you know it's non-existent?"

"We use the same wax girl at the spa, doll. Now, spill."

I laughed, but I felt my smile quickly fade when I remembered feeling like a two-bit whore for sleeping with Beck and that I was apparently unworthy of the call he'd promised. After huffing out a long breath and closing my eyes, I finally spoke. "I did something stupid. Well, I didn't *think* it was stupid while it was happening and I certainly didn't *think* it was stupid when he told me I'd be hearing from him today, but now... I just *feel* very stupid." Four stupids in one tiny answer. I was explaining myself rather well, wasn't I?

"First off, sounds like you did *someone* stupid, not something. Second, who is this stupid? I want deets."

Sounded easy enough. We'd been down this road plenty of times before, but once I told him it was Beck, all bets would be off. I could just hear the impending shriek of OMGs now.

"Promise not to have a titty attack when I tell you?" I pleaded. I wasn't in the mood to relive every toe-curling detail, and since Fallon already had a thing for men in uniform, he was going to want me to elaborate on every single kiss, lick, and suck. Right now all I wanted was someone to vent to—I wanted validation that I wasn't crazy for feeling like there was something there. Maybe I was wrong for calling Fallon. Maybe I should've called one of the girls instead. "You know what, Fal, I just remembered I have to—"

"Oh no you don't, bitch," he interrupted. "You are going to tell me who you have your skimpy little panties all in a bunch about. And if you don't tell me now, I'll come over there and go all Patrick Swayze in *Ghost* and sing outside your door until you let me in."

He wasn't kidding, either. He'd serenaded me with worse than Henry the Eighth for holding out on him in the past. My neighbors wouldn't appreciate Fallon's off-key rendition of *It's Raining Men* at this time of night. Taking one final breath for courage, I winced in anticipation of his reaction as I said his name, "Beck Matthews."

I could swear the bastard's phone dropped to the floor, but listening closer I heard what sounded like over exaggerated hyperventilating. "Are you effin serious, Riles? Beck Matthews as in your brother's best friend, Beck Matthews? As in FDNY calendar material, Beck Matthews? As in I fantasize about him at least once a week, *Beck Matthews*?" Fallon always found a way to put the queen in drama queen.

"That would be the one." I smiled to myself, feeling kind of proud of my Fallon-approved accomplishment. My friend had just made it like I'd conquered someone far out of my league. I couldn't deny that it felt insanely good to have gotten a taste of one hot hunk of desirable man.

"Well, hot diggity damn, girl. What the hell is stupid about fucking the shit out of Beck Matthews? I'd switch places with you any day."

"Okay, well, I don't think he'd be too keen on that considering he's straight, and the reason I feel stupid is because… " I paused, trying to think of the reason that sounded best. There were plenty of them, but I didn't want Fallon to know how truly pathetic I felt for allowing my fling with Beck to hold any significance.

"Oh, shit, Riles. You like him, don't you?" Even through the damn phone this guy knew the real deal.

I deflated against the cushions, wishing I could sink into their warmth and bask in it. The plush cushiness brought back memories of my legs wrapped around Beck, fisting the soft material as he made me scream out his name. *Mmmm, yummy.*

Snapping back to reality, I let out a frustrated whimper. "See. I really am stupid. Why do I let these things happen to me, Fal?"

"Before I make you rehash your whole evening to me with complete, colorful descriptions, let me ask you something."

"Go."

"Do you want to do it again?"

Of course I did, but did Beck want to do it again? He was on a break with Marissa, but he left this morning because she called. For all I knew, he was at her place right now making up. I wasn't going to be the other woman. Hells no.

"I don't know if that matters. Things are complicated, Fal. Besides the fact that he's my brother's best friend and I've known him since he was a damn toddler, he also has a girlfriend, or had a girlfriend... I don't know. And then there's the little issue of me being the biggest hypocrite that ever walked the planet. I've been giving Tessa and Marcus the third degree over whatever it is they have going on. If I start up something with Beck, they're going to lynch me for it." Shit, this was more complicated than I'd thought.

"Can I ask another question? Kind of off topic, but I think it's still a valid one." Fallon's reactions had gone from curious to concerned. This was why I'd called him. I could always count on him when it came down to it.

"Of course," I answered, feeling like his questions would help me get the answers I needed.

"Why *do* you care if Marcus and Tessa are together?"

The question was easy enough, but the answer was a lot more complicated. "Because they don't belong together." That barely scratched the surface.

"Okaaaay, meddling sister and jealous friend, that still doesn't answer my question. Why. Do. You. Care? Let them figure it out for themselves. It has nothing to do with you."

"You're wrong. It has everything to do with me. Tessa barely has anyone in her life to lean on. She has me and I'm not sure exactly *how* close she *thinks* she's gotten to Marcus, but I guess we can say she kind of has him, too. But once he's done messing with her and tosses her aside like he always does—I'm all that's left. And that's if she allows me to stick around.

"It's not my story to tell so I won't, but she has a piece of shit for an ex who made her life a living hell. He was abusive and possessive and made her turn her back on me, on everything. I don't want to lose her again—this time because my brother can't commit. She can't handle the aftermath of being duped by Marcus Grayson after everything she's been through.

"I love Tessa with all my heart, but she's no good for Marcus either. If and when he does decide to actually date someone, I think he needs to test the waters slowly at first. He can't dive into the deep end with a woman full of baggage and emotional issues. They are just no good for each other. End of story. I want to protect them both from inevitable heartache." It was a mouthful, but it was what I'd been telling Marcus and Tessa all along. They were setting themselves up for doom and gloom, and I only wanted to prevent it for both of them.

"Riles, you can't live your life protecting other people all the time. Especially your brother. He's a grown man now, and just because your mother isn't around to give him a good ass-chewing now and then, doesn't mean you have to take her place. Wanna know what I think?"

That was the point of the phone call in the first place, but we were getting off tangent here. I wanted to know why I felt like a loser that Beck still hadn't called. "Yes, but what does any of this have to do with Beck?"

"A lot, actually. Hear me out before you bite my head off, okay?"

"Yes, Master," I sighed into the phone.

"I know you love your brother and your friend and you only want what's best for them. I get that. You are one selfless, albeit hard-core and stubborn, firecracker. I didn't know you that long while she was alive, but ever since your mom passed, you've been living your life for everyone but yourself. You worry about Marcus, about your dad, about the business and your friends. You overanalyze *everything* and don't enjoy the moment. Even on those few dates you do go on... you're too worried about the future to just live in the present. I'm not saying you've passed up your chance with a prince, because let's face it... you've dated some real winners, but I think you need to go with your heart instead of your brain sometimes, Riles.

"I think you see Tessa and Marcus doing exactly that— throwing caution to the wind, having fun together, not worrying about what comes next—and you're green with envy because you just can't allow yourself to do that, too."

"Fallon, you know I'm not the type to just fuck around for fun. And it's not only that, I *know* Beck. I'll *always* know Beck. There's history there. It will be awkward now because I *didn't* think with my brain the other night. And because for whatever reason, I'm thinking things about him that I didn't expect."

"And there's my point exactly—stop thinking. Just let it be. Just live. Isn't that what she told you to do?"

He was talking about my mother's dying words. I wanted nothing more than to follow through with her hopes and dreams for me, but life wasn't just about hopes and dreams. It was about being responsible and realistic too. Fucking around with Beck and hoping it could be more was neither of those—it was stupid. *There was that word again.*

"Girl, I hear your brain juice working from here. Didn't I just tell you to stop thinking so hard? Let this be your first experience with letting loose and having fun. Don't make me chant it... *live, live, live, live*! Why make it a big deal if he doesn't call?"

I let out a small laugh, trying to make light of everything. Fallon had some spot-on points. He knew me too well. I needed to stop being so damn serious and act like one of the Beatles... *let it be.* So what if Beck didn't call? He didn't owe me anything. We had a good time and I should be able to look back on it with an ear-to-ear grin. There was no need to make things awkward. It didn't have to be. He was still the same old Beck and I was still the same old Riley. The fact that we knew each other's naked bodies inside out should have no influence on how we reacted toward each other from here on out.

Except that for some reason, it did matter.

"Because I felt something, Fallon. Even in all the drunken sloppiness, the slurred words, and the silly jokes—there was something there. I don't know how to deal with all these emotions, or even *why* I have any emotions about Beck Matthews, period. But I am. And I do. And I want him to call and I'm really pissed off that he—"

The beep of the incoming call interrupted my rant. "Hold on. I have another call. Probably Ashworth finally getting back to me."

When I looked at the caller ID and saw Beck's name flash across the screen, I nearly shit myself. "Oh my god, Oh my god, Oh. My. Gawd," I yelled into the phone.

"What, you freak? What's the matter?"

"Fallon, it's him. Beck's calling."

"Oh my gawd, is right. Go answer that shit and call me as soon as you're done."

I didn't have time to respond. Instead, I cleared my throat, put on my best smile, and clicked over to the other line.

"Hello," I said, trying to accentuate the out-too-late-and-hung-over rasp in my voice.

Too much? Too soon? Ah, whatever. I was supposed to be having fun and living, right?

CHAPTER 7

Beck

So after dick move number one, which was lying to Marissa, I was about to go through with dick move number two, which was calling another girl right after I'd made my girlfriend my ex-girlfriend. Well, kind of.

After Marissa left my apartment, I couldn't get thoughts of Riley out of my head. I owed her a phone call and I wasn't about to go back on my word. Was I going to jump from one relationship to the next... can I get a hells no? But I'd be damned if I was going to make Riley feel like shit, either.

It was already almost nine o'clock and according to the rules set out by the dating gurus, I didn't have much time left to deliver on my promise without looking like I'd brushed her off. When had I become so attuned to what was morally acceptable dating policy? I had no fucking clue, but Riles deserved what was promised to her.

I quickly dialed her number, feeling all sorts of queasy waiting for her to answer. I could tell by the sound of the rings that she was on the other line. I hoped I was important enough to end the other call.

"Hello," she answered, with a dick-twitching sexy rasp.

"Hey, sweet thing. Sorry I took so long." At the sound of her voice, suddenly I *was* sorry. I'd wished I'd spent the entire day wrapped in the warmth of her soft blankets and silky skin.

"Yeah. Me too. I was ready to give up on you."

"I don't disappoint, Riles. I thought I proved that to you *multiple* times last night."

I'd never spoken to her on the phone as an *us*. Our conversations in the past always had something to do with Marcus, so while this was uncharted terrain, it was also pretty damn fun.

"That you did," she laughed, making me picture her with her head back, exposing the deliciously sweet skin of her neck.

"So, what did you do all day? Besides wait for my call, of course?"

"You're one cocky son of a gun, aren't you, Beckster?"

"Ugh, Riles. That damn name. Don't make me come over there and teach you a lesson."

There was silence for a second and then she asked something that surprised me. "*Can* you come over here?"

I looked at the time, contemplating. It was already after nine and I was due into the house tomorrow at five a.m. to start a shift of three twenty-fours. It probably wasn't a good idea, even though I really wanted to. "Tonight's no good, Riles, and I say that as I silently curse my work schedule. I have to be in really early and need to get to bed, but I just wanted to say hi." I wanted to do a lot more than say hi, but it would have to wait a few more days. "Tell you what, are you free on Thursday?"

She let out an adorable groan. "Now it's my turn to curse my work schedule. I have to tie up all my loose ends with my clients before the holiday weekend. I'll probably be working until the wee hours of the morning, knowing me. But, oh shit... aren't you coming to Marcus's Fourth of July thing at the lake house?"

Yes, I had planned on attending... with Marissa, but now that we were on our break, I'd be there as a single participant. However, the fact that Riley would be there... shit, this was about to get complicated. "I am going to be there. I take it you are too?"

"Yup."

"Well, good, but..." I hesitated to gather my thoughts. This had to come out the right way or I'd hurt her feelings. "Riles?"

"Yes?"

"We can't tell Marcus about this. At least not yet. He'll have my head—and my dick—for fucking around with you. I know he's doing the same thing with Tessa, but this is different. It's like a guy code thing. He won't be happy and I don't want to make you—"

"Beck, calm down." Her soothing voice interrupted me and instantly set me at ease. "I have no intention of telling Marcus. I'm just happy you'll be there. I know we won't get to be together, but... well, even if we can't see each other this week, we can make time for other things."

My interests were certainly piqued. "Like what kinds of *other things*?" I asked, extremely curious.

"B, I happen to be very good with words. In fact, I think I

missed my calling as a smutty romance novelist. You'd be surprised with my sexting abilities… and I only need one hand to do it."

Holy shit! Riley Grayson was holding out on me all this time. Even though I wouldn't get to see her until Friday, when we'd have to pretend things were the way they'd always been, this week was already starting off better than I'd expected.

"So, can I hang up now and see exactly what that dirty mind of yours can do?"

"No. I kind of like talking to you," she admitted in a much quieter voice. "Is that cheesy? I mean, in this day and age do people even talk on the phone anymore?"

I laughed at the adorableness of her honesty. "Texting certainly does make things a little easier, if you ask me, but I like talking to you too. Even if you're not drunk and sloppy."

"Hey, I wasn't that drunk."

"Oh, no? Riles, you sang that song for thirty minutes straight. I've been making up my own lyrics all day today."

At that, she let out a string of the most contagious giggles I'd ever heard. "Oh my god. Really? I'm sorry, but—"

I knew what she was going to say. "No. I don't sing. Not happening."

"Come on, B. *Please?* I want to hear what you came up with. Don't leave me hanging… I'll even start you off. Cabaret, ohhhh! Even though I used to tie your shoes, I like to share my bed with you."

Damn it! I would never get it out of my head now. And she was spewing them out, one after the other, with precision and ease. It was impossible not to laugh at the hilarious way she made each set of new lyrics about our situation. "Alright, already." I finally caved, wanting to join the fun. "Give a dude a chance. Anything not to hear your terrible screeching anymore." It was a lie. She actually had a really sweet voice, but I couldn't go giving her a million compliments right away. There'd be nothing to look forward to later.

"Fine, meanie. Let's hear what you got."

I thought long and hard. It was a catchy enough tune that was easy to put words to, but I wanted to make them about us, the same way she had. "Okay, I think I got one." I cleared my throat and swallowed my pride. Was I really about to sing into a phone? Yup, guess so. "Cabaret… ohhhh! Even though you like to call me Beckster, I still want to rock your world."

Her booming laughter made me smile wide. "Oh! I love it! See, I knew you had it in you. Come on, give me another one."

Fucking Justin Timberlake and Riley Grayson. The combination of the two was a force to be reckoned with.

The rest of the conversation went on with us singing and laughing for another hour. At around ten thirty, I reluctantly hung up because I had to shower and get to bed so I wouldn't be dragging ass in the morning.

The last thing I thought about before I closed my eyes and drifted off to sleep was how easy it was to talk to Riley. How much fun it was to just be ourselves. How surprising it was that we could be more than friends, yet not have to center our situation on sex. I also thought about how it scared the shit out of me that I was smiling like I hadn't smiled in forever. I was supposed to be the one rocking

Riley's world, but my best friend's knock-out sister was beginning to turn mine upside down.

"Dude, if you don't stop whistling that fucking tune, I'm gonna get the hose and blast the shit out of you," Derek barked from his usual spot on the community recliner in the rec room of the firehouse. There was nothing community about it when Derek was around.

I guess I really wasn't getting the song out of my head any time soon. In fact, it must have been a subconscious thing, because I didn't even know I was still whistling it. "Sorry, Derek. Kinda can't help it."

"What the fuck's got you all *whistle while you work* at fucking eight a.m. anyway? Last I heard, you and Marissa were on the outs. Things change over the weekend?"

"Things have certainly changed, but not with Marissa."

Derek's eyes went wide and his grin grew devilish. "Ah, so you finally took my advice, came to your senses, and ditched the bitch?" There was no hiding his feelings toward Marissa. He hadn't been a fan all along. He didn't like that she'd dismissed having a family from the start—that was his biggest gripe. He knew deep down that's what I wanted—whether or not it was what I wanted as a probie. But after spending time with these guys, they kind of reformed me.

Derek was a reformed frat boy himself. Now in his mid-thirties, he'd been married for ten years and had two boys and a baby girl on the way. His wife was a fucking gem and a saint for putting up with him and his rowdy sons. So when

Derek talked about women and whether or not they were wife material, it kind of made sense since he'd hit the jackpot with Kelly. I probably should've listened to him all along rather than wasting two good years of my life trying to convince Marissa I was husband material.

But I didn't want to talk about marriage, kids, and the future on this fine Monday morning. Unlike Marcus, Derek was the kind of person I could tell anything to without judgment. I wanted to bounce ideas off him and tell him all about Riley. It certainly couldn't hurt.

"So, are you gonna elaborate or make me pull it outta you? I may have been with the ball and chain for what seems like an eternity, but I can sense when a guy's sampled some new pussy after sticking it in the same one for a while."

What a way with words. "Yes, new pussy, Derek. You read me so well." I didn't look up from the stove, where I was preparing the usual massive breakfast for the guys.

"I fucking knew it! Anything worth regaling my underused one-pussy-for-the-rest-of-my-life dick with or was it just a one-nighter like old times?"

"Definitely not just a one-nighter. We're talking Riley Grayson here." It surprised me how easily that slipped off my tongue.

Without looking, I could tell by the loud thud and the squeak of the lever that Derek had propelled the recliner from lounged to upright rather swiftly. "You must have a death wish." He was making his way toward me. "What would possess you to fuck Marcus's sister, Beck? He's gonna freak." He attempted to steal a piece of bacon from the steaming pile, but I swatted his hand away.

"Precisely why we're not telling him," I answered matter-of-factly.

"Oh, *we're*, as in the two of you are an item? Why would you to start a new *we* when your old *we* is still warm on the slab?"

"Calm down, old man, there is no *we*. And back away from the pancakes. Can't you wait for me to finish, you fucking beast?"

"Stop thwarting the topic," he said, chewing with his mouth open.

"Thwarting? Seriously? Been reading the dictionary lately?"

"Yeah, exactly, smartass, but I'm serious. Why her? Don't you have enough problems with Marissa? Why complicate your friendship with Marcus *and* Riley?"

It was more complicated than I cared to admit, but talking on the phone with her, laughing and joking and just having a good time—it made all the other shit go away for a while. I wasn't ready to over complicate things, but I wasn't ready to stop whatever was going on with Riley before it even started. "I don't know, bro. It just kind of happened. It's not like I haven't thought about Riles like that before, but—I don't know. I kind of always stayed away from her because of the age difference, and Marcus, and then Marissa. But now that we're both adults the age thing isn't even a thought. Marissa and I are on a break so it's not like I'm cheating, and—"

"And that still leaves Marcus, and he's one big mother fucker. I have a sister, Beck. And even though I think you're a good kid, I wouldn't want you fucking around with her fresh out of a two-year relationship with someone else. It's not fair to her or you, and when you get your head out from between her legs and go back to Marissa, or realize this isn't going anywhere, Marcus is going to hand you your balls in a neat little package."

Did he think I was afraid of Marcus, physically? That was so not the case. I might not be as bulky, but I was just as strong, if not stronger. We benched the same weight at the gym together and with all my free time sitting around at the firehouse, I probably worked out at least three more times a week than he did. This wasn't about battling fist to fist. It was a head to head thing. It was about respect. In that aspect, Derek was right. I didn't want to fuck with Marcus because he was my oldest friend and I didn't want to piss him off over something that might turn out to be nothing.

"What are you pussies coffee-talking about in here? Sounds like the fucking Oprah show." Ramos came booming in from the back room, a towel wrapped around his waist. He headed straight for the bacon, barging his way into the conversation. He was one to talk about us being pussies. He was the most pussy-whipped of us all. His wife was also pregnant. They had a quick shotgun wedding when they found out about the baby, but Ramos wasn't suckered into anything. He'd loved Angel—as we liked to call her for being so damn sweet to everyone—since their first date in high school. He only pretended he was some macho, alpha male who wore the pants. We all knew otherwise.

"We're talking about your mother, Ramos. She was really good last night," Derek chuckled from his stool at the table.

"Your mother" jokes were always the lowest blow, but they also got the most laughs.

Following suit, I catcalled, "Ohhhh! Ramos's mother gets around. I had her the night before."

"Very funny, dick. But from what I heard while eavesdropping on you clucking hens, you fucked Marcus Grayson's sister and you're gonna be a dead man," he cackled, tightening the towel around his loose and flabby middle.

"What the fuck, guys? You really don't think I can take Grayson? Not that I plan on fighting him, but why are you all so hell bent on him kicking my ass?"

"Because you're gonna hurt his sister, and even though it's usually bros before hos, when you fuck with a dude's sister, your ass is grass."

I darted a frustrated glare at Ramos—now he was a poet? What the hell did he know? "And how do you know I'm going to hurt her? It's not like that. We're just having fun. She knows my situation with Marissa and she has no expectations. It'll be fine."

"Until he finds out," Derek added with a disapproving shake of his head.

"Jesus Christ, you two. So much for gloating about my hot piece of ass. You're taking all the fun out of this."

"And Marcus is gonna take the jizz out of your balls."

Derek nearly fell off the chair laughing at Ramos's remark. "Shit, kid. You're one stupid mother fucker, but do what you want. It's not like you forced her into it or anything, so I guess just go with it. But, when the shit hits the fan—and it will—just remember... we told you so."

Please. I knew what I was doing. I was just having a good time. There was no reason to overanalyze where this was going. Somewhere in between our *Cabaret* interpretations, we actually talked about not taking anything too serious. She was on board with that *and* not telling Marcus. We had all our ducks in a row and I wasn't gonna let these cocks make me think otherwise.

CHAPTER 8

Riley

Me: Don't you have a cat to rescue from a tree or something?

Beck: Nope. The only pussy that needs rescuing is yours.

Me: LOL. You're right. Come over.

Beck: Can't. 12 more hours and then I can finally get outta here.

Me: Aren't you exhausted?

Beck: No. Been doing nothing but sitting around. Not many fires to put out.

Me: I've got one for you to put out.

Beck: *Being a fireman leaves us with endless possibilities for innuendoes doesn't it?*

Me: *Seems that way. Can I play with your big, long hose?*

Beck: *LOL. That never gets old.*

Me: *So. Have you thought anymore about how we'll play it cool over the weekend?*

Beck: *I'd much rather you ask me about my hose ;)*

Me: *Seriously, B. Marcus isn't stupid. We're gonna have to keep our distance.*

Beck: *He's so far up Tessa's ass it'll give me plenty of opportunities to be all over yours.*

Me: *Yeah, or so you hope.*

Beck: *Don't you hope too?*

Me: *Mmmmhhhmmmm*

Beck: *Oh, baby. I love it when you text-moan.*

Me: *Are you wearing your gear right now?*

Beck: *That depends. Do you want me in my gear or in nothing at all?*

Me: *Gear = sexy*

Beck: *You = insanely sexy*

Me: *Me = horny*

Beck: *Me = really wish I didn't have to stay at this house tonight.*

Me: *I'm about to start a fire just so you can come here. What will cause the least damage but get you here the quickest?*

Beck: *LOL. Step away from the matches, Riles. We're not first responders to your hood.*

Me: *Darn it :(*

Beck: *You're cute, sweet thing.*

Me: *Just cute?*

Beck: *Hot as fuck too!*

Me: *Did you ever picture this?*

Beck: *What? Texting one of my oldest friends? Sure...totally normal.*

Me: *LOL. No, I mean THIS. I know it's not really a THIS but still. Did you ever think we'd wind up all flirty and sexty, and screwing around?*

Beck: *Want honesty?*

Me: *Always*

Beck: *No*

Me: *:(*

Beck: *But not because I didn't want it. I always thought you were hot. Always wanted to jump your bones, but the timing was never right and there were too many things in our way.*

Me: *Hate to break it to you, but all that shit still remains true.*

Beck: *Yeah, but I just don't give a fuck right now. Feels too good to care.*

Me: *Why, Beckster. You rebel!*

Beck: *I HATE THAT NAME!*

Me: *Beckster, Beckster, Beckster...*

Beck: *Okay, I'm going now.*

Me: *NO! Wait. Sorry. Couldn't help myself.*

Beck: *Like I won't be able to help myself to another taste of your sweet, delicious pussy again the next time I see you.*

Me: COME OVER NOW

5 minutes later

Beck: Sorry. We got a call. Gotta go. I'll text you when I get back if it's not too late.

Me: Bye. Be safe :)

Beck: ;)

I clutched the phone to my chest and leaned back in my swivel chair, swooning. These frequent text conversations were killing me. Meaning: I loved every minute of them.

"What the hell are you so smiley about?"

I jumped out of my skin when Fallon crept up behind me. "Shit, Fal. Give a girl her space."

"That was him, wasn't it?" he asked, tracing a finger around the rim of his coffee mug.

"As a matter of fact it was," I said, adjusting my faux leather pencil skirt and smoothing out a wrinkle in my teal silk top. I turned to stare at my laptop screen as if I could focus on anything but the swarm of butterflies flapping in my stomach.

"Look at you," he poked me on the shoulder with a smile. "You're happy. You're smiling. You're in way too deep."

Tucking a strand of my choppy side bang behind my ear, I swiveled around to face him and huffed, "Why am I in too deep? I'm just having fun... isn't that what you told me to do?"

"Yes. And I'm glad you're listening for a change, but I know you, leopard. Your spots are still in season... you wear them well."

I swatted him on the shoulder, laughing. "Would you just shut it? I know what I'm doing. *We* know what we're doing. I don't expect anything from him... we've talked about this. He's still got Marissa on the back burner, we get along great, and the sex... well, that one time... was *insane.*" I smiled thinking back to that night. A tingly hot flash washed over me, causing me to shudder. "Oh, never mind. Fal, just let me enjoy this while it lasts without making me worry about what comes next."

Pointing a finger in the air obnoxiously, he shouted, "Bingo, doll! That's what I *want* you to do. So keep up that attitude and don't get sucked over to the dark side. As long as you keep telling yourself what you just told me... you're safe."

And that's what I'd intended to do. Stay safe—guard my heart, protect my emotions, and defend my actions. But with every string of texts, my safety and security was being hacked into by a clever thief.

Beck was the smoothest of all criminals of his kind. Half the time I didn't know if *he* even knew how good he was at what he did. Or was he even doing it intentionally? He was perfect parts smoldering sexy beast and sweet talking teddy bear. It was confusing because I'd always known guys to be either one or the other. Not Beck. He was the total package. He'd matured a lot over the years and grown into a man that possessed all the qualities I'd ever looked for. He even had the one quality no one I'd ever meet after him would have—he'd known my mom.

Even better—she'd loved him.

Growing up, he was a permanent fixture at my house, like a third Grayson kid. Not that his parents weren't great too, but Marcus and Beck always spent more time at our house. I guess that's why I never looked at him as anything other than a brother. Especially when he started coming into his own. He was one good-looking kid, even at fifteen when he was still growing into himself. But by the time he'd reached seventeen... *damn*. I'd find myself staring at a shirtless Beck, all sweaty and panting after shooting some hoops with Marcus and really liking the view. But staring was as far as it went. Well, except for the flirting.

Yeah, come to think of it, there'd been a lot of red flags in the past, but still... I never imagined this. I never pictured myself actually going through with the fantasy.

And the fantasies continued that evening, when Beck was back at the firehouse after his run and I was curled up on my bed watching HGTV.

I muted the television at the sound of the incoming text.

Beck: *Wanna come ride my pole?*

The fireman jokes *were* endless, but I didn't always have to give in.

Me: *I've always wanted to slide down a firehouse pole! It's on my bucket list.*

Beck: *Bucket list, huh? Guess what, sweet thing?*

I loved when he called me that. It was even better when it rolled off his tongue. But I'd take what I could get for now.

Me: *What?*

Beck: *I marked quite a few things off my own bucket list with you the other night.*

Me: *Oh yeah? Like what?*

Beck: *Like kissing your gorgeous lips, licking the smooth skin of your neck, tasting your perfect tits, playing with that perky ass, making you scream my name.*

Memories came flooding in, causing a pleasant tug of tension in my core and a dampness pooling in my panties. I played along as if he wasn't having any effect on me.

Me: *I'm sure you've done that all before.*

Beck: *Not with you.*

Me: *I was on your bucket list?*

Beck: *Yup*

Me: *Well, well, well.*

It wasn't exactly unexpected, but getting the confirmation that he'd wanted me in a sexual way for some time made me feel good.

Beck: *Yes, you do it very well.*

Me: *So do you ;)*

Beck: *How well?*

Playful Beck was one huge turn-on, even through text messages.

Me: *So well I want more.*

Beck: *How bad do you want it?*

Me: *Real bad.*

Beck: *Bad enough for you to take off your panties and pretend I'm there.*

And there we went.

Me: *Hmmm... maybe.*

Beck: *Don't be a tease.*

Me: *How do you know they're not already off?*

They weren't, but now they were going to be. I hooked my thumbs inside my Victoria's Secret sweat pants and boy short ensemble and slid them down my legs.

Beck: Ah, just how I like it. Now, bring your finger to your lips.

Me: *Which ones?*

Beck: Not so fast, sweet thing. Mouth first.

Me: *Ok*

Beck: Suck your finger into your mouth, and twirl your tongue around it to make it nice and wet.

Me: *It's definitely wet.*

Beck: Now take that finger and trail it from your mouth, down your neck, to the center of your chest.

I still had on a ribbed tank top, so I quickly removed it and tossed it aside. I was lying on my bed, completely naked. And practically panting.

Me: *Ok*

Beck: Roll your hard, rosy nipple between your fingers, pulling gently. Feel good?

Me: So good. But it would be better if you were doing it.

Beck: Close your eyes.

Me: Done

Well, at least he thought so. I couldn't exactly text with my eyes closed.

Beck: Now it's me. Now, move that hand down lower. Over your smooth, tight stomach and down to your throbbing clit.

I continued to do as he said. I felt so self-conscious even though I was alone and no one could see.

Me: Still wish it were you.

Beck: Me too, baby, believe me.

Me: And what am I supposed to do when I come? It's not exactly like you can hear me.

Beck: Your texts are awfully wordy. You sure you're doing this with one hand?

Me: LOL. Yes. Okay. No more talking. I'm playing.

Beck: Good... me too.

Oh, I liked that. I just hoped he wasn't doing this with an audience of rowdy fireman. Would he do that?

Me: Where are you?

Beck: In the bathroom.

Me: Ok, continue...

Beck: Now, close your eyes again and pretend your wet finger is my tongue flicking your clit and finger fuck yourself, Riles. Hard and fast.

I minute later

Beck: You there?

Me: Mmmmhmmmm... thank you. You were wonderful.

Beck: LOL, but I'M not done yet.

Me: Well I'm spent. Go jerk it. TTYL. ;)

I couldn't have thrown the phone out of my hands quick enough. It hit the floor with a soft thud and I took a deep breath, allowing my lingering release to finish its delicious decent through my nerve endings. There I lay on my bed, alone, sprawled out, naked, and breathless.

What was Beck Matthews doing to me?

Wow! I laughed to myself. That was certainly... fun. I'd told him I did this sort of thing all the time, but... consider that another item to check off the list.

CHAPTER 9

Beck

Jerking off with my cell phone in the other hand, while definitely fun, was getting a little... lonely. Riley was working late tonight so she could have the rest of the long weekend off for the Fourth, but I wanted to actually *see* her instead of texting or talking over the phone.

I thought long and hard about the message it would give to Riley and her co-workers—especially that Fallon dude who was always all up in my grill—if I showed up unexpectedly at her job to take her out for lunch. It seemed like a boyfriend thing to do, and I definitely wasn't her boyfriend, but friends could grab lunch together too. Right?

Throwing on a fitted grey V-neck and a pair of my favorite worn jeans, I plucked my keys from the hook by the door and donned my tattered Yankees cap. Casual and comfortable—nothing about my attire would make her think I was trying too hard. In fact, I hoped it made her think I was just in the neighborhood, happening to pass by her office, doing the nice thing by dropping in to say hi.

And that's exactly what I'd tell her when I made my way across town and whisked her away for her lunch hour. I just had this need to see her again. Alone. Only the two of us. I'd see her again this weekend at the lake house, but there'd be too many eyes watching us. We wouldn't be able to be our normal selves—well, our *new* normal selves.

As I rang the intercom to be buzzed into her building, I gulped down the nerves that stood as a warning. *Play it cool and let it be.* It's just two friends enjoying each other's company.

The door swung open and Fallon's eyes roamed my body from top to bottom, making me squirm uncomfortably. "Well, hello there, handsome! Oh, Riles, look what the cat dragged in," he called over his shoulder. "What a pleasant surprise."

"Nice to see you too, Fallon. Can I come in?" As if it weren't weird enough being scrutinized like some piece of fucking meat, he blocked my entrance into the office like a drooling guard dog.

"Depends. Are you here for business or pleasure?" He brushed his palm over the top of his spiky Mohawk, grinning.

"I'm here to take Riley to lunch," I said, exasperated. What was taking Riley so long anyway?

He slapped his tongue against the roof of his mouth and threw his hand on his hip. "Bitch didn't tell me she had a lunch date with a hot fireman. She's holding out on me."

That made me laugh. He was good people, even if he was a bit eccentric at times. "No she's not. She didn't know. I thought I'd surprise her."

Fallon's cat-like green eyes popped open to triple the size.

"Oh mister, you just scored mucho points with the BFF," he sang, as he patted me on the shoulder. "Come on in. She's on the phone with a client." Fallon hooked a plaid-covered arm in mine and escorted me into the bright, spacious office.

The place screamed Riley. It was eye-catching and contemporary. Classy. Bright yellows and turquoises accentuated the white washed furniture. A few of the pieces were paneled in mirrors and elaborate crystal chandeliers hung from the ceiling. Her office made *me* want to redecorate my drab apartment. I could see why RG Interior Design was becoming the name on everyone's lips. It made me proud for her. She deserved this kind of success.

"Nice right?" Fallon asked, nudging me with his elbow.

"Really nice. She's made quite a name for herself." I smiled, and Fallon clapped his hands in front of his mouth, clearly proud of his friend. "Her desk is over there to the right. This client is making her skin crawl, so when you sneak up on her I'm sure she'll be thrilled."

I nodded as I started walking in her direction. "Thanks, Fallon. Wanna join us for lunch?" I hoped he'd say no, but I thought it was the right thing to do. He and Riley were inseparable at work and I didn't want to infringe on their afternoon plans.

"Awww, sweetie. More points, but no thank you. You two need your alone time. Her fingers are starting to blister from all that texting." He winked, making me think he knew more than he should about those private conversations. Damn girls and their gossip.

When I reached her desk, I crept up slowly, listening to her conversation.

"Ginny, the shipments are off because of the holiday. I

know we promised it would be done this week, but they'll be in first thing Monday. I'll even hand deliver them to you myself." She sounded stressed and I could hear the voice on the other end growing louder and louder.

"I'm sorry you feel what way, but—" She spun around in her chair, fisting a chunk of her short hair and the look in her eyes when she spotted me brought a huge smile to my face. "Ginny, I have to go. You can yell at me later."

She hung up and jumped out of her white leather chair. "Oh my god. What are you doing here?"

For a quick second I felt awkward, not knowing how to greet her. This was the first time we'd seen each other since I left her house Saturday morning. Did I kiss her on the cheek? On the lips? I wanted to do what came naturally, but I didn't want to make it weirder than it had to be.

Thankfully, she made the decision for me and wrapped her arms around me, landing a sweet peck on my clean shaven face. "This is a nice surprise. What are you doing here?" She backed up from our embrace, grasping my hands in hers and looked into my eyes.

"I was in the neighborhood and I thought we could grab some lunch."

"You buying?" she asked, tilting her head.

"Well, from the looks of things around here I might make you my sugar mama, but lunch is definitely my treat."

She giggled, brushing a strand of dark hair out of her eyes. "Sometimes these pains in the ass aren't worth the money they pay me. They're all pretentious and impatient and driving me insane. Wherever you take me must have cocktails. I need a drink."

"You're on," I laughed, taking in how put together she

looked in her long summer dress. "You ready to go now or do you need a few minutes?"

She grabbed her cell phone and plopped it into an oversized purse, swinging it over her bare shoulder. "I was ready for a drink at nine a.m. Let's go."

I turned to Fallon and asked if he wanted us to bring anything back for him, but he simply shook his head and winked at me. I'd have to ask Riley exactly how much she'd told him about us.

"An extra large mojito for me, please," she ordered, still holding the menu in front of her face.

"And I'll take a Stella," I said to the waiter, placing my menu down on the table. I couldn't help but admire Riley as her stunning blue eyes perused the menu, deciding on a selection. Was she a salad girl? A burger girl? It occurred to me that as well as I knew her from hanging around with Marcus all these years, there was still so much I *didn't* know. And getting to know her was the fun part. It seemed I learned something new every day.

Sensing my eyes on her, she looked up from the food choices and smiled. "What?"

"Nothing," I shrugged, smiling back. "You just... you look pretty today." I didn't know why I said it; I just felt the need to. It was like that with Riley, honesty just poured out of me without regret.

"Thank you," she said, gazing down and biting her lip. After the initial bashfulness passed, she tapped the lid of my cap. "You look pretty adorable yourself."

"Adorable?" I pouted.

"Yes, totes adorbs," she giggled.

"You know what I think is pretty adorable?" I leaned closer to her, pulling one of her hands over the table in mine.

"What?" she asked, staring down at our joined hands.

The restaurant was noisy and busy with their workday lunch crowd. I leaned forward for a little privacy, looking into her blue eyes. "The way you're all kinky and uninhibited in your texts and then shy and modest when I tell you how pretty you are." God, I liked looking at this woman. Did she have any idea how gorgeous she was? Crazy how I was just realizing it now myself.

"B, you're sweet. But... I'm the worst at taking compliments. Sorry. Girl thing."

"You've known me forever, Riles. You don't need to be shy with me."

"That's exactly *why* I feel so shy around you. This is kind of crazy, no? Us sitting here," she looked down at our hands again, "holding hands, on a surprise lunch date. It's almost easier to hide behind the flirty texts and the sex... the attraction is easy to explain. It's everything else that's so... weird."

It was weird, but not necessarily *bad* weird. Just *different* weird. "I like our weird. It's fun."

She leaned closer, whispering, "Me too." Then slanting back in her chair, she blew out a huff of air, causing her feathery bangs to fly up and out of her eyes. "Shit. This weekend is going to be hard."

"I know. Wanna ditch it?" Now, that was actually a clever idea.

"We can't. I promised Marcus I'd help him out. Plus a few of our mutual friends will be there—and then there's the whole Marcus/Tessa thing." She rolled her eyes and it was obvious to see that her brother and Tessa being together didn't exactly make her happy.

Before I could ask her why, the waiter was there with our drinks and to take our orders. Riley ordered a soup and salad combo and I ordered a BLT with fries.

When he'd left, jotting everything down on his pad, I clinked my bottle to her glass and brought her attention back to the topic of our friends. "So, why are you so against Marcus and Tessa being together?"

"Oh, not you too?" She tilted her head and took a sip of her mojito. "First those two, then Fallon, and now *you*? Is everyone fucking blind, deaf, and dumb?" She was clearly agitated, her hand gestures becoming more and more animated as she spoke. "They're a disaster waiting to happen, Beck. He's a man-whore with commitment issues and she's a single mother with more baggage than an airport conveyer belt."

"Nice way to talk about your brother and your best friend." I laughed, pulling back on my beer.

"Hey," she tsked. "You know I don't mean it like that. I love them both. I only worry because I care. I don't want either of them to get hurt."

"Well—" I had to think about how to say this, because here we were teetering on the same slippery slope ourselves. "What if they're just having fun... like us? No expectations, no worries about the future. Just enjoying the way they make each other feel." There. That summed it up.

She sighed, fluffing her hair up with her fingers. "You're right. Everyone's right. I shouldn't care and I should just lighten up, but... I don't know, B. As much as I worry about Tessa, I'm actually more concerned for Marcus. He's never done this before. You're different. You've... been in love." She struggled getting that part out, but I admired her grace in explaining herself. "My dad is useless when it comes to advice. Mom was always the shoulder to cry on, our cheerleader. I feel like I owe it to my mother to take her place when it comes to these big, momentous things in his life. Marcus is so damn pigheaded and now he's a grown man, for God's sake. I don't expect him to come to his big sister for advice about girls."

"That's what he has a strapping, experienced, genius of a best friend for." I pointed my thumbs at my chest, winking.

"That's true," she laughed. "And thank God you're pretty sensible and responsible, but... I can't help worrying about him. We're getting older and even though he's like ten times the size of me, he's my baby brother and I'll always want the best for him."

Voices and laughter from the other tables surrounded us, but looking at her, sharing this with her—it was just the two of us. I stared into her eyes, getting another look into the surprising things I was learning about this girl I'd known my whole life. "I hope he knows how lucky he is, sweet thing. You are one amazing big sister."

"Yeah, fat chance of getting him to see it that way. He just thinks I'm a pain in the ass nag."

"Well, yes," I admitted; Marcus did see Riley as overbearing at times. "But he also loves you very much. On more than one occasion he's told me how much he values the special friendship you have and how, even though you guys are five years apart, you still hang out together all the time. He appreciates how you stepped up to the plate with your dad when your mom died... and for him too, Riles.

"You've been more than just a sister to him for as long as I can remember. So don't be hard on yourself, and cut him some slack too. I know he's got a thick skull and he's still got a hell of a long way to go, but he's different when it comes to Tessa. I think she could be good for him. She's a lot like you. He needs more women like that in his life."

She seemed to think about what I said as she bobbed the straw up and down in her drink. When her eyes finally met mine again she smiled shyly, but I could see a sadness wash over her soft features. "I hope you're right, because quite honestly—" She let out a huff of air that seemed to deflate her whole body as she released it, eliminating a world of stress "—I'm so freaking tired of worrying about everyone else.

"I don't know why I'm telling you this. I don't really like to talk about her because it's still so hard sometimes, but..." She sipped her mojito through the straw, staining it with her lipstick. "Since Mom's gone, I feel like I do everything as if she's watching me. As if she's in the background nodding in approval or pointing her finger to warn me before I do something I'll regret. It sounds crazy because that wasn't her and it's not how she would've wanted me to live my life.

"Not to boast, but she knew I'd always land on my feet and that I could take care of myself. She even told me not to worry too much about Dad and Marcus, but I took it upon myself to meddle in their lives only because it's my way of holding on to her. Without my nagging daily reminders or my attempt at keeping the traditions of Sunday dinners and holidays alive, I feel like she'll just disappear for good.

"But it goes beyond that and it's something I just need to get over on my own. I can't replace her for them and I can't be her, as hard as I try. She always had the right thing to say and the most sensible way to solve a problem. Marcus was putty in her hands, for whatever reason."

"Riles, you're doing an amazing job of everything. She'd be so fucking proud of you. For keeping an eye on Marcus, for loving your dad the way you do, for accomplishing so much." I took her hand again, staring deeply into her eyes. The tears were welling up, but she held them back. The server showed up to check our drinks, but I waved her away until Riley could compose herself. I needed to lighten the subject before this impromptu lunch turned into something way too serious for her.

"I nearly shit myself when I saw your office today, babe. You're an interior design rock-star. You even got me hard thinking about adding some sconces and wainscoting to my place."

She laughed at my joke, and the sadness slowly faded. I lifted my beer, motioning for her to do the same with the rest of her mojito. "A toast."

"To what?" she asked, confused.

"To lightening up and having a good fucking time."

"Are you saying I have a stick up my ass?" She squinted and pouted, withholding her drink from my toast.

"No, you definitely do not have a stick up your ass, but... I can certainly give you one," I winked.

Finally clinking her glass to my bottle, she bit her lip and smiled. "I'll drink to that! Now, let's hope the food comes quick so you can deliver on that promise before I have to get back to work."

CHAPTER 10

Riley

Thank God he lightened the mood and changed the topic. I definitely was *not* about to take it in the back door my first time as some quickie on the way back from lunch, but I'd risk risqué sexual banter over a near emotional breakdown any day.

I was way too close to telling him about *all* my fears. All the things I was afraid of doing without my mom. All the reasons I missed her so much. Confessing secrets and talking freely with Beck just came so naturally. I guess it was that we'd known each other so long, but since hooking up and getting to know each other more intimately—I don't know. I felt like I'd grown so much closer to him in this last week. I could let my guard down with him. I liked that. I was pretty sure he did too.

And there were those *feelings* coming into play again. Confiding in him as a friend was one thing, but getting comfortable enough to actually think he cared about what I was telling him... that was dangerous ground

I probably shouldn't tread on.

After lunch, we walked back to my office where I offered to have him come in and hang out for a bit. He sweetly declined, saying he had errands to run, giving me a soft goodbye kiss on the mouth. That kiss said something the previous ones we shared hadn't. While our kisses on Saturday night were empowered by pure lust and desire, our "see ya later" kiss meant so much more.

It meant we'd reached a comfortable place in whatever this was. One where we didn't have to think about who we were to each other, just what we felt for each other. That simple kiss spoke volumes about the little time we'd spent together. And even though it wasn't much, I already knew that I liked spending time with him. A lot.

Something unexplainable was tugging at me and I wasn't sure how to analyze it. *Yeah, that's right.* My internal rational, mother-hen of a subconscious reminded me. *Keep overthinking, you freak! You've been alone with him all of two times, and one of those times you were completely intoxicated and mauling each other. This is Beck we're talking about. Stop making it more than it is.*

Was I making it more than it was? It didn't seem that way at lunch when we were laughing and sharing confidences effortlessly. I didn't want to cross a line and ask Beck where he saw this going because he kept mentioning that we were just having fun. He was fresh out of a two-year relationship with Marissa. Maybe he was just occupying his time with me until she wanted him back.

These were all questions I wanted answers to, but there was no way I'd ask them. I wasn't about to fuck up this good feeling I had when I was with Beck. I wanted to just let it be without putting too much weight into it, even if there was this unexplainable warmth and giddiness every time I thought about him. It was probably just the idea of something new, the idea of being wanted by someone. But, was I crazy to think we could be more than some friend-turned-fling situation? I mean, look at Marcus and Tessa. They were trying to make it work and that seemed pretty absurd to me.

Either way, it was all too much to think about with the kind of weekend we had ahead of us. Sitting at my desk and scrolling through my to-do list without really paying attention, I thought about how everything would play out at the lake house.

We'd have to be super discreet in front of Marcus. For one thing, he would think I was playing tit-for-tat by hooking up with his friend since I told him not to hook up with mine. And secondly, I didn't want to justify myself to him. Right now, my feelings were all over the place. Explaining to my brother that I was enjoying meaningless sex with his best friend would not go over well. And describing it as meaningless sex wasn't fully true—on my end at least.

I had a lot to think about before I went and said anything I'd regret to anyone. Most of all, Beck. I'd have to feel him out before I made a fool out of myself by asking him a million questions about our situation, or lack thereof.

"Hey, boo. Have a second?" Fallon broke me of the internal struggle between my brain and my heart.

"Sure, what's up?" I didn't bother to look up from my desk, because Fallon would be sure to read right through me and see I'd been overthinking all things Beck since the moment I sat back down.

"We got a call from a new client today. I wanted to go over your calendar with you so that we could schedule—Ah! Who the fuck am I kidding? I want to know about your lunch date with the young, hot fireman."

I turned around to face him, arching an eyebrow incredulously. "Smooth one, Fal. But there's nothing to tell. It went great, he's a sweetheart, and somehow I'll screw this whole thing up because I already feel that I like him more than I should."

He plopped into the chair next to my desk, pulling it as close to me as humanly possible. "Yeah. Okay... nothing to tell, wench. That's quite a mouth full. Oh and speaking of mouthfuls, is he one?"

"Fallon! Can't you be serious for one damn second, you perv?"

"I'm sorry, but my mind was wandering the whole time you were at lunch. Did he really take you to eat or did you go, you know, act out some of those schmexy-ass texts in person?"

"Okay, that's enough. Back to work."

I usually didn't mind sharing all the gory details with Fallon, but today my mind was racing with too many warring emotions to hash it all out in a timely fashion. I had shit to get done if I wanted to have a decent Fourth of July weekend dodging my brother and Tessa's make-out sessions and trying to hide my feelings toward Beck from everyone, including him. This was going to be fun. I could hardly wait.

That night, when I'd finally left the lonely office around nine thirty, picked up a fast food salad from a late-night drive thru, and settled in on the couch to catch up on my recorded shows, my cell phone chirped with an incoming text and my hopes immediately soared.

When I reached over to the end table and saw it was from Beck, a huge smile grew on my face. I couldn't help but bounce up and down on the cushions. Pausing an episode of *The Voice,* I blew a kiss to Adam Levine and told him I had another man to deal with. Yes, I was obsessed with far too many male musicians to count, but there was no harm in my outlandish obsessions over the unattainable. It was the one I had with my brother's best friend that I had to worry about.

Beck: *Whatcha doing?*

Me: *Drooling over Adam Levine.*

Beck: *God, my competition is fierce. First JT and now Adam?*

Me: *They've got nothing on the Beckster.*

Beck: *rolling my eyes*

Me: *I love getting under your skin.*

Beck: *I love getting over your skin—with my tongue.*

I loved our schmexy texts, as Fallon had put it, but I was seriously bone tired and couldn't see myself being that creative tonight.

Me: *Oh, B. Don't get me riled up. I'm exhausted and I have to be on the road early tomorrow to help Marcus set up.*

Beck: *Well, that's actually why I'm texting you.*

Me: *To rile me up? ;)*

Beck: *That and... I wanted to see if you needed a ride. We can go together.*

Together? Was he kidding? My fingers typed "yes" then erased the letters, then typed "no" and erased those too. I was stuck with no way to answer this reasonably. Finally, I decided on what was best.

Me: *Probably not a good idea. We don't want to give anyone anything to talk about.*

Beck: *Ah, fuck 'em. Let's let 'em talk!*

Me: *Yeah? You're ready to deal with Marcus and tell him you're banging his sister?*

Beck: *Correction: BANGED his sister. You've been holding out on me all week.*

Me: *Me? You had work!*

Beck: *And now you're tired. I could've come over tonight and really wore you out.*

Me: *LOL. As appealing as that sounds, I still have to pack, tie up some loose ends, and do all those fun things us women have to do in order to look decent in a bathing suit.*

Beck: *All you have to do is put one on and you'll look drop dead gorgeous.*

Me: *Aw, thanks*

Beck: *Now, seriously. Want to drive up together?*

I wanted to say yes so badly, but it was a bad idea for so many different reasons. The biggest one being that if anything went wrong over the next few days I'd have to figure out another way to get home.

Me: *B, thanks for the offer, but I still think it's a bad idea.*

Beck: *Can I ask you something?*

Me: *Sure.*

Beck: Are you afraid this whole thing is a bad idea?

Was this his way of letting me off easy because he thought exactly that? Or did he genuinely want to know what I thought?

Me: You first.

Beck: You're a PITA, but fine my answer is... no. I don't think this is a bad idea.

Why did that make me so damn happy?

Me: I don't think so either, and I'm glad we got this out in the open, even if it IS over text, but I still think we need to lay low. Don't you?

Beck: Yes, oh wise one. As much as I'd love to shock the shit out of a few people with our unexpected canoodling, I think you're right. No need to rock the boat just yet.

Me: B?

Beck: Hmm?

Me: I really like canoodling and rocking the boat with you. And I don't know where this is going or IF it's going anywhere but can you promise me one thing?

Beck: *I'll try.*

Me: *Please don't hurt me.*

It was a tall order to ask of someone, but I already sensed that my heart was a part of this complicated equation. I'd had it painfully bruised in the past; I needed all the assurance I could get.

Beck: *Sweet thing, I wouldn't dream of it.*

Once we'd finished our conversation and texted each other goodnight, I felt a huge wave of relief wash over me. Not because I had the answers to all my questions. Not because I was sure this was going to work out between us. But because as uncharacteristically vulnerable as I felt, I also believed I was safe in Beck's presence. Beck was a good man—a decent man who seemed to have my best interests at heart. I could trust him. The problem was I couldn't trust myself not to get in over my head.

CHAPTER 11

Beck

Marcus had me under lock and key, playing idiotic games like flip-cup and quarters as if that shit still entertained me. When I walked in without Marissa, he started with the questions. I finally told him, without mentioning my involvement with Riley of course, that we were on a break. He decided that meant I needed babysitting. I didn't feel the need to give him all the details or a reason to hook me up with one of his random single guests. I had no intention of doing something like that with Riley around, anyway. Hooking up with anyone besides her wasn't even a thought in my mind, but there was no way to get that through Marcus's head now that he knew my status with Marissa. So I downplayed the break so he wouldn't think I was fair game.

I'd only gotten a quick chance to say hi to Riley since arriving at the lake house two hours ago, and it wasn't the kind of welcome I wanted to give her. Not that I'd be able to give her that proper welcome with the hawk on my tail. I couldn't help noticing her watching me out of the corner of her eye while she sat and talked with Tessa and some of her other friends, all the while fussing over Tessa's son, Luca. Every time I caught her looking in my direction I'd wink or smile, but the last few times she seemed to glance away, rolling her eyes. I had to get over there and find out what was bothering her. We left off fine—actually more than fine—last night; I couldn't imagine what I did to piss her off.

Marcus was mumbling something about me wallowing in my pity as he downed a water bottle to try and dilute all the alcohol he'd already consumed. I shooed him away, still focusing on Riley. "Oh fuck off. I just want to talk to Riley about something."

He narrowed his eyes, but before I gave him reason to think about why I needed to talk to his sister all of a sudden, I blurted out, "She... uh... she dropped her lipstick in the cab last week, so I brought it to give to her."

He clapped his hand on my shoulder, smiling. "Oh, how sweet of you." Sarcastic bastard.

I rolled my eyes and elbowed him in the gut as we made our way to the girls. As soon as Tessa and Marcus were within three feet of each other, they started eye-fucking each other. Marcus made a crude comment about Tessa in her bathing suit, and she quickly scolded him, clearly embarrassed in front of Riley's friends. When they were gone, the rest of the crowd kind of broke apart and I took the opportunity to single Riley out.

"Hey, sweet thing," I whispered to her.

"Oh, don't you sweet thing me. You liar." She turned to walk in the direction of her friends, but I tugged at her elbow and spun her around.

"Hey, what's this all about? I knew you looked pissed for some reason, but why am I a liar?" I seriously had no fucking clue what she was talking about.

She said one word, "Marissa." And instead of it clearing things up it just made me all the more confused.

"What about her? You see she's not here, right?"

"When exactly were you going to tell me you're making your relationship even *more* permanent while texting me all kinds of crazy things? Tessa told me you're asking her to move in with you."

Whoa! She clearly had her timing mixed up. "Riles, I think you have the story all wrong. Come on," I motioned toward the empty dock. We could sit and talk, far enough away from Marcus, without him thinking it was anything but two friends chatting. "I can explain, if you'll let me."

Her expression looked doubtful, but once she let me tell her everything, she'd understand. "Fine," she huffed, walking in front of me. She was wearing a turquoise blue string bikini that left absolutely nothing to the imagination. Her bronzed skin glistened in the scorching afternoon sun from the lotion I'd seen her apply earlier on. I couldn't stop staring at her ass as it swayed perfectly, finally stopping at the end of the dock and taking a seat. She dangled her legs over the planks and dipped her feet in the cool water.

"Sit. Explain. I feel like an idiot," she admitted. Even angry, this girl made me want to smile.

I kicked off my Converse, took a seat next to her, and dunked my own feet in the refreshing lake. "This is nice." I hummed, discreetly tracing a finger along her thigh.

"No touching. Just talking."

"How about talking *and* touching?" I pressed my luck.

"Come on, B. What's going on? Are you and Marissa back together? Are you really asking her to move in with you?" Her features softened from angry to upset. I had to clear this up so she could go back to smiling and laughing, the way I liked her best. Oh, and so I could touch her again too.

"To answer your questions respectively, no and yes."

"Wait, *what*? She's moving in with you?"

"No," I laughed. "I'm sorry. Let me clarify. No, we are *not* back together, but yes I did ask her to move in with me." I might be busting her balls, but I wasn't lying to her.

"Are you serious?" she whisper-screamed. "Why in the hell would you ask your ex-girlfriend to move in with you? Beck, this means we can't—"

"Calm down," I inched closer, placing a hand on her beautifully bare shoulder. Her skin was warm from the sun and as soft as I remembered.

She shrugged me off, picking her ass off the wood and scooting further away from me.

I lifted myself up and scooted closer in her direction. "She's not moving in with me and I asked her *before* we broke up, Riles. It's actually one of the reasons we're on this break in the first place. I don't think she wants all the things I want—at least not yet." I didn't want to talk about all this stuff with her, unless she wanted to hear it. I told her I wouldn't hurt her, and knowing the way a girl's mind worked, hearing about an ex was something that caused unnecessary pain.

"Then why would Tessa make it like I should tread lightly with you? Someone's not telling the truth here." She wasn't as pissed as she was before, but I could tell she was still confused.

"Marcus and Tessa are in their own little world, Riles. He didn't know Marissa and I were on a break until I told him today. Besides, you have some explaining to do yourself." I arched an eyebrow, placing my hand on my hip like a girl. When she remained silent, I figured she wasn't picking up on my question. "You told Tessa about us? First your other girlfriend, Fallon, gives me the third degree about our texts and then this? I thought we were keeping this on the DL." I wasn't actually annoyed. In fact, I was happy she cared enough about our situation to tell her friends about me. It meant a whole shit load of things—good things. But if she had questions, so did I.

"Okay, you got me there. But you can't expect me to keep completely quiet about all this, B." She hid her eyes with her hands, finally admitting, "I might've spontaneously combusted if I didn't tell someone."

I laughed at how adorable she was, but then grew serious. "You don't think she'll tell Marcus, do you?" It was my only concern. Not that I was afraid to tell him—I would, when the time was right—but things were so new and unclear between us. I didn't want to rush into telling him when it might only cause awkwardness and hard feelings— for everyone. Besides, it was none of his business right now. We were adults. We could do whatever we wanted with each other, for each other, to each other.

Staring out at the lake where a group of teenagers tubed recklessly off the back of their boat, she seemed to ponder her answer. "No, we can trust her. And considering she still thought you were with Marissa until just a few hours ago…

she won't let Marcus think you're cheating on your girlfriend with me. As much as he didn't exactly love Marissa, he does love me and being some guy's mistress is not exactly something he'd take lightly."

"Is she against us being together? Not that she should really have a say, considering she snuck around with Marcus for God knows how long, but I'm curious about her take on this." I'd like to know that at least one person was rooting for us on some level.

"Like any friend, she's skeptical because of the whole 'break' thing and she doesn't want to see me get hurt, but—" She brought her attention back to me, staring at my lips and biting her own nervously. I could tell she was holding back. I didn't want her to.

"Just say it. But what?"

"Beck, I know we're nothing and I'm not asking for any kind of commitment, but I don't make a habit of sleeping with more than one guy at a time. I don't expect you to—" I lifted a finger to her lips, shushing her.

"Would you please stop saying we're nothing. I know it's been like three minutes and things are not—I don't know, 'the norm'—but we're definitely something and I want to give us a shot. I haven't been able to stop thinking about you, Riles."

Her eyes lit up at my admission. Hell, my stomach dropped and I felt my heart rate pick up when I said it. This was all so fucking crazy and fast. I never expected to feel something for another girl two seconds after breaking up with another. Shit, I never expected *another girl* to be Riley Grayson. But what came as the biggest surprise was that I wasn't upset any longer about not being with Marissa. Not because Riley was a replacement, but because Riley was an incredible person. I was getting to know her on a whole different level, and the more time I spent with her, the more I liked her. And the more I liked her, the more I realized I wanted to see where this would go.

Looking past me toward the house to make sure no one was watching, she inched closer to me and gave me a soft peck on the cheek.

"What was that for?" I asked, loving the feel of her lips on me again.

"For being you. For making me feel like I'm not insane for feeling all these things about you too. I'm sorry; I jumped to conclusions and got all jealous for no reason."

Tapping her on the nose, I said, "I like jealous Riley."

"Oh, do you?" She smirked.

"So far there's not one side of you I don't like, Riles. What are we going to do about that?" This was going far beyond flirtatious fun and I really didn't care.

"God," she moaned, letting her head fall back. "Why do we have to be *here* right now? Can't all these people disappear?"

I felt her frustration. I wanted nothing more than to pull her into the lake with me and swim off to have my way with her. But we were surrounded by people who wouldn't understand the situation. If we gave in to what we wanted to do to each other right now, it would only come off as a random hookup. I didn't want people judging either of us without knowing the truth.

"I'll tell ya what." I had a plan.

"Go ahead," she smiled, swirling her feet in the lake and making ripples spread across the smooth water.

"Marcus is already pretty intoxicated. If he keeps up this pace, he'll be passed out and comatose before the fireworks even go off."

"Continue," she said, her grin growing wider.

"Once he's asleep for the night and all the rest of the guests are gone, I'll sneak into your room and we can have some fun of our own. Sound like a plan?"

Biting her lip and clapping her hands, she butt-danced. "The perfect plan. So perfect I want to break out in song. Caberet ohhhh…even though Marcus has no clue, we're still getting our groove on!"

Putting my arm around her shoulders and bringing her close, I kissed her on the top of her head and laughed. "That fucking song. I have to admit it's growing on me."

"Good, because I'm just getting started. Caba—"

"Don't make me shut you up with a big wet kiss. If people haven't noticed the touchy feely-ness, they'll be sure to notice my tongue down your throat."

"Oh, Marcus!!" she called out, standing up. "Let's go do some shots." Looking down at me, she extended her hand to help me up. "Come on, let's get him good and zonked. I want your tongue down my throat."

CHAPTER 12
Riley

When Marcus had the brainchild to fix up the lake house and then throw the party of the century, I doubted him and his ambitious attitude. My little brother didn't always follow things through. But his efforts to execute the ultimate remodel—together, as a team—brought on an onslaught of other emotions besides anticipation. As excited as I was that Marcus wanted my help and that I'd get some well-needed quality time with Marcus, the thought of erasing my mom, and happy childhood memories, was a bitter pill to swallow.

"Fuck a duck!" Marcus shouted over the stereo that boomed with Mom's old albums.

"What now?" I looked over to where he stood on the stepstool, trying to suck away the pain from his thumb.

"Who hung this shit? Had to be Dad. Nails sticking out all over the place."

I laughed as I dropped the paint brush to tend to Marcus's boo boo. "Probably. You know Mom was more of a handyman than he is."

"No shit. And that's why the damn ducks have grins across their stupid beaks. She's mocking me and punishing us for ripping down her beloved décor."

Mom and her country chic. Back then, it was acceptable. Today... "Yeah, as much as I hate to strip this place of her charm, it really needs it." It pained me to say it. It actually hurt. None of us had been back to the lake house since Mom died, but when Marcus asked me to help him redecorate and modernize the place, I jumped at the chance. It was time I could spend bonding with my little brother and reminiscing about old times. We needed this. I just never imagined it would be so hard.

"I still can't believe she's gone, Marcus." I didn't want to cry. It made Marcus uncomfortable, but watching him rid the kitchen of something that symbolized my mom... it sucked. No other way to put it. It was like we were erasing her—adding another layer of dirt to the grave.

Clearing his throat and climbing down from the stool with the dusty curtains in his hands, Marcus groaned, "Oh, Ry. Come on. These ducks have quacked their last quack. Please don't lose it over these ancient things."

"It's not about the curtains," I whispered, wiping the tears with the back of my hand. "I miss her so much, Marcus. She should be here."

Slumping into a rickety kitchen chair—those were going too; we'd ordered a new set from Pottery Barn that would arrive tomorrow—Marcus ran his hands through his hair. "She is here." He smiled, obviously reflecting on a fond memory. "Do you remember the year Beck and I almost killed those people fueling up at the gas station?"

I shook my head at the memory and grabbed a couple beers from the fridge. "I don't know what Dad was thinking, letting a fourteen-year-old Beck drive the boat."

"It wasn't our fault Dad fell asleep."

With two cold bottles on the table, I took a seat across from my brother. "No, but it was your fault that you two hot-shots thought you could handle docking and gassing up the boat."

Marcus tried to hide his grin, but it was impossible. He clinked the neck of his bottle against mine and took a long pull. "Shit, that poor innocent puppy was in the wrong place at the wrong time. I guess it was kind of a disaster. Funny now. Then—not so much."

"You two put Mom and Dad through fucking hell."

"Oh, 'cause you were Miss Perfect. Mom saved your ass that time you came home drunk and fell asleep on the floor of the shower stall."

"Mom ripped me a new one for that. I was grounded for three weeks."

"Oh! Three weeks. Call social services. You got off easy."

"You always thought that, but I definitely had it harder than you. Being the first, they always expected more from me, but you, Marcus, you were her favorite." I sipped my beer, thinking back on how she doted over her only son. It made me resentful, but it also made me smile. My mom loved with all her heart. Even if she coddled Marcus a little more than she did me, our bond was so strong I still felt it today, even in her absence.

"Riley, you're fucking crazy if you think I was her favorite. I appreciate the gesture, but what the two of you had... I was so damn jealous. Dad and I were never that close and as much as Mom loved me... Shit, Ry—the sun rose and set with you. You have to know that."

Did I know that? There was a part of me that did, but there was a part of me that always wondered if I'd done right by my mom. Maybe an outsider had the power to see it better than someone who experienced it every day, took it for granted.

God, I missed her.

Fingering the raggedy old table cloth, full of snags and stains from years of use and reuse, I let the tears fall, unashamed. "I'm so glad we're doing this together, Marcus." I reached out to grab his hand.

He didn't reject my touch, he didn't roll his eyes. He let me latch on, comforting me with tiny circles on my palm as I cried. "She would be happy we're doing this together. She'd hate that Dad let this place go to shit," I said between sniffles.

He finished off his beer, setting the empty glass down on the table and wiping his mouth with the back of his hand. "Oh, totally. She's probably dancing along to the tunes as we speak." He looked up, as if peeking into heaven. "Hey, Ma. The ducks can suck it! Next—we move onto those ridiculous toile bedspreads."

Dropping my hand from his, I stood from the table to race up the stairs, calling out behind me. "You're not touching those!"

"Like hell I'm not," he bellowed, chasing after me. "I'll fucking burn them as soon as you leave."

"Not if I take them with me."

"Be my guest, Ry. But don't tell your clients you're

holding onto that tacky shit. It will ruin your credibility."

We joked around like that the entire time we worked on the remodel. There were memories in every nook and cranny of the house—reminders in silly things like stolen salt and pepper shakers, rusted lounge chairs, old board games shoved into the back of the closet. Marcus was right—my mom was there. She always would be. And she'd be happy we were going on with living our lives as normally as we could with the gaping hole in our hearts.

After bonding with Marcus over the remodel and talking with Beck a little while ago, Fourth of July was turning into my favorite holiday of the year.

Tessa and I were on good terms—now that I had the stick out of my ass about her relationship with Marcus. I had to admit, it took me calling *her* out on being a bad friend for not supporting my craziness with Beck. *Hypocrite.* Spelled out letter by letter, enunciated syllable by syllable—that's what I was. But luckily that was water under the bridge, thanks to my understanding and forgiving BFF.

Life was freaking good. Everything seemed right. I couldn't help but smile as I held Luca in my arms, keeping an eye on him for Tessa, who'd gone to find Marcus.

Dancing to the summer soundtrack I'd programmed into Marcus's iPod, I bounced Luca up and down. As I swirled him around the edge of the deck, I saw Beck making his way toward me with two beers and a dazzling smile.

When he reached the two of us, he put my beer down on

the bar and tickled Luca under his chin with his free hand. "What have we got here? Auntie Riley getting some practice?"

My eyes popped open at how free he was becoming with his thoughts. Things were going fast, but not that fast. "B, you're joking right?"

He looked and me, confused at first, and then realization set in. "Oh, no! That's not what I meant. Oh my god, you must think I'm fucking crazy. What I meant was—Shit, total foot in mouth moment. What an ass." He was stuttering his words and backing away from Luca like he had some infectious disease. The only thing infectious about this little boy was his cuteness. Apparently, he made everyone baby crazy.

"It's okay. I know that's not what you meant. Don't worry, I won't be asking you to make me a mommy any time soon. We've got plenty of time for that."

"Shit," he huffed, brushing a hand through his hair and gulping down his beer. "Sometimes things just slip out of my mouth without consulting my brain. Can't help my tongue around you, sweet thing." The old cool and confident Beck was back. I liked every side of Beck... sweet, sexy, confident, and vulnerable. I couldn't wait to uncover more.

"So, do you have a status update on Marcus's intoxication level, yet?"

Shifting Luca to my other hip, I shook my head. "That's a negative. I actually haven't seen him in a while. I wonder if Tessa ever—" The sound of screaming from inside the house broke my attention. Beck and I looked at each other for a split second before darting toward the sliding doors to see what was going on.

Through the glass I could see a crowd huddled around Marcus and Tessa—Marcus was yelling and Tessa was crying. *What the fuck?* Without hesitation, I shoved the doors open to see what was going on.

When Tessa spotted me, she jetted in my direction and tore Luca out of my arms. "I'm leaving," she whispered, tears rolling down her cheeks.

"Tessa, what—"

"I. Need. To. Leave." She spoke out of desperation. "Pack my stuff and bring it home with you, okay?" I nodded, not knowing what else to say. Not understanding what the hell had happened.

After Tessa whooshed past me in a frantic hurry, and the only sounds that filled the silence were the revving of her car engine and the crunching of gravel as she peeled out, I turned to look to Marcus for an answer.

He stood there, sobbing, blood dripping from his hand.

"Jesus Christ, what goes on?" I mumbled to myself.

Beck was already at his side, trying to calm him down. I started to walk over to them to find out what the hell had just taken place, and then I saw *her*—A raven-haired, half-dressed, sly-looking thing, parading down the steps like a stripper on stage, wiping the smeared lipstick from her face.

Taking it all in, I gasped in horror. You'd have to be blind not to put two and two together. "You son of a bitch!" I screamed, lunging at my asshole of a brother. "I knew this would fucking happen. I *knew* it!" Marcus didn't need to say a word, the evidence of his betrayal of Tessa was staring straight at me, wearing a shit-eating grin.

Marcus turned to the bitch in question and spat, "Get the

fuck out of my house!" before running to the front door and clumsily attempting to grab his keys off the hook.

The nosy crowd of onlookers parted as Satin-the-slut slithered her way out the back door. Beck rushed to Marcus's side, blocking him. "Whoa, buddy. Not so fast. Where do you think you're going? You've been drinking all day. You can't drive."

Marcus put up a good fight against Beck, who was restraining his arms. My brother pushed him a few times, banging him against the wall in their struggle, but when he realized Beck wasn't budging, Marcus finally relented.

Deflating against the wall and dropping to his knees, I could see the pain wash over his usually flawless face. "I can't lose her, Riley. I have to go after her."

As tortured as he seemed, I had no pity on him. This was exactly what I'd been warning Tessa about. I knew in time he'd fuck up. I just didn't think he'd do it with such a skank. And with Tessa right under his nose. "You should have thought about that before you went and fucked Little Miss Twat-wad." I ranted and raved and truly let him have it. He deserved to feel like shit for this. Someone had to make him hurt the way Tessa was hurting right now.

But no matter how low my blows fell, Marcus was still trying to go after her. "Let me go," he begged. "I have to go after her." He stood again, trying to bypass the brick wall that was Beck, guarding the front door.

Grabbing fistfuls of his hair and taking deep, exasperated breaths, Marcus finally looked at me with the most pathetic of expressions. His eyes pleaded with me for mercy as he cried, "I fucking love her! Don't you see that? I love her, Riley. I can't let her go!"

It was the first time I'd ever heard Marcus say those words about anyone. I had a feeling he and Tessa had been sneaking around for a while and things were more serious than they'd let on, but I had no idea he'd fallen in love with her.

Hot, hateful tears sprang to my own eyes. Tears for my brother, who had finally given his heart to someone. Tears for Tessa, who was now broken-hearted because of his mistakes. Tears for myself for not nurturing their love from the beginning. Perhaps I would have had the power to stop something like this from happening by allowing them to do their thing without judgment. I was all over the place—I just wanted to make this all go away.

Beck, witnessing my breakdown, came to my side and placed a consoling arm around my shaking body. After scanning the room he raised his voice over the murmurs of the forgotten crowd. "Show's over, everyone. Beer's outside." At their grumbles he shouted, "Everybody out," then rounded them up like cattle and steered them through the sliders.

I couldn't stop staring at my brother. "Why?" I finally asked. "If you love her, why the hell did you do this?"

Finally giving up his fight to chase Tessa down, he stared me in the eye with intensity. "I didn't. It's all a misunderstanding. I swear to Christ, Ry. I did not touch that girl. Tessa walked in on me pushing her off me. I would never hurt Tessa, Ry. Never. I love her so damn much. You have to help me get her back." His words were so desperate I wanted to believe him. Could I?

I turned to Beck, who was also staring at a distraught Marcus, probably wondering the same things I was. "Do you think he's telling the truth?" Beck had to have the answers. Someone besides my drunken brother had to have the answers.

"Stop fucking talking about me like I'm not here! I can hear you and I'm telling you the fucking truth!" Marcus was irate, even from his feeble position crumpled up on the floor.

Beck went to him and kneeled down, comforting his friend. "Bro, calm down. I know you didn't screw that girl. I know you love Tessa, but you have to let her cool off and you need to sober up. Maybe even take a cold shower. We'll bandage up that hand and tomorrow will be a new day."

"Tomorrow will be too late," Marcus said, hanging his head.

"It won't be. I promise." Beck placed a hand on Marcus's shoulder and then looked up to me. "*We* promise. Don't we, Riles?"

In that moment, Marcus looked to me for guidance, for reassurance, for unconditional acceptance. All those years that I had tried to take my mother's place—being strong for my brother and hoping to teach him life's lessons—meant shit. Now was when he needed me to believe in him most. I couldn't let him down. "Marcus, we'll get her back for you, sweetie. I promise."

CHAPTER 13

Beck

Getting Marcus to calm down was like trying to wrangle a pack of rabid wolves. He'd clawed and barked, sometimes foaming at the mouth to try and get past me and Riley for his car keys. Finally, we had to hide them in a box of Hostess Devil Dogs way in the back of the pantry. There was no way he was looking in there, even out of desperation.

The rest of the guests dispersed after the scene, eventually realizing that neither Marcus nor Riley were in a mood to entertain anymore. Once the drama was over, they also realized there was nothing left to see. Unfortunately for their host, the fireworks that went on indoors were much more of a crowd pleaser than the ones that lit up the summer sky.

Once Marcus was done trashing the kitchen and breaking whatever was in his path, he sat down on the couch, staring out the window like an abandoned puppy. There was no doubt in my mind he was praying and pleading with God for

Tessa to come back. It was a pitiful sight—the phone in his hand, pressing redial over and over again, wiping the tears from his face every time he wound up with the same empty result. Riley finally had to pry the phone out of his vice-like grip and send Tessa a text herself, letting her know she was worried about her getting home okay and asking her to call when she did.

In the time it should have taken Tessa to arrive safely home, she still hadn't called. But Marcus was now passed out in his spot by the window, where he was keeping vigil for his girl. I kept telling him he needed to give her more time and to let it all cool down. He didn't want rationalities and friendly, logical advice. He wanted his girl back. He wanted to erase the whole night and make it fucking disappear. Besides, who was I to promise him anything? I had no idea how this would turn out.

What a fucking mess. That was all I kept thinking. Marcus had *finally* given up his game for a special girl, *the* girl. He'd done what everyone who knew him thought was an impossibility for Marcus Grayson, Man-Whore, Underwear-Modeling Bachelor-for-Life—he'd fallen in love. And as with most first loves, he was experiencing his first heartbreak.

I felt so sorry for the bastard, knowing what it was like to have my own heart ripped out of my chest by the woman I loved. But watching this all play out, I also felt something else. Something totally unexpected. It was this overwhelming need to let Riley know exactly how I felt about her. To allow myself to give in to what my heart was telling me to do. To let go of the past—even though it was something I once wanted for my future—in order to make room for something that had taken me by total surprise.

As shocking and quick as this whole thing had happened with her, if I gave in to the chance of starting something up with Riley (without the prospect of Marissa coming back into the picture one day), it would be incredible. So why was I fighting it? Because of time? Because of her brother? Thinking about it now, they seemed like ridiculous reasons to stop myself from giving in to what I was beginning to feel for Riley. We'd connected in a way I'd never imagined, and I owed it to myself, and to her, to see where it could go.

I checked on a snoring Marcus one more time, propping his head up with a pillow in case he decided to chuck up all the extra alcohol he'd consumed trying to numb his pain. When it was safe to assume he would be alive again for at least another twelve hours, I walked through the sliders into the dim light of the moon to find Riley star-gazing on the dock.

She'd changed out of her bathing suit and into a pair of shorts and an oversized sweatshirt. She still looked beautiful, but she also looked sad. The night air was cooler than it had been all day, but the way she hugged her arms around herself made me think she was cold.

"Chilly?" I asked, startling her.

"Oh, hey. How long have you been standing there?" She pulled her feet up out of the water and curled them underneath her.

"Long enough to see you're upset." Crickets chirped in the distance as I sat down next to her and pulled her close, hooking my arm around her waist.

"Perceptive, B. Another adorably attractive attribute of yours." She smiled, looking into my eyes.

"Nothing tops all your adorable attributes," I said, losing myself in her warm, soothing gaze. Staring a bit too long, maybe making her uncomfortable. Her eyes left mine and she looked down at our joined hands.

Lifting them up, I brought her hand to my lips. "Hey, what gives? You okay?" What went on earlier wasn't exactly fun for any of us, but she seemed to be taking it personally.

"Yeah, I'm okay. I guess... I just feel bad."

"For?"

She shrugged. "For Marcus, for Tessa, for... me."

"Riles," I swiped at a strand of her hair that was stuck to the corner of her mouth. My finger lingered on her moist lips, and I traced my thumb against the perfect heart shape. "Once this blows over, Marcus and Tessa will be fine. She'll eventually cool off and let him explain. He loves her and from the looks of things, she loves him too. So, don't worry about them."

She pondered what I said, even nodding her head in agreement, but when her eyes met mine again, they were glistening with tears. "And what about me?"

"What about you, babe?" My heart squeezed for her. I didn't like seeing her upset, but I had no idea what this argument between her brother and Tessa had to do with her. "This isn't your fault, you know?"

"I know it's not. And I've even wracked my brain, going over the things I've said to them the last few months. No matter how harsh I was, I still came around and wound up being truly happy for them. What happened today sucks, and has nothing to do with me doubting them—I'm okay with that. It's not why I'm upset." She stopped there, but I nudged her to continue.

"So? Why the tears, sweet thing. This will be okay before we know it."

She huffed out a long breath, closing her eyes. "It will and they'll be happy and maybe even get married and have a family and live happily ever after." Those things should have made her happy, but instead I could see her growing more upset.

"Riles, I'm a guy—a dumb one. You're gonna to have to spell it out, nice and slow."

"It's stupid," she finally said, standing up and shaking her legs out. "Forget it."

I stood and walked to the edge of the dock to meet her, wrapping my arms around her middle and snuggling into her neck. "I don't like seeing you like this. I only want to make you smile around me. So, if you don't tell me what has you all weepy I'm going to scoop you up and toss you in this lake."

She leaned into my embrace, and I felt her laughter vibrate against my chest. At least she wasn't crying anymore. But she also wasn't talking.

Abruptly, I spun her around to face me and kissed her roughly. She hooked her hands around my neck, her fingers creeping into my hair and anchoring our lips together. She let out a soft moan as my tongue flicked hers, but when I reached up to cup her face, I felt the tears. I immediately backed away, "Hey. Why are you crying?"

"B, I want what they have. Is that too much to ask?"

I just looked at her, my heart melting for her, unable to answer. I didn't know if she was being rhetorical or if she genuinely wanted an answer from *me* about *us.*

Before I had the chance to answer, and possibly screw

this up with the wrong words, she continued. "All this time I thought they were only messing around. If someone like Marcus can find love, find someone who understands him for all his crude, rude, and pigheaded ways, why can't I? I mean, we're talking about a guy who has *never* thought of a girl as more than a piece of ass. It may have started that way with Tessa, and it probably did, but—he's totally reformed because of her. And I'm so happy for him—this is all I've ever wanted, but... what does he have that I don't? Why the hell am I so jealous of them, B?"

I wanted to tell her she was crazy. She was so much *more* than what Marcus was. She was a beautiful person, inside and out. A girl that anyone would be happy to call their own... forever. Why she hadn't met that guy yet, I had no idea. But suddenly I was happy she hadn't. It left her available for...

"Riles, don't you know how special you are? How beautiful? And smart? And loving? And selfless? And sexy?" I ran my fingers through her hair with one hand, holding her tight against my body with my other hand at her back. "I've always thought those things. Can't remember a time I didn't. And now... now that we've gotten closer, I realize so much more." Did I continue? Did I dare to tell her the things she made me feel? I didn't want her to think her tears made me confess these things. The water lapped against the dock, breaking the silence as I held back a bit, wanting to gauge her reaction.

"Then why I am alone?"

It didn't matter how many compliments I gave her—she had to have heard those all before. What she needed now was to know that I didn't want her to feel alone. I wanted to be the one to fill that void. "You're not alone, Riles. You have me."

"I have you for now... until she comes back and realizes what she gave up. I know you love her, Beck. I know you can't just turn off your feelings for someone. This is all fun and it's a nice distraction for you, but once she comes to her senses—when she wants you back—where does that leave me?"

I thought about it for a second. I thought about Marissa asking me to come back to her, changing her mind about the things that tore us apart, about how happy we'd been over the last two years. At one time, all those things brought a smile to my face. There was a time when I wanted nothing more than Marissa to be my future, but now... being with Riley, getting to know the real her, feeling her under my fingertips, sharing intimate moments and secrets—Marissa was no longer the one I wanted to be with. "Riles, can I say something without you thinking I'm crazy?"

She looked at me, wiping away her tears as she laughed. "Nothing can make you look any crazier than I must seem right now."

"Yeah? How about this," I blurted out. "I want to be with you. Not because you're a rebound, not because I'm using you to forget someone else, not because this is fun or convenient, and certainly not because I feel bad for you for feeling lonely. I want to be with you because the idea of *not* being with you makes me crazy.

"The idea of sneaking around through 'schmexy' texts and secret lunch dates and late night, dockside heart-to-hearts—it's not enough. In our ridiculously short amount of time together you made me realize I wasted two years of my life with the wrong girl. I did love her, but… the idea of being without her, it sits fine with me, it does nothing to me. The idea of being without *you*… it crushes me, hurts my insides, makes me sweat with worry. So now, who's the fucking crazy one, Riles?" I lifted her chin so she saw the truth in my eyes. "Want to take a chance on crazy?"

Riley's tears went from sad to happy, I could tell by the huge smile on her face. They fell from her eyes and I patted them away, kissing her on the tip of her nose. The words came to me in a flash, knowing she'd get a kick out of them. Whispering in her ear, I sang, "Cabaret… ohhhh! Even though we're two crazy fools, I wanna do crazy with you."

"B, you had me at Cabaret," she laughed, inching up on her toes to kiss me. "Crazy sounds really fucking good."

I melted into our kiss, licking her lips and speaking against her mouth, "Crazy *tastes* really fucking good."

Nuzzling into the crook of my neck, she sniffed in and moaned, "Crazy *smells* really fucking good."

With that, I scooped her up in into my arms, walking back toward the house. "Let's go inside and make some crazy together."

CHAPTER 14

Riley

Was this really happening? Was *this* really happening? By *this*, I didn't mean having my shirt and bra peeled off sensually and slowly by my brother's childhood friend. By *this*, I didn't mean gripping his ass and urging him to grind against me, causing me to moan in ecstasy while my brother was in the other room. By *this*, I meant—was I really falling for Beck Matthews?

After that conversation on the dock, after he bared his soul to me with honesty and sincerity I never imagined could come from a man, I realized that's exactly what was happening. No doubt, no mistake, no fucking shit—I was falling *hard* for Beck Matthews.

"Please don't stop that. Please," I begged as he teased one taut nipple with his tongue, his fingers parting my sex and thrusting in and out of me under my panties.

"Let me get you undressed first, baby. I want to go slow tonight. There's no rush."

I loved the sound of that, but I couldn't help but worry

that Marcus would wake from his drunken slumber to find us. And worse, I wasn't sure I could withstand the slow, delicious torture Beck was capable of. I needed this release—now—and I didn't care how I got it. I just knew I wanted it from him.

Helping his cause, I pulled at the hem of my shorts, sliding them down my legs. Kicking them to the side, Beck hooked his fingers into the sides of my panties and snapped the lace elastic against my skin.

I giggled at his playfulness, pulling him down to my face by his neck and getting lost in a deep kiss. "Take them off," I groaned against his mouth.

"Yes, love," he said, complying.

Love. I wanted to hear that word come out of his mouth many more times. In many contexts. For many years. God, I was in too deep. Way too deep for the short amount of time we'd spent together. It was ridiculous when I thought about it, but our connection—both in and out of the bedroom—there was nothing ridiculous about that.

Stepping out of my head to enjoy the feel of Beck's body hovering over mine, I traced my finger along the waistline of his jeans, finally unbuttoning them. "Your turn," I said, feeling too naked underneath him while he was still fully clothed.

I yanked at the denim, needing him to be free, craving the feel of him rocking in and out of me. The way he'd made me imagine it in our texts—fast, hard, rough. But by the way he was worshiping my body with kisses, I could tell this would be so much more than a quick, wild, meaningless romp.

Finally ridding him of his pants and underwear, I stroked

his hard length, guiding him toward me. "Not yet, baby," he whispered, his voice practically quivering. "I want to be inside of you, but not yet."

"Please?" I begged.

He let out a breathy laugh, lifting his shirt above his head. I stared in awe at his defined body, wanting to reach out and touch, to wrap my legs around his tanned muscles, to beg him to take me. But before I could do any of those things, he was hovering over me again, his tongue traveling the length of my naked body. "I said slow. Let me enjoy this beautiful body."

I wanted to enjoy his too. Preferably *inside* mine. How was he not aching to thrust into me? Just the thought of it alone had me on the edge of coming undone, but when his tongue traced circles on my inner thigh, and his fingers cupped me from behind, I felt the warmth of his breath between my legs and shuddered underneath him. "Oh, God," I moaned prematurely.

"I haven't even touched you yet, Riles."

"I know!" I squealed, unable to contain it. "Please? Please touch me already!"

I felt his breath escape through his nose as he laughed and then turned serious, groaning,"Mmmmm."

When his tongue finally darted out to taste me, I thought I would die from the slight relief it brought on. I didn't die, but it was heaven. I let out a whimper, arching my hips off the bed as he sucked my clit and tugged lightly with his teeth. It was so raw and carnal, yet so intimate. I'd never felt this comfortable during oral sex. Beck had a way of making it as if we'd explored each other's bodies a million times before. He already knew exactly how and where to touch me to elicit the most pleasure. I smiled, thinking it could only get even *better* with time.

When I felt his hands grip my ass and tilt me upward, I readied myself for the intensity that was sure to come. Making his tongue stiff, he breached my entrance with a hot dampness that surged through me like lightening electrifying each and every nerve ending. He brought one hand around to continue circling my pulsing clit, and within seconds, I was exploding. He drank each drop with the most sensual sounds I'd ever heard.

"God, I love making you do that," he gloated, crawling over my quaking body and placing a soft, salty kiss on my lips. "You okay?" he asked, smirking.

"More than okay. Great. Fantastic. Wonderful." I was still breathless, but I wanted more. I wanted so much more from Beck than I ever imagined. But I needed a minute to come down from my high.

Resting his head against my heaving chest, I tangled my fingers in his unruly hair, enjoying the skin-on-skin contact, the closeness, the comfortable silence. After a few seconds of relishing in my bliss, my vision became clear again, and my breath less hurried.

Beck looked up at me, resting his chin between my breasts and smiling. "What are you thinking?"

"Lots of things," I admitted, not willing to tell him how my heart was not only racing because of the incredible orgasm he just gave me, but because it was ready to leap out of my chest from the way he was looking at me. Happy, enamored, fulfilled.

Bringing his hands up under his chin, he continued his magnetic gaze. I broke eye contact and sunk into the soft pillow beneath my head. "B, I think you broke me," I huffed.

He scooted up, curling against me, bringing my face to his with his gentle touch. "I hurt you? How?"

"No," I laughed, realizing he was clueless. "I'm done for, B. I think you ruined me for any other man. That wasn't even *sex* and I'm completely exhausted from the workout you just gave my body. That tongue is... it's magic," I sighed.

Bending his elbow and leaning his head against his open palm, he looked at me intently. "First of all, no talk about other men while you're in my bed."

"Technically it's *my* bed, but go on..."

"You know what I mean, smartass. And secondly, you better dig deep and find some more strength." He looked past me to the alarm clock on my nightstand. "That fiasco made everyone go home early... the night's still young, sweet thing. I've been waiting all week to be with you again."

Even if I was completely worn-out, my limbs deliciously languid, hearing those words had me craving more.

In one quick movement, Beck lifted me by my waist and sat me on top of him. I straddled his perfect body, admiring him. He flexed his pecs, lifting his eyebrows. "Like what you see?"

Licking my lips, I took on a role I never thought I could play—sexy and domineering, rather than the shy and submissive girl I'd always been in bed. I felt at ease with Beck—confident. "I love what I see," I purred, running my hands along his smooth chest, tracing my fingers along the rigid dips and valleys his muscles created. I eagerly surveyed every inch of him, rubbing my body against his as I explored. My fingers trailed the narrow patch of dark hair that led from his belly button to the center of his deliciously shaped V. Just looking at him was enough to get my body blistering with desire.

"Sweet thing, your eyes say it all."

I stared at him, deeply, scanning his beautiful, chiseled features. "And what exactly are they saying?"

"Want me to spell it out?"

"Mmmhmmm," I encouraged him, grinding my sex against his stiff erection.

"You want me to fuck you, hard, and rough, and dirty like that first night." He reached around, grabbing my ass with force. It would leave a mark. Was it sick that I'd fondly think of the bruise as a token of our night together?

Pressing my body against his, I leaned down and sucked his lower lip into my mouth, biting softly. "That's exactly what I want," I whispered.

In a fast movement that left me nearly dizzy, he flipped us over so he was now on top of me, caging my body in his strong limbs. "Too bad. Not tonight. I told you, we're going slow." He kissed my neck right below my ear and whispered, "Gentle." Bringing his lips to mine, he teased me with a soft kiss and brought his mouth to my other ear where he whispered again, "Inch by inch. I want to come together. I want to make this last."

I allowed Beck to take over control and set the pace. His fingers kneaded my shoulders from behind, as we got lost in another spine-tingling kiss. When I felt his thick stiffness prodding against my thighs, I sucked his tongue into my mouth, trying to show him just how badly I wanted him.

My obvious need for him did not make him hasty. If anything, he took his sweet time even more.

With our bodies fused together, he kissed the tip of my nose, sweeping strands of unruly hair out of my eyes. He kissed each of my eyes, humming in enjoyment. The look on his face as he feathered my skin with these sweet kisses made me even needier for his touch.

His musky scent invaded my senses and I dug my fingers into the wavy tufts at the back of his head, as his lips continued praising my neck. "Beck, please."

"Baby, I waited too long to just get this over with. Let me savor you." It was a simple request, but it didn't relieve the ache that was growing more and more intense each moment he deprived me of what I wanted most.

"You're killing me, B. I want you. I *need* you! Just... please..." I sounded desperate, and maybe in that moment I was actually desperate for him. All those texts and phone calls, and the memory of our one night together—they made me frantic for the real thing.

Collapsing on top of my body, he lifted his head from where he was nibbling my collarbone, and arched an eyebrow. "So, you want me to fuck you, huh?"

"Yes." I stopped myself from nodding my head up and down like a panting puppy, waiting for a treat. "That's what I want. Right now." Clear and to the point. I couldn't wait any longer.

Jolting upright and settling between my legs, he spread them wide, watching me. I arched my hips, indicating my eagerness and with one slow thrust, he guided himself inside me.

"Ahhh," I moaned in pure delight. I almost wanted to

thank him for finally satisfying the emptiness begging to be filled... by him. So I did. "Thank you. Jesus Christ, thank you." I sighed as he slid in and out of me, picking up his unhurried pace.

He cupped my face in his hands, prompting me to open my eyes. "Look at me, Riles," he said, fixing his warm brown eyes on mine. Plunging deeper and causing me to writhe underneath him again, he then looked down to where our bodies were joined. "Look at how perfectly we fit together. How beautifully your body reacts to my touch."

My body certainly loved his touch. It was magical, and I never wanted it to end. I never wanted *this* to end. And the more I thought about what was happening, the more I realized that as badly as I wanted Beck to fuck me over and over again, I craved the effortlessness in our lovemaking too.

That's what we were doing. There was a definite difference between the reckless wildness of the other night compared to the tenderness and warmth between us tonight.

As our bodies moved together in a passionate dance, I felt the need for him to be even closer. I wrapped my arms around him, pulling him tighter. I never wanted to let go. I had no idea it could feel this good. I guess it was all about being with the right person.

Was Beck that right person? God, it certainly seemed that way. I wanted to tell him, to let him know that these moments of intimacy between us were some of the best of my life. And I wasn't just talking about sex. It was the connection—feeling for the first time that I was totally in sync with someone who knew me on so many levels. "So good," I hummed, not wanting to make any confessions just yet. He didn't need to know what I was thinking—that I wanted to be with him, really be with him, all the time, more than I'd ever wanted anything.

"It's perfect. Not just good, baby. *Perfect.*" It came out in a throaty whisper that caused my insides to contract. He felt it too. His words were my validation that I wasn't on this crazy ride of emotions alone.

The idea of us being perfect together swam through my brain and traveled through my veins as the friction between us grew more and more intense. I allowed the powerful combination of internal emotions and physical sensations to flood my body. It was unbelievably liberating, yet astonishingly terrifying. I wanted to give myself fully to this man whom I'd only been with twice. To a man I'd once known as a boy, as a lifelong friend, as someone else's boyfriend. Did any of that matter anymore? Did it matter who Beck was in the past? Or was it about who he could be in my future?

"Look at me, baby," he demanded softly, breaking me from my internal analyzing. Even during amazing sex I couldn't shut off my brain. *Stupid brain! Stupid heart! Let me enjoy the moment!*

I shook off the thousands of thoughts ruining my focus on the incredibly skillful man anchored to me. Bringing my eyes to his, I smiled, realizing that all those thoughts had a rightful place in my head. I was staring into the eyes of someone who had the ability to make me happier than I'd ever been. He could fill the void by being mine. I just wanted him to be mine.

He smiled back at me; his warm chocolate eyes had

turned darker and coal-like. Gliding in and out of me so that I could feel every solid inch of him as he did, he dug his hands into my thighs and closed his eyes. "I never want to stop, Riles, but..." I didn't want to hear a reason for him to stop. Ever. My mind jumped to silly conclusions, but catapulted back to my happy place when he continued. "Oh, God... I'm gonna come, baby. Are you close?"

I wasn't—not that his performance was at fault. It was my damn head, making me think instead of feel. *Stop thinking, damn it!* I wanted to do this together.

Inching myself up on my elbows, Beck helped to pull me upright and I draped my legs over his in a sitting position. Gazing into his eyes, I wrapped my arms around his neck as I lifted my body up and down over his, forcing him deeper and deeper.

He groaned and his head fell back as I sped up the pace. I leaned down to kiss his neck, lingering over his Adam's apple and feeling the gentle vibrations of his growls beneath my tongue.

Rocking faster and faster over him, I felt him stiffen and pulsate inside me. Feeling the incredible signal of his impending rupture was all I needed to fall over the edge myself. I tangled my fingers into the hair at the base of his neck and pulled him to me. Our mouths crashed together and our tongues tangled wildly as we rode out the explosions our bodies created together.

"So fucking good, Riley," he sighed against my lips.

"So fucking *perfect*," I corrected him, resting my forehead against his and trying to catch my breath.

It was in that heated moment, damp with sweat and clinging to each other, spiraling back down to reality, that I knew he was the one for me. I didn't want to admit my feelings, but it was impossible to hold them back. "Beck?" I finally spoke, my voice still shaky.

"Mmmmhmmm?" he hummed against my neck, still embracing me in his warmth.

"I want to be with you."

Lifting his head, he looked at me with a sly grin. "You'll have to give me a few minutes, sweet thing. That was intense."

Moving off his lap and lying beside him on the bed, I rolled my eyes. Such a guy. "That's not what I meant, silly."

"Oh, no?" he asked playfully, spooning me and tracing his fingers along my neck.

"I meant outside of the bedroom, B. I want to *be* with you. As in, be your girl." I was starting to get nervous. I was glad I couldn't see his face. I didn't want to know what he was thinking before he said it. Trying to calm my nerves and lighten things up before I got my heart stomped on, I blurted out, "Is it too soon? Am I acting like a crazy clinger thinking that we could be more than just great sex?"

"Just great? I thought that was fan-fucking-tastic!"

Swiveling around to face him, I smacked him on the shoulder and he laughed, rubbing the spot I'd hit. "Focus here, Beck. Unless of course, you don't want to. I'm sorry I'm letting it all flow like some verbal brain vomit, but I just felt... I don't know... that was so different... special, almost."

His eyes went wide and I was afraid he'd think I'd gone postal with my impulsive confessions. "Almost? You really are crazy if you're going to classify what we just did as *almost special.*" His words brought on a relief that washed over me and calmed my frazzled nerves. I smiled, bringing my hand up to his cheek. He cupped his hand over mine and kissed me on the tip of the nose. It was so intimate and heartwarming, I felt a tingle spread across my entire body.

"Riles, with you everything feels special. And not *almost* special. *Definitely* special. I know it's all happening fast and furious and without thinking, but sometimes—sometimes the best decisions are made without thinking everything through. Without pie charts, and spreadsheets, and deep conversations about pros and cons. I'm going to sound so cheesy for saying this, and you better never repeat it because I'll deny it for as long as I live."

I smiled so big that it actually hurt. I loved that he was comfortable like this with me. It made me feel powerful, like he had this draw to me that he'd had to no one else. "Shoot. I won't judge."

He held my hand at our sides, rubbing his thumb along my skin. I relaxed, readying myself for what he was about to say. He swallowed audibly as if he was nervous, but the look on his face was confident and sure as he spoke. "We don't get to choose who we fall for. Sure, we can *try* to pick based on appearance, or personality, or compatibility. But sometimes, like in our case, it's right under your nose and you don't even know it. Yeah, it's all crazy and complicated, but who gives a fuck about all that? It'll take time to work around some things, but I think it will be worth it. What I'm trying to say is, sometimes the heart wants what the heart wants and right now... my heart wants you, Riley."

Without giving my brain time to think, I blurted, "Oh, B. You have no idea how happy that makes me!" I kissed him hard, reveling in the moment.

I never imagined Beck to be such a romantic. He was full of wonderful surprises at every turn. Surprises that had my heart doing somersaults and jumping into my throat. He was right in saying we'd have a lot to work around—my brother and his judgment, Marissa and the unfinished nature of Beck's relationship with her, the almost irrational speed at which this was all unfolding. But it was worth hurdling those obstacles if it meant Beck was the prize.

CHAPTER 15

Beck

It took everything in my power to sneak out of her bed and leave her side. We'd made love another time, spoken more about what we wanted for our futures, tried to figure out how to work around the things that would hinder our growth as a couple. But it was getting late and we were still mindful of the sleeping, drunk, angry giant sharing our quarters. If he woke up to find us together he wouldn't understand, and I didn't want to have to explain it to him while he was still in a heartbroken-drunken stupor.

After kissing Riley goodnight and wishing her sweet dreams (this girl was melting me and turning me into the ultimate pussy—I kinda loved it!) I headed downstairs for a glass of water and to check on Marcus. I tried to tiptoe past him, as gracefully as a clumsy man can tiptoe, without waking him, but when I stubbed my toe on the clunky coffee table, it shifted and I muffled an "*ow*", causing Marcus to stir.

Waking from his coma, he grumbled, "Fuck!" He

brought his bandaged hand to his head, confused. "Shit, what the fuck... Oh, no! Tessa!" He darted up and off the couch, obviously remembering everything from the night before. "What time is it, bro? I gotta get to her."

I walked over to him, clapping my hands on his shoulders. "You're not going anywhere. It's the middle of the night. You're still half-drunk and half-asleep. I told you I'll help you in the morning."

He glared at me, dragging in heavy breaths. "I can't just sit here and wait and make her think I don't care. I've never told her I love her. I have to tell her, Beck. I can't live another minute without telling her."

The pain showed through his eyes, seeped through his words, and as much as I felt that pain for him, he needed to give it time—at least until the morning—until he went chasing after her.

"You'll get to tell her, bro. I promise. Didn't I promise you last night?"

He nodded his head, slumping his shoulders. This dude was still not sober and probably emotionally exhausted from having his heart ripped out. I needed to get him back to sleep so he was in a better way tomorrow. "Come on," I said, ushering him to the staircase. "Go back to sleep. Get a good night's rest and tomorrow's a new day. 'Kay, asshat?"

Conceding, he held onto the banister and started walking up the steps one by one. When he was halfway up and I was feeling like a champ for getting him to listen, he turned around, shaking his head. "I'll tell ya one thing, Beck."

"What's that?" I asked, curious. Marcus was never that enlightening, so I could only imagine what he'd taken from all of this.

"It's damn near impossible to live without something you love. I learned that lesson the hard way with my mother and I'm in fucking agony right now thinking I've lost Tessa. And I know you, man. You're a good guy. You love with your whole heart. So, be smart. Whatever shit is going on with you and Marissa, fuck it... work it out. I know now how much you love her and need her. Don't let that slip away."

After he was done with his speech, he turned and walked up the rest of the steps, entering his bedroom and shutting the door behind him. I was left at the foot of the stairs, completely baffled.

Marcus had never given me advice on life or love. He wasn't a deep thoughts kind of guy. But the one damn time he chose to go all Dr. Phil on me, he had to mention Marissa—and after I'd just put her behind me and decided to move on with his sister.

It wasn't that I was having second thoughts about Riley or that I was thinking about getting back together with Marissa. But I was all kinds of worked up by what he'd said. If I announced to him tomorrow morning that Riley and I were together, that we were starting a relationship out of the blue, he would never understand it. He thought I was technically still with Marissa. He would assume I cheated on her with Riley. He'd think I was acting on impulse rather than true emotions. He'd think it was only sex. He'd accuse me of being an asshole for jumping from one girl that I supposedly loved and wanted to spend the rest of my life with up until seven days ago, to his innocent, sweet sister.

I'd want to kick my ass, too, if the tables were turned!

If there was one thing I didn't want to do in all of this, it was hide my feelings for Riley. Oh, that and hurt her. And telling her that we had to hide our relationship and sneak around until we figured out a way to ease Marcus into things—yeah, that was going to sting no matter how pretty I made it sound. "Fuck," I huffed, exhausted and frustrated and just plain stumped.

Marcus had made a point with his little speech about not letting what you want slip away. Only thing he was wrong about was the girl. It was good in the hood to encourage me to go after the girl when the girl was Marissa, but would he be so encouraging when he found out who I truly wanted was Riley? Yeah, I didn't know about that.

I couldn't think about this shit right now. It wasn't the time or place. So instead I went to the fridge and grabbed a water bottle, downing it as I made my way back upstairs to the guest bedroom.

The bedroom was at the end of the hallway, past Marcus's, the bathroom, and across from Riley's. Marcus's door was closed shut, but Riley's was open just a crack. I approached the room with trepidation—I wanted to barge in there and crawl back into bed with her, wrapping my arms around her until we woke up together in the morning. Unfortunately, we'd have to delay our adult slumber party until Marcus wasn't under the same roof.

I inched closer to the room to check if she was still awake. I told myself it didn't matter if she was or wasn't—I couldn't risk going back in there no matter what. Aw, fuck, who was I kidding? If she was awake, I was going back in there to give her a kiss that would hold us over until we were able to be alone again.

But luckily, or unluckily, however you decided to look at it, she was sound asleep with her hands tucked adorably underneath her cheek, curled in the fetal position. She was beautiful—and not just beautiful in that peaceful, sleeping angel way. Her presence alone lit up that dim room even as she slept, reminding me of all the things I already couldn't get enough of.

The next morning I woke up to the sound of crashing and cursing. It took me a minute to figure out what was going on and where I was, but when my eyes adjusted to the bright light, I remembered everything—and that explained the ruckus going on downstairs.

Jumping out of bed, I bypassed the T-shirt that lay where I threw it after waking in a sweat from a rather interesting dream—one starring Riley and me as the main characters. Flinging the door open, I flew down the steps.

Riley sat at the kitchen table with her head in her hands, crying. Marcus was tearing the kitchen apart in search of… something. I wanted to run to her and comfort her and then smack the shit out of Marcus for making her upset. Instead I added to the noise. "What the fuck, man? Look at this mess! What the hell are you looking for?"

Riley's head popped up when she heard my voice. Her eyes were wet with tears, her face red and blotchy from crying. She was still breathtaking, even more so after the night we spent together. I gave her a friendly nod when I saw that Marcus was watching me, but when he turned around to continue his tirade, I winked and smiled, bringing a shy smile to her own lips.

"Where the fuck are they, Riley? What the hell did you do with my fucking keys?"

Riley sat stoically at the table. She didn't turn around, she didn't raise her voice. "She doesn't want to see you right now, Marcus. I'm not gonna let you drive like a lunatic to go home to someone who's only going to kick you back out. Give her time. Leave her alone," she said, as if she'd said it a million times already.

This only seemed to make Marcus more irate. He wasn't taking no for an answer, and he was taking it out on the pots and pans. And Riley. "Bitch!" he yelled as he rummaged around. (He was getting closer to the Devil Dog box, dammit). I wanted to run over to him and punch him in the face for talking to her like that when all she was trying to do was protect him. I had to be cool and inconspicuous, but I didn't have to stand for him talking to his sister that way. "Hey, calm the fuck down. It's not her fault, so don't take it out on her."

He stormed toward me with his hands clenched at his sides. I'd seen him like this before and there was no reasoning with him when he was going off the deep end. I didn't want it to come to blows, especially not in front of Riley. So as he got in my face, cursing and yelling about how I had no idea what I was talking about and that I was being a dick for keeping him from her, I took a deep breath, swallowed my pride, and simply backed away with my hands on his chest. "Dude! I'm not gonna say it again. Calm. The. Fuck. Down."

Riley was at my side now, her hand on my shoulder. There was nothing suspicious about the minor physical contact. An outsider would see it as a friend trying to ease a heated situation and prevent a fight. But even the slightest touch of her hand on my bare shoulder had me wanting to reach out and hold it there. I glanced at her, biting my lip to suppress any sound that might escape me, and then quickly looked away.

Sensing the frustration that not being able to respond to her touch was bringing me, she dropped her hand and stood between me and Marcus. "Enough. Beck. Why don't you two go for a run or something? I think he needs to exert some of this energy. I'll clean up his mess—can't fucking wait—and you talk some sense into him about leaving Tessa be."

"I don't *want* to leave her be. I want to apologize to her and she's not answering my fucking phone calls!" He was so tense, a good, sweaty run around the lake was probably the best thing for him right now.

"She's right, Marcus. Let's get some fresh air, sweat out the stress, and then by the time we get back and pack up we can head home, beat the traffic, and maybe Riley will have heard from Tessa by then." It was like coddling a toddler. I'd bet Luca was easier to talk to than he was.

Rolling his eyes and raking his fingers through his messed-up hair, he finally calmed down and gave in. "Fine! I'll be ready and down in ten."

He stalked off, ignoring the humongous mess and the sour mood he'd managed to create.

When he was gone and I heard the door to his bedroom slam shut, I turned to Riley and wrapped my arms around her. "You okay, babe?"

"Yeah, I'm fine," she sighed against my neck. "He's out of control. I've never seen him like this, B. I'm worried."

Stepping back and appraising her concerned features, I tucked a hair behind her ear and pulled her close to me, trying to comfort her. "He'll be fine. He's just in love. Love can make you do some crazy ass things sometimes, right?"

"The craziest," she giggled.

I didn't want to prod or push, or take this to a place it was nowhere near yet, but by her giggle and the redness in her cheeks I could see she was thinking the same thing that had crossed my mind. *Love.* It certainly was the cause for some epic, unexplained behavior. And right now, tangled in each other's arms, our lips inches apart, the stiffness in my pants growing harder and harder—we were acting pretty fucking crazy.

"This isn't a good idea. He can come down any second," I whispered, my nose touching hers.

"You're right; he might find us," she whispered back, still not backing away.

"And if he was mad before, just imagine how mad he'll be when he sees my hands all over his sister's..." I dropped my hands to her ass, gripping the perfect round cheeks with a pinch.

"Ow!" she squealed and then repeated the same motions with her hands on my ass. "B?" she finally asked, nipping at my neck.

"What, sweet thing?" I pulled her tighter against me. I never wanted to let go. In fact, I wanted to take this a little further—okay, a lot further—upstairs.

"When do we get to see each other again? I can't go another week with just sexts and phone calls. Plus, now that we have to keep it a secret—"

I pulled back, a little confused. I knew we had to keep it a secret. I had intentions of talking to her about it today. I'd originally thought it would take a lot of convincing and sweet talking to make her understand that I wasn't treating her like some illicit affair, but rather was protecting her and *us* from judgment. But hearing her speak my concerns out in the open and totally doubtless about it too—God, this woman got better by the second.

"Hey," she asked, taking inventory of the mixed emotions playing across my face. "You're not mad that I said that, are you?"

"No, I'm not mad at all." I said, kissing her right below her ear.

"Then why are you quiet?"

"Because you're amazing and I need to soak it all in, babe."

"What's so amazing about me telling my equally amazing... lover... that we have to keep our feelings private from everyone we know and love? I'm not ashamed of this at all, you know? It has nothing to do with how I feel about—"

"Shhh," I said, placing a finger at her lips. "I know. I get it and I couldn't agree more. Now come here and give me a kiss before he comes stalking back down here like a mad dog."

With that she shut up and allowed me to take her in my arms and show her exactly how amazing she was.

When Marcus came back downstairs it was almost impossible not to laugh like two kids who were hiding something from their parents. Throwing each other knowing glances here and there, I pretended to help her clean up.

"Why the fuck aren't you ready? You waiting for an engraved invitation?" *Such fucking couth, Marcus. You're really helping your cause.*

"I was helping Riley clean up your tantrum, asshole. All I need is five minutes to get on a shirt and my sneakers." I stacked another pile of napkins on the counter, brushing my arm against Riley's in the meanwhile.

She looked back to Marcus, who was lacing up his shoes and whispered toward me, "Ask him for ten and I'll make it worth your while."

My eyes went wide when I thought of the possibilities that ten minutes alone with Riley could bring, but I cleared my throat, pretending she hadn't said anything.

This would not be easy. And the hardest part wouldn't be keeping it from Marcus. The hardest part would be keeping my hands to myself all damn day.

CHAPTER 16

Riley

Damn it all to hell! If he was fuming before, he would be super fuming now. Tessa had finally made contact with me, but I wasn't allowed to tell Marcus about our conversation. Every single molecule in my body fought the urge to be loyal to my own flesh and blood and tell him what he desperately wanted to know. But I also had to stay true to my friend's wishes. At least until she landed safe and sound in the comfort of her parents' home, all the way across the country in Arizona.

Did I say he was going to freak out? Marcus was going to lose his fucking bird when he found out I didn't tell him she was flying to another state to get away from him for God knew how long.

God, I felt so guilty. When had I become such a despicable liar? First I was keeping my relationship with Marcus's best friend from him, and now I was acting all harboring-the-fugitive with the girl he loved. He was going to rip me a new one for being a horrible sister. I probably deserved it too. But by the time we'd made it back to Brooklyn—in three separate cars, in holiday traffic—Marcus's stress level had finally lowered a few notches and I wasn't about to rock that boat.

"You okay?" I asked him as I stocked his fridge with the last of the leftover food from the party.

"Yeah, I just wish she'd let me talk to her. If she'd just let me explain..."

I truly felt sorry for him. It was the first time since our mother died that my heart ached for him because of the way he was handling his "loss."

Whereas most people used sadness as their outlet, Marcus turned grief into anger. I could tell he was definitely miserable without her, but his irritation at her running away without giving him a chance was what shone through the most.

Joining him on the couch, where he'd plopped down with a beer, I sat next to him and took the bottle out of his hand.

He immediately darted a look at me as if to say, "stop judging me," but I couldn't help it. I didn't want him turning to a bottle when I was there to help. He wasn't *that* guy. Tessa didn't need *that* guy in her life again. Numbing his pain—the way he did with clubbing and whoring around after our mother died—was not going to solve this problem.

"So," I finally said, breaking the silence. "Tessa Bradley, huh?"

"What about her, Ry. Why are you busting my balls... now?"

"I'm not busting balls. I'm trying to talk to you. You think you can turn off the angry caveman for a few minutes to talk to your older, wiser sister?"

He wouldn't look me in the eye. He stared ahead, cracking his knuckles, still visibly enraged, but seeming like he was trying to keep his anger at bay. "I'm listening," he sang, like the immature brat he used to be.

"I know you don't think so, but... I'm happy for you two."

He shook his head and started to laugh so hard I thought he was putting on an act.

"What? What's so funny, Marcus?" I asked, a little taken aback by his reaction.

"Thanks, but no thanks, sis. Now that I've fucked it all up and she's out of the picture, you're happy for me? You tortured me for hitting on her and flirting with her when you had no idea what we were all about. You judged me and ridiculed me and said who the fuck knows what to her to make her think I was a bad guy. I kind of blame you for her running off the way she did, you know? If you hadn't planted it in her head that I was a fuck up, maybe she would have seen what she saw in a different light. Maybe she wouldn't have doubted me the way you did. Did you ever think of that?" He was spitting it out as if it were poison on his tongue.

The words stung. They ripped me apart. I'd been hard on him. I'd warned Tessa about him and told her to stay away, but that was because I didn't think he was capable of love. I had no clue he'd finally fallen for someone. I had no clue he was in this deep. If he had opened up to me, maybe tried to reason with me—who was I kidding? I was such a stubborn bitch these last few months, maybe I *was* at fault for the mess they were in right now. There was nothing left to say except, "I'm sorry, Marcus. I truly am. I had no idea how you really felt. I didn't think it was serious. I just thought you were fucking around and I wanted to protect you both. Can't you understand that?"

His attention was still focused on the picture of Yankee Stadium that hung on the wall opposite the couch. He didn't have to look at me for me to know what he was feeling. The wall that Marcus had built around his heart after our mother died was finally coming down. He'd allowed Tessa in and now that she was gone, he was lost.

"She'll come around, Marcus. I know she will. Just give her time."

He finally looked at me, and the pain in his eyes—there were actual tears—almost made me crumble. "Why won't you tell me where she is? Why are you doing this to me?"

Suddenly, I couldn't think of a good enough reason *not* to tell him. I wanted to buy him the plane ticket myself and let him confess his love to her so they could live their happily ever after. But then I remembered my words to Tessa and wished I hadn't promised to keep her location on the DL. She'd already been broken, hurt, disappointed, and scarred by one man in her life—she needed to figure this out without Marcus in her head. She'd given him her trust and in her eyes he'd broken that trust. She needed time to realize what she was missing. She needed time to sort things out. I hated that I had the power to take that all away with one word. I hated that I had the power to erase Marcus's pain with one word.

Before I had the chance to go back on that word, Marcus interrupted my mental hate-fest with a chuckle. He was typing something into his phone, but I couldn't imagine what could be so funny.

"Is that her? Did she finally text you back?" I asked, hopeful.

"I wish. It's just Beck."

I tried to hide my reaction—the way my back straightened and my cheeks warmed at the sound of his name. "He get home okay?" I asked, nonchalantly.

"Yeah, he's good... but Marissa isn't."

Marissa? Why the hell was he mentioning her name? "Oh, no? What's up?" I played dumb.

"Sounds like she was waiting on his doorstep for him to come back. Poor fucker got the third degree as soon as he pulled up to his place. Guess they'll be making up tonight. At least someone will be back in the arms of the love of his life."

His words caused a shiver of disgust to roll over my body. I felt weak, helpless, totally out of control hearing that Beck was with her right now. She could only be there for one reason and that was to get him back.

Would he cave? Was what we had strong enough to push her away? He told me he wanted me. Did he still want her too? Oh God. My happy bubble that I'd been in with Beck was about to pop in my face and I couldn't even react.

"What the fuck's your problem? You look as white as a ghost." Marcus broke me from my thoughts, making me very aware of my rapid heartbeat and the sweat forming on my upper lip.

"Yeah... um... I'm fine." I stood, trying to think of an excuse to jet the hell out of there. "I just remembered that I have to get a whole sample display together for a client consultation tomorrow. I put it off, thinking we'd be home earlier and I totally forgot." I could tell by the dismissive look on his face that he'd bought it. "You okay if I go?"

Shaking his head and rolling his eyes, he returned his attention to his phone, dismissing me. "I'm fine, Ry. I don't need a babysitter. And I *will* keep calling her, even if she doesn't answer."

I wanted so badly to know what he and Beck were talking about. I fought the urge to lunge at him and grab his phone to read the texts for myself, but that would just come off as absolutely ridiculous. In his uninformed mind I had no reason to give a shit what he and his best friend were talking about. In my mind—I couldn't even keep track of all the rampant thoughts freight-training through my brain right now.

"I'm gonna go, okay?"

He shooed me away, not even looking up. I guessed he was still pissed at me for not giving him any info about Tessa. I saw myself out, blowing him a kiss, and as soon as I shut the door behind me, I was dialing Beck's number.

When he didn't answer the first time, my heart sank a little. In that moment I understood Marcus. I was losing Beck. After the amazing night we'd spent together. After sharing and admitting so many things to each other, he was returning to the familiarity of Marissa and abandoning his feelings for me.

Was I crazy to ever think he had feelings for me? Was it all just a rebound, even though he said it wasn't? Was he second-guessing our connection to give the woman he'd loved for two years another shot?

I had no fucking clue. And I wouldn't know until I spoke to him, but there was no way in hell I would stoop to the level of some crazy-ass jealous girlfriend. I could drive to his house and see what the hell was going on. I could call him over and over again until my thumb was blistered from hitting send. Or I could face the reality that maybe what we thought we felt was just hurried, hasty, and harried.

Maybe it was nothing.

Maybe I imagined it all because I wanted it so badly. Maybe I hoped for this to work because I was tired of being alone. Maybe I was so jealous of Marcus and Tessa that I was grasping at straws. Maybe, maybe, maybe. There were a million different scenarios that left me doubtful.

When I got to my car and deflated into the driver's seat, reality sank in. *No!* It wasn't any of those things. I wasn't fucking crazy. Beck and I had an irrevocable connection. It was real. It was perfect. It was solid. I hadn't imagined it.

But I had to hold on to my pride. So, instead of dialing his number again or saving my curiosity for when he did answer my calls, I texted him with the truth.

> **Me:** *I know she's there. I was with Marcus when you texted him. I don't want to bother you, but I just want to make sure you're okay.*

I waited for what seemed like hours, staring at the screen for his response. When I finally saw the three little dots, indicating that he was typing something, I thought I'd die from the suspense.

Beck: *Don't worry your sweet little head, babe. It's not what you think. I'll call you in the morning.*

Morning? His carefree tone and his sweet words made me feel better, but—*Gah!*—I was going to lose my mind until then. I thanked my lucky stars that this was a text conversation and not a face-to-face. This way I could hide my insecure side and come off like the graceful, carefree girl he knew me to be.

Scouring my brain for a proper response, I finally settled on…

Me: *KK*

It was indifferent, cool. It would make *him* think. If I had to wrack my brain all night about what was going on over at his place with Marissa, the least I could do was make him wonder what *I* thought about the situation.

What *did* I think about the situation? It wasn't cut and dried—not at all. My mind was racing and so were my nerves. To me that meant I was feeling things I didn't even *know* I was feeling. I'd only invested a week's time with Beck, but in those seven days we'd shared more than I'd ever shared with any other man. It was special, and different, and—just like me to put myself all out there and wind up getting hurt.

As I drove home, I tried to distract myself and drown out the voices in my head with the radio. Of course, as if it were a blaring warning that my mind was only allowed to focus on one thing, Justin Timberlake's *Mirrors* was the first song that came on.

In the last week with Beck we'd referenced JT and *Cabaret* at least a hundred times. It was becoming an ongoing joke—*our* ongoing joke. I wasn't crazy! We already had our own private things. That's how great relationships started. Unfortunately, exes coming back into the picture was one of the reasons great relationships ended.

The song continued in the background while my worries ran on in the forefront of my mind, but when Justin sang *'Cause I don't wanna lose you now, I'm lookin' right at the other half of me,* my eyes began to tear up. The thought of not being with Beck was something I didn't want to face. But the idea of not being with him *and* having to see him around Marcus, *with* Marissa—now that just made me want to rip her eyeballs out. I'd let down my guard for Beck, but I wasn't about to give him the power to crush my heart.

CHAPTER 17

Beck

Imagine my surprise when I turned the corner, pulled my car into the driveway, and nearly ran over my ex-girlfriend. Not the welcome home I was expecting—I wasn't expecting *any* welcome home. In fact, after I settled in I'd planned on texting Riley and asking her to come over to continue what we'd re-started this weekend. I didn't want to be alone tonight. Not after seeing how distraught Marcus was since Tessa walked out. The idea of one more second apart from Riley rattled my cage in a weird way. And now—now my cage would have to remain locked tight as I dealt with the dramatic bullshit that was about to unfold.

As I put the car in park and swung my door open, Marissa strolled over to me with her head hung low. She looked unruffled, no sign of crying, but I knew her better than that. She didn't usually cry when she was upset—she paced, overthought, lost sleep. She would dissect the problem endlessly, coming up with scenarios that were so far-fetched they were impossible. In hindsight, I'd *rather* see her cry when something bothered her. Her analytical way of dealing with her emotions only made her seem cold and calculated now. Like it wasn't her heart she was worried about, rather her reputation or her dignity that she needed to uphold. She wasn't upset over losing me because she loved me and couldn't live without me. She was upset that she'd lost something in general. Marissa always needed to win.

"Hey," she finally said, still looking down at her feet, but acting as if it were completely normal to be here waiting for me.

"What are you doing here, Ris?" There was no reason to beat around the bush.

"Hi to you too." This time her tone matched mine.

I wasn't exactly happy to see her. Not that I had any ill feelings toward her, but I wasn't ready to face her just yet. She had said she wanted a break and I was giving her that break. I couldn't exactly tell her, *"Oh, by the way, while we've been on our break for what, seven days, I started seeing someone else. And I really like her and I want to see where it goes with her, so, mind leaving now so I can call her to come over?"*

"I miss you, Beck. I think I made a mistake." This time her eyes met mine, and for the first time since I'd known her, sadness was clear on her face.

Shit. Wasn't expecting that. I couldn't tell her to leave. *I* wasn't heartless. Just because I didn't want to be with her anymore, didn't mean I could be a dick. "Let me get my stuff and we'll go inside," I offered, waving my hand toward my front door and then turning around to grab my duffel from the back seat.

She stood behind me in silence as I unlocked the door to the apartment. Something we'd done together so many times before—usually with her hand in mine, or resting on my shoulder—seemed odd and uncomfortable now. It was funny how I'd managed to change my whole perception of our relationship in such a short amount of time. I guess I was right when I'd told Riley love makes you do crazy things. It apparently had me thinking I wanted to spend the rest of my life with someone I didn't feel like spending the rest of my evening with.

It sounded harsh, but I really wasn't trying to be. I was rejected by Marissa when I asked her to move in and forced into a break that I didn't want. Followed by the truth about what people thought of my girlfriend all this time. All topped off with a kicker—connecting the way I did with Riley Grayson.

It was a lot to deal with in only a week's time. A lot to hold resentment about. A lot to change my mind about.

Switching on the light, I plopped my bag down on the floor and made my way into the tiny room where we'd spent so many nights cuddled up on my couch, watching a movie or making out. I almost suggested sitting at the kitchen table so she wouldn't get the idea of falling into old habits, but again—I didn't want to be a prick. I wanted this to end as amicably as possible.

"Come. Sit. Tell me what's up." I tried smiling and making light of the situation, but I was so nervous about letting her down that I couldn't be comfortable in my own place.

"Were you at the lake house?" She started with small talk. She knew where I was, she didn't need to ask.

"Yup. You knew I'd be there. You were supposed to be there with me."

Leaning her head back on the couch, she sighed. "I know. And I'm kicking myself for *not* being there. It would have been a good time—together. I miss us—together."

I had to deflect the serious tone of the conversation. She thought she was here to get back together. I didn't want that anymore. "Ris, it's only been a week. You haven't even had time to miss me yet."

She rose from slouching and grabbed my hands in hers. "That's just it. When we were together a week seemed to fly by because of work and school and studying. But this week—it was the longest week of my life. I thought about you every second. About what a mistake I made. How stupid I was for panicking when you asked me to move in. I want all of those things with you, Beck. I thought it was too soon, but I'd rather do it your way than no way at all."

She might have meant well, but she wouldn't have said that if she knew how it sounded to me. "Listen to what you're saying, Marissa. It's normal to miss someone after seeing them regularly and then quitting them cold turkey. I'm sorry things turned out this way." I tugged at the hem of my T-shirt to keep my hands busy; any physical contact would be misleading. "I missed you, too, but I don't want you to take the next step and move in with me just because you're afraid the chance won't come up again. Doing something for someone else only leads to resentment. I don't ever want you to resent me because I made you do something you weren't ready to do."

"I thought I wasn't ready. I think I am now. I'm scared to let you slip away, Beck."

I wanted to ease her worry, but I couldn't lie. I didn't still want the things I wanted last week—I didn't want the *person* I wanted last week. *Seven days. Seven days.* It only took seven days for my world as I knew it to be completely transformed. It took less than seven minutes of seeing Marissa again to know she wasn't my future anymore. "I don't know. I'm sorry. I don't want to hurt you, but I can't promise you that anymore."

Her eyes grew scary wide. Like pop-out-of-your-skull wide. "*What?* Seriously? This break wasn't meant to be a break-up, Beck. It was just a temporary separation to take a breather from each other. To clear our heads and focus on other things."

How could I tell her that that was exactly what I *had been* doing? I'd certainly been focusing on other things— Riley in particular. If I wasn't flirting with her in a cab, screwing her brains out on her couch, sexting her from the firehouse, making love to her at the lake house, or having dirty dreams about her, I was thinking about her non-stop.

My brain was warped by the newness of it all. And where I thought this weekend was one of the best I'd ever had with any girl—our connection insurmountable, our time together crazy and intense—maybe I was jumping the gun. It had nothing to do with seeing Marissa again. I didn't want to be with her anymore, but maybe this was an eye opener. Maybe I needed to take a step back and regroup before I hurt anyone else.

"Say something!" she yelled, breaking me of my fucked-up realization. "What are you thinking right now?"

Without making it any harder than it had to be, I just came out with it. "I'm thinking that it's over. We don't want the same things we used to want, babe. It took being apart to make me realize it and I'm sorry. I am truly sorry that it didn't work out for us because I did love you and I do think you are an incredible person, but—"

"But I'm just not the person for you anymore." She finished my sentence better than I could have. When she gulped back what seemed to be the first sign of tears all night, I reached up to wipe away the single one that escaped and trickled down her cheek.

"I'm sorry, Ris. Please don't cry."

"I'm sorry too. I feel like I ruined the best thing that ever happened to me."

"Pssssh." I lifted her chin with my finger and smiled. "There are so many better things that are going to happen to you. You're going to be one hot-to-trot kick-ass lawyer, for starters. And once you've changed the legal world with your tough-as-nails, no-bullshit attitude, you're going to do all the things I was trying to make you do way too soon."

Shaking her head and sniffling back the last of the tears, she said, "I hope so. I hope this isn't a huge mistake... for either of us."

It was her truth about what she was feeling and a warning all rolled into one. It was as if she was saying, *"Here's your last chance, Buster."* But I was firm in what I felt. This was the best thing for us. We needed to sever our ties and go our separate ways. It was the only way to move on.

After Marissa and I said our final goodbyes and promised to remain friends with that vow that most couples pledge at the end of a break-up, I kicked my feet up on the couch and took out my phone.

I wanted to text Riley. I was dying to talk to her again, but the whole thing with Marissa had me thinking. What kind of moron jumps into something serious two minutes after leaving something serious? It was a recipe for disaster. I didn't want Riley and me to end up a disaster. I wanted to do things right with her. When the time was right. I needed more time before I spoke to her again.

So I decided to text Marcus to check in on him.

Me: Dude, you holding up okay?

Marcus: Just fucking perfect! You sure you don't know where she is?

Me: Nope, sorry. No word from her I guess.

Marcus: Nope. What are you up to? Want to grab a beer?

Me: Nah. Exhausted. Just had it out with Marissa and I need to call it a night.

Marcus: She called? You back together?

Me: No. She was here waiting for me when I got home. Not good, but we'll talk about that later.

Marcus: *Wow, stalker much? You okay?*

Me: *Yes. Fine. I think.*

Marcus: *Shit. Look at us two. Erase this fucking text history before anyone sees it and thinks we are the most pathetic, love-sick assholes ever.*

Me: *LOL. True. Consider it done.*

I threw the phone on the coffee table in front of me to prevent myself from dialing the next number stored in my brain. I fought with myself to forget it was there and paid attention to the game on television. The Yankees were losing and the game was uneventful, so I started to doze off. Just as I was about to go to that happy, sleepy place, the phone started buzzing on the table. I reached over to silence it and saw that it was an incoming text from Riley. *Shit!* I wasn't going to ignore her. I'd have to answer her back.

Riley: *I know she's there. I was with Marcus when you texted him. I don't want to bother you, but I just want to make sure you're okay.*

Fuck! I hadn't thought about that. I'd have to be mindful of shit like this in the future. Whatever I said to Marcus about anything would always have the possibility of getting back to Riley. The hazards of carrying on a secret affair with your best friend's sister—apparently there were more than I thought.

I didn't want her to know what was going on in my head.

I owed it to her to be fair and I owed myself more time to iron things out. Without much thought, I typed a response that gave nothing away, yet gave me more time.

> *Me: Don't worry your sweet little head, babe. It's not what you think. I'll call you in the morning.*

It wasn't a lie. I was omitting nothing and not leading her on. Plus it gave me until tomorrow to figure out what the hell I was going to do.

CHAPTER 18

Riley

The men in my life would drive me to drink.

First there was Marcus, who I'd put on my own version of suicide watch. I still hadn't told him Tessa was in Arizona and he was taking it out on inanimate objects, from what I'd seen of his place last night. After I'd settled in for the night, thinking about how I'd left off with Beck, Marcus called me up, demanding I take him to Tessa's. I told him there was no use because she wasn't there, but he'd been adamant. If it eased his mind to see things for himself, I figured I owed it to him as his sister to help him out.

But when he found her place empty—like I told him it would be—he really upped the let's-take-it-out-on-Riley ante. First, he called me all kinds of hurtful names for not telling him where Tessa was. *That was strike one.* Then he blamed me over and over again for causing her to run off. *Strike two.* But the worst was when he accused me of being jealous of him because I was still alone. *Strike three—you're out!* I couldn't take the mental abuse from him at that point—even if he wasn't himself. I understood he was hurt and needed an outlet for it all, but there was only so much I could take before I actually started to believe him.

After he refused to let me drive him back home, I'd left him alone at her house, wallowing in his self-pity. I drove home to my own loneliness, wishing I could call Beck to come over and make me feel better.

But Beck was one of the reasons I was currently on the verge of spiking my Monday morning protein shake. He and the chatter-happy Fallon, who was gloating about his blissful July Fourth weekend with his latest boy-toy.

Geez, I sounded bitter. I *was* bitter. I went from my own state of bliss over my blossoming relationship with Beck, to flat-lining it and not knowing where the hell I stood with him. All in a matter of hours. It was so damn odd it made my head spin.

"What's with you, cookie face? You haven't said much about the smoking hot fireman yet today." Fallon finally came up for air.

"That's because *you* haven't shut up and there's not much to say, anyway." What *was* I supposed to say? I couldn't understand it myself, so how could I explain it out loud.

"Wasn't he there? I thought you said—"

"Yes, he was there. And yes we... spent some time together. But when he got home yesterday, Marissa, his ex, or whatever she is, was waiting for him. I haven't heard from him since last night when he told me, in a text, that he would give me a call in the morning. It's..." I looked down at my watch to see how long it'd been since I looked at it last. "It's almost noon and he still hasn't called. Safe to say,

I'm thinking the worst." There. That cat was out of the bag.

"Oh, honey. Here I am going on and on about Roger—why didn't you tell me to shut up?" He stood from the seat by my desk to give me a comforting hug.

"I didn't tell you to shut up because apparently I'm a jealous bitch who can't be happy for anyone because I'm alone and will be forever." I didn't spit it out the way Marcus had, but rather tried to repeat the insult as if they weren't words intended to hurt me.

"Who said that to you? Was it Beck? That hot little prick. I'll—"

"You'll what, Fallon?" I laughed, tilting my head. "He'd kick your ass and you know it, but that's not who said it, anyway. He's even bulkier and more hot headed, and a much bigger prick!"

"Marcus?"

"Yup."

"But why?"

I went on to tell Fallon what had happened with Marcus and Tessa at the lake house. Fallon ate it up as if it were a soap opera instead of real life people that I cared about. He was the biggest gossipmonger I'd ever met—he had to be kicking himself for not accepting my invitation to the party. But, after I explained everything about Marcus and Tessa, the hardest thing left to decipher was what went on with Beck.

Fallon seemed just as baffled as I was. "It sounds like things went great, Ry. I don't understand."

"*You* don't understand? How do you think *I* feel? One minute he was practically telling me he loved me," —well, maybe not, but it seemed like things were headed that way—"and now he won't even call me to tell me if he's still freaking available. I should've known not to get my hopes up. Things were going too good. That's usually a clear sign that the shit's about to hit the fan. I just didn't expect it to be so soon." That's what bothered me so much. It was how quickly it all changed. I didn't expect promises, but I also didn't expect to be let down… like this. Without so much as a phone call.

"Do I call him, Fal? I really want to call him." I sounded impossibly pathetic, but for once I didn't care. I had to be truthful with Fallon. I'd like to say he wouldn't judge—but he would. It was fine though, because his judgment was always critical, in a good way.

"Over my Jimmy-Choo-wearing lifeless body, you will!"

"Jimmy Choos?"

"I want to be buried in Jimmy Choos. We've been over this before, doll. An homage to my queens, my roots, my fashion-loving soul."

I rolled my eyes, annoyed that I'd allowed him to get me off topic. "Ugh! Fine! Jimmies in the casket, but can we get back to Beck? Why can't I call him?"

I joked around about how dramatic Fallon was, but when it came down to the nitty gritty, no one had better advice. He dragged a chair over beside me, sat and grabbed my hands in his. "Because he's spooked. And if you call him after he told you he'd call, you're gonna spook him even more.

"I don't know what sent him running—whether he's giving the ex another shot or not—but you need to let him chase *you*, honey, not the other way around. It sounds like he's a good guy who's probably scared of his intense feelings for you. He's just coming off a two-year thing with that chick—whose profile we will stalk on Facebook all day today, by the way—and now he's falling for you. Give the dude time. I bet he'll come around a lot sooner than you think."

It made me feel better, but it still didn't make sense. Beck had never acted *spooked* by the way we fell so fast into whatever it was we had going on. I didn't think the normal dating rules applied in this case, but maybe they did. Maybe I needed to let someone—even if it was Beck—chase me for a change.

I knew what I had to do. After years and years of doing the wrong thing when it came to guys, I had to change it up a bit. It mattered this time. I didn't want to lose Beck, and if this was the only way to do it—let the games begin.

Fallon loved the word *aloof.* It was bound to be the next word out of his mouth if I let him go on. I wanted him to see he'd taught me something over the years. "I guess it's time to put your training into action for once and for all, huh?"

"Why, darling. Whatever do you mean?" He batted his eyes, waiting for me to say it.

"Operation: Aloof Riley commences now."

"That's my girl! I knew you could do this!"

I *could* do this. I'd done it before. Beck was no different. I pulled up my big girl panties and fought to not check my watch or my cell phone too often. I kept busy consulting with the clients on my waiting list, and had Fallon schedule appointments for them. My calendar was starting to book well into the New Year and that made me happy. My career always made me happy; at least I had one constant in my life. But I wanted more. I wanted Beck. I wanted the happily ever after with the knight in shining armor. I'd done what my mom had told me by kissing lots of frogs, but I was tired of always winding up the damsel in distress when the frog turned out to be anything *but* a prince. Up until last night, Beck had seemed liked Prince Charming—forget charming, he was sexy, sweet, romantic, en-freaking-chanting. And now I had no idea if we'd ever be together again and there was nothing I could do about it.

"Hey, Miss Aloof—stop thinking." Fallon caught me staring into space from the other side of the office and shook me out of my mental musings. He was right. I had a few more hours left in my workday and plenty of things to occupy my time. I could get through one day of not worrying.

The day was one thing, but the night was a whole different beast. After work, I went to the market to get a few things to make my dinner for one. I picked up a bottle of wine and some flowers to replace the ones that were wilting in my kitchen. All of this just reminded me of how alone I was. Strong, confident, witty, smart—I was all those things and wasn't too shy to admit it, but I was also lonely.

Up until recently, I didn't realize how badly I longed for someone to be home waiting for me with a home cooked meal, a bouquet of just-because-I-love-you flowers, and two wine glasses to toast our happiness. Was that too much to ask for? I really didn't think so. Maybe I was just looking in the wrong places. Even though I thought for a fleeting moment that I could have all those things with Beck, it looked like I might have to start the search all over again.

Sipping my glass of Chianti and watching another rerun episode of *Friends*, I decided to check on Marcus. I dialed his number and waited for him to pick up, laughing at the awkward ways Chandler and Monica had to hide their relationship from Ross. *How ironic. I can't even escape the memories in sitcom syndication heaven... sheesh.*

"What?" He finally answered. He was obviously still brooding.

"Hi, Marcus. How you doing?" I ignored his tone and went on with my reason for calling.

"Same as yesterday. Can't get in touch with her, so nothing much has changed unless you're calling to tell me—"

"Nope. Sorry. Just wanted to check in."

"Bitch!"

"Enough, Marcus. You can't be mad at me forever. It's not my fault. I'm sorry she's not answering your calls, but when she's ready she'll let you know what's going on." Easy enough advice—would Beck do the same thing? I hoped so. I couldn't stay guessing like this forever. It was torture. I understood exactly what Marcus was going through.

"I'm sorry. I know it's not your fault. I'm just so scared of losing her."

I understood that too. "I know, hun. But you won't. Promise. I'll help this time. Once she's cooled down, I'll help you get her back." One of us deserved to be happy, right?

"If you really mean that, then thanks." His voice was raspy and subdued now. Maybe he was finally calming down and taking my advice. Or maybe he was putting on the aloof act too. It was all about how you made people see you, not the truth that was churning and bubbling the doubt inside.

I may've had to be aloof in front of Fallon, but Marcus had no clue. "Hey, talk to Beck? Is he okay? You said Marissa was giving him shit?"

"He didn't say much when I spoke to him today. He was at work. Took on a few extra days because one of the guys had a family emergency or something."

Why that made me smile, I didn't know. Okay. I did know. Beck was busy. It made me hopeful. Maybe he wasn't avoiding me. Maybe he was just working.

"Oh, okay. Sorry you two are both having girl trouble," I said, trying to give a reason for my Beck-inquiry without looking suspicious. "At least you have each other."

"Yup. Guess so."

"You have me too, you know?" I wanted him to know that even though I'd given him and Tessa shit for everything I was ready to make up for all of that now.

"I know Ry, and thank you. I just hope she comes around soon."

"She will. I'm pretty sure she loves you too. The few times she spoke about you to me she could barely hide her smile. That says a lot. Believe me, I know."

"God, I hope so." It sounded like he was actually praying.

I was about to ask if he wanted some company for a little while when my phone alerted me of an incoming text. "Hold on a sec?"

"Yup."

I moved the phone from my ear to see Beck's name light

up the screen. My heart thudded quickly and my smile spread wide. Even if it only said one tiny word, he'd reached out and I needed to see what it said. "Marcus, I gotta go. Fallon's texting me about work stuff. You sure you're good? I can come over if you—"

"I'm good. I'm gonna call it a night soon. Tomorrow's another day."

"Maybe tomorrow's *the* day. I have a good feeling." I said it just to appease him, but apparently it did because I could almost hear the smile through the phone.

"From your mouth, sis. Good night."

"'Night, love. Talk to you tomorrow."

I hung up the phone and rushed to check the message.

Beck: *Hey*

So it was only one word. It meant that whatever I said next would set the tone for the rest of the conversation. I took a deep breath and put on my Aloof Riley hat.

Me: *Hey*

Two could play the indifferent game.

Beck: *Sorry I never called this morning. I went in to work and took on a few extra shifts.*

Me: *That's okay.*

Beck: *Talk to Marcus?*

Me: Yup. He's still upset, but a little calmer. Hope she comes around soon and doesn't keep him waiting in agony.

I meant that for both me and Marcus. Would he pick up on it?

Beck: Ry?

Me: Beck?

Beck: I didn't get back together with her if that's what you're thinking.

I closed my eyes and did a happy dance in my head. That was good, but I wasn't about to let him think that was what I'd been waiting for.

Me: Sorry to hear that?

Beck: Not sorry at all.

Me: Well then, I'm happy it worked out the way you wanted it to.

Beck: Ry?

Me: Beck?

Beck: I want to be with you... I really do, but I think we need to take a step back. Last week was amazing and intense and I loved every minute of it, but I don't think I'm in a good position to start a new relationship right out of an old one. It wouldn't be fair to you either.

Seriously? Did I just read that right? My heart sank to my toes, the blood left my brain, and the tears started to well up in my eyes. Was he freaking kidding me? I wanted to throw the phone across the room, but I also wanted to forget this texting bullshit and call him up to scream at him. Had I imagined our whole magical weekend? Was I a total sucker for thinking Beck and I were on the same page? God, this hurt. I'd been rejected before, broken hearted even, but this... this fucking sucked. I really liked him. I wanted more than just fun. I thought he did too.

Aloof Riley. Aloof Riley—where the hell are you right now? Please take over my fingers and ignore what my brain is telling me to type.

Me: *Ok*

Beck: *Ok? That's all you have for me?*

Screw you, Aloof Riley. Say what's on your mind.

Me: *No, I have a lot more for you, but it seems you don't want it right now.*

Beck: *Oh, Riles. That's not it at all. I'm sorry it came out that way. I want to try this. I just can't make you promises.*

Me: *I totally understand. No worries.*

Beck: *Can I see you one night this week?*

I wanted to say yes. I wanted to see him more than he could possibly imagine, but I also couldn't be just a good time to him. I wanted more than that, and he wasn't ready to give it to me. What was the use in getting my feelings dragged through the proverbial mud while he figured himself out? That was the story of my life. It was time for me to change that ending.

Me: *I'm really busy this week. I took on a few extra clients. Maybe next week?*

Beck: *You blowing me off, sweet thing?*

Me: *Nope, wouldn't dream of it.*

Beck: *LOL ok good.*

Me: *Perfect*

Beck: *Just like you*

Before this went somewhere I couldn't handle it going, I decided to cut him short.

Me: *So sweet. Thanks, B. I gotta go do a little work before bed. Talk to you later?*

Beck: *Night, babe.*

Me: *Night*

After I texted my last response, I threw the phone to the opposite side of the couch to prevent myself from writing what I really wanted to. My plan to play it cool seemed to work, but it was all a lie. Inside I was nothing close to calm and aloof. I was heated, anxious, bursting with a thousand different uncontrollable emotions. I wanted what Beck couldn't give me right now and I didn't want to settle for less and take the chance that he'd never be ready to give it to me. Deep down, I felt that if I gave him the time he needed, it would work out the way I wanted it to, but it was all about coping now.

Playing this game of pretending I was someone I wasn't was no fun at all.

CHAPTER 19

Beck

Almost one week of brush offs and oneworded texts. I was losing my fucking mind trying not to overreact. After all, it was my dumbass idea to back off from Riley. It was my idiotic idea to plant it in her head that I didn't want anything serious. It was my stupid mistake to think I could live without her now that I'd gotten a taste of how good we could be together.

So many times this week I wanted to show up at her place and tell her to forget all about it. To tell her I'd take her however I could get her, even if it meant going all in, hasty, rushed, and frenzied—the way it all started.

But something kept holding me back. I didn't think my conscience was smart enough to be convincing so the only explanation was that I had Riley's best interests at heart. If she was being standoff-ish—and she was—it had to be for good reason. Maybe she was second-guessing things herself. Maybe I wasn't worth the trouble. Maybe she'd already moved on. The possibilities were endless and driving me fucking mad.

I kept busy—well, as busy as a fireman with no fires to put out could be—at the firehouse, but today was my first day off and I found myself moping around my apartment with absolutely nothing to do.

So it was like a fucking miracle from the heavens above when I received a text from Marcus, asking me to come over to Tessa's and watch the game with them, and... Riley. When I heard she was there the hope that coursed through my body was electrifying. I got dressed and ready so quickly it had to be a record for the Guinness Book. I set another world record for getting to her place and finding a parking spot on her usually crowded block in under twenty minutes. Eager much? Yup... you betchya. I needed to see this girl again, even if it wouldn't be the reunion I was hoping for.

After ringing the bell, Tessa opened the door to greet me. Instead of a warm, welcoming smile, she shot me an intentional look that told me she knew exactly what was going on with Riley and me... even though I had no idea myself.

"Hey, Tess. Thanks for inviting me over. This is for you." I handed her the six pack of beer and leaned in to kiss her cheek.

She pulled back, arching an eyebrow. "Mmm hmm. Thanks for the beer, but I'm not happy with you right now."

"Me? What did I do?"

She gestured me inside, putting her finger over her mouth. "Shh. We don't need Marcus knowing about you and Riley, especially since there isn't exactly a you and Riley anymore, is there?"

I followed behind her, shaking my head. Girls were so confusing. It was Riley who'd backed off lately, not me. I could only imagine the conversations these two had been having since she came back from Arizona and went back to being all gooey eyed around Marcus. "Listen, Tess. I don't know what she's told you, but—"

"Hey, stop monopolizing my girl and get in here. The Yanks are losing—again. I think we need to do our old ritual to get them out of their slump."

Marcus was seated on the couch with Luca bouncing up and down on his knee. My friend was so chipper it was almost sickening. But it was a nice change from the miserable grouch he'd been while Tessa was gone. Now that she was back, now that they were in love and the whole world knew it, he was happy. I needed to be happy for him.

"Hey, bro. What's the score?" Ignoring the hole Tessa was burning into my back with her disapproving stare, I joined my friend on the couch and sat back to hopefully watch the Yankees rally up a win.

Riley still hadn't made an appearance, but I heard her voice coming from the kitchen and assumed she was in there on the phone—probably with a client. She did say she'd been extra busy these days; I had no choice but to believe her. Even though I didn't.

She was avoiding me. Avoiding her feelings. But the fact that they'd invited me over with her here meant she didn't totally hate me and wasn't afraid to be in the same room.

I'd have to wait to see her to gauge her feelings toward me. Had she encouraged Marcus to invite me? Did she even know I was here? God, it was killing me to wait. I was visibly squirming in my chair and Marcus noticed.

"What the fuck, dude? You all right over there?"

"Yeah, sorry. Hurt my back working out the other day. Can't get comfortable."

He bought my excuse, and I stretched out my muscles, looking over to the door that separated the living room from the kitchen for the hundredth time in a minute.

When it swung open, my eyes met with hers and the air escaped my lungs in a *whoosh* as if I'd been holding it in since I got here. She looked effortlessly beautiful, like always. Her short hair was pinned back and off her face, revealing the stark icy blue of her eyes. She was wearing little if any make-up at all, and it looked like she'd just thrown together her outfit without any thought—a tight fitting ribbed tank top and a pair of casual shorts that showed off her silky tan legs. Even when she went for the natural look she was smoking hot.

I mentally devoured her entire body, staring a beat too long. Tessa cleared her throat, noticing my ogling and my eyes darted up to meet Riley's again. "Hey, Riles." I said as nonchalantly as possible.

"Hey," she said back, looking down at her fidgeting hands. Fidgeting was good. In this case at least. It meant she'd noticed how I was looking at her, how she affected me. I wanted to have the same effect on her. Her fidgeting made me think I did.

I unwillingly broke my gaze from hers to make it like I was paying attention to the game. I cursed something at the screen, seeing how Pettitte had just blown another run for the opposing team, and everything started to fall into its usual place. That was, until Riley sat down next to me and I nearly let out a girly pussy-like gasp. She was so close, all I wanted to do was touch her. I could smell her perfume and her fruity shampoo and I just wanted to reach over and sniff all of her in.

Tessa must've sensed that I was acting like a blood-starved vampire in the company of a virgin victim and broke the silence. "Beck, can you help me grab a few more beers from the kitchen?"

Marcus responded something barbaric about him being able to help out his girl before I could answer, but Tessa shushed him and I got up from my seat to follow her into the kitchen, leaving Marcus, Luca, and Riley alone. I hoped Luca would be the center of attention for however long Tessa decided to keep me hostage, ripping me my new asshole. I didn't need Riley confessing to him now of all times.

When the door had swung closed behind us, Tessa turned to me and asked, "So? Want to explain why you chickened out and broke my girl's heart?"

Broke her heart? Riley was acting completely indifferent. "Whoa. Hold up a minute," I defended myself with my arms up in front of my chest. "She's been avoiding me, declining my invitations to hang out. Did she tell you any of that?"

"She told me plenty. Especially about how you changed your tune after Marissa showed up last week. She's only giving you the space you asked for, Beck. You're obviously not trying hard enough—unless of course you don't *want* to try harder." She gave me that look again. It made me wonder if all mothers were taught that you're-in-trouble glare the second they gave birth.

I geared myself up for the wrath that would probably ensue after I told Tessa the truth. But what the hell? I was already on her shit list. "I can't try any harder, Tess. I don't want to lead her on. Don't get me wrong. I want her. I really do. I have a great time with her and not just in bed—she's an incredible woman. I can see myself with her."

"I'm sensing a *but*, even though it seems simple to me."

"There's nothing simple about it. It's very complicated— you of all people have to understand that, Tess. I don't want Marcus to think I'm fucking around with his sister. He wouldn't understand me jumping into something with Riley right out of my relationship with Marissa. Hell, he doesn't even know the whole story with her because he's been so preoccupied with chasing you around the country."

"Never mind me and Marcus, go on."

"I can't give her everything she wants right now. Maybe someday, but until then, I don't want anyone getting the wrong idea. I'm willing to do this casually and have fun and even be discreet for the sake of not making Marcus have a coronary, but I don't think she wants that. I think that's why she's been avoiding me." It was the only explanation. Our connection was fucking insane, but where our hearts were involved, we were on two totally different pages.

Tessa huffed, pulling her hair back into a ponytail. She'd been through so much, a lot of it similar to my situation with Riley, since starting things up with Marcus. This wasn't easy for her, either. She was invested in the Graysons... that was clear. "What a clusterfuck. I wish I had a solution, but I'm still trying to figure out my own screwed up life. I'm finally getting there and I couldn't ask for more when it comes to Marcus, but—let's just say I understand complicated. It's been a theme in my life, and while it worked out to my benefit this time, sometimes people aren't fit to deal with complicated. Sometimes people just want what comes easy. Riley needs easy—she's had enough hardship. If you can't give that to her then you need to walk away... for good."

I wanted to be Riley's easy. I wanted it with every single bone in my body, but I didn't know if I could be that for her right now. "You're asking the impossible of me, Tessa. I can't give her what she needs, but I can't stay away either."

Coming closer, she looked me square in the eye as if warning me, even though her voice was soft and sweet. "Make your decision, Beck. You can't hurt her. I won't let you. And think about what would happen if Marcus finds out."

She was right. I didn't want to hurt Riley and I didn't want to ruin my friendship with Marcus. He was like a brother to me. I couldn't throw that away for a maybe chance with Riley. If it didn't work out in the end, things would be all screwed up with no way to salvage any of it.

It would be easier for me and Riley to get over this now because we hadn't gotten too involved. But if we took it any further—there'd be no turning back. I had to keep my distance. Even if it killed me. I had to say goodbye to the chance I thought we'd had and just go back to watching her from afar as my best friend's beautiful older sister.

I did the best I could of making it like everything was the way it used to be. We watched the game, drank our beers, laughed at each other's expense and passed Luca around as if he were some toy. Kid was stinkin' adorable. And also actually stinky. Dude needed a diaper change and his mother had just sniffed it out.

"Hey, Ry. Come help me with Luca?" Tessa winked in Marcus's direction and Riley stood to follow her.

I had a feeling this was Tessa's idea to get me alone with Marcus. We hadn't had much guy time lately—him flying to Arizona to win back his girl, me working crazy shifts to drown out my own girl problems. We hadn't had the chance to watch a game together in a long time so this was good, even if the ladies were only a few feet away, upstairs.

"Shit! They're all tied up. How'd they do that?" Marcus asked, focusing on the game for the first time in a while. When Tessa was in the room, he had eyes for one thing only.

Channeling the old-Beck that used to talk baseball and chicks with my best friend all the time, I faked my answer. He'd have no idea anyway, unless he watched the highlights. "Jeter homered and brought in two runs. Reminds me of the playoff days. I hope they make it this year. We could catch a post-season game together—bleacher seats, of course." I threw the last part in for good measure to make it like my mind wasn't totally preoccupied by something other than baseball.

He looked up to where the girls were, as if to make sure they weren't listening. When the coast was clear he asked, "You all right, dude? Riley told me about Marissa. I'm sorry I've been a shitty friend. Wanna tell me what's going on?"

I thought about brushing off his question, making like it was no big deal, but suddenly I wanted my best friend to weigh in on my issues. I'd have to make it like my issues were mostly about the break up with Marissa, because I couldn't tell him the whole truth. But without thinking too hard, I just blurted it out. "There's someone else."

Marcus looked shocked. "Who? Marissa's fucking around on you?"

"No! *I've* met someone else."

Now he looked even more stunned. And he was actually grinning. "Whoa! Really? I didn't see this one coming." He was actually grinning. "You were about to ask Marissa to move in with you, no? Who is she?"

Hearing all of his questions and how little he actually knew of the situation brought out my frustrations. This was complicated. So far from the *easy* Riley needed. I scrubbed my face with my hands, standing up. I started to pace, trying to make sense of it all. "You don't know her," I lied, becoming more frustrated.

"Are you sure you want to leave Marissa for this girl? I mean, is it serious or just a cold feet kinda thing?"

This would be so much easier if I could tell him who the girl was. But I couldn't. I just had to solicit half-assed advice because I had to give him half-assed information. "No, dude. I'm all fucked up. I really like this girl. It's different and unexpected, but I can't pass this up. So, I did the right thing. I ended it with Marissa, came forward and told her the truth, but... I don't know..."

"Listen," he finally spoke. "You have to go with your gut, man. You can't stay with someone just because you want to be the nice guy. I may be late to the love fest, but I get it now. Everyone deserves to be happy—in love—with that special someone and if Marissa isn't that girl, maybe new girl is."

New girl. Nice. He'd even given his sister a nickname without knowing it. I'm sure she'd appreciate that. "It's complicated." I mocked the situation.

"Oh, I don't know complicated? Complications mean shit. If she's worth it, you look past all that and fight for what you want."

Marcus made a good point. But then again, so did Tessa. My brain was playing tug of war with my heart. I wanted to do the right thing—in this corner stood Tessa and her advice to stay away until I was ready to give my all. But I also wanted to fight for what I so desperately wanted, and that was to be with Riley anyway I could—in the far corner stood Marcus and his surprisingly stellar advice to fuck it all and go for your dreams.

"You okay, dude?"

No I wasn't, but just like all the other secrets, I couldn't tell him that. As I heard the girls making their way back downstairs, I sucked it all up and pretended my head wasn't splitting from the turmoil taking place in my brain. "Yeah, I'll be fine," I lied. This night needed to be over. I couldn't be in the same room as Riley and not be able to touch her. I couldn't be in the same room as Marcus and Tessa, feeling like a chump for lying to my best friend and making a fool out of him in front of his girl and his sister for keeping secrets.

Clusterfuck—that's what Tessa had said before, right? I had to assume that if I searched that word in Google, images of me, Riley, Marissa, and Marcus would show up.

My life was officially a clusterfuck.

CHAPTER 20
Riley

"Wow. This little bugger is really turning one? I can't believe it, Tess. It happened so fast." Of course that sounded silly, considering I'd only first met Luca a few months ago. But it was still exciting to be a part of his life—I planned to be a part of all the milestones he would be celebrating from here on out.

"Tell me about it. It feels like just yesterday I found out I was pregnant." She was smiling at her curly haired boy as he giggled on her lap, but I could sense a sadness I didn't understand.

"Hey, you okay?"

"Yeah," she said, kissing Luca atop his blond ringlets. "Just hate thinking about the past, even though it all worked out in the end. Zack wasn't exactly thrilled when he found out I was pregnant... neither was I, to be honest. I was trying to find a way to get away from him, not tie myself to him forever. But... I guess everything really does happen for a reason. I can't imagine my life without Luca man. Having him opened my eyes and made me realize I couldn't be with a man like that anymore. He truly is a blessing and that is why he deserves the best first birthday ever." She said the last part with her eyes wide, her smile even wider, and her voice high-pitched and sing-song like. Luca took in his mother's happiness and reached for her nose with a handful of drool.

I sat back and admired the connection these two had. I wanted that so badly, drool and all. Not just because I felt even lonelier in the last few weeks since Beck and I decided not to pursue a relationship, but because I was starting to concede the fact that kids may not be in my future. I was almost thirty with no boyfriend and no time, thanks to my booming business, to meet anyone new. I hadn't been out socially the last few weekends because of other things that kept me busy—tending to my dad as the anniversary of my mom's death came closer, helping Tessa plan Luca's upcoming birthday party, taking business trips around the tri-state area to brush up on some of the new interior design trends at conferences I'd been looking forward to.

While all of that was fun, rewarding, and time consuming, in the back of my mind I always thought about the coming home part. It was depressing. I came home to emptiness. To microwaveable dinners on the couch, to a half-unoccupied bed, to silence only filled by the voices on the television or stereo. I was starting to think about putting an ad in the paper for a roommate. I could always move back home with Dad and rent out my place or sell it altogether, but I'd gotten used to being independent. Something about moving back home felt like taking a step back. That would make things even more depressing.

"Hey, Auntie Riley," Tessa broke me out of my pity-party, dangling Luca in front of me. "Wanna go to the beach tomorrow?"

I usually made sure to spend Sunday afternoons with Dad, but a change of pace and some vitamin-D might be good for my soul—and my paling skin. "I'd actually love that. Will Marcus be joining us?"

"No, just us girls and the Luca man. Marcus has plans with... Beck. I think some firehouse poker tournament or something."

"You don't have to do that, you know?"

"What?" she pretended not to get what I was saying.

"Beck and I are fine. I just talked to him a few days ago. There're no hard feelings." It was a half-truth. Beck and I still kept in contact through texts—just not as colorful as the ones from a few weeks ago. I liked having him in my life, even if only as a friend, but there were definitely hard feelings. On my side at least. I didn't like the way things ended so suddenly. It wasn't even like we talked about ending it. It just did. And with no explanation.

"Bullshit," she whispered, holding Luca's ears so he couldn't sponge up her dirty word. "I know you're still hung up on him. I'm not blind, Ry."

"Well, then check your eyesight because I am indeed fine. See," I said, exaggerating a smile and pointing to it. "Really. I'm not kidding. He obviously doesn't want to be with me and he's got shit to figure out. I can't wait around for him to change his mind—that would just be stupid. Beck Matthews is not the only guy in the world. There will be others... one day." The head-scratching question was *when*.

"I'm sorry, Ry. I really am, but I think he did the right

thing. And if it's any consolation, he definitely does want you. From what Marcus tells me he hasn't had any contact with Marissa and he hasn't seen anyone new since... well, since you. You want to know what I think?"

What did it matter? She wasn't a fortune teller. The sooner I got the idea of Beck out of my mind, the better. There was no use holding on to hope when it was only false hope. "Sure, lay it on me, sista." I shrugged, promising myself not to put any weight into what she was about to say.

"I think the two of you would make an amazing couple. Sometimes the best things come totally unexpected—like me and Marcus, for example. I just think you guys started things up at the wrong time. You're practically dying for your happily ever after and he's not ready for that. I don't doubt that he's done with Marissa—she wasn't for him either, but he can't start a new relationship, the kind you deserve, wholeheartedly. Whether he admits it or not, his heart is still a little broken by what went on with her. You want a man who has his whole heart to give. Give him time. It heals all wounds."

She meant well and had great points, but she couldn't predict my future. And she had no idea what Beck felt. Smiling just to pacify her, I gave her kudos for being a dutiful friend. "You're one big cliché, Tessa Bradley. Your words are wise and I sincerely appreciate the pep talk, but I don't want to think about Beck anymore right now. I'll save my wallowing for when I'm all alone tonight in my half-empty bed. Right now, I want to talk centerpieces and favors for this little guy's bash. October is only two months away and we need to get a move on it if we want it all to be perfect."

"I wouldn't expect anything less from you," she said with a wink.

That's right—no one expected anything less than perfect from me. But I couldn't help thinking that was a façade I'd created. On the outside it all seemed perfect, but on the inside, I was anything but.

The next day at the beach, I sat with my feet buried deep in the warm sand as Luca crawled across his blanket, flinging Cheerios in the air. The seagulls were swarming, picking up Luca's discards and creating a spectacle in our little section.

"Oh, shoo, you annoying fuckers. Go feast off someone else's crap. Tessa, can you make your adorable son stop?" I hated seagulls. They were gross and needy and causing a scene. Some of the nearby people rolled their eyes, some laughed at Luca's antics, but one in particular caught my attention and was smiling directly at me. His chest muscles tightened, glistening in the sunlight as he laughed at the scene going on with the dirty birds.

I adjusted my sun hat so I could see him a little better, and smiled shyly as I took in his slim but defined physique when he stood from his lounge chair. Taking my eye contact for interest, he ran his fingers through his salt and pepper spikes and licked his plump lips. Slick. And full of himself, it seemed. I shook my head, rolling my eyes at his obvious cockiness, hoping he'd get the hint and fuck off.

But that didn't happen. He was headed my way.

Just as he was getting closer, Tessa rolled over from her tanning position on her stomach, and caught my admirer making his way to our blanket.

"Oh, yummy, and it looks like he's got his sights set on you, doll."

I giggled as I watched Tessa's eyebrows wiggle up and down, but became serious as Mr. Middle-Aged but Smoking Hot made his way closer.

Adjusting my bathing suit so I wasn't giving anyone a free show, I sat back in my chair and waited for my suitor to approach. When he was within a foot or two, his tight, fit, and tattooed body casting a shadow over me, I slid my sunglasses down my nose, and addressed Mr. Full of Himself. "Do you mind? You're blocking my sun."

"I don't mind at all. The sun causes cancer, love," he said with an adorable wink and a smile that displayed a dimple in his scruff-covered cheek. Oh, I was a sucker for dimples. "Hi, I'm Griffin. The seagulls sent me your way." He introduced himself, extending his hand with a breathtaking smile.

Before I had a chance to answer, momentarily stunned by this guy's forwardness *and* goodlookingness, Tessa stood up behind Griffin, holding a sandy Luca. "Griffin, this is Riley. Her nephew Luca and I are quite happy that his Cheerio throwing caused the seagulls to swoop in, prompting you to come over and join us. But as you can see, my son has more breading covering him than a fried chicken cutlet. So I'm going to wash him off in the water while you two get acquainted. Ciao." She spoke in a whirlwind of words, not so much as taking a breath to get it all out. Before I could scold her for being a tool, she took off, holding Luca like a football at her side. All that was left for me to do was laugh. Oh, and talk to this handsome stranger.

"As my blabbermouth of a friend just pointed out, I'm Riley."

"That's one cute kid she's got there… quite a wingman too."

"Cute, yes. Wingman, not so much."

"Oh, no? How so, love?"

I didn't know what it was, but something about this cocky dude irritated me. In a good way. I didn't like that one bit. The last guy who'd gotten under my skin—in a good way—dumped me via text message. It was in that moment that I took my Beck anger out on poor Griffin. "First of all, Griff, I'm not your *love*. Second of all, a wingman is someone who comes out with you to help you pick someone up. I did not come to this beach today to pick anyone up. I came here to spend time with my friend and my nephew and to relax in the sun. So, if you don't mind, you can stop making presumptions for me, and let me get back to my magazine and my tan lines." I sat back in my chair, pushing my sunglasses back up my nose and ignoring the delicious man who was sure to stomp all over what was left of my dignity if I allowed him to reel me in.

"I love them feisty. Seems like the seagulls sent me in the right direction." Instead of stalking off like I'd hoped he would, he plopped down into Tessa's vacant lounge chair and made himself comfortable.

"And what exactly do you think you're doing?"

Sitting straight in Tessa's chair, he leaned over and grabbed my sunscreen. He popped the top open, squeezed the white lotion into his palm, and began applying it to his sinewy shoulders.

"You see, Riley, I *did* come to this beach today to pick someone up. I've been sitting here all day people watching, and not one girl has caught my interest the way you have. Forgive me for sounding like a dirty old man, but I've been observing you for quite some time. I watched you with your nephew. I saw how loveable you can be, how much you care for him and his mother. I noticed how you weren't like ninety percent of the girls on this beach, squealing and squirming every time a grain of sand touched their skin or attempted to ruin their pedicure. And as if all that didn't make me want to get to know you, you are absolutely gorgeous in that little number you have on there. So, let's try this again: Hi, I'm Griffin and I've gotten to know you from afar for the last few hours, but I'd love to take you out some time and get to know you better."

Humina humina humina. I was speechless. There were no words. How did I come back from something like that? Not one wiseass remark fluttered through my stupefied brain. Somehow I stopped my mouth from dropping open and making me look more dumbfounded than I already was. Instead I summoned my inner gumption and decided to… flirt.

"Well, since you twisted my arm, I guess it's not a sin for you to sit and join me until my friend comes back for her seat." From the look of things, she wasn't returning any time soon. They were literally frolicking in the waves—Luca laughing uncontrollably every time the water rolled in and slapped him and Tessa in the face. Tessa was laughing so hard herself I was afraid she might drop Luca in the water and let the sea carry him away. Yeah, that would never happen. She'd never let any harm come to that kid. He was her life.

"Hey," Griffin snapped his fingers, pulling my gaze from the ocean back to him. "I'm here. Where'd *you* just go?"

I mentally evaluated his sharp features—brown eyes with flecks of green and gold and surrounded by the tiny lines of age that just made him seem all the more interesting. His face was covered in just the right amount of scruff that matched his hair color—the dark brown locks he'd probably been born with, accentuated by the perfect amount of silver that gave him that distinguished gentleman look. But what threw the whole package slightly out of whack were the tattoos. He had one rather large one covering his neck. It was a dragon tattoo, full of vivid color and so animated and detailed it seemed to jump off his skin. The dragon reminded me of Beck, the other tattoos scattered across his arms and chest reminded me of my brother. *Please tell me he's nothing like those two. I can't handle another boy—I need a man this time.*

"I gotta say, I'm digging the tattoos, but... I don't know, forgive me for being so blunt. You seem a little *mature* for some of them."

"Mature, huh? Is that your way of calling me old?"

Oh, I didn't want to insult him. I mean, he was definitely nowhere close to my age, but I didn't have to point it out to him and make him feel older than he was. "I'm sorry. I didn't mean it like that. It's just... I can picture you in a suit, with a briefcase, commuting to the city for your big important hedge fund job."

Griffin slapped his knee and laughed so hard I found it a

bit rude. "Hedge fund? What in the world would give you that impression?"

"Well, so-*rry*! What is it you do for a living, then? No, wait. Let me guess…"

"This should be fun… considering you were so off with your first guess."

"Shhh. Okay," I eyed him up and down and went for the obvious. "A tattoo artist."

"Nope. And now you're stereotyping me." He frowned.

"Hmmm," I thought, tapping my finger on my chin. "Please don't say firefighter."

"Nope. Don't like them very much either."

Think, Riley, think. This guy was more than your run of the mill businessman. "Artist?"

"Getting warmer." His eyes brightened.

"Singer?"

"Can't hold a tune to save my life."

"Musician?"

"Tone deaf."

This was infuriating and fun all at the same time. "Ugh. Okay. One more and if I get it right you owe me a Fudgie Wudgie from the ice cream guy over there."

"And if you *don't* get it?" His eyebrow twitched upward.

"You can take me out."

He narrowed his eyes, shaking his head as if he were confused. "Well, where's the fun in that? I was taking you out anyway."

"No. That's what you *thought*. I had no intention of saying yes to your advances, Griff. I don't just go out with random, *old* strangers who try to pick up girls on the beach. You could be a serial killer, for all I know."

"Serial killer? Was that your final guess? No Fudgie Wudgie for you."

"Hey! No fair. That wasn't my guess."

"Yup, too bad. You lose. I'm a photographer. And tonight I'm taking you to my favorite restaurant in Williamsburg. Want to give me your number so I can call you, or are you still scared I'll hunt you down and chop you into little pieces?"

I was not afraid about my body being chopped into little pieces—it was my heart that couldn't take the mutilation. And if Salt and Pepper Griffin kept looking at me like that, my heart, my lungs, and my sanity were all goners.

CHAPTER 21

Beck

"Someone steal your Teddy Bear, dude? You've been one mopey motherfucker. What's your problem?" Ramos was a dick. An irritating, pain in the ass dick. He'd been on my case for the last few weeks, making jokes like this and singing randomly made up songs about Marissa and Riley just to bust my balls.

The funny thing was—I couldn't disagree with him on most of his lyrics. The ones about her bitchiness even made me laugh. Like the ridiculous ditty he sang about her begging me to leave the fireman's ball because she'd forgotten to DVR *The Shahs of Sunset*.

Oh, Marissa, you should only know,
Lieutenant McNabb watches the same show.
He'd ditch his bitch and the ball,
for a chance with the Shahs and to fuck you against the wall.

But the songs about Riley—those tore me up and made me miss her even more. Even the mention of her name made me edgy. And the guys knew it. So when Ramos started up a new one:

Beck's a schmuck for letting that one go.
He was too afraid of Marcus to let his feelings show.
He ended things with the poor broad
with the swipe of his thumb
and now it's been three weeks since the dude's spilled his
cum.

Derrick and Sean had to hold me back from decking him. "Really, asshole? Aren't you tired of screwing with me yet?"

"Never. When have any of us ever relented on a pussy-whipped brother? You're still cracking jokes about the way I cried at my wedding. It's not my fault I was raised to show my emotions. Angel looked fucking gorgeous—all pregnant and glowing and shit."

He had a point. There wasn't a shift we'd worked together since his wedding that I hadn't made fun of him for his theatrical waterworks.

But *this* was torture.

I couldn't be the boyfriend Riley deserved, and I couldn't stand to be the one to hurt her. Tessa's argument in the debate was strong because she understood all the circumstances. If Marcus only realized it was his sister who was my "other woman," he might not be so keen on advising me to go for what I wanted.

The rec room was hip deep in testosterone and flying insults by now. I exited the sausage party and found myself at my locker, scrolling through my cell phone in hopes of finding a text from Riley.

Was she as tormented as I was? I'd heard she'd been traveling a lot, racking up new clients left and right. I was happy for her. In my eyes, that girl would always deserve the best—yet another reason to stay away.

After scrolling through random notifications from Facebook and Instagram, I caught a text message from her— not the *her* I'd wanted to text me but the other *her*. Marissa.

What could she possibly want? The last time we spoke it was for me to come over and pick up some stuff I'd left at her place. When I got to her apartment she tried to convince me to stay for dinner, attempting to persuade me with a skimpy outfit and a few tasteless come-ons. In the past, I might have fallen for it. But Marissa's advances were not what I craved. If it was Riley putting the moves on me and asking for another shot—I wouldn't be as resistant.

Opening the text, I took a deep breath to ready myself for something I didn't want to see.

> ***Marissa:*** *Hey, was wondering if you're doing anything next Saturday. My cousin Jodi is getting married (remember?) and I RSVP'd for two. Can you still make it as my plus one?*

No. I was no longer her plus one and I had no intention of leading her to believe I ever would be again. But I didn't want to hurt her feelings, so I came up with an excuse.

Me: Sorry. Hate to miss it, but I'm pulling a double that weekend. It's my turn on the rotation, thanks to Ramos. His baby is due soon.

Okay. So it was an elaborate excuse, but she would buy it because she knew the way things worked around here.

Marissa: That sucks. Guess I'll have to go stag.

Me: Sorry

Marissa: Don't be. It's not like you haven't let me down before.

Guilt trips were unappealing, even through text messages. I really didn't want to deal with that now—or ever.

Me: Ris? Please, not again.

I readied myself for the long, drawn out text I was about to receive, but was surprised by her clipped response.

Marissa: Good night, Beck. Sorry to bother you.

Me: Good night, Ris. No bother. Be good.

There was no reason to burn bridges or be an asshole. After all, it wasn't Marissa's fault that our break brought me to another woman. And it certainly wasn't her fault that the other woman was consuming my mind. Still, something made me angry with her, as if it *were* her fault. Deep down I truly believed that Marissa was the reason I couldn't pursue a relationship with Riley right now.

If it weren't for things ending so abruptly with Marissa, my heart, my mind, and my soul would be untainted and completely up for grabs. For Riley. All I needed was a little more time to prove to Riley that Marissa was my past and I wasn't rushing into anything. Once I could show her that she was more than a rebound and more than a good time— I'd be at her doorstep promising her forever. If she'd have me.

Later that night when I got home, I rifled through the mail—a bunch of bills, a few magazines, a flier for a handyman trying to gain more business—until something caught my attention. It was a large orange envelope addressed to *Mr. Beck Matthews & Guest.* When I flipped it over to check the return address, I remembered that Tessa was planning a big first birthday party for Luca. If I recalled correctly his birthday wasn't until October, but it must be the proper protocol to send these things out early to do all those annoying party planning things like seating arrangements and shit.

When I opened it, a smile crept to my lips when I saw the addition of Marcus's name to the invitation.

Mommy & Marcus would be thrilled if you could join me,
Luca Thomas
As I celebrate the first year of my life with a Halloween
Birthday Bash...

Wow! Those two had clearly taken things to the next level. Whenever stationary was involved, it had to be serious. Good for them!

Marcus had spoken to me a few times about taking the next step and asking Tessa to marry him, but he also had other, more permanent plans. The same plans I'd had with Marissa before things went south and eventually nosedived. He'd been looking to buy a bigger place for all of them to live in. As a family. It was crazy how things had changed. I couldn't believe the turnaround he'd made since meeting Tessa. It was like he was never that man-whore we knew him to be. He'd even taken on some more subtle gigs, not wanting to be unnecessarily *exposed* for just anyone anymore. He had no reason to be. He'd found the woman who made him happy—he didn't need to search for that anywhere else. I'd be lying if I said I wasn't a little jealous, but I was also sincerely happy for the guy. For all of them. Together that threesome made quite a team.

Tucking the invitation and the rest of the mail under my arm, I unlocked my door and walked into my empty apartment. Entering the darkness and the silence, the reminders of all the things I didn't have that Marcus did, I decided I couldn't take it anymore. I needed to talk to her.

Switching on a light and then collapsing onto the couch, I kicked off my shoes, typed out a text, and let my thumb hover over the send button.

Me: *I miss you. Can we talk?*

I sat there staring at that screen for what seemed like hours. In the end, I chickened out. Just a little more time. That's all we needed. I thought back to that invitation—it could be a start. She'd be at that party. It was only a few months away. Maybe by then I'd be able to make promises. Promises that could be kept, not broken.

CHAPTER 22

Riley

After my first date with Griffin, two nights after our meeting at the beach, he convinced me with his good manners, witty conversation and that to-die-for dimple to go out with him again a few nights later.

This time we were headed to a restaurant his friend owned in SoHo. Rather than drive and pay a fortune to park, we decided to take the train into the city and enjoy the warm summer breeze as we walked from the train station to our destination. It was the perfect beginning to a second date.

He hooked his arm in mine as we strolled and laughed, and it occurred to me that I already felt at ease with him for only knowing him a short time. While I was definitely attracted to Griffin—did I mention he was smoking hot—I was not jumping that gun again. Whatever was happening between us already felt very different than anything I'd ever experienced with a guy.

Maybe it was that he was older and more mature. Maybe

it was that he was reserved and old fashioned, not trying any funny business on our first date. Or maybe it was just that even though I had fun spending time with Griffin, my mind was still preoccupied with thoughts of Beck.

Whatever it was, I owed it to Griffin to be in the moment and give him my full attention. "So how do you know this friend?" I asked, curious to find out more about my enigmatic date.

"Buddy from high school. Great guy. We spent a summer in Europe together on one of those student exchange type things. He decided to take in the culture through his mouth—big dude, by the way—and I took it all in through my eyes. Bought my first camera as soon as I got back to the states. Haven't stop snapping since."

"For someone who *snaps* so often, I haven't seen your camera once."

"You haven't seen it, but it's seen you." He winked.

"Huh?"

"I took a few candids on the beach that day. Haven't had a chance to really look over them yet, but I know they're beautiful." He smiled, focusing those smoldering eyes on my mouth.

That look right there secured him the first kiss green light. If he didn't try to at least do that tonight, I might go in for the kill myself.

"Creepy," I joked, trying to hide the way my heart was thumping, thinking about his lips on mine.

"Creepy? Do you make a habit of letting creepy men take you out twice in one week?"

"Maybe," I shrugged.

He laughed, a hearty, deep laugh, and pulled me closer to

him as he continued to guide me down a few more blocks.

When we arrived at a restaurant sporting a yellow and red awning and emitting mouth-watering aromas, he unhooked our arms. Opening the door, he placed his hand on my back and led me inside. "After you."

"Thanks." It was a simple gesture, but it again proved what a gentleman he was.

We stood at the hostess's podium for a few seconds and Griffin took out his phone to call someone. I thought it was weird timing to make a phone call, but when he started to speak, I realized what he was doing. "Hey. We're here," he said. He must've been calling his friend, the restaurant owner.

He put his phone back in his pocket and motioned for me to sit on a bench in the lobby. "He should be right out. When I told him I was bringing you he went all out. Seems we'll have a private table and special attention tonight."

"That's very sweet, Griffin, but he didn't have to do that." I looked around to the other tables in the dining area. Although it wasn't necessary, having our own private area might actually be a great idea. This place was loud. There'd be no way to carry on a normal conversation over the noise.

"Well, he did. And here he comes." Griffin stood, extending his hand to me.

I willingly grabbed it and stood to join him.

"Griffin, buddy," the large, round man bombarded my date with a hug, clapping him on the back a few times.

"Sonny! So good to see you again. It's been too long."

"Well, I guess I have to thank this lovely creature for finally getting you out here. Not like you don't live right over the damn bridge or anything."

"I know. I have no excuse. I guess I've been a bit of a recluse these days."

"A rude recluse. Introduce me to this stunner." Griffin's friend had a warm smile and welcoming eyes. He used them to eye me up and down, but there was nothing scrutinizing about it.

"Sorry, Sonny, this is Riley. Riley, this is Sonny."

"So nice to meet you. Your place looks—and smells—amazing." Extending my hand to shake Sonny's, he grabbed it and brought me in for an unexpected hug.

"Any friend of Griffin's is a friend of mine. Come on. If you think it smells great, wait 'til you taste what I prepared for you two tonight."

Sonny did not disappoint. Everything from the signature martini he'd created just for me to the homemade gnocchi pesto entrée I was currently polishing off my plate.

"I take it you didn't like the food?" Griffin joked, watching me stuff my face.

Suddenly embarrassed, I dropped my fork and picked up my napkin to wipe my mouth. "I don't usually indulge like this. I actually haven't had a carb in way too long, but this—" I stared at the few gnocchi left, dying to finish them off. "This was incredible. Your friend is quite the chef."

Griffin laughed, taking another sip of his own drink—some kind of scotch that was supposedly aged to perfection and a beverage he and Sonny had had many fun times sharing in the past. "Yeah, he knows a thing or two about how to make the taste buds happy."

I couldn't help myself at that comment. I was having a great time—again—and he deserved to know. "And you know a thing or two about how to make the ladies happy."

Tilting his head and arching a brow, he leaned in closer and took my hand from across the table. "I want to take you back to my place."

I quickly withdrew my hand from his, disappointed that my one tiny compliment made him think I was ready to sleep with him. I mean, it's not that I wasn't wondering when he'd make that type of pass at me, but I kind of liked that he wasn't like so many other guys I'd dated in the past. It was nice to take things slow and get to know each other—to be wooed—before taking to the sheets.

Sensing my discontent with his comment, Griffin shook his head apologetically. "Oh, no. I didn't mean it like that, Riley. I guess I shouldn't have blurted it out like that."

"It's not the way you blurted it out. It's the way you looked at me when you said it." He was looking at me the way I must have been looking at my gnocchi a few minutes ago. Starving for satisfaction and the taste of something rich.

"Well, can you blame me for looking at you that way? You're beautiful. I can't help that my eyes are pleased with what they see."

"Your eyes or what's inside your jeans?"

He laughed, that hearty laugh that made my insides melt. "Okay, so not just my eyes. Let's just say you have an effect over *all* of me, but that's still not why I want to take you home. Promise."

I leaned forward. He really had my attention now. "Why, then?"

Taking the final sip of his scotch, he said, "I need some advice on my home studio. I spend a lot of time there and I'd like your decorating expertise. Would you mind mixing business with pleasure?" *Subtle and cute, but still an innuendo.*

I definitely didn't mind helping him out, but if I wound up back at his place I'd probably end up helping myself out too—to him. "I don't know. Maybe we should set up a real appointment—make it more professional. Besides, by the time we get back to Brooklyn it'll be dark. I'd need to see the place in daylight to get a sense of what I'm working with."

"Are you scared of me, Riley?"

No. I wasn't. I was afraid of my own lack of self-control, but I couldn't exactly tell him that without looking like a hooch. "Do I need to be scared, Griffin?"

Reaching for my hand again, his lips curled up into a warm grin; that dimple making its appearance again. "I thought we cleared that up on the beach. You already know I'm not a serial killer. Come back to my place with me. I won't bite."

If only he knew how badly I wanted him to bite. My lips, my neck, the fleshy skin of my inner thigh—"Ah... I don't know." I squirmed in my seat trying to think of an excuse, but there was none good enough to keep me away. "Okay, maybe just for a little while." God, I probably sounded like an indecisive tease. If this was his way of testing the waters to see how far I was willing to go, I was like a yo-yo of mixed signals.

"Really?" His eyes brightened, the lines surrounding them appearing deeper as he smiled.

"Yes. Really. But I'm still checking your freezer for Ziploc baggies of dismembered limbs, buddy."

"Be my guest. You'll find nothing but ice in there."

"Oh, man, no mint chocolate chip?"

"Nope. I almost never eat at home. Sorry, kid. We can pick something up on the way back if you'd like."

"Nah, it's okay. I'm stuffed from this wonderful dinner and besides... I'm only going back there for one thing."

"Oh my goodness, Riley!" He gasped, straightening to attention and placing a hand over his heart. "What kind of man do you think I am? I don't give it up on the second date. It takes at least three to get me into bed. That one thing will just have to wait."

Rolling my eyes, I balled up my napkin and chucked it at him. "You're a regular comedian, aren't you? You know what I meant: the studio. I only agreed to go back to your place to see your studio, wiseass."

Chuckling, he motioned for the check and then brought his attention back to me with a mega-watt grin. "I'm only messing with you, Riley. But I've been going on dates since you were in kindergarten. You're fidgety, and tense, and your cheeks took on a beautiful blush when I mentioned going back to my place.

"And?"

"And you worried whether I'll kiss you goodnight, and if I'll try to go further." He locked his eyes on mine, his gaze intense. "I'm a gentleman, Riley. I don't expect you to fall all over me because I took you to a few nice restaurants. Don't confuse my manners for my lack of interest—that's definitely not the case—but when I do take you to bed you'll go willingly, and not out of obligation. And we'll know more about each other than what our favorite ice cream flavors are."

"I never told you my—"

"Mint chocolate chip. You licked your lips right after you mentioned it before. Mine's plain old vanilla."

His smoothness *was* pretty impressive. I had to hand it to him. He was attentive—did I like that or not? Time to throw him off kilter a little. "Vanilla? That's all you got? Shit, now I just might have to let you take me to bed. You're not vanilla in there too, are you?"

Choking on the last bit of his scotch, he raised his napkin to catch the dribble that spurted from his lips at my reference to his bedroom skills.

"What?" I asked, cocking a brow. Two could play at this game.

"As much as I'd like to think I can read you, Riley, you are full of surprises."

"Yes. I am, so stop trying to mind fuck me with your I-can-read-all-women ESP. I'm not like all women."

"No, you most definitely are not."

"Good. Now that you know I'm *not* screwing you tonight, and that I'm different from the harem of ladies you've been dating since I was five... wanna show me that studio?"

The dimple was back and Griffin had this dreamy look in his eyes that practically made them sparkle.

"Why are you looking at me like that?"

Shaking his head and straightening the collar of his shirt that was unbuttoned just enough for the tattoo on his neck to peak through, he smiled and asked, "Wanna cut through all the red tape and just agree to marry me now?"

Running my fingers through my hair, I flipped it to the side, tilting my head. "What a schmoozer."

"This has nothing to do with schmoozing. I don't want to mention the... harem, as you put it... again, but I've never met someone quite like you."

He wasn't serious. I knew that. But it still made me the slightest bit uncomfortable. "That's not a reason to marry someone, Griffin." Not that I knew anything about the reasons for marrying someone. I'd once wanted to marry a guy because the way he growled my name when we had sex made me come right on the spot. It didn't matter that he smoked more pot than Snoop Dog and had two illegitimate kids. Perfect husband material, that one.

"It's a perfect reason to marry someone, Riley. But I'll give you until date five to make that decision."

"Date *five*? How do you even know there'll be a date *three*?" Cocky bastard. Let me rephrase that... cocky, *panty-melting* bastard.

"Oh, there will be. You'll see."

Date three was on a Saturday afternoon (a week after date two) at Griffin's apartment, where he had invited me to go over some of the samples he'd picked out for his studio. He was also going to attempt to cook me a meal. I brought over a bunch of my favorite take-out menus, just in case. From the way he'd described things when I was at his apartment last, he lived minimally and very rarely ate something that wasn't prepared by someone else. I wasn't in the mood to be his Guinea pig for the sake of him trying to impress me. Winding up with salmonella or the runs was not on my agenda—especially not while in the presence of Griffin.

"What're these?" he asked when I handed him the bag of menus.

"Our back up plan."

He poked through the bag, and when he realized what they were, his expression changed from happy-to-see-me to how-could-you-doubt-me. "Huh! That's a first. I say I'm cooking and you bring take out menus?"

"I told you I'm not like other women, Griffin. I thought it would have sunk in by date three."

Shutting the door behind me, he took the bottle of wine from my hand and motioned for me to walk toward his kitchen. "And I thought you would've started to trust me a little more. You're putting a kink in my plans, love. I'm gonna get you to say yes to my proposal by date five."

I laughed at how relentless he was. It was becoming a turn on. But as turned on as I was, I still wanted to take things slow. So when he placed his hand on my back, right above the low waistline of my jeans, I hurried on ahead to rid my mind of the way his touch made me feel. Warm, tingly, needy, ready. *Nope! None of that. Not yet, at least.*

"So," I said, cutting right to the chase. "I got some of the swatches we talked about and brought a few catalogs for you to look through." I lifted my work bag onto the kitchen table and started to pull things out for him to look at. I figured if I avoided all things date-like and made this more about his studio, I'd be safe from his charm.

But when he grabbed my hands to stop me from rummaging and our eyes met, that was the moment I knew he was about to change our friendship into something more. "What are you doing, Griffin? Don't you want to see what I brought?"

"Yes, but not now," he said, closing the distance between us. "I know it's customary to *end* a date with a kiss, but since you're so different from everyone else I thought you might like it if we started off with one."

Without giving me time to disagree with his clever trick, he brought one hand up to cup my face and the other tangled itself in my hair. I stared into his eyes for a brief second before his lips brushed mine, and for the first time since ending things with Beck, I wanted this man to kiss me. It was time to forget Beck and what we could've been. It was time to move on and be grateful for what was right in front of me. Griffin was a wonderful man—and so far, a wonderful kisser—and I enjoyed spending time with him. I owed it to both of us to be here fully. Allowing Beck into my mind while I was with Griffin was anything but fair.

And now it was ruining our first kiss.

Shooing the Beckster far from my thoughts, I wrapped my arms around Griffin's neck and allowed myself to surrender to him. Our tongues danced together, relishing in our first intimate moment. It felt good to let go and give in. So I abandoned every inhibition, every fear, every uncertainty and just lived in those few minutes.

When our hands started to roam and our breathing quickened to more of a panting rhythm, I pulled away and took it all in. His eyes were still closed as if he were savoring our connection. His arms were still wrapped around me at my waist and his lips were damp and slightly swollen from our kiss.

I thought about going in for another, because—well, what the hell, right? Once you've already done it, the rest was just icing on the cake. But before I could claim his mouth again, his doorbell rang, startling us both from our tender after-kiss embrace.

"Expecting someone?" I asked.

He stood stoically, still holding me in his arms as he rolled his eyes and let out an irritated huff. "Actually, yes. I forgot my sister was stopping by to pick up some pictures I took for our parents' wedding anniversary. Their party's next week and we're putting together a montage of candids I've been taking all year to surprise them."

Trying to hide my nervousness over how he would introduce me to his sister, I simply complimented him on being such a thoughtful son. "Griffin, that's a wonderful idea. I bet they'll love it. I'll just stay in here and get the um, samples out while you get her what she needs."

He furrowed his brows and gave me a quizzical look. "Don't you want to meet her?"

I didn't want to make it a bigger deal than it was, so I just played dumb. "Oh, how silly of me. Of course. Want to ask her to stay for dinner too?" *Please say no! Please say no!* I wasn't ready to spend an evening with his family just yet. I'd just kissed him for the first time, what... three seconds ago?

Walking toward the unanswered door, he spoke over his shoulder. "I wouldn't go *that* far. She'll come in for a minute and then she can go. I want to finish what we started a few minutes ago, anyway."

Now I was praying she *would* stay. I wasn't ready for more than that kiss—no matter how sweet it was. If Griffin was indeed the gentleman he said he was, his intention was probably to *start off* sweet and then pull out all the stops later. "Okay. Let her in already. She's gonna think we're up to no good in here!"

"Good," he whispered, ruffling his hair to make it look messy and unbuttoning the first few buttons of his shirt. "Maybe she'll get the picture and leave quicker."

"Griffi—" I started to scold him, but I was too late.

He swung the door open and when his sister spun around I nearly shrieked.

"Took you long enough," she said, barging in.

"Sorry. I was putting something in the oven. Riley, come here, meet my sister—"

"—Marissa," I finished for him. "If it isn't a small freaking world." It felt like all the breath had been knocked out of me. I mean really—it wasn't that small of a world. How could this be happening?

"Riley? Oh my god. How funny is this? *You're* the girl my brother can't stop talking about?"

"Wait a minute," Griffin interrupted, trying not to look too embarrassed by his sister's confession. "You two know each other?"

"Well not really, but yes. Her brother is Beck's best friend."

Hearing her say Beck's name made my insides turn. Clearly one kiss from Griffin was not enough for me to let go of my past.

"Marcus Grayson is your brother?" The way Griffin said it made it seem like it was an impossibility.

"Yup." It was all I could say, still trying to wrap my head around this coincidence.

"I did a few of his shoots in the past. Nice guy. His best friend, not so much."

"Who? Beck?" I suddenly felt defensive. What did he have against him?

Marissa flailed her hands in the air. "Whoa. Calm down, big brother bear. Don't go saying anything stupid and making things awkward. Beck and I have been talking again. Who knows? We could end up back together." She said it with such a giddiness I could tell she meant it. Or at least she was hoping it was possible.

Griffin and Marissa shared a few words back and forth. I assumed they were about his disapproval of Beck, but I couldn't make out one damn word of it. All that kept ringing in my ears over and over again, causing my head to spin and my heart to squeeze, were Marissa's words: *Beck and I have been talking again.* For the second time since seeing Marissa, I wanted to vomit. This was no good. No good at all. There was no way I'd be able to play it cool with Griffin once she left. I had to make up an excuse and get out of there. I needed time to process this whole ridiculous, too-close-for-comfort situation.

CHAPTER 23

Beck

What a loser. An exhausted loser too. It was barely ten o'clock on a Saturday night and I was ready for lights out. I'd had two sleepless nights at the firehouse because of a three a.m. call two nights ago and then a snoring Ramos last night. Curling up underneath the blanket, I welcomed the grogginess and heavy lids and got ready to catch my well-deserved z's.

I was dozing off with an image of myself and Riley in the back of that cab when my doorbell rang and nearly jolted me out of my skivvies.

"Who the fuck?" I scratched my head, reluctantly swinging my legs over the side of the bed.

I had no idea who it could be. I worried that I might have forgotten plans for the guys to come over and watch the game, but as I hurried down the steps, the doorbell chimed over and over again as the person knocked like an obnoxious asshole.

When I opened the door, ready to rip whoever it was a

new one, my jaw dropped wide open at the sight of my unexpected visitor. "Riley? What are you—?"

"You're getting back together with Marissa? Is that why you ended things with me? You... you... *asshole*!" She'd been crying. I could tell by the black smudges of makeup in the corners of her eyes. But what flashed through more than her sadness was her anger. She barged past the threshold, pushing my chest with her tiny hands.

"Whoa. Hold up, sweet thing. What's this all about?" I grabbed her wrists and leaned down so my eyes met hers.

"Don't call me that, Beck. I'm not your sweet thing. I'm not your *any* thing. You made that pretty clear when you just ended things out of fucking nowhere. But to find out that you couldn't be honest and tell me it was because you were getting back together with her. That's just... you're really... fucked up. You know that?"

My head was spinning. Not only was this completely unexpected, but Riley seemed really effected by the chance of me getting back together with Marissa. The thought of her being jealous... over me... it made my insides feel uncharacteristically warm and gooey.

Unable to wrap my head around the range of emotions invading my brain, I invited her into the living room. "First of all, come in and get out of the doorway." I ushered her inside and flipped on a light so we weren't in complete darkness. "Second of all, I'm not getting back with Marissa. Who told you that?" I wanted to know who fed her this false information. It couldn't have been Marcus or Tessa, because they knew that wasn't the truth. Especially Tessa. She *did* know the truth. I was doing what was best for Riley by staying away, even though it was driving me mad.

"*She* told me, Beck. I ran into Marissa and she told me you two are still talking and are most likely getting back together."

I raked my fingers through my hair, narrowing my eyes at her and trying to make sense of all the confusion. It made *no* sense. None of it. "She lied to you, Riles. We've texted back and forth a few times, but I assure you we are *not* getting back together. I don't know why she'd say that. I've made it clear that it's over. I don't want to be with her anymore. It couldn't *be* more over, Riles."

I thought that would put her at ease. I figured once she knew the truth her anger would subside, her tears would stop, but that wasn't the case.

"Then why did you end it with me? Why didn't you even give me a reason?" The tears came down in fat drops from her eyes. Had I known she was this upset over the way things had turned out with us…

"I'm so sorry. I didn't mean to—" I didn't mean to what? I had no idea how to finish that sentence. I'd wanted to be with her all this time, but according to Tessa, and even a few of the guys at the house, giving in to what I wanted was selfish. They didn't think I was ready to be serious yet. But maybe *they* were fucking crazy. It wasn't their life. They weren't in my head. What the fuck did they know? "I was trying to do the right thing, Riley. I didn't want to hurt you."

"You don't think the way you ended things hurt me? I've been left wondering what I did wrong all this time. Why I wasn't good enough. And then Marissa says what she said and at least I felt there was a reason, but now—I'm still so fucking lost here, Beck. What am I missing?"

She couldn't feel inadequate. No. I couldn't make her feel that about herself. She was perfect. Every single thing about her was fucking perfect. She needed to know how I felt. Inching closer, I reached out to hold her but she backed away. "Baby, there's nothing wrong with you. You're perfect. You are *the* girl. Everything I've ever wanted. I'm the one with the flaws. I'm the one at fault. Everyone made me believe that if I rushed into things with you right after breaking up with Marissa—it wasn't right. I needed time to be completely yours." I felt so vulnerable, telling her everything, baring my soul. But it was about time. I was tired of pretending I was okay without her. I wasn't. And obviously she was not okay without me either.

"There hasn't been a day since our last time together that I haven't missed you." I reached out to her again and when I saw she wasn't rejecting my touch this time, I grabbed her hand and pulled her closer to me. Cupping her face with the other hand, I gazed into her blue eyes and spoke more truth. "I want you so bad, Riley. Not just for fun, not on the side, not as a distraction. I want you because I can't stand to be *without* you. I want you because you are the most incredible woman I've ever known and even though we weren't together long, I know without a doubt that we're supposed to be together. You've been right under my nose all these years—I can't believe I was so blind. I can't believe I ever let you go."

She gulped back her tears and a shy smile spread across her lips. It seemed like she was mentally appraising everything I'd just confessed, then she rested her head against my chest and let me hold her. "I missed you so much, B."

Kissing the top of her head, I closed my eyes and sniffed in the scent I'd dreamt about since our last night together. "I missed you too. No more time apart. No matter what anyone says."

As tired as I'd been before Riley showed up, I was now full of energy and wanting to make up for lost time. We'd been apart nearly a month, but in all honesty, it felt like a lifetime. My hands ached to touch her soft skin, my lips craved hers, my tongue begged to taste her. I'd never felt this empty or disoriented by the loss of someone before. Not even Marissa—and not just because I'd had Riley to help ease that loss. Forcing myself to be without Riley and not tell her what was going on in my mind was like being shackled and restrained unwillingly. It took more willpower than anyone could ever imagine.

But I did it for her.

I did it because I thought it was right to wait it out and revisit my feelings when I had more to give. I should've known by the way my head was cluttered and distracted this whole month that none of that mattered. There were no guidelines and time limits when it came to love. And while this might not be love just *yet*, I was certain it wouldn't take long.

Not wanting to waste one more second apart, I crashed my mouth against hers. Her lips parted as soon as our mouths touched, allowing my tongue the access it was starved for. Our tongues flicked together in a familiar rhythm, but it was also hurried and frenzied as if making up for what we'd been missing.

"I'm sorry, Riles. I wanted to come to you so many times. It was so hard to stay away." I spoke between frantic kisses, finally pulling away to make sure this wasn't a dream. I needed to see her, smell her, hold her to know she was *actually* here.

The way she anchored herself to me by tangling her hands in my hair told me that she felt the same urgency. Letting out a long breath of air as if she'd been holding it in all this time, she pressed her forehead to mine and whispered, "Then why did you?"

"I wanted to be able to give you all of me. I can do that now. I can give you everything. If you let me."

Closing her eyes and melting my heart when a few more tears escaped, she pleaded with me. "Please don't hurt me again, B. I thought I was okay, but... well, look at me like a psycho ex, showing up here unannounced. You must think I'm crazy!" She stared down at the floor, avoiding eye contact, but I lifted her chin with my finger bringing her gaze back to mine.

"I don't care how it looks. I'm just glad you're here. It's been fucking torture."

"Good." She grinned. The first sign of happiness on her face since she showed up on my doorstep.

Although I was glad to see some of the sadness disappear, I was confused. "Good?"

"Yes, good. I hope you were in agony. You deserve to suffer for making me wonder all this time."

I couldn't argue with her there. I knew the suffering she was referring to because I was dealing with it too. While it was noble to keep my distance, it also stung like a mother fucker to think I could lose her in the end. But I didn't want to focus on how I'd almost screwed this up. I wanted to move forward. It was time to fuck the past, forget about what everyone else thought, and live in the goddamn moment. YOLO, right?

Making light of the situation, I jabbed her in the ribs with my finger, making her squirm. "Suffer? Ha! I'll show you suffering... upstairs."

She let out an adorable, almost musical giggle as I picked her up and flung her over my shoulder like a caveman. "If we're going up to your bed, suffering is an impossibility."

Happy to hear her mood turned playful, I started our journey to my room. "Oh, we'll see about that." I ignored her fists drumming on my back and continued up the steps, two at a time. "Hey, you never told me how you ran into Marissa."

"Please don't ever say her name while holding me again," she scolded and her body stiffened under my grip.

"Sorry. Point taken, but—"

"It's not important. It was just a casual run-in."

I could tell the topic bothered her and I didn't want to screw up our reunion, so I changed the subject. "Can you stay the night?"

"Sure can."

"Those two words never sounded so fucking beautiful."

Once we made it to my bedroom, I tossed her onto the bed and she let out a girly squeal. "Such a gentleman."

Crawling over her body, making sure to grind my stiffening cock against her as I made my way up to claim her mouth again, I said, "Sweet thing, I'm pretty sure you don't want me to be a gentleman when I fuck you."

Her eyes widened, her smile brightened, and her cheeks flushed. I brought my hand up to caress her embarrassment away. "All of a sudden you're shy? Would you rather we take it slow?" I pressed against her again, demonstrating how gentle it could be. Bringing my hand down to wrap her leg around my waist, I whispered against her ear, "We can take our time getting reacquainted if you'd like that better."

Her leg tightened around me as her hips arched off the bed to meet my gentle thrusts. She was eager—just the way I wanted her.

"Or you can let me fuck you the way I've been dreaming of—with your sweet pussy swallowing me deep and milking me dry."

"That," she panted into my neck. "Let's do that!"

I collapsed on top of her, laughing at how needy the two of us were for each other. She joined me with a cute giggle that soon turned into uncontrollable laughter. Our bodies rocked and jiggled as we clutched our stomachs, lying next to each other. When we'd caught our breaths, I turned to face her, resting my head on a propped up pillow. "Damn, I missed you, Riles. I'm sorry I didn't come to my senses sooner."

"Mmm hmm," she groaned sarcastically.

"No. I'm serious. Listening to everyone was a mistake. I should have taken Marcus's advice instead."

"Wait? What?" She shot into a sitting position, staring down at me. "You told him about us?"

Shaking my head, I grabbed her hand and brought it to my lips to kiss her knuckles. "No. Not exactly."

Pulling her hand from my grasp, she arched a brow and pursed her lips. "Speak."

"Yes, Mistress," I chuckled, but there was no amusement on her face. "Fine. When I was over at Tessa's that night we watched the game together, the two lovebirds offered some advice. Tessa, knowing the situation, was the one who convinced me to keep my distance."

"I should kill her," she grumbled.

"No. She meant well, babe. She knew my head was all fucked up and she worried that I'd be stringing you along. In the end, even though your amateur Casanova of a brother was very convincing, Tessa's advice made more sense. It was the least selfish thing to do."

"And what *did* my idiot brother tell you to do?" she mused, with an unconvinced expression.

"He told me to go for the girl. Of course, he didn't know the girl was his sister, but still—"

Scooting down to settle in my arms, she interrupted me. "I can't believe I'm gonna say this, but you should've listened to him. Would've saved us both a lot of heartache."

Brushing a few strands of hair off her face, I focused on her plump lips, wanting to take a bite. "Your heart was aching? Over me?"

"Don't sound so stunned, Beckster. We had a connection at the lake house. One of those I-think-I-met-my-soulmate moments. Don't tell me you didn't feel that too."

"Of course I did." With one hand still playing with her silky hair, I laced the fingers of my other hand with hers.

"So, how can you think I wasn't affected by you just up and leaving after that? It was such a mind-fuck. I played it cool because I didn't want to come on too strong or make it more than it was. I thought maybe you *weren't* feeling the same way I was, after all."

"I was *definitely* feeling the same thing. There's no doubt about that. I guess—I just guess I didn't know how to process it all. It seemed wrong to be able to let go of Marissa so easily. I had no regrets and I worried that maybe the way you and I rushed into things so hastily was what kept me from actually... mourning... the end of a two-year relationship."

"Are you still *mourning*?" she asked quietly, as if she were afraid to hear the answer.

"There's nothing to mourn, babe. As heartless as it sounds, I don't feel anything at all when it comes to her. I really hate that stupid expression about everything happening for a reason, but I do think we got together at the perfect time. I was ready to take the next step with Marissa because I thought it was right. I thought I loved her unconditionally. But when things got a little rocky—" I combed my fingers through my hair, trying to find the right words. "—let's just say we didn't have a future. We don't want the same things. We probably never did. I guess I just stayed, holding on to hope that I could change her mind." I hated talking to her about Marissa, but she wasn't stopping me. Maybe this was her way of understanding.

"Do you really want to hear all this?" I finally asked, not wanting to make things awkward.

"Yes and no. I don't like the idea of you with another woman, even if it was before me, but maybe you're right. Maybe things happen the way they do for a reason."

"What do you mean?"

"I mean maybe it was smart that you took Tessa's advice

and we came back to each other this way. Now you *know* how you feel. You have your closure and the rest can just be called his-to-ry." She sang that last word with giddy excitement.

Talking to my current girl about my past girl could not have gone smoother. I was a lucky mofo.

"Now there's only one thing left to do," I said, leaning down and nibbling at her collarbone.

"Yes. Please." She stuck her fingers in the waistband of her skirt and started to shimmy it down her hips.

Reluctantly stopping her efforts, I corrected her. "Okay, maybe two things."

Tilting her head, she eyed me, confused. "Huh?"

"We need to tell Marcus, Riles."

Collapsing against the pillow with a huff, she whimpered, "Can't we just live in our bubble a little longer? I know we're two consenting adults, and it's really none of his business, but... once he knows, things will be different. I don't want to be scrutinized or *worse*—I don't need him messing with me the same way I messed with him about Tessa. Can't we just leave it our little secret for now?" Her hands clasped together as if she were praying as she exaggerated the batting of her long lashes.

"Embarrassed by your younger man?" I joked.

"Has nothing to do with age. I've dated younger... and older, if you must know."

Now it was my turn to be uncomfortable about *her* past. I hated the idea of her with another man. Loathed it, actually. I was not about to listen to details about *any* of the clowns she'd been with before. Nope—not no way, not no how. "Okay, let's leave it at that. End of story."

Inching up on her elbows and then hooking her arms around my neck, she leaned closer, pressing her lips to mine. "Jealous?"

"Very," I answered, nipping on her lower lip.

"Good. I have to keep you on your toes."

"And I'm gonna do things to you that will curl *your* toes."

After that we fell silent, except for the sounds of heavy breathing and pleasure-filled moans. She shed her clothes, revealing a skimpy lace number that had me pawing at it just to experience it with a sense other than sight. She looked fucking incredible, but she felt even better under my fingertips.

Unhooking her bra, I dropped the straps over her tanned shoulders and trailed kisses across her chest as her head fell back to give me access to her gorgeous tits. Her nipples perked to attention as my lips caressed her skin. My hands instinctively reached up to knead her, causing her to writhe against me. We were both still clothed from the waist down, but not for too much longer. It was as if our brains were in sync as we both reached for the other's clothing and slid the obstructions down and out of the way.

I pulled back from our kiss—a heated swirling of tongues and lips and hands groping skin—to guide her down on the bed. But with a firm grip on my wrist and a bold push at my shoulder, Riley shoved me down and positioned herself on top of me, leaving me in awe.

Her legs were draped along either side of me, her pussy wet and throbbing against my own aching arousal. I wanted to be inside of her so badly I was afraid I might prematurely shoot my load from neediness alone. Sensing what I so desperately craved, or experiencing the same yearning herself, she stroked me as if her hand were hugging my cock and directed the tip of my head to her slick opening.

I gave in to her control, loving that she knew what she wanted. I didn't mind being at the mercy of this woman, it only mattered that we were back where we belonged— together.

When my cock was finally buried deep inside her, her hips grinding in a seductive rhythm, I allowed myself to appreciate all I'd been missing, all I thought I'd never have again. "Riley?" I muttered, almost unable to speak from the way her hips worked their magic.

"Yes?" she moaned, rocking our bodies to a tune that allowed me to feel depths I never knew I could.

"I'm gonna fall in love with you." It was such a pussy thing to announce in the middle of having the hottest girl known to man riding me like there was no tomorrow, but I couldn't help myself. Holding back was what caused us all the unnecessary time apart. I didn't want that anymore. Only truth from here on out.

"Good. Because I'm pretty sure I'm falling in love with you too."

Her words almost felt better than the sweet warmth of her pussy. I did say *almost* right? I wasn't about to lose my man card over the mere mention of the "L" word. But that word did make me want more.

Gripping her hips, I urged her to pound against me without mercy, taking me even deeper. I was pretty sure I could get off just from the moans she made as our bodies crushed together. It was an intensity I'd never felt before— like we would die without the connection. I was so close to finishing, but I wanted to hold on because I didn't want it to end. I didn't want to just let loose because the urge to do so was building inside me like rapid fire. I wanted us to do this together. I wanted her to know I was committed to her in more ways than one.

"Sweet thing, let's do this together. Come with me." I anchored her to me, still clutching her tiny hips. As sinfully sexy as she was—with the sweat from our exertions glistening off her bronzed skin and her dark hair messily draped over her hooded lids—she was angelic.

Leaning down and pressing her damp skin against mine, she trailed her tongue across my lips, across my jawbone, and up to my ear. "Yes. Let's do this together. *Always* together."

This time her words fueled me even further. I lifted my hips off the mattress, plunging into her with driving force. Moving my hand between our bodies, I reached between her legs to where our bodies were joined, and fingered her clit with my thumb.

"Yes, Beck. Yes. Yes. *Yes.*" It was erotic music at its best.

Her grinding became wild and her pussy clenched around me, gripping my cock as if sending it an invitation to explode inside her. With her fingers digging into the tensing muscles of my arms, I thrust into her one last time. She screamed out my name as her warm release seeped between us. It was too late to even think of pulling out, my brain was too far gone and my dick was bringing it home. Emptying myself inside her as if draining everything I had, I held her tight and let the waves of pleasure roll through me.

Wrapped in each other's arms, our bodies still connected, I kissed her shoulder and combed my fingers through her hair. The gentle exchanges and skin-on-skin contact lulled us both into a drowsy after-sex stupor. When her breathing slowed and her grip slackened, I realized she'd fallen asleep in my arms.

It was the best way to start our new beginning.

CHAPTER 24

Riley

"My boyfriend *and* my brother? Wow! You get around. Just like your whore of a brother. Guess that makes you quite the slut, yourself." Her words dripped with pure hatred and disdain.

"You have no idea what you're talking about, Marissa." It was unnerving being cornered and attacked this way. I feared she might do something stupid out of rage and jealousy. But the only thing that kept me calm was that I hadn't done anything wrong. I shouldn't have to defend myself. I wasn't a whore. But the idea that she thought that—that she might put the idea in Beck *or* Griffin's head— "Just leave me alone. This has nothing to do with you." I tried to stand my ground, but the way my body quaked gave me away.

Stalking closer and pointing a threatening finger in my face, she barked, "It has everything to do with me, you bitch! Griffin and I... My brother deserves better than you. Stay the fuck away from him! And just to make things clear… Beck. Is. Mine. He loves *me*. You're nothing to him." Her words stung. I didn't know much about Griffin's past—I guess I hadn't really given him enough time to tell me. But it didn't matter anymore. I would never get to know him better. I was with him for all the wrong reasons. I needed a distraction from the man I *really* wanted. And that man was no longer in love with this evil witch before me.

It was time to tell this bitch how things would go down. I wasn't a coward. She was no one to me. No one to him now. "You're wrong, Marissa. He doesn't love you anymore. He wants *me*. He loves *me*."

Wrong move. Her face became the mottled crimson of a blood orange, her eyes popping out of their sockets. "You motherfucking whore!" she shouted, lunging at me with her claws ready to dig into my skin.

I backed up, shielding my face with my arms, knowing I had nowhere to hide. "Please! Stop! Don't hurt me!"

"Riles? *Riley!* Wake up!" Beck's voice and his strong grip on my arms woke me from my nightmare.

When I opened my eyes, I realized my arms were still in front of my face, my heart was thumping so rapidly I could taste it in my throat, and my skin was damp from my dream-induced sweat. "Oh my god. How embarrassing." I finally spoke, panting and coming back down to reality. "I must've been dreaming."

Swiping away the hairs that stuck to my forehead, Beck studied my face with a worried expression. "That was some dream, sweet thing. You sure you're okay?"

"I'll be fine." There was no reason to overanalyze it. Marissa wasn't a psycho, Griffin and I hadn't been *together* long, and everyone else would understand—when the time was right.

"I'll make you some coffee. Stay put." Beck covered me with the blanket that I'd kicked off in my slumber-scuffle and stood from the bed to go downstairs.

Before he could take a step further, I grabbed his hand to stop him. "No. Really. I'm good. Just come back to bed. I'm not ready to get up yet." Stupid dream behind me, it was time I started enjoying this for what it finally was. I hadn't slept in—with a handsome man in my arms—in a very long time.

"I wouldn't mind staying in bed all damn day if that's what you have in mind."

It was a wonderful plan, but I did have work to do. And some explaining to do to poor Griffin.

After Marissa left his apartment last night, I'd made up an excuse to cut our night short. Looking at the clock now, I realized I should call him to let him know I was okay. That would of course be after I told him that I couldn't see him anymore. I wasn't about to fill him in on every detail of my dating life—especially not the *who* part—but I did owe him honesty. He deserved to know I was seeing someone else. And Griffin wasn't the only one who deserved an explanation. I wanted to tell Beck about Griffin before he heard it through the grapevine.

"Sure you're okay?" Beck leaned against the headboard, appraising my distractedness.

Already I felt like I was starting this off on the wrong foot. I didn't want to be dishonest about anything. Keeping things from each other this early on was not the most stellar way to build a trusting foundation for our future. And if I knew one thing after this whole hot mess, it was that I wanted a future with Beck. A strong, solid, long lasting one.

I owed him some truth.

"It's not the dream. B, I need to tell you something." I inched up so our bodies were level with one another, pulling the blanket higher for some form of comfort and protection.

"Anything," he said in the sweetest, most understanding way possible. *Perfect. Just perfect.*

"I was seeing someone else while we were apart. I just thought you should know before we started this and you found out and it looked like I was hiding it from you. If we're going to do this right, I want to make sure that—"

Shaking his head, he interrupted me before letting me get to the good part. "I'm not an idiot, Riles. Well, actually I am a pretty big jerk for letting you go in the first place, but that's not what I mean. You are one of a kind and you deserve only the best. I didn't expect you to sit around and mope over me—I also didn't expect you to just date the next bozo that came around, either—but I get it and it's okay. I can't judge you for what you did or who you spent your time with when we weren't together. It's none of my business and you owe me no explanation. But, from this moment on… clean slate, fresh start, balls to the wall."

All worry vanished for a fleeting second and I smirked, unable to suppress a giggle from his comment. "Balls to the wall? What the hell does that have to do with it?"

"I don't know," he shrugged adorably. "Just sounded right."

"In some strange way, it's true. This all just sounds so right." I didn't want to get all mushy and girly on him, but I wanted him to know I was serious about us. I didn't want to press the Griffin issue because he'd managed to change the subject, but was that omitting a truth? Wasn't that the same as lying?

"Wanna know what else is right?" he asked, nudging me in the stomach with his elbow.

"What?" I mused, looking into his eyes and forgetting all about the things weighing heavy on my mind.

He stripped the blanket off of us, stood up on the mattress, and started dancing. "Breaking out in song! And this one's just for you since I'm bringing sexy *Beck*."

I busted out laughing so hard I thought I might pee in his bed and ruin the sheets. He stood there doing a little strip tease while singing the lyrics to *Sexy Back*, causing tears to burst from my eyes.

"*Dirty babe. You see these shackles, baby, I'm your slave. I'll let you whip me if I misbehave. It's just that no one makes me feel this way... Take 'em to the chorus!*"

"Beck, you're killing me," I managed to get out between snorts and giggles. "Come back down here."

He curled his finger, gesturing for me to join him in his dance and continued serenading me so much better than JT ever could. "*Come here girl. Go ahead, be gone with it. Come to the* Beck. *Go ahead, be gone with it...*"

As if of their own accord, my legs made the decision for me. I jumped up to dance and Beck grabbed my hands, swaying me around as if we were on a dance floor and not a queen-sized pillow-top mattress. "I'm so glad you showed up and brought my sexy back."

"Yeah, well, *those other boys don't know how to act.*"

Tilting his head and rewarding me with a soft peck, he arched a brow. "I'm glad we've moved from *Cabaret* to this, but I don't even like that dude, Riles. Can't we paraphrase Zeppelin or The Who?"

"Who?" I exaggerated, as if I was clueless.

"The Who. You know, *Baba O'Riley, Won't Get Fooled Again.*"

"I know *who* The Who is, B. But I'm dating a younger man, not an old fart. You should be hip to Justin and Drake and Usher."

Pulling me closer to him and nuzzling his scruffy face in the crook of my neck, he laughed against my skin. "My little hip-hop lovin' freak. I learn something new about you every day."

There were a lot of things he didn't know about me. A lot I wanted to tell him, so much I didn't. But I was getting ahead of myself. I needed to be present in our moment. I owed it to myself—to Beck—to enjoy this and worry about the rest later.

"Do you have plans today?" I asked, hoping he didn't have to pull a three day shift or something like that. I knew little about his schedule, except that it was erratic. There would be times he'd be off for weeks and then others when he'd probably be MIA for a while. I hoped we could spend some time together, getting reacquainted and reconnected.

"As a matter of fact I do," he said pointedly.

I couldn't help hide my disappointment. I was very comfortable wrapped in his arms, dancing like a fool in nothing but one of his oversized T-shirts. "Really?"

"Yup. With you." He leaned down and kissed the tip of my nose. "I let you go once and I'm not letting it happen again."

"B, that sounds like the fairytale I've always wanted, but unfortunately this is reality."

"Not in this room it ain't. When you're in here..." he crooned, guiding me back down to our still-warm pillows. "... it's all about the fantasies, baby. And I plan on living them out all damn day."

There was this saying I'd heard a couple of times that popped into my head as I stared into Beck's hungry dark eyes. *I still believe in fairytales, they're just a little dirtier now.* I loved the idea of living out my knight-in-shining-armor, white-picket fence, picture-perfect fantasies with Beck—I wanted to make them a reality.

After living out quite a few fantasies, napping while spooning, and snacking on the only unexpired thing in his cupboard—peanut butter and jelly—I convinced Beck to release me as his sex prisoner. I wanted to go home, take a shower and change into my own clothes. I felt grimy from all our... reacquainting... and I wanted to look nice for my man.

We made plans to head into Hoboken and had reservations at one of my favorite Cuban restaurants. Not only was their sangria the best in town, but we also picked the spot to be discreet. Marcus and Tessa rarely had the opportunity for fine-dining since they had Luca to take care of, but Beck and I decided that keeping things on the DL for a little longer wasn't the most terrible idea.

As I got in my car and plugged my cell phone into the car

charger, I felt a pang of guilt over Griffin. It was mid-afternoon and I still hadn't called him. He was probably worried or annoyed and I really didn't want there to be any hard feelings between us. Aside from having fun together, we'd formed a friendship that I hoped would remain plutonic. Especially since he'd hired me to work on his studio.

Turning at the green light, I slid my sunglasses from the top of my head to shield my eyes from the sun, and decided to give him a call.

"Get it over with before you make it worse," I told myself. I couldn't just ignore the last few weeks and pretend he didn't exist. That would be the most immature thing I could do. And Griffin was far from immature. From what I'd seen he was a secure and confident man. He didn't need to play games, and he certainly didn't seem like the type to stand for them either. Having knowledge of what it was like to be on the shit end of the game-playing stick, I struck up the nerve to speak the truth as his phone continued to ring.

Just as I thought his voicemail would pick up, and wondered if I should punk out and let him down in a message, his gruff, sexy voice filled my car on the Bluetooth. "Thank God, you're alive!" He was clearly being sarcastic, probably ticked off that I'd taken so long to give him a call.

For whatever reason, Griffin's opinion of me mattered. He was a good person, someone I liked having around; if not on a romantic level, at least as someone I could call a friend. I didn't want him to be irritated with me, so I started off with an apology. "Yes, I'm alive and I'm so sorry I didn't call sooner, but I was... tied up." The simple phrase could be interpreted in many ways. It was his choice to decipher it before I explained myself.

He cleared his throat and spoke in a sultry voice. "That's quite a vision you're painting for me, Riley. I would have liked to see it for myself."

That was the one scenario I'd hoped he didn't envision. "Listen, Griffin."

"Uh, oh. I've been on the other end of those words in that tone before. What's up?" Poor Griffin. I should have known not to get involved with such a perfect person so soon after Beck. I always had the hope we'd find our way back to each other so maybe I was a bitch for agreeing to spend time with Griffin. Was I that girl? *God, I was that girl!*

"Griffin, I hate to be *that* girl and I hope you understand, but..." Why was this so hard? I didn't owe him anything. We'd barely kissed. It wasn't like I'd led him on. These things happened all the time. Right? "I really think you're a great guy. Like *really* great, but I just... I shouldn't have gotten involved with you in the first place. You see, there's someone else and I thought... it doesn't matter, really. I'll spare you the details and just let you know that I can't go out with you again. I want to give it a shot with this guy and it wouldn't be fair... to either of you... to continue whatever it is you and I started. I had a lot of fun with you and I would still love to work for you, that's if you'll still have me, and even though this sounds like a shitty cliché-like thing to say, I would really like to stay friends."

The line fell silent for a few seconds and I worried that I'd gone through a bad area and dropped the call. I really didn't want to have to say that all over again. My body was a little shaky from getting it out the first time. I was thankful I didn't live too far from Beck's—driving while preoccupied and jittery wasn't exactly safe.

Unable to stand the silence any longer I blurted out, "Hello? Griffin? Did I lose you?"

"I'm here. I'm just... well, this blows." He finally admitted, huffing. "I like you a lot, Riley. You're a very unique woman and I wanted to get to know you better, but... I understand and it was very noble of you to come out and just say it. So, thank you."

"You're welcome?" It came out as a question because, really, was this guy serious? Thanking me for breaking up with him out of the blue.

Chuckling, the musical rasp in his voice spread a comforting warmth through my nerve-chilled body. "Don't sound so surprised, Riley. What did you think I was going to do? Demand you to continue dating me? Give you a hard time for being honest? You're a sweetheart, and I'm sorry we can't be more because I really dig you, but... I'd love to remain friends. There's no reason we can't be. Unless of course your boyfriend is jealous of the older, rugged, artsy gentleman type?"

I laughed, relieved by his cool response. "Oh, Griffin, you are one perfect gentleman, for sure. I'm happy we met on the beach that day."

"Me too. Let's just say it's your loss, babe."

"Hey!" I shrieked.

His booming laugh filled my car before his words made me sigh. "He's one lucky guy, Riley. I can't help feeling like a sore loser."

"There are no winners or losers, Griffin. It just... is what it is."

"I guess so and thank you for being honest with me. I'll just have to take what I can get."

A bit mournful over the premature ending to whatever it was we'd yet to even start, I tried to hide my melancholy over the situation. I couldn't have my cake and eat it too. And I wasn't about to date two men at the same time just to figure out who was the right fit. Besides, I already knew who I wanted to be with. My feelings for Beck were so much stronger than the tiny bit of regret I felt ending things with Griffin. It was time to make this professional and amicable with just the right amount of sincerity. "Now you're making it like it's goodbye. It's definitely not goodbye... we'll need to meet up in a week or two to go over all the ideas I have for that impressive studio."

"I look forward to that. And Riley?"

"Yes?"

"You're one special lady. Don't ever forget that."

"Thank you, I won't." I hesitated for a second before saying what had to come next. "Bye, Griffin."

"Bye. Call me to set up our appointment."

"Okay. Have a good one."

"You too, love. Ciao."

He hung up the phone just as I turned into my driveway. I put the car in park and rested my head against the seat. That totally sucked. I hated doing things like that. I shouldn't feel any remorse—I was ending things with Griffin to start things with a man I was pretty sure I was falling in love with.

As I let it all sink in—getting back with Beck, letting go of Griffin—I smiled, knowing this was what my mother meant when she told me to live. Part of living was losing. Part of living was loving. I'd done my fair share of the first, I intended to spend the rest of my meager life doing the latter.

CHAPTER 25

Beck

October

Riley and I had hit the three month mark. Three months since our first time together—a drunken night of what we thought was a mistake and turned into the best decision of my life. Three months of sneaking around—even keeping the wool over Tessa's eyes since getting back together—and enjoying the thrill of it all the while. Three months of taking things slow—learning new things about each other, enjoying making sweet love and fucking like animals, and just doing what any normal couple did in the beginning of a relationship. Three months of holding in how much I loved this girl—that part was unbearable. I only held off because I wanted the timing to be *perfect*. But now I was at the point where I couldn't wait one more day to express how deeply I'd fallen in love with Riley Grayson.

Up until this moment, I couldn't have asked for more. We spent as much time together as we could without letting anyone now how serious things were becoming. Other than Fallon, who was actually becoming a good friend to me as well, we'd made a fun game of keeping everyone out of the know. Tessa and Marcus were so wrapped up in themselves and Luca turning one that they didn't even notice we'd spent less time with them and more time on our own. Together.

I tried not to pry into Tessa and Riley's friendship. It was their own special connection, much like the bromance they all joked I had with Marcus. But even though we'd decided to keep things discreet, I was pretty sure Riley was feeding Tessa some gossipy version of us fooling around. I was certain, though, that it was impossible for Tessa to know Marcus was no longer the only Grayson sibling planning a future with someone special.

Riley and I had our own plans. And we talked about them often. Once this damn birthday party was over and Marcus and Tessa were moved into their brand new surprise-this-is-our-new-home present he'd bought for Tessa and Luca, we'd come out as a couple. Then everyone would just have to deal. It was none of their business anyway. If Riley could accept her best friend and her baby brother shacking up and starting a new life together as a family, then Marcus would have to give his blessing to *his* best friend and his big sister.

"So what time do you have to be there tonight?" I asked, curling a strand of her hair that she'd grown a bit longer since the summer. I liked it. There was more to grab during sex. And just like that I was hard again and ready for another Saturday afternoon quickie.

"Whoa, partner. Tame the beast." She wedged a pillow between my package and her ass. "I have to get back to my place to take care of a few things and then head over to Tessa's. They're going to an early dinner and then he's bringing her by the new house. Oh, and he's showing her the motorcycle today too."

First the new house and then the Harley—Marcus was making all kinds of outlandish purchases these days. "Dude's losing his mind. He's too young for a mid-life crisis, so he must be booking those underwear gigs left and right. Making big bucks."

She laughed at the way I swayed my hips and snapped my waistband at the mention of her brother's underwear. "Or maybe he's just happy. He's finally settled down and doing the right thing. I'm happy for him. For all of them. It's about time someone got a happy ending around here."

My eyes went wide and I snorted, trying to hold in my laughter. "Yeah, you're right. I could totally use a happy ending, sweet thing. What's say we get started right now?" I inched my hand down my stomach seductively and grabbed my junk, jiggling the overflowing (yup—perfect adjective) handful.

"God, B. Always about the pecker." She ignored the suggestive stroking motion I made with my fist, and started to get up from the bed. I yanked her around the waist and pulled her back down to me.

"I was kidding about the pecker's happy ending, Riles. You left yourself wide open for that one." I kissed her on the cheek, sniffing in her sweet, ruffled after-sex aroma. "Marcus and Tessa aren't the only ones who'll get their happy ending. I promise." I should've just come out with it right then and there. *I love you, Riley. And we're going to spend the rest of our lives together. We'll get our happy ending—the one you want (and me too—wink wink). I haven't been able to think of anything other than our future since you came back to me.*

Sounded easy enough—maybe not poetic, but it was the truth. So why was I keeping those three words to myself when she deserved more than anyone to hear them? One reason was that we couldn't keep our hands off each other. While there was nothing wrong with that, I had a method to my madness. My rotations at work were so wonky lately, I didn't know whether I was coming or going most of the time. And when *I* wasn't working Riley was busy with her ever-growing client list or off at the latest convention. So when we were together—you bet your ass we were all over each other. I didn't want to blurt out those words during sex. The first time I told her I loved her I wanted us to be fully clothed, completely sober, and not groggy from another sleepless night of screwing. She needed to know those words were not just the result of a mind-blowing fuck.

And then there was this teensy ounce of doubt I had. Could it be I was afraid she didn't feel the same? I *thought* she did. The signs were all there. Besides, she was the one who got all mopey-eyed and envious when she mentioned Marcus and Tessa getting their silver lining. There was no denying she was waiting for me to make the right move— she didn't want to go first and I respected her for that. She was a stubborn little firecracker, but I owed her the honor of confessing my love before she did. It was the proper order of things. Guy meets girl, guy falls for girl, guy tells girl how much he loves her. Of course our meeting had taken place years before I could even spell half that shit, but whatever— our history didn't matter. What mattered was what came next. And the beginning to our "next" would happen tonight when I surprised her at Tessa's.

"Okay, I really have to go now. It's getting late." She stretched and sat upright, then leaned down to leave me with a soft kiss. "You sure you can't babysit Luca with me tonight? We can pretend we're like teenagers. I'll sneak you in through the back door after Luca falls asleep and you can sneak back out before Tessa gets home."

That's exactly what I had planned, but she didn't need to know that. "I wish, babe. But I promised Ramos I'd help him with the last of the baby's nursery. Angel's about to pop any second. If I put him off any longer he'll have my balls." It wasn't a complete lie. I would help Ramos put together a few pieces of furniture for his little rugrat and then I'd make my way over to tell my girl I loved her.

"Fine," she huffed, rolling her eyes. "But I'm coming over right after, so keep your phone handy so I can text you when I'm done there. Okay?"

"Sounds perfect, doll." I slapped her on the ass, and watched as she shook her head and walked out of my bedroom.

"Want me to walk you out?" I yelled out to her, realizing it might be nice for me to see her to the door like a gentleman.

"Nope. I'm good," she answered from the living room. "I'll see you in that exact same spot in about eight hours. Make sure Pecker's ready."

"He's always ready for you." I tucked my hands under my head, even though they itched to stroke out the throbbing ache Riley left me with at the mention of my pecker. God, would this ever get old? I doubted it.

"Shit, man! Keeping you from something? Look at your phone one more time and I'm gonna shove it up your—"

"Victor, watch it. You have to start curbing that mouth of yours once the baby gets here."

Angel was rubbing her massive bump, overseeing our efforts to put together the crib.

I nodded in her direction and gave her a wink. "Tell him, Mamacita. Kid's first word's gonna be pretty colorful with this dude's repertoire."

She leaned down and biffed her husband on the head. "Not if I have anything to do with it. You guys want anything from the kitchen? I want more ice cream—did you pick up that hot sauce I asked you to get, Vic?"

"Yup. Middle shelf."

Angel waddled out of the soon-to-be baby's room and I eyed Ramos suspiciously. "What does hot sauce have to do with ice cream?"

He shook his head with his mouth agape. "Don't even ask. You're worried about my kid's mouth? I'm worried about its poor stomach. She's been eating such spicy shit the kid's gonna come out with a sombrero and an ulcer, God forbid." He made the sign of the cross and just as I was about to ask him if he was warding off the ridiculous hat or the latter, my cell phone buzzed.

"What the hell?"

"What's wrong?" he asked, taking note of my disappointment.

"It's Marissa. I haven't heard from her in over a month. I

don't really want to answer it."

"So don't." He had a point. I didn't have to. And I wasn't about to let her ruin what I had planned for Riley tonight.

"Fuck! Of all nights." I tossed the phone to the side and got back to tightening a screw with an Allen wrench.

"Why? Is there ever a good night to hear from your ex?"

"I'm telling Riley I love her tonight. And then I want to tell Marcus about us tomorrow. It's time we cut the shit and stop worrying about everyone else. I'm not ashamed and I'm tired of worrying what people will think. We've kept it to ourselves long enough. But once I tell her how I feel— shit! I want the world to know." Ramos was the perfect guy to have this conversation with. Any other guy in the firehouse would've laughed his ass off at how pussy-whipped I sounded—again. Marissa was the first girl to wear that crown, but with Riley it was different. I didn't give a shit what they said. As long as I was being pussy-whipped by Riley—bring on the leather belt!

"Good for you, bro. I'm happy for you."

"Thank you. She's the real deal, Ramos. I thought I had it all figured out with Marissa, but this—there is not one single thing lacking. Not one doubt. She's it. I know it."

My phone buzzed again, vibrating against the oak floors. "Then you better tell that one to leave you alone. There's no reason to keep in touch if you're not friends."

"We're not, but—"

"Dude, answer that shit."

I crawled over to the phone and scowled at the screen. It was her again. I had to answer.

"Hello?"

"Beck? Oh my god, Beck. I need you." She sobbed in

between words, bellowing out moans and blowing her nose. "Please come here. My life is falling apart. I failed the goddamn bar, Beck. I don't know what the hell I'm going to do now. I need you," she begged.

I looked at Ramos, who had to have heard her through the phone. He shook his head, disapprovingly. "Don't do it, dude." He mouthed.

He was right. It was a disaster waiting to happen. It was a kink in my plans. But leaving her feeling this way was a dick thing to do. "I can stop by for a few minutes. Just to make sure you're okay. But I can't stay, Marissa. You know that, right?"

"Yes. Please. Just come. I need you. Everything's... falling... apart."

"Calm down and hang tight." I ended the call and ignored the hole Ramos was burning into me with his critical stare as I searched the contacts in my phone and pressed send.

The phone rang twice and his deep, gruff voice sounded annoyed when he picked up. "Beck? What do you—?"

"Griffin, hey buddy. Listen, Marissa just called. She sounds like—I don't know. I'm worried. I promised her I'd go there to make sure she's okay, but... I don't want to give her the wrong impression. Can I swing by and pick you up on the way? You free?"

"What the hell's going on? I just spoke to her earlier this week. She's been a little screwed up since you two split, but she seemed fine." I could tell he was worried. He was a good older brother. He cared a lot about Marissa, even though she wasn't his full-blooded sibling.

"She failed the bar. She sounded... desperate."

"Shit! I'll meet you there in twenty."

We hung up and I jetted out of Ramos and Angel's, waving goodbye and slamming the door behind me. My whole night was officially fucked.

"You called my brother, Beck? You called my *brother?* Are you that scared to be alone with me? What? Does your new girl have some kind of golden whoo-ha or something? I can't *believe* you called my brother."

Her eyes were red and swollen from crying. Her hair greasy and unruly, her clothing wrinkled and mismatched. She was always a beautiful girl—still was, even if she was a mess. But something just wasn't right about all this. Becoming a lawyer was her life, so failing the bar definitely had to have rocked her, but there was something more. Something about the irrational look in her eye as she watched my mental exchange with Griffin.

"You can take it again, Rissy. Why are you so worked up? Why didn't you call *me*, or Dad? We would have been here in a second."

She flopped onto the couch, turning off the Pandora channel. She'd been listening to the Mumford & Sons station—I'd always told her they were too damn depressing. "My whole life is falling apart. Everything is just... gone." She held her head in her hands, her shoulders jutting up and down as the sobs wracked her body.

I'd never seen her so out of control. This so uncharacteristic of the strong, confident, career-hungry woman I used to call my girlfriend. Unable to make sense of it all, I stood, stunned-still, behind the couch.

Griffin took the initiative and sat next to her, wrapping an arm around her small frame. "Rissy, stop this. Nothing's falling apart. You're just upset. This too shall pass, remember?"

Marissa took a long, deep, shaky breath, and let her hands fall from her face. She swiveled around to face me and zeroed in on my eyes. Her lip quivered and her tears flowed freely. "Why did you leave me, Beck? I thought we'd work things out. I never imagined it would be over for good. I can change. Maybe I'm not cut out to be a hard-assed lawyer after all. I can't even pass the damn test. I can put that aside and be the woman you wanted. Marriage and babies. I want that all with you."

Shit! This wasn't about me. She was just overwhelmed and confused and it was all coming to a head—here, in front of her brother who was eyeing me like I was Jeffry Dahmer incarnate. Not tonight. I couldn't talk my ex-girlfriend off the ledge with her brother ready to pounce and my heart belonging to someone else—someone who was unknowingly waiting for me to surprise her with our first I love you. *Not fucking tonight!*

"Marissa, you don't mean that. I know you better than this. Sure, I miss you too." I didn't really, but I wasn't about to pour salt in her wounds. "But we're just not right for each other anymore. You're going to pass that test, land the sickest job in the most prestigious law firm and when you're ready—not when someone tells you to be ready—you're going to make some guy the luckiest bastard on the planet." I'd walked around the couch during my speech and sat in front of her on the coffee table. I reached out to grab her hands, to comfort her, but Griffin's scowl warned me not to.

"Why don't *you* want to be that lucky bastard? Why am I not good enough anymore?"

I hated to see her so weak. I hated to think I made her this way, but I couldn't do anything about it. I didn't love her anymore. It wasn't my place to fix her.

"Rissy, have you eaten yet today?" Griffin tried to divert his sister's attention from me, rubbing circles on her back with his thumb. "I can order from that Thai place you like. It will make you feel better."

Ignoring Griffin, Marissa's eyes never left mine. "Will you stay? Just to eat?"

"You have me here, sis. Aren't I good enough?" Griffin faked a smile, nudging his sister.

"Of course you are, Griff, but... he's already here. And who knows when I'll see him again."

Griffin stared me down again. I wasn't afraid of him, but I wanted to respect his wishes for his sister. He had her best interests at heart. I was just here because she called. "I can stay until you've calmed down. Until I know you're okay. But I have plans. I have to finish helping Ramos with his baby's room."

"Okay," she conceded, still disappointed. "I'll take what I can get."

I never wanted to run out of a place so badly in my life. This was wrong. Everything about it felt wrong. I shouldn't be here comforting Marissa. She had her brother for that, but I couldn't just up and go and leave her in this state. There was a sense of security that I guessed only I could give her right now. I'd spend an hour here, getting her to come to her senses and then hand her off to Griffin so I could get on with my night.

But she dragged an extra hour out of me, playing on my guilty nerve and convincing me to stay for the rest of the Yankees game. During the last inning of the longest playoff game in history, my nightmare of an evening quickly turned into a full on horrific reality.

My cell phone rang, reminding me that I had somewhere else to be. I figured it would be Riley, checking in, but when Tessa's number appeared on the screen, the blood drained from my face. "Beck! It's Tessa. Get to Methodist Hospital as soon as you can. It's Marcus *and* Riley, Beck. They're both... Zack almost..." Her sobs broke her and before I could ask her to explain, I was beckoned by a pleading, desperate woman for the second time tonight. "Just come quick, Beck. Please!"

CHAPTER 26
Riley

"*Miss Grayson. Can you hear me? Miss Grayson?*" The angelic voice sounded like it was in the distance. "Doctor, she's awake," she buzzed an intercom. "And, sir, you really can't be in here. Please let us do our jobs." The angelic voice turned stern and became clearer.

And then there was another, more familiar male voice trying to make its way through my groggy haze. He was frantic, concerned, scared.

It didn't take long to figure out who it was. *Beck.* If I didn't recognize him by sound, I certainly knew it was him by the touch of his hand on my face. *Ouch!* His soft touch actually hurt. My cheek felt swollen and my jaw ached as I tried to open my mouth to speak. "Where am I?" I managed to croak out through gritted teeth. I took in the white coats, the beeping, the tubes protruding from my arm. "Am I in the hospital?"

I tried to sit up, but Beck stopped me in place and the throbbing in my brain backed him up. *Not a good idea to move,* it told me. *Stay put and relax.*

"Riley, baby. Do you remember what happened? Do you know why you're here?"

I searched the room, looking for answers. My vision was a little fuzzy and my memories grainy, but one glance at the police officers standing guard by my door and it all came back to me in a fury of flashes.

"Call her again, you bitch!" He held the gun against my head, tightening his grip on my wrist.

"Tessa's not answering, Zack. Please, just let me go get Luca." The baby was upstairs screaming bloody murder for at least ten minutes already. I prayed I'd left his bedroom window open so a nosy neighbor would hear him and come over to see if we needed help. We did, desperately, because I wasn't one of those courageous women you saw on those survival stories. The fight or flight instinct was all flight for me. I was too scared to fight back. I didn't know how. There was no outsmart-the-bad-guy plan hatching in my terrified brain. Suddenly, I was praying more than I had in a long time. To God, to my mother. Please don't let this psycho kill me or that little boy. Please, Mom, watch over us and keep us safe.

"You are a useless piece of shit," he spat at me as I dialed the phone for what had to be the twentieth time. I was glad she hadn't answered. As helpless as I felt, I was hoping I could take care of this myself so she and Marcus didn't have to come home to face her lunatic, alcoholic, homicidal, ex-husband.

"Please, Zack. Tell me what you want. It doesn't have to be like this, you know?" I tried to remain composed, but the

stone-cold look in his bloodshot eyes scared me more than the gun digging into my temple.

"Shut the fuck up and try her again. And this time if she doesn't answer..."

He didn't finish but I knew where he was going with his threats. He was irrational and his actions were way beyond that. Even though it was obviously not my fault Tessa wasn't picking up her phone, to Zack it was my problem.

When she didn't pick up again, my heart dropped, but instead of giving in and finding out exactly what he would do to me for not getting him what he wanted... I lied. Her voicemail picked up and I pretended I was speaking to a live person. "Oh, hi, Tess." I paused for effect hoping he would buy it. His eyes were wide now. I could see very little white peeking through the veiny lines of red that masked what used to be an attractive hazel-green. "Yes, sorry for calling so many times, but... Luca's really cranky; you think you can—"

"Give that to me!" He ripped the phone from my hand and in that moment I sincerely feared for my life. Not only had I failed in getting through to Tessa, again, but now I'd lied to the psycho.

"Tessa, baby, is that you?" His face softened for a moment. I almost felt sorry for him. As sick and maniacal as he was, he was a human being who was hurting. It was too bad that his alcoholism and abusive behavior turned my compassion into disgust.

"Hello? Hello!" When he realized Tessa wasn't on the other end, that I'd made up the whole thing, anger seeped out of every crevice in his body. "You must think I'm some kind of idiot, don't you, Riley?" He mimicked a little boy's *voice when he said, it as if he was making fun of me.*

I shook my head, holding back tears. The closer he got, the more I wanted to scream. What did it matter at this point? Luca was still wailing and Zack had me cornered with a gun pointed in my face.

So that's what I did. I dug deep down into my core and released the loudest, most blood-curdling scream I could. "Heeeellllppppppp!"

Before I could beg for mercy again, his fist was flying at me, the metal of the gun shining in the dim light. The last thing I remember before the floor fell out from under me was praying that he didn't harm his innocent son.

"That mother fucker," Beck growled, after I'd recounted my story to the police officer.

He jotted everything down, nodding as I spoke. He wasn't very informative; but then again, how could he be? We were putting together the pieces as best we could, with the little we had to go on.

"Beck? Oh my god. Did he... How's Luca? And what about Tessa and Marcus?" I had no idea how I'd gotten to the hospital or how Beck even knew to find me here. Someone needed to fill me in... and soon. I was starting to feel like an amnesia patient. *Shit!* Did I have amnesia? As I rummaged through my mind for every fact about myself, I didn't fall short. *Okay, no amnesia.*

Before Beck could calm my fears, the nurse was interrupting with an update. "You need to take it easy, hun. Try to relax. The attending doctor will be in shortly to see you." She adjusted a few contraptions and then scurried to the doorway.

When she'd disappeared into the great hospital unknown, everyone else followed suit. One by one the two policemen and the orderly who'd delivered my tray of food left me and Beck to our privacy.

I focused on my poor worried man, who hadn't let go of my hand since I'd woken. Although I was the one who needed comforting, I wanted to take away his pain. I squeezed his hand and smiled. When his worry lines smoothed and his lips curled up out of a serious straight line, I asked about everyone again. "How are they? Please tell me everyone's okay."

He brought his hand up to my face, steering clear of what I assumed were the bruises that throbbed under my skin. "They're all fine now. I promise. We'll talk about them later. I have to say something first."

Shit! Was he stalling? He was making me nervous. "Okay. But you're kind of freaking me out. You're not lying to me about them are you? Are you trying to change the subject? Oh god. Something happened, didn't it?"

Beck sat on the bed next to me, careful not to disturb any wires or harm my already bruised body parts. He cupped my face softly and sucked in a long, heavy breath. "No, baby. I promised, didn't I? I wouldn't lie about something like that. Now, there's something I've been wanting to tell you, so let me say this. It can't wait."

I nodded and he continued with a shy smile. "I was supposed to come over to Tessa's and tell you this tonight. I should have come sooner, dammit. I hate that I wasn't there so that asshole couldn't do this to you, but—" His frustration vanished as he caressed the top of my hand with his thumb. "I can't wait another second to tell you, Riley. I don't want another minute to go by. I don't want to be scared of ever losing you again. Nothing else matters. Nothing can get in the way of this ever again. I love you, Riley. I've loved you for a long time and I should have told you the first time I realized it, but I wanted it to be right... perfect. And here I am, telling you this in a damn hospital bed. I'm so sorry I wasn't there to protect you. I'm so sorry he hurt you and I'm—"

"I love you too, B." I cut him off. I had been wanting to hear those words for a while now. Wanting to say them myself. I loved him so damn much it didn't matter how or where he told me. I was just happy he felt the same. Tears filled my eyes, this time from the astounding warmth and happiness coursing through my exhausted body. For a brief minute the horror of Zack and the pain and everything else vanished as we had our little moment. "This *is* perfect. This is exactly how it was supposed to happen." It wasn't pretty—shit, I couldn't look pretty right now, but it was ours. If anything good could come out of this nightmare, it was that I knew I never wanted to live without this man by my side.

When his lips touched mine I could tell he was trying to be careful, as if I would break. But little did he know every tiny piece of me that felt shattered before this moment, felt complete when our lips met. He held me in his arms for a few silent seconds and we caressed each other, not wanting to let go.

But when the doctor cleared his throat from the doorway we had no choice but to temporarily separate.

Beck jumped back abruptly as if he were caught doing something forbidden and I laughed at how adorable he looked, trying to straighten his appearance for the doctor.

"I'm sorry to interrupt," he said with a warm smile. "I'm Dr. Craig." He extended a hand to Beck and Beck took it with a firm grip and a grateful smile.

"Nice to meet you, doctor. How's my girl doing?"

The young doctor didn't return Beck's smile this time. Instead he focused on me with a seriousness that brought chills to my body. "I know you must have a million questions, Ms. Grayson, but I'd like to go over a few things with you if that's okay?"

I had questions and I wanted to fill in all the blanks, but the doctor's tone made me uneasy. Had I been permanently injured? *Oh my god, was I paralyzed or something?* I wiggled my toes, and moved my hips. Thank the Lord, I was still intact.

Dr. Craig silently looked over at Beck and then back to me. "I need to discuss Ms. Grayson's personal health records. Would you mind leaving the room, sir?"

Beck reluctantly stood, following the doctor's command, but I yanked on his hand. "No, you can stay."

"You sure, Riles?"

"Doctor, he's my boyfriend." I clutched Beck's hand. "Anything you have to say to me you can say in front of him."

Dr. Craig nodded and fingered through the papers in my file, getting straight to business. "There's not much here to report. So we'll just go over the results and then you two can get back to... well, let me just get on with your evaluation." A rosy flush warmed Dr. Craig's pale cheeks, but he cleared his throat and adjusted his coat to get back in the doctor-zone. "Okay, so, you suffered a mild concussion from the fall. You have some bruising from where the assailant struck you, right here." He lightly grazed my temple, pushing my hair to the side. I winced when his finger caught on a stray hair and pulled at the tender flesh. "Sorry about that. I just wanted to check for any lacerations. It looks worse than it actually is, but there should be no permanent scarring. The outer wounds will heal nicely; it's the inner ones I want to talk to you about."

The ginger-haired doctor sat beside me and his expression softened as his voice did the same. "I am recommending you to a therapist who specializes in situations like this—post traumatic stress and victims of assault and abuse. I think it's best, especially in your condition, to have someone to talk to on a weekly basis so you don't cause any unnecessary stress to your body."

I was ninety percent convinced he knew what he was talking about. It seemed like a smart move to talk this out. Seek professional help after something so near-death. All of his words made sense... except for three. "What do you mean: *in your condition?* You said my head injuries are nothing to worry about. Is there something else you're not telling me?"

Beck looked concerned as he grabbed my hand and stared down the doctor for an explanation. "Yea, Doc. Isn't she going to be okay?"

"Yes." He smiled. "They both are. Assuming you two have been together for the last few months, your girlfriend *and* your baby are going to be just fine."

That was it! Zack must have done a number on my hearing when he knocked me out. I could have sworn I heard him say something about a *baby.* "Wait. What?

Whose baby? Luca belongs to Tessa. We don't have any kids. He," I pointed a sideways thumb at Beck before continuing, "doesn't have any kids. What are you—?"

"I take it you didn't know you were eight weeks along."

Beck's brows scrunched together, the lines in his forehead creasing. "Along what?"

"In her pregnancy. Ms. Grayson, congratulations. You'll need to take it easy for a few days. We've administered an IV to rehydrate you and I've managed to grab a few prenatal vitamin samples for you for the time being. But you'll want to make an appointment with your regular OB as soon as possible so you can get the proper prenatal care..."

Dr. Craig rambled on and on about this baby that I had no idea was growing inside my belly for the last eight weeks. This baby that Beck and I had created together. This baby who I could have lost before even knowing it existed because of that sick bastard.

It was all so overwhelming. I was going to be a mom. I wanted *my* mom. I needed my mom. Oh my god, it was too much to handle.

"Baby, why are you crying? What's the matter?" Beck was first to register my thoughts. From the looks of things he had to think I was upset about the news. I wasn't upset. I wanted this baby. After only finding out three seconds ago, I was certain I never wanted anything so badly in my life.

"I can't believe... I just... Oh. My. God, B. We're going to be parents. I'm having your baby." Saying those words was surreal. Was this really happening? Shit! How did Beck feel about all this? "What are you thinking? Please tell me you want to keep her?"

Dr. Craig stood and excused himself with a smile. "You

two talk and I'll be back later to check in on you. You're fine to be discharged in the morning. And congratulations again, Ms. Grayson."

I nodded a thank you and focused on Beck. His face didn't give much away. Was he scared? Was he angry? Was he happy? "B, talk to me. We have to keep her."

"Why do you keep saying *her*? There's a fifty-fifty shot here, Riles. It can be a boy."

"It's a girl, Beck. I know it. This is our miracle. This is my mother's doing. I always wanted a little girl and this is her. I just know it. Now please, please tell me you're okay with this."

He sat silent for a few more beats and my heart sank, thinking he wasn't as happy as I was over this unexpected news. We weren't married, we'd only just spoken the words "I love you" minutes ago, no one knew we were together and we'd only been a couple for a few months. This was extremely unconventional, but it just seemed... right.

"Of course we're keeping her, Riles. How can you think I'd want to give her up?"

I felt the air return to my lungs when I heard him say those words, but he still seemed off. "You're quiet... pensive... are you upset?"

He stood and started pacing with his hands in his hair. Not exactly the reaction I was hoping for, but when he finally stopped wearing out the tile of the hospital floor, the wide grin on his face was the reaction I'd been waiting on. "It's a fucking shock, but... a baby! A baby that *we* created. Riles, I honestly couldn't be happier." He joined me on the bed again, cupping my face and kissing me on the tip of the nose.

"Promise?" I asked for good measure.

"Swear on my first born... I mean, swear to Christ. Sorry," he corrected himself and gazed at my stomach. "How did you not know this? He said two months. Haven't you missed your..."

"I'm on the pill, B. Not to give you TMI, but sometimes I hardly get it at all. I guess I didn't notice that last month's cycle was extra extra light. And speaking of the pill... guess I'm that point zero zero one percent they always warn about." I shrugged, but there was nothing apologetic about it. I was so happy our form of contraception had failed us. *Take that, birth control! You're no match for me and my man's sperm!*

Beck chuckled as he traced his thumb back and forth over my hand. "For a girl who was just nearly killed by a psychopath, you're awfully chipper."

I laughed at what the situation had to look like. Bruised, battered, and bloody, in this get-up for a hospital gown with a ginormous smile on my face. "Crazy, right?"

"You can totally say that again."

"We do crazy really well, B. I'm starting to like it."

He nuzzled closer, lying next to me on the pillow and placing my hand in his. "I'm starting to *love* it, but... things are about to go all kinds of crazy when we share this news with your brother."

"Ah, piece of cake. Let me handle him."

In the blink of a freaking eye everything can change. A few hours ago I was afraid for my life, trembling and helpless at the mercy of another man. A man that had hurt my best friend in the past and done God-knows-what to her and my brother tonight. I should be lying in this bed sobbing and shaken, broken and torn, but that's not at all what I felt. I felt blessed. Blessed to be loved by Beck. Blessed to have survived that ordeal. Blessed to be carrying my little Claire—my daughter. *Our* daughter. She'd be named after my mother, there was no doubt about that. And regardless of the way I'd found out about her, or when she was conceived, or how unconventional this whole situation was... this child would be loved.

CHAPTER 27

Beck

In the week since I'd found out I was going to be a father, I'd done more adapting than any wildlife rescue case there ever was. Don't get me wrong—every single change was one I accepted willingly and happily, but my life had taken on more upheaval in the last seven days than it ever had.

For starters there was spilling the beans to Marcus. Tessa was all smiles and tears as soon as I rolled Riley's wheelchair into Marcus's room at the hospital that night. Marcus took a while to grasp it. In fact, we practically had to sound it out syllable by syllable. At one point I sounded like Darth Vader—"Marcus, I am the father."

I thought he would wind up and knock me out for boinking his sister. But thanks to Tessa and Riley—oh, and the fact that he was bed ridden because of the gunshot wound he sported from the Zack-attack—he took the news better than expected. Everyone was in a good place. Everyone was happy. Everyone was paired off with the person they loved and adored. And all of us were excited about what the future held. Weddings, babies, memories—you wouldn't hear any complaints from me.

But, of course, to plan and execute the perfect fairytale future, the present needed to alter somewhat. For me and Riley, learning that we'd be welcoming a baby into this world in less than six months meant switching things up a bit—*and* getting used to them.

The first thing we needed to check off the list was living arrangements. If circumstances were different—baby not on board—we would've waited to discuss the whole moving in together thing. It hadn't worked out so well for me the first time I took that step with a girl—God really did work in mysterious ways, I guess. But there was no way me and my baby mama were living under separate roofs while she was growing my little sprout.

We decided I'd run out the lease on my apartment (thankfully there were only five more months) and I would move in to Riley's place. She lived on the second story of a two family home that had three bedrooms and lot more space than my studio. No brainer. For the time being we'd split our time between apartments, but eventually Riley's place would be *our* place. Nursery and all.

Other than that, and the idea of Riley's belly growing plump and round with our daughter (my lady was insufferable) the only thing that took getting used to was being together in public around Marcus—and Mr. Grayson too.

Today's celebration was our first as an outed couple. Family members from the Grayson side, who'd known me as Marcus's tag along buddy all these years eyed me skeptically as I walked hand-in-hand with Riley. I paid them no mind. Everyone would get used to it, and if they didn't, they could fuck off. We were happy. We were in love. What else mattered?

I looked on with a smile as Marcus toted Luca in his thick, tattooed arms like a proud and doting father. He brought him over to his mother and stood for a family photo by Luca's birthday cake. They were dressed in Flinstones' costumes—Fred, Wilma and little Bam Bam. I had to admit, it was adorable.

Riley and I had settled on Superman and Wonder Woman. She looked sexy as hell in the skintight get-up— you'd never know she was more than two months along. But me—I had to look ridiculous. My balls were jacked up so high in this thing, I'd been squirming all night.

"I feel like I'm in a dream," Riley whispered in my ear, resting a red-gloved hand on her still-nonexistent bump.

Ignoring my crushed nads for a few seconds, I pressed up against my very own super heroine. "Why?" It was a silly question because this was all still as surreal as fuck.

She nodded in her brother's direction, smiling. "Look at him, B. Look how happy he is with that little boy in his arms. Luca loves him as if he's his real daddy, and Tessa—I have never seen her so at peace since I've known her."

In the past, when Riley reflected on other people's happiness, there was a hint of jealousy. But this time it was genuine. We had our own happiness to celebrate.

"You're right, sweet thing. This is a dream come true."

"Thank you," she hummed, turning her head to gift me with an acceptable-in-public kiss on the mouth.

"For?" I asked when she pulled away, leaving me wanting

more. I tugged on the hem of her cape and brought her back to me.

"Everything, B. I know this is all fast and sudden and a whole lot more than you signed up for when you got forced to take that cab ride home with me that night, but—you've handled it all so well I'm starting to wonder if you actually are Superman." She poked at the big "S" on my costume.

I grabbed her hand and brought it up to my lips, kissing her knuckles. "Would you stop this?" She'd been more insecure in this last week than I'd ever known her to be. Any other guy might've run after he heard his girlfriend of three months was pregnant with his child, but I had no reason to flee. I wanted this. I wanted a future full of kids with Riley Grayson. I was hell-bent on marrying this girl and loving her until the day I died. I didn't need ten years of dating to convince me it was right. It was fucking right. Plain and simple. I felt it in my bones. "I love you, babe. That's all that matters. So quit your worrying and just deal with it, Wonder Woman."

"See, you really are my Superman." She leaned in for another kiss just as her father made his way over from congratulating his soon-to-be daughter-in-law and one-day grandson.

"Well, you've already gotten her pregnant, so what can I warn you about now?" He glared at the two of us, but there was no anger in his eyes. Mr. G was the happiest I'd seen him since he'd lost Mrs. G. Even the news of the pregnancy didn't make him lose his cool the way I was sure he would.

When Riley told him how happy she was, that was all he needed to hear. He loved his little girl and was appreciative of the way she took over as the matriarch in keeping their family together. Besides, they'd been through too much turmoil and loss to let the good things in life go uncelebrated. An out of wedlock, unplanned, and complete fucking shock—this baby was a good thing. For all of us.

"Oh, Daddy, you'll get used to it," Riley laughed, draping her arm around her father.

"I don't know about that," he chuckled. "This one and your brother have been up to no good since the day they met. They may be all grown up, but it's gonna take a little more convincing for me to trust that you and Tessa are in good hands."

That was Mr. Grayson—perpetual ball buster. Especially when it came to Marcus and me. Not to say we didn't deserve a dislocated nutsack for the shenanigans we'd pulled in the past. Like the time we climbed into the neighbor's treehouse to spy on Mandy Piccardelli while she undressed for bed. We got caught by Mr. Piccardelli, Mr. G's neighbor and bowling buddy, and Marcus placed the entire blame on me, saying it was my idea. I still didn't know why his parents believed him, but either way, Marcus landed us both a week's worth of grounding and my parents made me write an apology note to Mandy. I wasn't exactly Mr. Popular with the ladies in school after that. No one liked a peeping Tom, it seemed.

But that was *nothing* in comparison to the time Marcus snuck Mr. G's car out before we had our licenses. Typical, cliché, teenage boy story. You'd think we'd taken a joy ride and got caught by the cops or caused an unnecessary fender bender. Nope. Not me and Marcus. We forgot to open the garage door before we put the car in reverse. There was no joy ride that night. But there was a pile of splintered wood and cracked brake lights piled in the Grayson's driveway. It took a whole year of paper route money to help pay for the damages. And after that Mr. G always eyed me with this look as if to say, "I'm watching you, boy."

Miraculously, that look vanished just in time for me to tell him my intentions with Riley. Holy shit, was that divine intervention or what? I didn't need him breathing down my neck and making me feel inadequate as the man his daughter chose to love. I wanted his blessing. I needed him to accept me as a permanent part of this family and not just some irresponsible friend of his son.

"Hey, Riley, would you mind grabbing me and Beck a slice of cake? Maybe some coffee too?"

"Yup," she smiled. "Anything for my men." She had to have added the last part in for good measure, maybe even as a warning to her dad. He'd have to share her now. I hoped he'd be okay with that eventually.

Clapping a hand on my shoulder, Mr. G cleared his throat to get my attention. It got my attention all right. In fact, that look that I'd said was non-existent just two seconds ago—it was back with a vengeance. "Um, everything okay, Mr. G?" I gulped.

"Calm down, Beck. Everything's fine. Let an old man have some fun, would ya?"

"Why is scaring the shit out of me fun?"

"Because it means I haven't lost my touch, son." He was by no means an old man and he certainly hadn't lost his touch. I once feared for my life around this man. He didn't have to raise his voice to show you he was mad either—the color of his face did that for you.

But his grip on my shoulder slackened and the look in his

eyes softened. "I want to give you Claire's ring."

I took a breath, ready to object, but he stopped me by bringing his hand up. "Marcus and I already discussed this. It's Riley's. Claire wanted her to have it. And I don't want to step on your toes or tell you that you have to marry her right now—but I think that's where this is headed, no?"

I nodded my head up and down, intimidated, unable to speak. Of course that's where this was headed, but hearing Riley's father offer me her mother's ring—this was a big deal. It meant he trusted me. That he approved. That he was giving us his blessing.

"Sir, I'd be honored. But are you sure?"

"Is there a reason I shouldn't be?" He stared at me with one eyebrow cocked. That look could give any grown man the runs.

"Of course not. I mean, I intend to... I mean, we want to... it's just that." I was a stuttering moron.

Tapping me upside the head in the most loving way possible, Mr. G calmed my nerves. "Shit, son, talk about tongue tied. Just relax. This is harder for me than it is for you, remember that."

I truly felt for him in that moment. I couldn't imagine what it was like to give your daughter away to another man. No matter how good of a guy he was. Shit, one day I'd be doing this myself if Riley was right in predicting we had our own daughter on the way. I didn't envy Mr. G right now. He had to have a million different emotions running through his body. Poor son of a bitch. It was my turn to put *him* at ease. "Mr. G, I promise I will take care of her. This baby too. I've never loved anyone like this before and I'm not just telling you what you want to hear. She means everything to me. I won't mess this up."

I saw a glimmer in this tough-as-nails man's eyes. He looked down, hiding the imminent tears, and cleared his throat as his voice became stern again. "Damn right, you won't. If I can't kick your ass, I'll sic Marcus on you."

Fuck! Another one who thought Marcus could take me. Didn't they know I did this shit for a living? I could lift men twice my size, wearing my gear, out of a burning building. Marcus didn't have a chance against me. But if it made Mr. G feel safer, I'd let him think he did. "I don't doubt it. In fact, I'll count on it, but don't worry. I'm a man of my word. She's in good hands and I won't ever let her go."

CHAPTER 28
Riley

This was business. There was no difference between *this* meeting with *this* client and any other meeting I had lined up for the week. Except of course that I hadn't kissed Mrs. Mitchell, or gone on three dates with Nanette Briggs, oh, and Mr. Shen wasn't my boyfriend's ex-girlfriend's brother.

Yes, I had a meeting with Griffin today and for some reason it felt like I was cheating on Beck by doing so. Beck still didn't know that I'd briefly "dated" Griffin and Griffin had no idea I was having Beck's baby. I hated thinking of it like that too. I had nothing to be ashamed of. I wanted this. *We* wanted this. Regardless of the baby, Beck and I had made plans to move forward. Instead of doing it at a normal pace, we were going a little more high-speed. Whatever. I didn't mind, so if anyone else did—they could take their opinion elsewhere.

"Are you going to tell him?" Fallon asked, peeking over his prized Starbuck's mug.

"Tell who?"

Rolling his eyes, he clicked his tongue and planted his hand on his hip. "John Lennon that you didn't approve of his marriage to Yoko... Snap out of it, Riles. You're guilty of lying by omission right now, hun. You need to tell him about this or shit is gonna hit the fan."

I shook my head and went about getting my desk in order. "Griffin doesn't need to know about my baby *or* about Beck. I owe him nothing, Fal. And by the way, Yoko *was* a bitch. She broke up The Beatles. If Lennon were alive I'd march right up to him and..."

He interrupted me with an obnoxious *tsk.* "Just as I suspected."

Slamming down a stack of files, I whined, "What now?"

"You're completely off topic. You're rambling. You totally have baby brain."

"Screw you!"

"No, I'm serious. I wasn't talking about telling Griffin. You don't have to tell him anything if you don't want to, doll. But your *man*—you know, that kid's daddy—you need to tell him that you dated Griffin. If he finds out somehow *before* you tell him—especially since he's still your client— you're going to look guilty."

That was absurd. He had no idea what he was talking about. Now I was defensive. "But I'm guilty of nothing. I didn't do anything wrong."

"No, you didn't and that's why you should tell him. You know that game telephone?"

Now who was off topic? "Of course, I know the game. What's the point?" I was starting to get irritated.

"The point is that when you play that game the beginning message goes through so many different people, with different inflection in their tones, or varying opinions about the message they heard, or even a mouthful of fucking marbles, that by the time it gets passed around, the end result isn't always the truth."

Okay, maybe I did have baby brain. I had no clue how this had anything to do with the game telephone. I stared at him, clueless as to what the hell he was getting at.

"Oh my god, Riley. It's sucking the brain cells by the minute!" He snapped his fingers in front of my face. "If you don't tell Beck, someone else might, and by the time it gets back to him the whole message can be distorted. Get it?"

"But there's nothing to distort, Fallon. I went on a few dates with Griffin and then ended it *for* Beck. It never went further than a kiss. What's there to tell?"

Huffing, he placed his coffee on his desk and coiffed his hair. "Just do it. I'm serious, Riles. The longer you hold it in, the longer it will stress you out." He grabbed my hand, scowling at my ruined manicure. "Look at your nails. Nice. Great nutrition for your fireman-in-training."

"It's a girl, Fallon. How many times—"

"As many times as I have to tell to you to *tell your boyfriend about Griffin!*"

"You know what, Fal? Take the rest of the day off. I don't need you fucking with me while Griffin's here."

"You fucking wish, love. I've been dying to see Gruff Griff since the last meeting. And, besides, you might need me for back up. Who knows what that baby brain is capable—or incapable—of these days."

"I despise you." I scowled.

"You adore me." He blew me a kiss.

Halfway through my meeting with Griffin, I had lost total focus. No, it wasn't baby brain, like Fallon had accused me of having. It was guilt. I felt awful for sitting in front of Griffin—who was smiling at me with that adorably, flirty dimple—knowing that I was keeping the news about my pregnancy from him. And the more time that passed with me gaping over this man's beauty, that guilty-by-association thing Fallon spoke to me about—it was festering inside of me. I was withholding something from the man I loved and I hated that. I wouldn't like it if the shoe was on the other foot. I'd have to tell Beck about my brief stint with Griffin Dennison just to clear myself of all incrimination.

But the dude kept staring at me like I was his lunch. "So," I tried to get his focus off me and back to the design board. "This is what I had in mind for the window treatments. Since we're closing off that part over there for a darkroom you can actually filter some light into the main room."

"Sounds nice," Griffin said, still staring at me and ignoring my designs.

"Why do you keep looking at me like that?" I finally had to come out with it.

With a hardy chuckle, he admitted, "Because you're beautiful. Actually, there's something different about you this time. Like you're..." he trailed off in thought, tapping his finger on his salt and pepper scruffed chin.

If he chose the word "glowing" I was going to piss myself. That was all I needed.

"Glowing. That's it! You have this absolute radiant glow about you, Riles."

Well, slap me silly and call me Milly. "Griffin, seriously?"

"Yes, seriously. You look gorgeous. Let me take you out again." He leaned closer, giving me access to a strong whiff of his intoxicating scent.

Oh, baby brain, stop letting other men flood your senses. "I'm with someone else. You know that." Thank God Fallon had been called out on an errand. If he saw the way I was squirming, or heard what was going on—I didn't even want to think about what he'd do.

"Yes, so you've said, but you've also been very reserved in your mention of said boyfriend. Could it be you're just blowing me off?" The combination of the cocked eyebrow, the flirty dimple, and the devilish grin—no good. And I'd be damned if he was going to call me a liar.

"I'm pregnant, Griffin. So, no, there will be no more dates with you. I only intend to date the father of this child. Now, let's get back to my designs, unless my *condition* is a problem for you going forward."

Griffin's eyes went so wide I could see every single fleck of the multi-colored hazel irises. He remained silent for an uncomfortable amount of time, before scratching his head and taking a breath. "Well, that explains the glow."

"I guess it does."

"How far along?"

"Almost three months."

"Did you know you were when we were... ?"

"Oh my god, Griffin! Of course not. I would have never started dating another man knowing I was pregnant. What kind of person do you think I am?"

He didn't answer me, just continued with his interrogation-like questions. "Are you with him *because* of this baby?"

Fuck you, Griffin. "I'm with him because I love him."

"Then why did you break up in the first place?"

"Listen, I don't have to explain myself to you and I'm sorry for how this all turned out, but... this is how it has to be. I love my boyfriend. We were separated for a little while—during which time you and I, whatever—all because of a misunderstanding. It worked out, the rest is history, or in our case, future. I'm happy, Griffin. I love Beck and I'm sorry for being a bitch, but—"

Shit! What had I just done? *Fuck, fuck, fuck. Damn you, baby brain!*

"Wait? You love *who?* Did you just say *Beck?* As in *Beck Matthews?*" Every time he said his name it reeked of disdain. Whatever Marissa had told Griffin about their breakup did not put Beck in a good light.

Narrowing his eyes, he asked again. "The father of your baby, the baby you've been carrying for almost three months, is Beck Matthews?"

"Yes." It came out as a barely audible squeak.

Standing from his chair and plucking his keys from my desk, he dug something out of his pocket and placed it in the empty spot left by his keys. "This is my card. It has my assistant's phone number on it. I'll tell her you'll be contacting her from here on out with all the plans for the studio." He tucked a hand in one pocket, combed the other through his short hair, and shook his head. "Good luck to you, Riley. You'll need it."

And then he left.

CHAPTER 29

Beck

The smell of Riley's doctor's office made me as uncomfortable as a Montana farm boy sipping tea and crumpets with Queen Elizabeth. It was all so clinical and sanitized and... *womanly*. I guess it could've been worse, considering *what* the doctor was examining in those back rooms, but the pink and floral decor just made me uneasy. Riley should leave them her card. Do her magic and modernize this joint with some flat screens tuned to SportsCenter. Put us expectant fathers in our element, for Christ's sake.

As Riley flipped through a parenting magazine, I people watched. Scoping out the waiting patients—each one larger than the next with bellies that resembled beach balls—I wondered if Riley's ankles would swell like that one's over there. Or if her nose would spread across her whole face like that one's over there. It wasn't exactly the nicest thing to do, sit there and judge the appearance of these women carrying God's greatest gift, but—whatever. We'd been in the waiting room for almost an hour. I had to pass the time somehow.

"You okay?" Riley asked, placing a hand on my knee to stop it from bobbing.

Grasping her hand, I tried to reassure her. "Yup. Just impatient. I hate doctors ever since that quack examined me for the fire academy." He was ancient—he must've graduated medical school at the turn of the century. If he graduated at all. He had me take the stress test part of the exam four times, each time making me think I had some kind of incurable heart condition. The PA in his practice finally came in on the fourth try and had to show the guy how to read the damn results. I hoped Riley's doctor wouldn't give us anything to worry about. I was already a ball of nerves as it was.

"There's nothing to worry about. You'll love Betsy. She's awesome. Not at all what you'd expect. She's young and cool. Promise."

Whoa. I didn't want some Doogie Howser delivering my kid. "How young? Does she know what she's doing? We have to have the best for our baby, Riles. I won't settle for less."

Leaning over, she planted a loud, wet kiss on my cheek. "You are adorable. Do you know that?"

"The sweat dripping off my head and the accelerated heart rate—that does it for you, huh?" Shaking my head, I went back to bobbing my leg up and down.

Swiveling in her chair to face me, her eyes met mine and glistened with such warmth it almost erased all my fears about this visit. "I love how much you already care about this baby. It makes me so proud. I feel so lucky.

You're going to be an incredible father, B."

I rolled my eyes, certain she was just trying to butter me up so I didn't act all crazy in the examination room. "You're just all mushy and sentimental because of all those hormones."

Arching a brow, she pulled back. "You'd be wise not to use the hormone card too much. Just a warning. And if you must know, I'm all mushy and sentimental because I'm excited to see our baby for the first time."

"What do you mean, see our baby? How?"

Huffing, she smiled. "Didn't I tell you this already? The sonogram. I'm already about ten weeks along so the baby has arms and legs—it's the size of a kumquat right now."

"A kum *what?*"

Riley's giggle filled the whole room. A few people turned to look our way with a smile. We must've looked like a happy couple. We *were* a happy couple. Leaning in for another kiss, this time smack on the lips, Riley baby-talked me. "See, you're adorable. Now sit back and relax. We're next. And try not to pass out when you hear the baby's heartbeat."

Heartbeat? I was going to hear my baby's heartbeat from inside her stomach? Holy crap! Modern technology was fucking incredible. I needed to start reading up on this shit.

A woman in scrubs peeked into the lobby with a file in her hands. "Riley Grayson?"

The two of us stood.

"Betsy will see you now." With a warm smile and a polite nod in our direction, we followed the nurse down a corridor lined with closed doors.

After Riley was weighed, changed into a maroon paper-like gown, and peed in a cup, the nurse ushered us to another room that had some kind of large equipment in it. When she explained that this was where Riley would have her sonogram I tried to relax, but it just wasn't possible. This was crazy. I'd known for two weeks that I was going to be a father, but suddenly this was all so fucking real it made me weak in the knees. Not because I wasn't ecstatic—I was—but I was scared shitless.

From the moment this baby would be born I had to worry about how *not* to fuck it up. She would rely on me to protect her, teach her right from wrong, serve as a role model and example of what a good man should be. I would be responsible for her well-being for the rest of my life and it wasn't the food, clothing and shelter that freaked me out—it was all the emotional stuff. The stuff good parents were made of. Did I have all that stuff?

"Beck, baby? You're white as a ghost. You okay? Do you want me to get the nurse?"

And now I was doing a shitty job as Riley's man. She was about to get some condom wrapped wand stuffed up her crotch and here I was pacing like a fucking fool. Taking a deep breath and raking my shaky fingers through my hair, I turned to her a new, confident man. "I'm perfect. Just wish she'd get in here already. You'll be ready to deliver by the time they get to you."

And just as I was about to rant and rave about this so-called OB wonder named Betsy, in she walked.

"Well, congratulations Mommy and Daddy. Riley you must be over the fucking moon."

Her tone, her language, the long hippie skirt she wore under her white coat—thank you Betsy for calming my jumping nerves.

"Yes. That's an understatement. I'm so happy I could cry."

"Nope. No crying yet. Let's save that for the twenty fourth hour of shitty labor, shall we?" Typing into the machine connected to the condom wrapped wand, Betsy turned and wiped her hands, walking toward me. "This baby is going to be drop dead gorgeous. You are some sight, Daddy. Riley?" she asked, never taking her eyes off me. "Introduce me to this delicious specimen."

Laughing so hard her gown started to creep open, Riley gestured her hands between Betsy and me. "Betsy, this is Beck Matthews, my boyfriend. Beck this is the well-renowned OB of Brooklyn Heights. We're in the best hands ever."

"Why? Did you doubt me, Mr. Matthews?" At first, Betsy's vicious looking glare could burn a hole through me, but when she smiled and winked I knew she was only joking.

"It's a pleasure to meet you, Betsy. Riley can't stop raving about you." She shook my hand and held it a little too long, then dropped it and plopped into the stool between Riley's legs. Watching her movements, the way she hummed around as she went about her doctorly duties, she reminded me of Barbara Streisand in *Meet the Fockers,* only younger. I prayed to Jesus she wasn't as unconventional as the character she portrayed in the movie. I couldn't handle that. I was a hippie lover, but not when it came to delivering my baby. Betsy had something to prove, whether Riley thought so or not.

"Now that we got that intro out of the way, let's meet this little one. I'm going to squirt this cold crap on your belly. Sorry about the chilliness, babe." She did as she said she would and then spread it around Riley's smooth belly with a wider wand than the one shaped like a skinny dildo. I inched over to Riley's side to observe and when I was close enough she grabbed my hand and pulled me even closer.

The room filled with an echo-type whooshing. Riley's eyes watered. Betsy's smile spread wide across her jovial face. And me—I looked around the room to see where the odd sound was coming from.

"That's your baby's heartbeat, gorgeous. It's coming from the monitor." She snapped the fingers of her free hand, grabbing my attention.

"That's the heartbeat?" I asked, stunned. Why had I never watched any of those TLC programs or paid attention in sex-ed. I felt like such an amateur.

"Oh my god, B. That's her." Riley smiled through her tears and grasped my hand even tighter. "Betsy, does everything sound good?"

"It sounds wonderful, doll. But what's this *she* stuff?" Betsy asked, smirking. "You're too early for me to tell you the sex."

Wiping the rest of the goo from her stomach with a napkin Betsy handed her, Riley answered, "I don't need you to tell me the sex. I *know* it's a girl. From the moment we found out, from the second we decided to keep her. I just knew."

Betsy glanced over to me and rolled her eyes. I simply shrugged. "She's a real know it all. I just go along with it to avoid the backlash."

Chuckling, Betsy pinched me on the cheek. "Smart move, gorgeous. Her hormones are gonna be all kinds of whacked out... yes her to death."

Riley was right, I loved Betsy. She no longer had anything to prove. She was good people.

Staring at the black and white sonogram photo plastered to my fridge, I now knew what a kumquat was. In fact, I knew that next week the baby would be the size of a fig. Our goal, which seemed a long way off, was a nice ripe mini-watermelon. Fruits and veggies—the comparison creeped me out, but after doing my research I was starting to get a clear visual of things.

Over dinner Riley and I were all goo goo ga ga over our little girl. Yup. She'd convinced me we were having a little ballerina of our own. Claire Elyse Matthews was the name we'd chosen in memory of Mrs. G. She was a wonderful woman. Baby Claire had humungo shoes to fill. We didn't want to jinx anything so starting the nursery was a no-no for Riley, but I could tell her design ideas were dying to burst out of her.

Once we were done eating, cleaning up and relaxing, Riley had decided to head back to her place for the night. She'd run out of clean clothes for the week and had an early morning meeting the next day. I hated spending a night apart—I didn't like parting with my kumquat now either—but I kept reminding myself that this transition stage would all be over soon.

We were going to be a family. The thoughts that had me uneasy and anxious this afternoon now had the complete opposite effect. I was excited and eager. I wanted to fast forward the next seven months and start our dream come true. I wanted to do all the things with Riley that I always imagined I'd do with my wife and the mother of my children. I couldn't pinpoint a time in my life that I'd been happier. This was my silver lining, Riley's fairytale.

There was only one thing left to do.

Since Luca's party I'd thought long and hard about what Mr. G had offered me. Claire Grayson's ring. I wanted to propose to Riley. Soon. But just like waiting to tell her I loved her, I wanted this to be perfect. Then again, look how that turned out. Maybe it was stupid to wait. The end result would be the same no matter when I decided to ask her. Riley would be my wife. And the more I thought about it, the more I wanted to do it before the baby got here in May.

Reaching for my phone to put in a call to Mr. G about setting these wheels in motion, I noticed a missed call and an unanswered text from a half hour ago.

Both were from Marissa.

What the fuck was it now?

I ignored the voicemail, but swiped the screen to check my text messages.

The two sentences I saw on that screen turned everything Riley and I had experienced today into a tainted, sour mess.

Marissa: *How do you even know this baby is yours? Your girlfriend was fucking my brother before you two got back together.*

Her message changed my entire outlook on this beautiful day, on my plans for our future, and planted a seed of doubt that I never imagined could be placed in my brain.

CHAPTER 30

Riley

My early morning meeting turned into a late afternoon nightmare. I never had a chance to drink my only allotted cup of coffee for the day and the bagel I'd brought into the conference room to stuff my face with earlier was certainly not enough to tide me over until now. I was a starving animal. Everyone had better steer clear of me until I ravaged the cheeseburger deluxe I'd just ordered from the diner around the corner.

When I returned to my desk, I flopped down into my chair and headed straight for the red blinking light on my office phone. As I punched in the code to retrieve my messages, my cell phone buzzed. Multitasking was my bitch—even with baby brain. I scrolled through what looked like a million unanswered texts as I listened to the messages from various vendors and clients. After three similar business-related messages, Beck's voice came through just as I was noticing that the majority of my missed calls and texts on my cell were from him too.

"Hey, Riles. Uh, we need to talk. I've been trying to get you, but I guess you're still in that meeting. Call me back as soon as you get this."

The rest of his texts said pretty much the same thing. Except for the last one that had a time stamp from only ten minutes ago.

Beck: *That's it. I'm coming there.*

I immediately dialed his number from my phone, worried that something might be wrong.

He didn't pick up. Straight to voicemail.

Irrational thoughts popped into my mind about our baby, but duh—I was the one carrying it. I would know if anything was wrong. Unless—*shit.* Had Betsy called him, unable to reach me? Beck's was the emergency contact number on my chart. Maybe she'd called him with results of some sort. What the hell else could he be rushing all the way over here to see me for?

"Fallon? Fallon? Where are you?" I screamed, feeling like the wind had been knocked out of me.

Darting out of the office kitchen with the creamer still in his hands, he jogged toward me and dropped everything on my desk. He could easily recognize my despair. He was a good friend and could read me well. When he wrapped his arms around me and asked, "What the hell's the matter? You feeling okay?" I slumped against his chest and wilted in his embrace, sobbing. "I think something's wrong with the baby, Fal. Something has to be wrong with my baby."

"Don't worry. There's nothing wrong with *your* baby, Riley." Beck's voice startled the both of us, forcing me out of my friend's embrace. I rushed over to hold on to Beck for dear life.

But when he stopped me an inch away from him and rejected my touch, I scowled at him, confused.

A cold, bitter resentment washed over his face. "Is this baby mine?"

The horror that eroded my veins with those words felt as if fire started at my core and spread through every single nerve ending. I could barely compose the proper words to answer him. Of course the answer was yes. Why was he even asking?

Fallon, noticing my state of utter shock and speechlessness, stepped in. "Are you serious, Beck?"

"Yes, I'm serious, Fallon." He never took his eyes off me, even as he spit out his venom-like words to Fallon. "Is. This. Baby. Mine? Answer the question, Riley."

"Hey," Fallon raised an arm, getting between me and Beck. "Don't talk to her like that. Whatever the hell is going on can be—"

"Shut him the fuck up before I do, Riley. We need to talk. *Now.*"

I'd never seen Beck this angry before. I'd never known him to have this side to him. He was always so calm and rational and loving. But he was right, whatever had prompted this should be spoken about without an audience.

"Fallon, we're okay. Can you hold down the fort while I go talk to Beck?"

It was Fallon's turn to stare Beck down. He continued his mental defensive, but nodded in answer to my question.

When he finally walked away, I pulled Beck by the arm and dragged him into the now empty conference room.

Slamming the glass door behind us, I got right to the point. "Yes. Of course this baby is yours. Where the hell do you get off accusing me that it isn't?" The more time I had to think about it the more time I realized that I was pissed. This was insane. Where did he get off accusing me of such heinous nonsense?

"Why didn't you tell me you were dating Griffin Dennison? Or that you're *still* working for him? Let me guess, he doesn't want the baby so you thought you'd stick it on me like I'm some sucker? Well, I'm not some sucker, Riley and I'm certainly not going to raise some other man's bastard and marry his whore."

Oh my god. Oh my ever loving God!

He'd found out about Griffin.

How?

Who?

Why?

I had an idea for every one of those questions, but still— that wasn't what had me in knots. The way he spoke to me. The things he just called our baby... "How fucking dare you." I croaked. I was so angry that it overpowered my tears, dried them up and made me furious. "You're going to be very sorry when I explain myself. Those are words you can never take back. Horrible, hateful, untrue words."

"Prove it." Was all he said back, barely even blinking.

Where was *my* Beck? The Beck who was so happy and satisfied yesterday. The Beck that promised me a forever full of love and togetherness. Surely, the person who'd fed him this bullshit was only out to get me. And that person could only be one of two people. Marissa or Griffin. But Griffin had no motive—Marissa, on the other hand...

"Who told you these lies? Was it Marissa?" I finally asked.

"What does it matter?" He gave himself away by looking down.

"Don't fucking defend her, Beck! *I* am the one carrying your child. *I* am the one you love. Now, tell me, was it her lies that forced you to come in here and accuse me of all this shit?"

Visibly broken, his shoulders slumped and he released a deep breath as he spoke. "Yes, it was Marissa, but she had a reliable source. She said she saw you two together with her own eyes. At his apartment. All over each other. Is she lying about that?" Of course she was lying about that. She was misconstruing the truth in her favor. I needed to get Griffin on the phone. He would explain everything to Beck. He would certainly do that for me. Right?

This was where I wanted to shoot myself in the foot for not taking Fallon's advice to tell Beck about Griffin. Had I gotten it all out in the open, like he told me to, I wouldn't have to defend myself now against a bunch of lies. It was Marissa's word against mine. It was a matter of who Beck believed more. It should be me, but who the fuck knew at this point. I could tell he was desperate. He didn't want to believe her, but there was a definite part of him that did anyway.

I owed him an explanation. It was time to lay it all out there. And thick. "Yes, B. She's lying. Not about me being at the apartment or dating Griffin, but this baby is *not* his. I never slept with him. I swear to you. We went on a few dates, we kissed *once*, but when I found out she was his sister... Beck, that's the night I came to you. That's the night

I ran into her. When she told me you were still talking. See how she was lying to me about getting back together with you? She's lying to you now. She's still hung up on you. She's only trying to break us up. You have to believe me."

His expression softened just the teensiest bit, but the doubt had been planted and true or not, it was still there. It was up to me to make sure that seed never sprouted into anything. Especially not the pesky ugly weed that would keep popping up when you thought it was gone for good.

"Say something, Beck. You believe me don't you? Don't you know me better than that? I would never lie about something like this. I would never hurt you that way. I love you. I love this baby. Please don't let Marissa ruin that." Now it was me who was desperate because I didn't see him budging any time soon.

"Why didn't you tell me about Griffin in the first place?" He pinched the bridge of his nose, scratching his head. This was far from over.

"I tried. The morning after we got back together. I was going to tell you, but you told me you didn't want to know details about what I'd done while we weren't together. I should have told you, especially since he's still a client, but I just—I didn't think it mattered."

"You had to know this would eventually get back to me, Riles. It's a small fucking world. People talk. I'm not sure how Marissa put two and two together, but I'm sure it wasn't that difficult."

"I know *exactly* how she found out about us. *Griffin.* At our last meeting I slipped about you and me. I never wanted it to get out because I had a feeling he would go and tell Marissa. But I never imagined it would turn into this. I knew she'd be jealous, but this—her lies could have ruined everything for us. I can tell you're still not convinced and I fucking blame those two for this. As a matter of fact, if you don't mind, I'm about to give him a call right now and give him a piece of my—"

Stopping me from picking up the conference room phone, he sighed. "Don't bother. I tried myself. He's out of the country for a job he took in Malaysia. Some big break from *Time* or something. I didn't really give a shit about listening to Marissa babble about Griffin's career. All I know is he's unreachable."

Fuck! If he'd tried to contact Griffin that meant—"Does that mean you still don't believe me? Do you... do you want me to get a paternity test to prove it?"

It looked as though he was contemplating that very thought. Fucking Marissa had just turned my life into the Maury Povich talk show! I wanted to kill her, but my hatred for that conniving, jealous twit might land me on Jerry Springer.

I felt so helpless. There was nothing I could say or do to make Beck believe me. The tears ran down my face, unrelenting. I felt my body weaken and I leaned against one of the chairs for support. "Everything was perfect yesterday. So beautiful... and happy and... *perfect.* How the hell did this happen? *Why* is this happening?" I clutched my middle, trying hard to protect my baby from the fears that overcame me. Loss, loneliness, defeat. But when Beck's arms wrapped around me and brought me close to his warmth, I knew I'd made a breakthrough.

"I believe you, Riley and I'm sorry. You just have to understand... please don't ever lie to me again. Please don't keep secrets. There's no reason to. It will only hurt us in the end. Nothing but our lies can tear us apart."

CHAPTER 31

Beck

"What do you think of this one?" Marcus was perched over a glass display of engagement rings, soliciting my advice on the proper cut, carat, and clarity.

"Dude, she's your girl. How am *I* supposed to know what she'll like?" I came along for moral support and because my best friend had asked me to, but my heart wasn't in this. Had this ring shopping taken place say, three days ago, I'd be gawking over the monstrous diamonds right along with him. But ever since Marissa put a snag in my trust in Riley—I hated to admit it, but things were different.

It's not that I didn't believe Riley about the baby, but the fact that she'd kept from me that she dated my ex's brother was enough to make me doubt the rest of her sincerity. I didn't want to fuck up Marcus's happy moment, but I needed to talk to him. He was the only person who knew Riley better than I did. Maybe he could help.

"Hey," I nudged him as his face nearly pressed up against the glass. "Can I ask you something about your sister?"

Standing at attention and ignoring the impatient saleswoman, Marcus looked me up and down with a smirk. "I thought you already got the old man's blessing? Want mine too? How *proper* of you to ask, bro."

"I'm not asking for your blessing, dick. I already know I have it. Your pops gave me your mom's ring and told me you were okay with it. That's the only reason I'm not draining my own savings account today for one of these." I pointed to the showcase full of sparkle with a pit in my gut. Having Claire's ring wasn't the only reason I wasn't making my own purchase today. Doubt had a lot to do with it too.

"Okay, then, what gives?"

"Marissa."

Marcus's happy demeanor switched to anger immediately. "You're fucking kidding, right? Don't even tell me you're screwing around on my sister, Beck. She's pregnant. With your baby. I'll fucking—" His fists balled at his side, probably by instinct. And that tattoo on his neck started pulsing over his pounding vein.

Raising my hands in defense, I motioned for him to quiet down and calm it. "No, you animal. It's nothing like that. Actually it's Riley I'm wondering about."

"How so?" His breathing calmed, but his fists were still white at the knuckles.

I took a breath and prayed that my friend could be loyal to me instead of his blood long enough to put me at ease. "Do you think she'd lie to get what she wants? Is she like that, Marcus? I know she's your sister and I don't want to tread on shaky ground with you, but you were my best friend before she was my girl. I need to know that I can trust her."

Eyeing the saleswoman, Marcus raised a finger. "Can you give us a minute? We'll be right back. Just gonna grab a coffee next door. Would you ladies like anything?" He offered the staff the chance to place an order, but they politely declined.

Ushering me toward the door, he gave me the game plan. "I need a break from all the bling. And some caffeine. Let's grab a cup of joe so you can tell me what the fuck is going on." It was the most rational I'd ever seen Marcus in my life. Tessa had done quite a number on him. *Way to go, Tess!*

After ordering two coffees and half a sub each, we took a seat on the upper level of the deli shop. Cracking his knuckles before he shoved the overflowing hero into his face, he spoke with lettuce sticking out of his mouth. "So? What did my sister do now?"

I unwrapped my sandwich and took a bite. After chewing and swallowing like a civilized human being, I pled my case. "You remember Marissa's brother?"

"Griffin? Yeah, nice dude. Why?"

"Nice dude, my ass. Seems Riley was seeing him a little while back. In between the first time she and I got together and since we made it official."

"No joke? He's a good looking guy. Right up Riley's alley. Wonder why it didn't work out." He continued chomping away on his food and I wanted to slap the damn sub right out of his hands.

"It didn't work out because *we* did, asshole. I thought you were over this shit. I thought you were happy for us? I am the father of your niece, you know? At least I think I am." I trailed off, hoping he'd take the bait.

"What the hell's that supposed to mean?" Bait taken.

"Marissa made it like Riley was sleeping with Griffin. Riley swears it never got that far, and I believe her, I really do, but—

"Let me guess, you're not a hundred percent sure? Bro, Riley would *never* lie to you about the baby. Even if she *did* sleep with Griffin, she would know who the father was. I hate thinking of this shit and my sister, but she's always been so organized and by the book. I doubt she would sleep with the two of you at the same time. That's not her MO. And not for nothing, but what makes you think Marissa isn't lying just to make you run back to her? She's always been a little off her rocker, if you ask me. I wouldn't put it past her to make something like this up."

He had an excellent point, but Marissa did have some validity to her story. "That's the thing. It's not a total lie. Marissa saw them together. Riley didn't deny that. And she actually kept it from me. She should have told me she was with Griffin as soon as she found out he was Marissa's brother. If she could keep that a secret—I just don't know, man. You know what it's like. We've all told a lie or two to cover our asses."

Wiping the mayo from his mouth, he tilted his head and narrowed his eyes on me. "Our lies didn't involve babies, Beck. Riley would never stoop that low. She's a good girl. She's the girl you told me you wanted to marry, so give her some credit and forget what Marissa told you. Marissa's trouble. *Talking* to her is trouble. Past, be gone!"

If it were only that easy. I wanted it to be, but my whole attitude about all of this was distorted now. I wished there was a way to get ahold of Griffin. I didn't want to go behind Riley's back to check her story, but hearing the truth from the horse's mouth would set me at ease and make all of this go away. Things needed to go back to normal. To when I was as happy as a pig in shit because I was in love and starting a family and ready to give my all to Riley and our daughter. The slightest thought that that little girl growing inside Riley wasn't mine—it made my stomach turn. I had to get rid of this feeling.

Riley

"You have to do this for me, Tess. I need to talk to her. I can't snoop through Beck's stuff because it will only make me look worse, but you—all you have to do it check Marcus's phone. I know he has her number in there. I *need* to talk to Marissa." That bitch needed to be put in her place.

Beck had been so distant and weird since our fight at the office the other day. We'd worked it out after I swore up and down and tried to redeem myself, but something was still off. He was still not himself. And it was all that bitch's fault!

"Do you really think it's a good idea, Ry?" Tessa peered over the pile of Luca's clean laundry with a disapproving glare.

Oh, screw that. I didn't need her disapproval. I needed her to help! "Why wouldn't it be?"

"Well, for starters, you're pregnant. You don't need her upsetting you and stressing you out."

"I'm pregnant, Tess, not a piece of glass. I'll be fine.

Besides, I'm already stressed out enough over this. Talking to her will make it go away—so would pulling her fucking fake red hair out of her head, too—but I'm not about to start a cat fight, preggers and all."

Standing to place the tiny paired-up socks in the laundry basket, she shrugged. "You should ask Beck. Tell him you want to meet with her. Together. I think that's the safest bet. If you go behind his back and he finds out—"

No! No! No! Not her too! "I already asked him to do that. He said no. He doesn't want to risk an altercation. I get it. He's worried about the baby, but I'm worried about *him*. He's not himself, Tess. She ruined that for us. She made him think I'm a liar. I need to prove her wrong."

I would not let her win. I'd already tried to get in touch with Griffin, but I was unsuccessful. There was no way to reach him by phone and I had no idea when he'd be back in the States. I couldn't wait a second longer to clear this up, to make it right. It was nagging at me like a festering sore. The more I picked at it, the worse it got.

I was innocent in all this. I couldn't allow Beck to think for one more day that I was pulling the wool over his eyes. He said he believed me, but I wasn't sold. I would not let Marissa ruin what Beck and I had worked so hard for. I couldn't believe I was in this predicament all because of that jealous bitch.

"Please, Tess? I wouldn't beg if I wasn't desperate. If I promise to keep it civil and under control will you please, please, pretty please get me her number?" I clasped my hands together. Luca thought I was clapping so he started his own happy commotion, distracting me and Tessa from the matter at hand.

"Fiiiine," she drawled out. "But none of this comes back to me or Marcus. I don't need to start a family war. We're all a close knit crew; siblings, BFFs, and little spawn. I don't want to spoil the good thing we have going. Got it?"

"Tess, this won't spoil a thing except for that rotten witch's plans to sabotage my relationship with Beck. You're the best. I can't thank you enough."

That night, Tessa sent me a text with Marissa's contact.

Tessa: Make sure you erase all evidence of where this came from. Good luck.

Me: Love you, chica. My lips are sealed.

Tessa: It's not your lips I'm worried about. It's your phone history. DELETE DELETE DELETE

Me: K, boss.

Tessa: Let me know what happens.

As soon as I ended the conversation with Tessa, I dialed Marissa's number.

"Hello?" she answered after a few rings. I guess she wasn't one of those to screen unknown calls. Lucky me. It made my life a lot easier.

"Hi, Marissa. It's your new BFF, Riley. How's it going?" I

sounded so fake it was almost comical. I wanted to call her a million different obscenities, but I could handle this with grace, if I dug down deep enough.

"What do *you* want?" She growled like the beast she was.

"It seems we have a bit of an issue. I wanted to clear it up before it got out of hand."

"I'm not helping you do anything, Riley. The sooner you realize it's not going to last with you and Beck, the better for both of us." Snarky witch. I'd show her, but first... more Grayson gracefulness.

"Is that what you really think? Listen, Marissa. I'm truly sorry if you're hurt or upset over losing Beck, but just so you know, the two of us didn't start anything up until you were out of the picture."

"Just so *you* know, I was never *out* of the picture. Did Beck tell you that he was at my place two weeks ago, on Saturday?"

She couldn't be telling the truth. How could she be? And if she was—I did the mental math in my head, calculating that the night she was talking about was the night I was attacked by Zack. "More lies, Marissa? Is that how this is gonna go? Beck was with Ramos that night, helping him put together the furniture for the nursery."

"Sure, he was there—*before* he came here. I invited him over to watch the playoff game with me and Griffin. He came by for a few hours. We had a nice time." I could hear her smirk through the phone. I couldn't confirm or deny what she was saying until I spoke to Beck. I wasn't going to take her word over his. She was no one to me. I'd give him the benefit of the doubt and the chance to tell me otherwise before I thought the worst.

"You know what, Marissa? Nothing you say holds any validity with me *or* Beck anymore. If you could lie to him about our baby just to get him to come back to you, I don't even want to know what else you're capable of. I called you to tell you to back off. Your plan failed. I *still* have Beck. He *still* loves me. *I'll* be the one sleeping in his bed tonight. So you can cut the shit and leave us alone. And as soon as your brother gets home from his trip, I'll be having a chat with him and Beck so he can tell him right to his face what a liar you are." It was as if I'd said it all in one breath. I sucked in the air through my nose to fill my lungs again. It felt good to get it off my chest.

But her obnoxious, villain-like laugh knocked me back down to size.

"You have no idea what—or *who*—you're messing with, Grayson. If I tell Griffin to lie about sleeping with you... he will. He'll do anything for me. Always has. All I have to do is say the word and he'll tell Beck whatever *I* tell him to say."

"You piece of shit!" Grace was officially gone. This was absurd. Unheard of. It was practically criminal. Why hadn't I recorded this phone conversation? Why? Because who knew I was dealing with a mental case? There was no reasoning with her and no use wasting my breath or my time trying to do so. So instead, I just told her where to go. "Marissa. Leave. Us. Alone. Get your own life and fuck off."

"Good night, Riley. I'm sure I'll be hearing from you again."

I hung up the phone so irritated and flustered I had to pace my angora rug in the living room in order to get my heart rate back to normal. This was why Tessa didn't want me talking to Marissa. This was why Beck told me no when I asked to meet with her. Feeling this way wasn't good for me, and what wasn't good for me wasn't good for my baby.

Feeling guilty for putting my baby in harm and going against Beck's wishes, I picked up the phone and dialed my boyfriend.

"Hey, sweet thing. What's up?"

"Please come here. I don't feel right. I don't think it's anything to worry about, but… I spoke to Marissa and it's my turn to ask the questions now."

CHAPTER 32

Beck

I was trained to deal with shit like this. I was qualified to handle stressful situations and remain composed while doing so. But hearing that something might be wrong with Riley or the baby—I could barely see straight, let alone keep my nerves calm.

There was nothing like this fear—an uncontrollable, all-consuming terror that something could go wrong and nothing I did would prevent it. Wishing I was on the rig so I could switch on the sirens and run every red light, I prayed my girls were okay.

I sped through the city, dodging the turtle fucking drivers as I weaved my way through the unexplainable evening traffic. By the time I made it to Riley's, a cold sweat soaked though my V-neck. In my haste to get to her, I forgot to grab a jacket so the cool fall air brought a shiver down my spine as I ran up the steps to her front door. I'd double parked on the narrow street and the possibility of a ticket or a tow was pretty great, but I didn't give a fuck. I needed to get to Riley and make sure she was okay.

"Riles, open the door." I banged on the wood as I pressed the doorbell down. "Baby, hurry. You're freaking me out."

When the door finally swung open, I took in her unusually haggard appearance and bum rushed the threshold to take her in my arms. Kissing her head and holding her close, I nearly cried, "Are you okay? Is the baby okay? Let's go to the emergency room. We have to make sure everything's right."

Pulling away from me and closing the door behind us, she motioned to the living room. "Calm down, Beck. I'm fine. I just got off the phone with Betsy. She walked me through a few breathing exercises and told me to have a cup of chamomile tea. I feel better already. Well, physically at least."

"Thank God." I breathed an actual sigh of relief. Other than looking a little frazzled, mismatched and... *angry*... she was in one piece and seemed to be walking around just fine. "This is why we can't keep spending our nights apart. When I'm not at the firehouse, we need to be together. I'll move the rest of my stuff in this week. I can't worry about not being here when you need me. It's too much. I nearly had a heart attack on the way here, worrying sick about you. The both of you." I deflated onto the couch, slouching against the soft cushions. After taking in a few more calming breaths, I patted the seat beside me, inviting Riley to sit with me.

Instead of joining me, she stood with her arms crossed against her body. "Nice to know you were worried sick—what a wonderful caring boyfriend you are, Beck. I wish you felt the same when I was passed out on Tessa's floor because that psycho slammed *his gun* across my head. But instead of protecting me and being with *me* when it mattered most, you were with *her*. Were you fucking worried sick then, Beck? Or do you think it's okay that you were watching a fucking ball game with that bitch while I was fighting for my life?"

How the hell did she find out?

The guilt over this exact thing had been eating me up. There were nights I literally tossed and turned and lost sleep over being at Marissa's that night instead of with Riley at Tessa's. Had I ignored Marissa's call and gone there earlier, I could have protected her from Zack. I could have saved her from what he did to her. It was something I had to live with every day. It was something I struggled with confessing to her every day. It was something I'd decided to keep buried and locked inside me every day. I knew that if she ever found out, she'd react this way. She had every right to hate me for betraying her like this. She had every right to resent me for not doing what any good man should do for the woman he loved—defend her, guard her, and be truthful with her.

There was nothing else to do but apologize for doing wrong by the woman I loved. "I'm so sorry, Riley. You have no idea how sorry I am that I wasn't there with you that night. I'll do anything to make it up to you. Anything." I nearly dropped to my knees and begged. I contemplated it, but when she started to cry, holding her middle and shaking uncontrollably, I needed to hold on to her.

I rushed to her to wrap my arms around her body, but she backed away and put her hand up between us. "So it's true, then? You're not denying you went there? I can't fucking believe this, Beck. I cannot believe you didn't tell me." Her words came out in pathetic drones. It killed me to see her hurt this way. It tore me apart to see I'd done this to her.

"I'm sorry, baby. I'm so, so sorry."

"How could you? You told me you couldn't babysit with me because of Ramos. Why would you leave him to go watch a fucking game with her? Are you still fucking her too? After you accused *me* of lying to you, you do the exact same fucking thing? I can't believe this is happening. I feel like—I feel like—I can't fucking breathe." She fisted her hair in her hands and bent over, dragging in labored breaths. When she stood upright again, her breathing was harsh, jarring, not right.

"Riley, you need to sit. This isn't good for the baby. Please." I grabbed her by the hand and brought her to the couch. "Sit down. Talk to me. Who told you this? Was it Griffin? Did you get in touch with him?"

"I called Marissa. I wanted to tell her to back off. I must've sounded like an idiot, telling her how much you love me, how happy we are. Here I am carrying your kid and you're there with her the night I—the night I—Beck he could have killed me and you were *there.* Do you know how that makes me feel? Do you know the fucking crazy shit going through my head?"

I could only imagine. There was no explanation for this. I wanted to take it back and make it go away, but I couldn't. Mostly, I just wanted her to calm down. I would say anything if she would just calm the fuck down. This wasn't good for the baby. She was going to have a nervous breakdown and it was freaking the shit out of me.

"Please listen to me. I don't know what she told you, but I didn't just go there to watch the game with her. It was not planned, Riley. She called me while I was at Ramos's, crying about failing the bar and her life falling apart. She sounded—I don't know—she sounded desperate. I was worried she might do something stupid. So I called Griffin and the two of us headed over there together.

"It's not at all what you think. I hate that I went there when you were in hell, all by yourself at Tessa's. You don't think I would change that whole night if I could? I would do anything for you, Riley. I love you so much I would fucking die for you."

"And lie for me too. Right? This whole relationship has been full of lies, Beck. From day one. Keeping it from Marcus, being on your break with Marissa. Me and Griffin. Nothing but lies—big ones, small ones, from me, from you."

She was right, but none of that shit mattered to me right now. Marissa was clearly fucking with the two of us and Riley was giving her exactly what she wanted. I'd made a horrible mistake by believing anything Marissa told me and now I had to worry that she'd made Riley believe more lies.

Where did she stand? Why did it sound like she was giving up? "What are you saying, Riley?"

"I'm saying we're doomed. I'm saying I don't know how this can work. Regardless of why, and even if it was out of goodness, you still went there. She called you, she needed you, and you dropped everything to be there for her. You couldn't have known what was going on over at Tessa's—I understand that. But now, when I picture it in my head, all I feel is resentment. You should have been with me. You should have come to save me. Instead, you were with her.

You went to her rescue. She won. She's always gonna fucking win."

She could only win if Riley allowed it. I would never fall for her shit again. "That's not true, baby. I see it now. I didn't realize it was this bad. I didn't believe you when you told me she'd do anything to get me back. I'll talk to her. We'll—" There was one saving grace in this situation. The only one who could help. "*Griffin!* We have to get in touch with Griffin. He'll clear it all up. He knows the truth. Baby, I can make this right."

Shaking her head and shedding more unrelenting tears, she sobbed. "Nothing can make this right, B. Nothing can make me feel that you didn't choose her over me."

"You're not being fair. I didn't know. You think I'd choose her over you if I'd known?" My voice was so desperate it squeaked. How could her thoughts be so misconstrued? How could she see it this way?

Riley stood from the couch and I followed her as she walked into the kitchen. She poured a glass of water and gulped the whole thing down in one quick motion. "Wanna know what I think?" she asked, with a strange calmness to her voice that was shaky and weak from her tears just a few moments ago.

I nodded, wanting her to continue.

"I think she's always going to be your weak spot. I think there's a part of you that still believes what she told you about me and Griffin. There's a part of you that will examine our baby when she's born to look for any resemblance of him. I think she did her fucking job in putting a wedge between us and I think—I think you need to fucking go!"

What? Really?

"Go? What do you mean? You're kicking me out? We're having a baby. I'm moving in. Riley, don't do this. You're being irrational." I tried to hide my devastation with a forced laugh. She had to be joking right? She was just on edge. She was just saying things out of anger.

"Too bad if I'm being irrational. I *feel* fucking irrational. I feel like I don't know what's right or wrong anymore. But I have to do what's best for this baby first and foremost. Right now, looking at you and resenting you—it makes my blood boil, it turns my insides, it makes my heart jump into my throat and prevents me from breathing.

"I can't handle this right now, Beck. I physically cannot take one more second of feeling this way." She closed her eyes as she spewed it out like vomit. Poisonous vomit, at that. Her words stung, pinched my heart, jabbed my gut. I didn't want to make her feel this way.

"So let me help you, baby. Please. Let me be here for you."

Turning away from me, she clutched the countertop and bowed her head. "It's too late for that now. I want you to go."

I reached for her, placing a hand at her shoulder. "Please don't do this, Riley. Please don't give up on us because of her."

Jerking away from my touch and stalking off, she let out one final wail. "Fucking go! I don't want to do this right now. Get out!"

My presence was only causing her pain, and her pain was harmful to our baby—the baby I loved as much as I loved its mother. I couldn't stay here and cause her anymore distress.

So, I walked out of her kitchen, out of her apartment, out to my car, which was thankfully still there.

And drove straight to Marissa's house.

CHAPTER 33

Beck

Why I hadn't figured it out sooner, I had no idea. I had a tendency to see the good in people, even if they weren't necessarily a good person. While Marissa wasn't a totally *bad* person, she was certainly *up to* no good. Her wires had crossed somewhere since we'd broken up and she failed the bar. There was no denying she was going through a lot of shit, but that wasn't my problem anymore.

There was a time when I loved Marissa and thought I would forever. We'd shared a lot of fun times before things went south, and those fun times, even though a part of my past, stood out in my mind when I reflected on our relationship. It didn't mean I regretted my decision to end what we had—we weren't right for each other anymore. Riley was right for me. Riley and our baby were my everything. But when someone I used to care about called me up in a bind, crying and pleading with me to help them—something clicked, making me think I owed her the decency of trying to calm her down.

Of course, that was before I knew she'd use it against me. That was before she had the audacity to feed me lies about the woman I loved just to make herself look better, or to make me want her back.

I was such an asshole for believing anything she had to say. I should've known, but Marissa was never malicious or jealous in all the time I'd known her. What was that expression? Fool me once shame on me, fool me twice—now you can go fuck yourself.

I drove to her house in a frenzy. I was on to her and she needed to know that. It all had to stop. She couldn't spew her garbage all over the place, ruining people's integrity, their relationships, their lives. That's exactly what her twisted game was doing and it would come to an end tonight.

Arriving in front of Marissa's house twenty minutes later, I pulled out my cell phone and dialed her number. I'd be erasing that shit from my phone tonight too. After this, there was no reason to hold on to anything that had to do with her.

"Beck?" She sounded surprised. "What's up?"

"I'm outside. Downstairs. Get in the car. We need to talk."

"You're... *here*?" She peeked through the blinds in her bedroom window. "Oh, shit. Look at that. Why don't you come up?"

Yeah. No. Not happening. This was happening on my terms. If I went up there she'd pull some shit or find a way to make it look like I spent the night or something like that. "No. We need to talk about all the lies you've been telling. Come down here so we can discuss this like two adults."

"There's nothing to discuss, Beck. But I'll come down anyway. I'd love to take a ride with you. Give me five minutes."

"Good." I rolled my eyes at her eagerness; then again, this was what I wanted. She had to hear from my mouth, to her face, that we were over for once and for all. No more games, no more lies, no more may-the-best-woman-win—she'd made it evident that the two of us couldn't even be friends. I had no place in my life for someone capable of shit like this.

She came out the door and down the steps, draping a jacket over her shoulders. Jogging to the car she opened the passenger side door and hopped in just like it was any old time. "Hey. Good to see you."

I gave her a half-assed nod and put the car in gear. I needed to drive. Maybe if I was distracted by the road and my focus was on getting to a destination I could fight the urge to lean over and strangle her. I wasn't a violent man, but the things she'd made me believe—the stuff she'd said— I pictured my hands around her neck with her gasping for air.

Shaking my head to try and erase the anger boiling in my blood, I turned to face her. "You know why I'm here?"

She leaned over and placed her hand on my thigh, rubbing it up and down. "Are we playing a guessing game?" She winked.

With one hand on the wheel I used the other to remove her claw from my leg. "Cut the shit, Marissa. You know damn well why I'm here. What the hell are you up to you? This isn't you. Why are you stirring the pot?"

"Oh." She giggled and it made my stomach turn. Was

this a game to her? My life wasn't a game that could be controlled and maneuvered by some woman-behind-the-curtains. This was real. My feelings were real. My relationship with Riley and my baby were real, tangible, meaningful things.

Focusing on the road, I gritted my teeth. "I know you're lying about Griffin, and as soon as I get ahold of him, I'll be talking to him about the rumors you're spreading about him. You two are tight and I'm sure his loyalty lies with you, but I don't think he'd appreciate you telling people he has some illegitimate kid out there. After all he's been through. After everything he's lost—you'd play with his life like that? What kind of person are you?"

"Don't you dare! Don't you point fingers at me. The kind of person *I* am? What about you? You left me because your ego was bruised when I wouldn't move in with you. You couldn't handle that I needed more time so you fucked the next thing that came along and knocked her up. Now, because of one mistake, because of one regret, I have to give you over to her willingly. I don't think so, Beck. We have too much history. Our story isn't over yet." My eyes were still on the dark night road but I could sense that her penetrating stare was trained on me.

How was I going to fix this? What would get through to her? Why the hell was Griffin out of town? *Damn it.* Tough love wasn't working. It was time to start reasoning with her.

"Marissa, I'm sorry it didn't work out. I'm sorry you failed the bar. You're going through a difficult time and I feel for you, I do, but you can't take it out on me. What we had is in the past. It's not Riley's fault we didn't work out— it's *our* fault. We spent two years pretending we had all the qualities we wanted in a spouse. We were fooling each other."

"How can you say that? You loved me. I know you did." Her voice cracked as she said it. She sniffled and without looking I knew the tears had started.

"I did love you, Ris. But it wasn't enough. I love Riley now. We're starting a family and I need you to respect that." It was blunt, but it was the truth. There was no reason to make her think we had a shot at anything again. She needed to know where my heart lay. It was with Riley and my baby.

She cried silently, except for a few snivels.

Realizing I'd driven further and further from her home in my aimless journey, I turned to face her at a red stoplight. "You're gonna be okay. Everything will be okay. But this shit needs to stop, Marissa. You can't keep lying to people. It won't win me back."

The traffic light remained a steady red for what seemed like an unending eternity. Her soft cries became sobs as her head fell in her hands. "Everything's falling apart. I can't believe I've lost everything."

Back to that tune again. I was sure she was more upset over failing the bar than losing me, but I wasn't about to weigh her losses against each other. That was for her to do. Those were her obstacles to overcome—without me. "Marissa, you'll take the bar again and pass. You'll do everything you've set out to do since as long as I've known you. I was holding you back. Your beliefs and dreams are different than mine, and that's okay. You'll get over me and realize that letting go of what you *thought* we had will only make you feel that much freer. Please believe me. Please listen to me. And if you can't listen to me, think about what

Griffin said the other night—this too shall pass. We've all had shit to deal with in our lives, but we can't let it break us." I was confident in my little pep-talk. I'd gotten my point across without being insincere.

Her sobs calmed as she wiped the tears from her face and the light finally changed from the intense red to a thank-you-God-Almighty green.

I lifted my foot from the brake pedal to the gas and started to make a U-turn. Marissa's arm flew across the dashboard, clutching the steering wheel.

"What are you doing? Let go," I yelled.

"No. You're not taking me home. You think you know it all. You think you can just tell me how *you* think it is and all will be right with the world. How could you do this to me?" Her cheeks were soaked and stained with her tears, her grip on the wheel becoming tighter. It was becoming hard to drive the car straight. I'd managed to only swerve over the double yellow lines once, but it was taking a lot of control.

"Marissa!" I yelled, making her jump. "Get off the wheel! I'll take you home and come upstairs. We'll talk it through." Like hell I would. This chick was going crazy right before my eyes. I'd drop her off and speed the fuck away. I'd give her mother a call to make sure she knew her daughter was acting out and becoming unstable. I couldn't have this shit on my hands.

"No you won't. You're patronizing me. I remember how you work, Beck. I'm not a stranger, even though you wish I was. I know things about you she can't possibly know. I helped you better yourself. It was because of me you got through the academy and it was because of me you turned your useless life around. Otherwise, you'd still be sitting home, waiting for the next bartending gig, spending your nights drinking and whoring with that winner of a friend of yours. And now that I've done all that for you, she gets to reap the rewards? The Graysons are nothing but garbage. Lucky you, you'll be bringing another one into this world."

Her grip on the wheel had slackened and her arms returned to her sides but the tension in her features made up for it. I'd never heard her speak this way. She was pretentious at times because of her upbringing and it was no surprise that she hated Marcus.

Before Tessa, he was *that* friend. The one your girlfriend forbid you to hang out with because trouble followed him. Or rather, he caused the trouble. But he wasn't that guy anymore.

Regardless of how Marissa thought she *molded* me into who I was today—she was fucking wrong. She helped me see things in a better light, but I'd made the changes for myself and no one else. I wouldn't take one more minute of her delusions. And I wouldn't stand for her badmouthing my unborn child.

It only made me angrier that I'd tried to reason with her, but I was done with that and done with arguing. Without even looking in her direction, I flipped my right signal to make the turn. "This conversation is over. I'm taking you home."

As I rounded the corner and accelerated, Marissa's arm shielded my vision and her hand held tight to the wheel again. This time, she succeeded in swerving the car. An oncoming vehicle blasted its horn and all I could see were glaring headlights.

"Get the fuck off!" I yelled, blinded. Thankfully, the other driver veered into the other lane and we avoided a head-on collision. "Are you fucking crazy? Let go of the wheel!"

"I'm not going home! I'm not letting go!" Even in my panic her double meaning bled through.

"Are you trying to get us killed?" The Marissa I'd once known wasn't the one struggling with me now.

"Maybe I am," she admitted through gritted teeth. "Maybe I'm tired of pretending to be perfect. Maybe I don't want to be a lawyer and pass the bar and be some doctor's wife. Maybe I want you to knock *me* up, and give everything up for *me,* and love *me* the way you say you love her."

There was a lot of desperation in her confession, but the only thing that stood out to me was her answer to my question. She was aiming to hurt us both. I wasn't too scared to admit that in that moment I did fear for my life. I worried I'd lose total control by showing my rage and going back at her. I worried that if I dropped her off she'd do something stupid. Either way, I'd feel responsible. How the hell would I be able to live with that? There was *no* way to live with that.

With one hand on the wheel, fighting against Marissa's strong hold, I shouted out to the Bluetooth, "Call Marissa's mom."

Her eyes darted to mine as the phone started ringing, echoing throughout the car. "Hang it up now." She warned with tears in her eyes. "Hang it the fuck up, Beck or I will—"

"You'll what? You're acting crazy. I can't trust you." I

held my hand over hers, stopping at another red light and putting the car in park.

She jerked the wheel, but it was no use. For good measure, I turned off the ignition. The phone continued to ring, and finally Marissa's mom's voice came through the device. "Hello? Beck? Is everything okay?"

"Hi, Mrs. Denni—"

"Mom, don't listen to him. He's lying! Don't listen to anything he says."

"Marissa? Honey? What's going on? Where are you?"

"He made me believe he was taking me out to get back together. He got me in his car and started going crazy, driving recklessly. He might even be drunk, Mom. I'm scared. I don't know what he'll do next."

"Oh my god!" Her mother screamed through the phone. "Where are you?"

I stared at her in disbelief. "You've lost your fucking mind." It came out in a whisper. I had no reaction, no defense. Her mother would believe her over me. I was the man who broke her daughter's heart. That's all she needed to form her opinion. "Mrs. Dennison, I would never do anything to hurt her. I haven't been drinking; she's the one acting irrational, but I'll let you see for yourself. We're at the corner of Eightieth and Elm. I pulled the car over and I'll stay here until someone comes to get her."

"Don't you go anywhere! Don't you dare move! We'll be there as soon as we can!" Her mother's voice was shaky, but determined. I had no doubt she'd be coming to rescue her daughter, and in turn rescuing us both.

As soon as I ended the call with Marissa's mom, I stepped out of the car—with the keys. I couldn't be in that tight space with her anymore. I had nothing left to say. There was no redeeming herself from this. She'd somehow lost all integrity and become a habitual liar all in the matter of a few months.

After twenty minutes of waiting and pacing, not so much as peering through the window to check on Marissa, I saw the lights. Bright, white headlights speeding toward me followed by blue and red spiraling lights and a deafening siren.

Fuck! They called the cops. Like everyone else—like me—they believed her lies. Now I would have to find a way to work myself out of them. Again.

CHAPTER 34

Riley

"I made him leave and now I can't get in touch with him. Where could he be, Tess? Has Marcus spoken to him?" Monstrous mistake. Big. Huge. What was I thinking? As soon as I realized what I'd done, I called Tessa in a tizzy. I didn't want to be without him for one second—let alone a lifetime—and now I couldn't find him!

"No. Marcus hasn't spoken to him, but calm down. I'm sure he's just blowing off steam. Send him a text and tell him to come home. When he's done sulking he'll come back, Ry. I know he will."

Maybe she was right. She was more rational than I was right now—pregnancy hormones were the fucking pits. It was as if someone else had invaded my body between the mood swings, the hot flashes, the cravings—and I still had a ways to go. Maybe one kid was enough. "Okay. Good idea. But if either of you hear from him, will you please let me know?"

"Of course. Now, get off your feet and stay calm. That

baby is going to be high strung because of you."

I rubbed my tiny bump, worrying even more. "Shit! Do you really think I'm fucking her up? God, I'm a terrible parent already and she isn't even here yet!" I wasn't doing the best job when it came to prenatal care. I mean, I hadn't exactly known I was pregnant for a good portion of my first trimester and now I was stressing myself out every second of the day.

"Would you just relax already? You're worrying for no—" she paused mid-sentence as Marcus mumbled something in the background. When she came back her tone was anything but soothing. "Uh, Ry?"

"Uh, yeah? What?"

"Be ready in ten minutes. We're going down to the precinct. Beck's been arrested. Marissa's pressing charges."

"*What?!* Are you freaking kidding me?" Could this night get any worse?

"Calm down, Ry. Please. Think of the baby."

How could I calm down at a time like this? What the hell was going on? Why was he with her? Why was she pressing charges against him? If he'd gotten physical with her—why? "Oh my god. Fuck my life, Tessa. When did it become a bad daytime talk show?"

"Just stay put and take deep breaths. Marcus and I will be there soon."

"What about Luca?" I couldn't expect her to drop everything for my drama.

"Your dad will come and stay with him. Marcus is already on the phone with him. We've got it covered, babe. Just sit tight." She tried her best to sound reassuring but I was anything but comforted.

My life was one sick, crazy joke right now. I was pregnant with a baby that my boyfriend didn't believe was his and he was about to be carted off to jail because of his psychopath ex. *Wonder-fucking-ful!*

By the time we arrived at the station, a commotion was in full gear. Beck was in cuffs arguing with a police officer as he gave Marissa the evil eye. Marissa was crying with melodramatic flair—for effect, I was sure. And an older couple—who I assumed were Marissa's parents—were speaking animatedly with two other police officers. Taking it all in, I shook off the shivers that swept over my body. Ever since Zack, I was weirded out by cops. Not because they weren't helpful, but because being around them brought back painful memories.

Marcus ran over to Beck and I followed with Tessa close to my side. "What the hell, man? You okay?"

He looked up to acknowledge his friend and then his eyes focused on me. "Riles, what are you—Marcus, why did you bring her here?"

His objection to me being there made me wonder if I had something to worry about. Was he innocent like I'd hoped? Had he done something to deserve the arrest? Did he have something to hide? What the ever-loving hell was going on?

"B, please tell me what's going on." My voice came out so shaky and frail it was barely recognizable to even my own ears.

"Riles, I wish you hadn't come. The baby—" He

instinctively brought his hand up to comb his fingers through his hair, but when the cuffs prevented him from raising one arm individually he dropped them both back to the officer's desk with a frustrated huff. "You shouldn't be here. We'll clear this up. They didn't need to worry you with this shit."

"Of course I need to be here," I cried. How could he say that? The man I loved was in trouble and I wanted to help him get through it. I needed to stand by his side and figure out how to make it go away. "Can you tell me what happened?"

Marcus, Tessa, and I huddled around Beck, who was still waiting to give his report as the officer scribbled some things on pad. Marissa stood with her parents, where I assumed she was giving her account of things. Whatever those *things* were.

As the metal wrapped around his wrists jangled against the wooden desk, Beck started to give us his side. The side I'd have to believe no matter what. I'd made the mistake of believing Marissa's lies once before—it was time I stood by my man. So long as his story made sense.

"After you and I had that argument I decided I needed to go over there and talk some sense into her."

"What would make you do that alone, bro?" Marcus interrupted. "You should have called me or Tessa. We could've come with you. We all know what she's up to. This has bad news written all over it. Her father knows people, Beck. Even if you're fucking right, they're gonna make you look dead wrong."

Marcus's words didn't put me at ease. They only made things worse. For Beck too. His complexion went from a heated tan to a pale white. "You don't think I know that? It was a stupid move, but I thought if I tried to reason with her... I just thought I could make it go away. But when she got in the car she went all kinds of crazy..." His eyes searched mine for forgiveness, for understanding, for anything to make him see I believed him. "Baby, I had no idea she would go to such great lengths to fuck with us. Had I known—I would've stayed away. She tried to kill us. She took the wheel and tried to swerve the car into oncoming traffic when I told her we were over. I was so scared... so scared I'd never see you again. So I called her mother. It was the only thing I could think of doing in that moment and as soon as I got her on the phone—Marissa fucking started spewing more lies. Lies. Lies. Lies. That's why I'm here. Because *I* believed her lies, *you* believed her lies—everyone believes her mother fucking lies."

I wanted to cry. I wanted to break down and just lose it right there. I'd had it with Marissa's games and now I was furious. She could have killed the love of my life, the father of my baby, all because she was a jealous bitch. "I'm gonna—let me talk to her!" I started to stalk in Marissa's direction, but my brother grabbed my arm, stopping me.

"Where do you think you're going, little girl? She's insane. You mess with crazy—and crazy's high and mighty daddy—and you'll be sharing a cell with your boyfriend tonight. Let me handle this, okay?"

I searched Marcus's eyes with desperation. I wanted to believe he could solve this whole ridiculous misunderstanding, but I feared irreparable damage had already been done. What lies had she told? If he was accused of hurting her physically or abusing a substance, he could be put on probation at work. Or moved to a shitty house in another borough. I couldn't have her ruining our lives any more than she already had. "Marcus, please? I need to let them know that she's been messing with us. Maybe they'll listen to me."

"Riley, there's no use, babe. I'm telling you. They'll believe whatever she says. It's always been like that." I didn't know if Beck was only trying to calm me down to avoid a brawl or if he was talking from experience.

Suddenly, I remembered what Marissa had said to me about Griffin lying for her at any cost. "What the fuck is it with her? Why does she have everyone wrapped around her finger?" It didn't make any sense. They couldn't protect her forever. There were consequences for shit like this.

"Just leave it alone, Riles. Please, baby?" Not Beck too. Why was he defending her?

"Screw you all!" I couldn't stand back and let this go down.

Fighting my way past Marcus and Tessa, and ignoring Beck's protests, I marched right up to the stuck-up family of bullshit artists and said my peace. "You have some nerve accusing him of *anything*. You know damn well he would never hurt you." I waved my finger in Marissa's face, holding myself back from balling it into a fist and slugging her.

Before I could get another word in, Marcus and Tessa were at my side, with their hands on my shoulders, holding me back.

"Come on, Ry. Let's sit with Beck. Let the cops handle this," Tessa whispered in my ear.

"No! They can't believe her! This is—this is fucking crazy!"

"Crazy?" Marissa finally said with an evil smirk. "I'll give you crazy. When he showed up at my house he reeked of booze and dragged me into his car. Do you know how scared I was?" All of a sudden her smirk turned into full-on theatrical waterworks. Her father rushed to her side to coddle her.

"It's okay, baby. He can't hurt you anymore." He cupped her head against his chest as she made herself look like the victim.

This had to be a fucking joke.

When she finally broke from her father's protective—and probably manipulative—arms, she stared me down as if to scare me away.

But I wasn't scared. I was enraged.

"You are despicable," I spat at her. The lies never ended, but there had to be a way to prove Beck's innocence without it just being his word against hers. Searching the room, I recognized a police officer who'd been sitting with Beck earlier. "Excuse me, officer?" I motioned to him and he strolled over. "Was my boyfriend given a Breathalyzer? If he's being accused of drinking and driving I assume he had to take one." We had to get to the bottom of this. There had to be an honest answer out there fucking somewhere.

"Ma'am, just relax. We're compiling all the information and filing the complaints. These things take time." His flippant response only irritated me more.

"Time, my ass. You're wasting yours. He did nothing wrong. She's a goddamn liar and you're all blinded by her last name and her fucking social status."

"Riley!" Beck yelled from across the room where he was now standing with his hands tethered together in front of him. "Enough. Just leave it alone."

With Marcus and Tessa holding on to me as if I were a fragile porcelain doll, I took in a long breath to try and even the raggedness out. My poor baby. She would hate me for making her wound tight. "Why is this happening?" I finally broke down. "I feel like I'm in a nightmare. I don't understand why no one will listen to me."

I'd never felt so helpless in my life. How could I fix this? I needed some kind of miracle.

"*Griffin?*" Marissa's eyes went wide. "What are you doing here?" She ran to him with open arms.

My head spun around like Linda Blair's in *The Exorcist.* Griffin was here! Was this my miracle? Holy shit, thank you, Jesus.

All eyes turned to the two siblings sharing a hug and a silent conversation. I wanted to run to him myself before she fed him more of what everyone else believed, but I held back out of respect for Beck.

The two of them walked over to our crowd, Griffin's eyes focused on me. "Riley," he said with a shy smile and a nod.

This was no time for something so composed. Everyone needed to snap the fuck out of their Marissa-trance and figure this shit out. "Griffin. When did you get back?" I asked.

"Last night. I was catching up on some sleep, trying to even out the time difference thing—guess that's why I missed my stepmother's call."

"Why are you explaining yourself to her? She's no one.

Come, Griff. You can help me fill out the forms for the restraining order." Marissa dug her claws into her brother's arm and I expected him to follow her like the other sheep.

But as she pulled, he didn't budge. "Marissa, why don't you go sit down and let me talk to Dad and your mother. We'll figure this all out. Promise."

"There's nothing to figure out. He's an animal and he needs to be punished. Are you going to let him get away with this?" The anguish that seeped through her voice almost made me feel sorry for her. She actually turned this whole thing around in her mind as if she was the one suffering and not causing the pain. She was good at what she did—no doubt about that.

Griffin patted her hair, tucking the red locks behind her ear. "Rissy," he hummed, tilting his head. He loved her. Deeply. You could tell just by the way he looked at her. How he spoke to her. Marcus and I were close and we'd always been protective over each other, but this was different. It was almost as if she depended on him in some way and they fed off each other because of it.

"You don't believe me? How can you not believe me?" She whimpered, staring into her brother's eyes.

"Because you've taken it too far this time. He hasn't done anything wrong. Falling in love with someone else isn't a crime, honey." He leaned down to her level and whispered something that sounded like, "You need help. I'll help you."

"*Griffin!*" Her mother's stone-cold eyes went wide. She didn't need to say anymore. It was obvious she was mortified that Griffin was airing their family's dirty laundry.

Marissa's face dropped as she lost all color in her usually rosy cheeks. "You can't be serious. Why would you defend him? Do you know how he's hurt me?"

Turning to face his sister with his hands planted on her arms, he spoke in a calm, soothing tone. "You're hurting and you're used to getting your way, but we both know Beck isn't capable of what you're accusing him of. I spoke to the cop who made the arrest—there wasn't a trace of alcohol. He passed the Breathalyzer. The stories don't match up and I'm not gonna sit back and let you ruin his life—or hers." He pointed to me over his shoulder. "They're good people. They don't deserve this."

Oh my God! Finally! Someone *finally* had enough sense to tell the damn truth.

"I hate you," Marissa whispered, like she was a bratty child who hadn't gotten her way.

Griffin kissed his sister on the top of her head. "No, you don't. And you don't hate him either. There are no charges to bring up and no restraining orders to file. Let's just go home."

"Can I fucking get out of these now?" Beck yelled, raising his arms above his head.

Griffin motioned to one of the officers. "Larry, uncuff him."

"Larry?" I asked, being nosy. "You're on a first name basis?

"Another friend. I told you I have a lot of them." He flashed his dimple, reminding me of all the good qualities he possessed—and not just in the looks department.

Larry ambled over to Beck, dangling a set of noisy keys. Marissa cried into her parents' embrace, looking more pathetic than ever. One of the police officers went over to them and then quickly walked off when her father shooed him away.

Marcus and Tessa stepped back, watching the show seemingly astonished by the events that had unfolded.

Beck walked over to join me and Griffin, grabbing my hand and kissing me on the cheek. "I'm sorry, babe. I am so sorry it came to this. I should've never doubted you."

"But you did doubt me, B." It still hurt. How could he think I would lie about the baby? I turned to Griffin, hoping he could finally rest this case.

"Can you please tell him?" I asked.

"Tell him what?" Griffin looked confused.

"Your sister told Beck the baby was yours."

"She what?" See... he hadn't even known. I knew he was a good guy! He had no reason to hate me the way Marissa made me think he did.

Beck jumped in, "Griffin, you're telling me you didn't know she was spreading this shit around? You had no part in this, no evil plot against me and Riley because she called things off with you?"

"No! Why would I? Riley, I liked you... a lot. But I have no animosity toward you for any of this. And Beck, not to get all up close and personal, but I barely even kissed her once. We never got far enough to... let's just say, there's not a chance that baby could be mine." I respected him for his choice of words. Beck must've too because a smile spread across his face.

"Oh my god, Riles. I'm so sorry I didn't believe you. I feel like such an asshole."

"You always were a bit of a jerk," Griffin joked.

"Very funny, bro." He punched Griffin in the arm. "Thank you for clearing this all up. I owe you, man. And you—" he turned to me. "I love you. I love you so damn much."

"I love you too, B. I guess we were both duped. I'm just happy it's all over." I inched up on my toes to kiss my boyfriend on the mouth.

Griffin cleared his throat and I worried I'd made things uncomfortable. Still grasping Beck's hand, I turned to Griffin. "Is this a recurring theme with her?" I finally asked, darting looks between the two men.

They shared a knowing glance. Beck shrugged and then Griffin spoke. "Let's just say we've been down this road before. Sometimes certain things set her off. When she was with Beck, things were under control—we didn't really have to worry, but she has a bit of a compulsion. It's a weakness we've unfortunately fed into to cover up for her, but I couldn't let her get away with it this time." Griffin raised a brow at Beck. "No offense, Beck, but I did it for her. I love my sister—we both know that—but Riley's a great girl. She deserves happiness. I guess *you're* her happiness." Griffin's eyes never left mine as he said it. His forlorn expression tugged at my heart, but his compassion brought an uncontrollable smile to my face.

"Thank you so much, Griffin." I beamed. He truly was a godsend today.

"Yeah, man. I can't thank you enough. I had no idea she would fly off the handle like that. She's under a lot of pressure from your folks, but this a new level of... out there. I'm sorry if it seems like I did wrong by her, but I assure you, I didn't. We were broken up before Riley and I became serious. We were stupid in telling our own lies to keep things secret, but now—I'm just glad this shit is all over."

"Glad I could help." Griffin nodded, this time only half the dimple showed. "Let me get back to my family. I'm truly sorry for any confusion."

"We're good." Beck fist bumped Griffin and it was like the world had returned to its normal state.

As Griffin walked away to escort the rest of the Dennisons from the precinct, my brother and my best friend came to meet us.

"The truth shall set you free, brother." Marcus joked, punching Beck in the arm.

Beck rolled his eyes and I slapped Marcus's brawny arm.

"What? Too soon?"

One day we'd be able to laugh about this—maybe. But for right now, I wanted to shelve this night along with the rest of the nights from my past that I wished I could erase from my memory for good.

As Marcus and Tessa walked ahead, Beck stopped me and spun me around to face him. "Do you know how worried I was when I saw you walk through those doors? I never want to feel that helpless again. I'm supposed to be your protector." He cupped my face, placing his other hand on my belly. "Yours and hers. You're my life, Riles. The both of you."

I smiled, trying to hold back the tears—both happy and sad—but it was impossible. The moment was too intense to fight the urge to let it all out. "You don't think I felt helpless... useless... watching you in those cuffs, listening to her weave her lies and have people believe them? I wanted to punch her in the face so bad, B. But it's over. I want to go home and never think of this shit again because the past is the past and I only want to think about our future."

"I couldn't have said it better myself, baby. I love you."

"I love you too. Like you have no idea."

He kissed me on the tip of my nose and I snuggled against him, wiping away the last of my tears against his T-shirt.

We caught up to Marcus and Tessa and the four of us walked arm-in-arm, like two matches made in heaven. Together we could probably weave a pretty gritty and interesting tell-all fit for a Lifetime network special. I'd recommend them calling it Fifty Shades of Grayson.

The somber mood was already passing, but in an attempt to lighten the mood, I asked, "You think she'll leave us alone now, B? Or do I have to worry she'll be a forever-stalker?"

Hooking an arm around my waist and kissing the spot below my ear, he reassured me, "I think we're good. We have Griffin in our corner and we both know not to believe her lies anymore. Consider it a thing of the *past*."

I wanted to. I wanted to be the bigger person too, but I couldn't resist the urge to belt out the way I really felt—with a JT song, of course. "You know what? Karma's a bitch so I really hope what goes around, goes around, goes around, comes all the way back around."

Beck laughed, surprising me with a different verse of his own. "Bridges were burned, and now it's her turn to cry... cry me a river."

It didn't matter that he sounded nothing like Justin. It didn't matter that I had no idea how he'd learned so many lyrics by a singer he supposedly didn't care for. All that mattered was that everything turned out the way it was meant to be.

Go freaking figure. Beck and I... meant to be!

My mother would be proud of me for ending up with him. And I was ecstatic that he was someone she'd known. It solved a dilemma I'd always feared would hang over my head—would my mother approve of the man I chose to spend my life with? If I hadn't fallen in love with my brother's best friend, this was something I would never know. But holding Beck's hand and imagining our future together—I somehow sensed I had her approval.

EPILOGUE
Riley
2 years later

"Get your ass over here, sweet thing," Beck growled as he lunged for me across the king-sized hotel bed.

"Do you *ever* get enough?" It had only been six hours since we'd fallen asleep naked from our last round of fun.

"I'm taking advantage... this is our first weekend alone since Claire was born and I want a piece of that ass." He pinched the flesh that felt flabby since the birth of our daughter, but Beck wasn't complaining about the extra junk in the trunk. If anything, that junk was a magnet to him.

Squealing when his tongue made contact with my thigh, I bucked off the bed. "She's in good hands with her aunt and uncle and I'm sure she's having a blast with Luca—but I kinda miss her, B."

"I miss her too," he admitted, but I didn't believe his words. His actions spoke louder: his hands roamed my skin and his lips. They were pretty close to distracting me from missing my eighteen-month-old too. "But she has no idea we're gone. This is good for all of us, baby. I've missed *this.*"

There was no denying our wild and crazy sex life had come to a halt midway through my pregnancy because of a scare with early labor. And once Claire was born—the bitch known as colic, an acid reflux disease called GERD (that inspired the nickname Gerdy from her uncle Marcus), and sleep patterns that could make any first time mother tie her tubes—yeah, I was lucky I remembered what the hell sex was.

"You know what, B? You're right. Let's screw like bunnies until we have to go home. I want your hands all over me, your tongue inside me, your lips tasting me, and that long, thick, pulsating co—"

"Okay, okay, shut up and let me fuck you already. I love your dirty talk, but I love your pussy more."

The two of us laughed as we tangled our limbs together, grinding our hips and kissing sloppily. I always hungered for him, always craved his touch, and lived for him to love me. It was our happily ever after.

The day he proposed to me—New Year's Eve in front of a just-wed Marcus and my sister-in-law, Tessa; with my father clutching his heart and nodding his approval; with my mother's ring as if it were her gift to the both of us—was the happiest day of my life. I'd like to be that perfect mother who says that the birth of her child was the best day of her life, but the freaking truth was… that day was not one ounce of fun. It was painful and scary, but I could still call it the *third* happiest day of my life. Because the second happiest was the day I married Beck.

We waited until after Claire was born so I could enjoy our special day and not have to worry about looking like an elephant in white or be unable to sip a glass of champagne. We chose the lake house as our venue and turned the adjoining dock into any bride's magical dream come true. The guest list was small—the few close relatives we had, Fallon and the boys from Beck's firehouse. Oh, and Griffin. He'd become a true friend, no awkwardness about our short-lived past. He was a good guy—who needed to find his own good girl.

All in all the day was surreal, a fairytale beginning to what was sure to be a lifetime of happiness—crazy and all. We'd always have ups and downs. It was inevitable that we'd want to wring each other's necks from time to time, but regardless of our rocky start, there was nothing but good things ahead.

And right now Beck's intention seemed to include giving Claire a little brother or sister.

"Dude, slow down a second. I don't want any of those swimmers making their way up." His eagerness was a turn on, but the idea of getting pregnant again so soon—not so much.

"Slow down? You're always begging me to go faster and harder." He thrust inside of me, causing me to moan.

Forgetting any concerns, I urged him to continue. "Oh, baby. Always harder. I love it!"

"And I love you," he groaned, pulling my hair and burying himself deeper. Breathless, he asked, "Can I tell you something?"

"Now?" We didn't usually converse during our

lovemaking. We were often panting and grunting with no room for words.

"When I was younger and you were in college—about the time Marcus started crushing on Tessa—"

"B, why are we talking about my brother while we're having sex?" It didn't stop me from grabbing his ass and pulling him closer while I wrapped my legs around his muscled back... but still, ew!

Kissing his way up from my chest to my neck, he laughed. "There's a point."

"Okay."

"I always wanted this. From the time I knew that a dick was good for more than just peeing."

"Wow, what a way with words."

"I'm serious, Riles. I think no matter what stood in our way—age, siblings, other lovers—I was determined to make you mine. I always knew I loved you."

I wanted to be able to say the same, but it would be a lie. And we'd vowed to never go down that road again. "I think that's the sweetest thing I've ever heard while being fucked to oblivion."

Staring into my eyes and rocking his hips with mine, Beck smiled. "I'm so glad we had to share that cab that night."

"Hey, I guess we do have Marcus to thank for this after all."

"Okay, no more Marcus talk. You're right. It's creepy."

Pulling his mouth down to mine, I lost myself in my husband's embrace, forgetting about who or what brought us together. "Make love to me, Beckster."

He laughed against my mouth and then swatted my rear as he continued to rock my world the way he had from the very start.

THE END

ACKNOWLEDGEMENTS

I'd like to do this without adding a hundred more pages to the back of this book, so I won't drone on and on. But every single mention included here is because you helped this story come to fruition in some way or another. Gratitude like that cannot go unmentioned. So even if I don't spell it out with some long winded 'thank you,' I can't express how much it means to me that you've been a part of all this craziness.

First and foremost, *Keep Her* would never have made it to the page had it not been for three of the most incredible betas on the planet. Ruthie, Tracey, and Trish; I thank you from the bottom of my heart for putting *your* hearts, brains, tears, guts, emotions (you name it) into this story. Your opinions matter to me, especially when it comes to my characters, but even in my personal life. This baby is as much yours as it is mine—you breathed it for the eight weeks it took me to create it and I thank you for spending so much time with me to get it right. You each connected with Riley, Beck, Griffin, Marissa and especially *me* throughout this process and I can't thank you enough for all of your eagerness, devotion, and hard work.

To my husband and my kids. Without going in depth, I couldn't have done this without you. A lot—and I mean A LOT—has changed in our lives, but one thing remains; the three of you (okay, Rocco counts too... so the four of you) are my heart and soul, always and forever. Don't ever forget it. You will never stop being my #1 priority, I love you.

To all my friends and family for your unending support. Thank you for being proud of me, for understanding a missed playdate or birthday party, but mostly for being a part of my life. There are too many of you to name, but you know who you are—parents, siblings, cousins, aunts, uncles, grandparents, nieces, nephews, in-laws, childhood friends, high school and college friends, new friends, Mommy friends, Facebook friends, author friends, blogger friends, neighbors, and acquaintances. I love you all.

To my indie chicks group—especially Elisabeth Grace, Livia Jamerlan, Celeste Grande, Ruthie Henrick, BA Wolfe, Eleanor Green, Niecey Roy, Gia Riley, Riley J. Ford, RE Hunter, Corinne Michaels, Ana Zaun, Mia Kayla, Michelle Lynn—girls, I have no words, and words are our lives. I don't know what I would do without you. *Any* of you. You are incredible friends, even though I've never actually met some of you, but our bond, connection, sisterhood is just untouchable. And the talent—I can't even go there. You all inspire me in different ways and I am ridiculously proud to be a fraction of our whole of strong, independent, kick-ass women! FYW! Indie Chicks Rock!

To all the blogs who have helped me make my name. You're all so selflessly incredible and if it weren't for your pimping, your encouragement, your willingness to help us indies out—we'd be unknowns, lost in a huge sea of amazing authors. I hope I name you all but in case I slip up and forget, please don't take it personally—I love you all, big and small, especially Schmexy Girl Book Blog, True Story Book Blog, A Book Whore's Obsession, K&T Book Reviews, Three Girls and A Book Obsession, Three Chicks and Their Books, BestSellers & BestStellars of Romance, Carver's Book Cravings, Panty Dropping Book Blog, Totally Booked, The SUBClubbooks, Lives & Breathes Book Blog, The Book Bellas, Read and Share Book Reviews, Devoured Words, The Book Vamps, For the Love of Books by Jaime, Sassy Savvy Fabulous, and many more.

To a few people that I want to single out—for good reason. Jen, I freaking love you too much for words. Tracey, hello friend, my days would be boring without you and our all day PM bitching fests. You are a true gem of a friend, I trust you with my life and I love that I have you in my life. Amy, I hate that you had to move even FURTHER, but I am so happy for all the good things that have happened for you this year and I love your face. Jennifer S, thank you for being so kind and easy to talk to. I am blessed to have met you. Lisa of Truly Schmexy Promotions for being the best at this gig. I love our chats and I can't tell you how much I appreciate all you've done for me. Christina Hernandez (Christina Leigh Designs)—you are a trip, girl, and a talented one at that. I can't thank you enough for all your hard work on the branding. Have I told you lately how much I love it? Angela Smith, I still think you're actually God. Thank you for too many things to list, but mostly for taking a chance on me. The future holds many long convos and a girls' weekend in NYC—promise!

To my dream team of amazingness; Regina Wamba of Mae I Designs & Photography for getting it (and me)—again, Angela McLaurin of Fictional Formats for the beautiful and clean fonts and squiggles you're looking at right now, Nichole of Perfectly Publishable for your spot-on, time-crunch of an incredible and professional proofread, and last but not least to my editor extraordinaire, Brenda Letendre, for taking time away from *your* love of writing to make mine better.

As always, I don't even know how to thank you, the readers, for taking this chance on my work. It touches my heart and brings a smile to my face every time I hear from one of you. I don't know if and when I'll ever consider myself a real author, but knowing that people are enjoying what I have to say and connecting with my stories—God, there is no way to describe that insane feeling. Okay, maybe there is—it's called happiness. Thank you for making me happy.

ABOUT THE AUTHOR

Faith Andrews lives in New York with her husband, two beautiful daughters, and a furry Yorkie son, Rocco. If she isn't listening to Mumford & Sons or busy being a Dance Mom, her nose is in a book or her laptop. She's a sucker for a happily ever after and believes her characters are out there living one somewhere...

Email: faithandrewsauthor@aol.com

Facebook: https://www.facebook.com/authorfaithandrews

Twitter: https://twitter.com/jessicafaith919

Blog: http://www.faithandrews.wordpress.com

Keep reading for a preview of

INDISCRETION: VOL. 1
by ELISABETH GRACE

Coming August, 2014

CHAPTER ONE
Chloe

"If you don't find a man soon, you're going to die a born-again virgin."

I directed an exasperated sigh at my best friend Jackie. "Well, It's a good thing I'm feeling adventurous then. Maybe we should find someone for me to flirt with tonight."

I set my half-empty martini down on the expensive chrome-and-glass VIP table I'd been able to secure at On The Rocks, New York City's newest high-end celebrity hangout. Tonight we were hear to celebrate Jackie's upcoming nuptials. Glancing around, I took in the carrera marble floors, black fabric-draped walls, and large circular banquettes running along the perimeter of the room. I was a long way from small-town Bar Harbor, Maine.

Jackie rubbed her hands together in obvious anticipation. "Ooooh, I like the sound of this. Let's pick one. Or should we wait for the rest of the girls to stop flirting with the bartender and get back here with the drinks?" I glanced over to the bar and sure enough the rest of the bridal party was there laughing it up with one of the workers. Before I could say anything, Jackie pointed across the room. "What about that guy over there?"

I looked across the dim bar to the wine-colored, velvet banquettes, where an attractive man sat pondering the wine list. "You know I'm not into blonds. Two blonds together, can you imagine? How would we ever figure out what body parts go where?" I batted my eyes feigning innocence.

Jackie chuckled at my lame attempt at a joke, while I continued my inspection of our fellow patrons. Not much to choose from, which was disappointing. On the one night I'd decided to let loose a little, there wasn't anyone worth letting loose with. I certainly wasn't interested in the middle-aged man with the small paunch and a wedding ring, trolling for women at the bar. Or the work-obsessed Wall Street type with the suspenders over his dress shirt who didn't seem to be letting his friends get a word in edgewise. And the artsy guy was too outside the box. His bright red jeans, painted on his ass, looked like they'd been dragged behind a bus. But this was New York City—they probably cost a small fortune.

I scrunched my face up in distaste then turned in the other direction and locked gazes with a set of piercing blue eyes. The wall sconces and the lighted glass behind the bar offered the only illumination in the room, but it didn't matter. I could see from here—this guy was smokin'. And not like a 'let's cook some marshmallows over the fire' kind of smokin'. He was three-alarm blaze, call-in-the-water-bombers smokin'.

I swallowed, my lips parting while my eyes took in his wholly male presence. He was standing beside a table, and his tailored grey suit hugged his body—a body that sure as hell had spent a lot of time at the gym. His dark hair had a slight wave to it and brushed the top of his back collar.

I held his gaze for a long moment as the rest of the people milling about the room seemed to fade away. The reality that I was blatantly staring at the stranger floated into my consciousness, and I cleared my throat as I diverted my gaze. But not before seeing his sexy, lopsided grin, complete with dimple and a perfect set of pearly whites.

Heat rose up my neck, and I traced the condensation pattern of a cup no longer there.

"Wow. He's something else."

I turned my attention back to my friend and gave her a weak smile. "He sure is."

With a suspicious smile, Jackie said, "I haven't seen this side of you in a while. I have to say, I like it."

I rolled my eyes. "I'm not that bad, am I?"

"Well, not at my bachelorette party, you're not," she said, sliding a shot in front of me. "I still can't believe you got us in this place."

It hadn't been easy. The group of us were only in town for the weekend, but luckily one of my past clients had a connection with the owner, who'd agreed to let us use the table without the usual bottle service requirement. Five hundred a bottle was too rich for my blood—and my bank account. In exchange for the table, I'd committed the ultimate sin and agreed to sell his oceanfront home at a reduced commission when the time came. Tit for tat, that was always the way. But a maid of honor couldn't put a price on keeping her nearest and dearest friend happy, now could she?

"Bottoms up," Jackie said, picking her shot up off the table.

I fidgeted in my seat, pulling down the too-short hem of my dress. How I'd let Jackie talk me into wearing this thing I'd never know. "I think I've had enough for now," I said and looked over at my friend.

"Come on," Jackie whined and placed the shot back on the table. "You've finally let loose. It's my bachelorette party... please?"

"Don't bat those eyes at me."

Jackie continued to give me her best version of a puppy-dog face, which in her inebriated state more closely resembled a botched Botox job.

I laughed. "You were always the noceur not me."

She rolled her eyes. "Alright word nerd, none of that tonight. I plan to have *way* too many drinks in me to try and figure out what the hell you're saying."

I shook my head and gave her a cheeky grin, knowing I'd used the word purposely just to bait her. I'd had a thing for words as long as I could remember. I loved discovering rarely used words, but my absolute favourite was finding words in other languages that had no English equivalent.

Jackie didn't share my love for all things literary. But it *was* just like my free-spirited friend to want to crank the party up a notch. We'd met twenty-eight years earlier when we were babies and both our moms had sent us to the same babysitter. I couldn't remember a time in our lives when we hadn't been there for each other.

"Fine, pass it over." I reached for the shot, sure it would be my undoing. "But I can't be held responsible for my actions," I laughed. Jackie always did have a way of talking me into things.

I sprinkled some salt on my wrist, licked it off, and tossed back the tequila. Grimacing, I grabbed a lime off the table, put it in my mouth, and sucked. The tequila burned my throat all the way down to my stomach. It was awful stuff, but a welcome distraction from the feeling of loneliness that seemed to have taken permanent residence inside me.

The idea of Jackie settling down still seemed so strange to me. "How is it that after all the sleeping around you did, you ended up being the one to find Prince Charming?" I asked.

Jackie laughed. "I keep telling you, Chloe, all work and no play won't make you happy. And it definitely won't get you laid." Her face turned serious and she bumped my shoulder with her own. "Come on, what gives? You haven't seemed yourself the past few weeks. It's almost been radio silence unless I call you. I love that you're having fun tonight, but I can tell something's been on your mind. Is it because you haven't been out with anyone in a while?"

I looked across the room and saw the rest of the girls were now sidled up to some guy at the bar, who looked to be buying them a round of drinks. "God, no," I muttered. "I haven't been out with anyone because there's no one worth going out with. We can't all be as lucky as you and have Prince Charming rescue us from the side of the road when we get a flat tire."

Jackie's eyes narrowed. "And you don't stand a chance of meeting Prince Charming unless he up and falls on your windshield while you're driving around town showing houses," Jackie countered. "I think you deliberately avoid situations where you might meet him."

"I don't need to meet Prince Charming...I'm perfectly fine with the way my life is now." The conviction in my voice almost made me believe it myself—almost. Attempting to lighten the mood, I added, "Maybe I'll become a nun, be celibate, and live happily ever after."

Jackie flicked her long, black hair off her shoulder and pressed her lips together, her green eyes unblinking as she stared impatiently at me. "Sounds like a lot of fun," she said dryly. "Can I make a suggestion? Try having fun for the time being. Find some hot guy, have lots of hot sex, and don't worry about whether he checks all the boxes on your extensive list of items meant to weed out any man with a pulse. Seriously, what's the worst that could happen?"

I twisted my lips to the side and pretended to think about it. "Hmm...I fall madly in love with said hot guy, not be able to live without him, and turn into Glenn Close's character in Fatal Attraction?" I laughed.

"Okay, smartass. Ever the optimist," Jackie quipped, sarcasm evident in her voice. "We all have needs. And you haven't gotten laid in forever. Hellooo—it's called sexual frustration."

I could always trust Jackie to put it all out there without softening the edges. "I'm not sexually frustrated. They make stuff to take care of that sort of thing," I teased.

"It's not the same and you know it. A vibrator isn't going to kiss you like it can't get enough. You can't feel the heat of its skin against you or gaze into its eyes when it's on top of you, just before it—"

I raised my hand up to stop her from continuing. "Okay, I get your point."

I had that familiar pang in my chest, a lonely ache coupled with another ache brewing further down as I imagined what it would be like to be with a man again. Having that intimacy with someone would be nice, but some things just weren't worth taking the risk for. Life had thrown a lot at me, and I'd learned that being that dependent on another person for my happiness wasn't worth the pain left behind in their absence. My sister was all I had left now.

"I understand," Jackie looked at me sadly. "After what happened with Jeff, I get it. But that was forever ago. Maybe you could keep it casual? You're gorgeous. You've never had a shortage of male attention."

I sighed. I was no fool. I knew exactly what Jackie's end game was. She hoped that if I put myself out there, I'd magically stumble into Mr. Right like she had. *Never. Going. To. Happen.* I just wasn't that girl who had everything fall into place for me. My past was proof enough.

Jackie's hand came down on top of mine. "I want you to be happy. I worry about you. What are you going to do once your sister's moved halfway across the country? I'm concerned about where that's going to leave you. Ever since Jeff, you've kept every guy at arm's length. And that was years ago. You need a man in your life."

I gulped. Jackie's concern was genuine, and none of what she'd said was news to me. I'd had those same thoughts plenty of times, but I kept pushing them away, telling myself I'd deal with them later. Well, later was fast approaching.

Hearing it from Jackie's mouth brought home the realization that I couldn't continue to put off dealing with the inevitable—my sister was leaving for college. Dread formed in the pit of my stomach as I tried to picture how I'd fill my days once she was gone. The person who had been my primary focus for the past ten years would soon no longer be a part of my daily routine. I'd taken a chance on Jeff and after how that turned out, well, I'd thought it was better to focus on raising my sister and securing my own future. My love life could wait.

"If you'd walked in on your boyfriend banging his secretary on his desk, you wouldn't be keen on dating either," I deadpanned. "But that's not it...I've been stressed out by work. I'm not sure I'm going to meet my sales quota by the deadline. I need that bonus," I said, massaging my temple. Impending loneliness had been the least of my concerns over the past few weeks. Ever since my Broker's offer to buy into the firm, I'd been working like mad to make every sale I could at the new condo building.

"Sales aren't going well?" Jackie asked.

"Well enough." I shrugged. "Still, I'd feel better if I'd reached my goal already, or if I was only a handful of sales away. That's the only way I'm ever going to have enough money to buy into the Brokerage."

Months ago, the broker in my office approached me with the deal of a lifetime. To semi-retire, he was going to need a partner to keep the brokerage afloat on a day-to-day basis. He'd offered me first dibs on the buy-in, saying he'd always admired my "grit and determination." I was ecstatic, of course. I needed this. I had no college education to fall back on, and years ago I'd grown tired of chasing the next deal.

God, if I could make this happen, it would change my life. It would mean that even after losing my mother so young, I'd have the stability and security I'd always sought.

"You're a great agent," Jackie assured me with an encouraging smile. "I'm sure it'll all come together."

I returned the smile though I didn't really feel it. "Thanks, but you're my best friend. You have to say that." I let out a heavy sigh, wishing I shared my friend's confidence, and pushed the feeling down. Now was not the time to reflect on life. I was here to have a good time and celebrate Jackie's happiness—to hell with my own issues. Tonight was all about my best friend, and I'd be damned if my own problems were going to bring my friend down. Jackie loved a good time, and as maid of honor it was my job to make sure I delivered.

"Enough talk about the heavy stuff. Let's get back to finding a guy for me to flirt with tonight."

"I thought we'd already found one." She nodded mischievously toward the insanely hot guy with the blue eyes.

"Yeah, right," I scoffed. "A little out of my league, I think."

"Oh please," Jackie frowned. "For all we know, he could be covered in back hair and have a small dick."

I burst out laughing and gave my friend a light smack across the arm. It took me a minute to catch my breath. "You're horrible." I grinned at her. "Do you know how long it's been since I flirted with someone? Maybe I should start with more of an average Joe."

I was in the mood for some innocent fun tonight. Being away from home and all the memories and responsibilities it held seemed to have had that affect. Even so, I had a feeling any conversation with the blue-eyed stranger had the potential to turn into something not entirely innocent.

"Alright then." Jackie leaned in to give me a hug as the rest of the bridal party returned from the bar and placed down a variety of drinks and shots. In the spirit of the evening, I picked up a shot of God-knows-what neon concoction and held it in the air. The other girls followed suit.

Smiling at my friend, I shoved down the lump of nostalgia. "I'd like to propose a toast to Jackie and her upcoming nuptials. May she and Rob have a long and happy life together, full of nothing but love, trust, joy... and because it's Jackie, a whole lot of mind-blowing sex."

All the girls cheered and clinked the assortment of drinks and shots before tossing them back. Jackie beamed. Whether a result of alcohol, love, or the fact that I was looking to have a little fun, I couldn't be sure. I hoped it wasn't the latter or my friend would end up disappointed. Despite what I'd said, I had no intention of pursuing anything beyond a mild flirtation with anyone—blue-eyed stranger included.

Ninety minutes, one drink, and two shots later, I stood in front of the gilded bathroom mirror, mulling over my earlier conversation with Jackie.

It was hard to admit she was right, but I knew it wasn't normal for a twenty-eight-year-old single female to put as much effort into avoiding a relationship as most others put into finding one. Even so, I wasn't interested in opening up my heart to be hurt again. My father, my mother, and my ex—all gone. My sister would be added to that list soon. All for different reasons, but gone just the same.

I had no illusions of a happily ever after for myself, but there was no denying that a little sexual satisfaction would be a welcome addition to my life. I'd never considered casual sex before, but I hadn't thought I'd be alone at this age either.

I smoothed the material down on the front of my dress. *Focus, Chloe.* No more thoughts about sex.

But my mind kept wandering.

Maybe if the sex came with no strings attached...and with someone who looked like that guy I'd noticed earlier in the bar. Spending a night between the sheets with a guy like that certainly wouldn't be a hardship.

Crap, I'd lasted all of five seconds not thinking about sex. I had the mind of a thirteen-year-old boy tonight. Had to be the booze talking; I sounded nothing like myself.

Whatever. It wasn't like I had to make a decision on the spot. For tonight, I'd have fun at my bestie's bachelorette party and see how I felt in the morning—after the effects of the alcohol wore off.

My arms were heavy as I fished a small comb out of my purse and ran it through my long blond strands. Some hairspray would be good, but there was no sign of the usual assortment of beauty products on the expansive granite counter. Too bad, especially since there hadn't been enough room to fit any in the microscopic cocktail bag I was carrying.

I returned the comb to my purse and straightened the pale yellow dress Jackie had talked me into wearing. Apparently hems that reached only mid-thigh were for streetwalkers and the trendy alike. As satisfied as I was going to get, I headed toward the bathroom door to re-join the girls. My legs felt leaden, like I'd spent hours in a hot tub, as my stilettos clicked on the marble floor.

With my hand on the door, I glanced back to make sure I hadn't left anything on the counter when I noticed...urinals?

What. The. Hell.

Shit. *Say it isn't so.* No, no. I did not go into the men's room. No freaking way. But with one more panicked glance, I realized I most definitely *did. Definitely blaming this one on the booze.* Either that or the artsy signage outside the door that left anyone guessing as to whether the figure resembled a man or a woman.

Turning quickly to make my escape, I whirled around and took a step forward, only to run straight into the opening bathroom door. Pain exploded in my nose and tears immediately pricked my eyes. Someone was entering the bathroom and pushing the door in.

Stunned, I took a step backward and shook my head. Warm hands settled on my upper arms and steadied me. I looked up and was speechless. The hands belonged to the man with the memorable blue eyes I'd spotted earlier. *Of course, why go for slight mortification when you could really out-do yourself?*

Sex on legs—that was my only coherent thought at that moment. And I was pretty sure from the grin on his face and the seduction in his eyes that I'd made his hit list.

Elisabeth Grace

Website: http://Elisabeth-Grace.com

Facebook: https://www.facebook.com/pages/Elisabeth-Grace-Author/637982532897100

Goodreads: https://www.goodreads.com/ElisabethGrace

Twitter: https://twitter.com/1elisabethgrace

19604501R00232

Made in the USA
Middletown, DE
27 April 2015